THE RAPIDS

CARLA NEGGERS

THE RAPIDS

DOUBLEDAY LARGE PRINT HOME LIBRARY EDITION

This Large Print Edition, prepared especially for
Doubleday Large Print Home Library, contains the
complete, unabridged text of the original
Publisher's Edition.

MIRA®

ISBN 0-7394-4911-7

THE RAPIDS

Copyright © 2004 by Carla Neggers.

MIRA and the Star Colophon are trademarks used under license and
registered in Australia, New Zealand, Philippines, United States
Patent and Trademark Office and in other countries.

Printed in U.S.A.

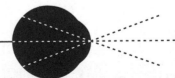

This Large Print Book carries the
Seal of Approval of N.A.V.H.

ACKNOWLEDGMENTS

A special thank-you to my Dutch cousins Henk and Christine Nouwen, Jan and Martha van de Leur, Amy Knechten, Sonja van den Akker and Bart, Leo, Marie Louise, Nanny and Rob Neggers for their warm welcome and many family stories on our visits to the Netherlands. Christine was my "Dutch pen pal" when I was growing up in small-town western Massachusetts and she was growing up in Eindhoven. Henk—who for some mysterious reason thinks the Neggers family is a bit argumentative!—went above and beyond the call of duty in answering my many questions for this book, and even put me in touch with a Dutch police inspector, who was equally generous with his time and expertise. I've promised to keep working on my Dutch vocabulary . . . but I'll never get those *g*'s down!

I'm so glad we got to see my cousin Carla, for whom I'm named, before her recent death. I will always remember our lunch in her beautiful garden. She and her husband, Daan, had the most gorgeous roses . . .

Many thanks to the deputy U.S. marshal who was so gracious and helpful in talking with me, and to my brother Mark and sister-in-law Kathy Neggers for showing me around the scenic and very special Hudson River Valley.

As I write this, hiking season is about to get under way here in northern New England. I'm still determined to hike all forty-eight peaks over 4,000 feet in the White Mountains . . . but it's going to take a while, because I also really like walking on the beach! I'm also diving into my next book, Juliet and Ethan's story—watch for it next summer. For an excerpt, and if you'd like to get in touch with me, please visit my Web site, www.carlaneggers.com.

Thank you, and take care!

Carla Neggers
P.O. Box 826
Quechee, VT 05059

To Kate Jewell and Conor Hansen

One

Maggie Spencer stood paralyzed in front of the glass case in a small Dutch bakery not far from her apartment. *Decisions, decisions.* She'd arrived at the American embassy in The Hague three weeks ago, her first foreign assignment as a diplomatic security officer and already had fallen in love with Dutch bread.

"You'll kill for a Krispy Kreme in another two months."

She laughed as Thomas Kopac, a mid-level diplomat at the embassy, joined her. "Be careful. I'm talking myself out of chocolate sprinkles."

"Ah. *Hagelslag.* It's more like dessert than breakfast."

"So's Krispy Kreme." Maggie smiled at him. "You said that so well. *Hagelslag.* My Dutch vocabulary is improving, but pronunciation? Forget it. Nobody understands what I'm saying."

But she'd had chocolate sprinkles on buttered bread two mornings in a row and decided, instead, on a whole-grain roll with smoked gouda.

Tom didn't order anything. "I just saw you in the window and figured I'd make you homesick."

"Do I look like the doughnut-eating type?"

"Uh-uh. I'm not going there."

They headed outside into the late August sun. A midnight rain had washed the humidity and pollution out of the air and perked up the summer roses and hydrangea blooming in dooryard gardens. The embassy was only a few blocks away. Maggie walked comfortably alongside Tom, a balding man in his midfifties who'd never married, a career foreign service officer who'd never rise to the top ranks of his profession. He was the sort who would wear the same suit for days on end. His job was his life. Maggie was trying to have more balance for herself, but it wasn't easy. Still, she'd turned thirty in July and had already learned the hard way that life was too short.

There was, mercifully, nothing romantic in Tom's offer of friendship.

"You can eat your *broodje* in front of me," he said. "I would."

"Do I look hungry?"

He smiled. "Starving."

"I'll have to pound the pavement after work to burn off the extra calories."

Dutch breakfasts notwithstanding, she kept in shape. At five-five, she couldn't count on her size to get her out of a jam. Fitness, training, experience and mental toughness were the trick.

And luck.

There was always the luck factor. But since luck wasn't her long suit, she didn't count on it, either.

"Look there," Tom said. "Your hair's the same color as those roses."

She noticed the cluster of orange-red roses in a dooryard. "It's not *that* red."

"Is the red hair from your mother or your father?"

"Father."

He hesitated. "I'm sorry. I didn't mean—"

"It's okay. I don't mind talking about him." She smiled to prove she wasn't just being nice. "My wanderlust is also a Spencer trait."

The day she'd arrived in The Hague was the eighteen-month anniversary of her father's death. Philip Spencer, ordinary American businessman, had walked into the middle of a bank robbery in Prague.

Talk about no luck.

The bank robbers still hadn't been caught. Nobody seemed to be looking too hard for them.

Maggie gave up on resisting, took her roll out of the bag and bit into it, welcoming the smokiness of the cheese and the softness of the bread. Normalcy. She had to establish her routines, focus on her job and continue to move forward with her life. She couldn't dwell on the past. And it wasn't her job to investigate her father's death.

She and Tom walked up Lange Voorhout, a tree-lined street of stately historic buildings that was said to be one of the prettiest in The Hague, or, as it was known formally in Dutch, *'s-Gravenhage,* which meant "the count's hedge." Even the Dutch shortened it to *Den Haag.* Although Amsterdam was the official capital, The Hague was the seat of the Dutch government and the residence of its royal family, as well as home to dozens of foreign embassies and the International Court of Justice.

The functional concrete American embassy was often called the ugliest building on Lange Voorhout, possibly in the entire city. The original embassy—presumably more graceful—had been accidentally destroyed by an Allied bomb during World War Two.

"Enjoy your bread and cheese," Tom said cheerfully when they arrived. "And don't work too hard."

"You're one to talk."

He laughed. "Not me. An eighteen-hour day's my limit."

Maggie made her way to her desk, pouring herself a mug of coffee before she sat down. As a special agent for the U.S. State Department's Diplomatic Security Service, she had a wide range of duties and responsibilities. First and foremost was the safety and security of the embassy's personnel, property and information, whether in or out of the building, and of American citizens in the country. She'd completed six months of training at the Federal Law Enforcement Training Center in Brunswick, Georgia, then worked in U.S. diplomatic security field offices for four years, investigating passport and visa fraud. She'd come to The Hague straight from the Chicago field office, on the heels of a major joint counterterrorism investigation that had culminated in the arrest of a sophisticated trio of Americans producing and selling fraudulent visas.

She ate the last bite of her roll and drank some of her coffee.

Having a father killed by bank robbers in Prague hadn't hurt her security clearance, nor did it even seem to trouble anyone—at least, not beyond sympathy for her loss.

It troubled her.

But she'd had to put her questions and doubts out of her mind, because there was nothing to be gained by sticking her nose into her father's murder investigation. The American embassy in Prague and the FBI would keep her informed of any progress. She had her own job to do.

She buried herself in it, and by midafternoon, she realized she'd forgotten lunch. She found some peanut butter crackers in her desk and opened up a bottle of water as she scanned her e-mail.

Re: Nick Janssen.

Now, there was a subject heading, she thought, noticing the message was from a free e-mail account she didn't recognize. She opened it up and took in the neatly typed words in a single glance, then read them over more slowly. Twice.

Special Agent Spencer,
You must hurry.
Nick Janssen is in 's-Hertogenbosch near the entrance of the Binnendieze boat tour. If necessary I can keep him there for another hour or so. But please hurry if you want him.
Sincerely,
A friend

Maggie read through the e-mail a fourth time.
A joke. It had to be.
Nick Janssen was an American fugitive

with the rare distinction of being on the "most wanted" lists of both the FBI and U.S. Marshals Service. He'd fled the country a year ago to avoid prosecution for tax evasion. That was enough to put him in hot water with the FBI and the marshals, but he wasn't considered violent. Then he tried to extort a presidential pardon, a disaster that had left three marshals wounded and three of his own men dead. That the whole mess had come to a climax in the backyard of the Tennessee boyhood home of the President of the United States didn't help matters.

As if that weren't plenty, Janssen's antics also exposed him as the violent, amoral mastermind of a lucrative criminal network of buyers and sellers of illegal arms, drugs and commodities.

Charlene Brooker, an American army captain, was the first person to suspect he was more than a simple tax evader. Janssen had ordered her killed last fall while she was in Amsterdam.

He was in Amsterdam himself during the pardon debacle in May and had managed to disappear shortly after it all blew apart.

Everyone wanted his hide.

Since arriving in the Netherlands, Maggie

had worked with various American and Dutch investigators on the Janssen case, but she couldn't think of a single "friend" who would know Nicholas Janssen's whereabouts and alert her by an anonymous e-mail.

'S-Hertogenbosch was a small city in the southern Dutch province of Noord-Brabant.

She didn't know what in blazes the Binnendieze was. The name of a canal? A boat tour company?

You must hurry.

It was almost four o'clock.

Maggie abandoned her peanut butter crackers and got up to go find her boss.

Libby Smith welcomed the breeze that seemed to float up from the Binnendieze, the shallow waterway that encircled most of the old city of 's-Hertogenbosch. "What happened to your dogs?"

"What?" Nick Janssen seemed confused, but it was obvious he hadn't liked anything about their meeting from the moment she'd joined him on his bench. It was, he'd said rather pathetically, his favorite spot nowadays. "How did you know about my dogs?"

"Rhodesian ridgebacks, weren't they?"

He'd dyed his distinctive silver hair a stupid-looking black. As notorious as he was, it was unlikely that anyone in the sleepy southern Dutch city would recognize him, even if he hadn't colored his hair.

Tourists—most of them Dutch themselves—stood in line for the boat tour of the Binnendieze.

Libby was bored out of her mind. She'd put on a frumpy denim skirt, a cheap tank top and ergonomic sandals and carried a canvas bag over her shoulder loaded with all the usual tourist paraphernalia. Her .22-caliber Beretta was tucked inside her foldable, packable, squishable traveler's rain jacket.

If necessary, she could get to the Beretta, shoot Nick Janssen and be gone before anyone realized what had happened. If people didn't expect him to be an international fugitive, they didn't expect her to be an accomplished killer.

But she hoped violence wouldn't be necessary. She had very big plans for her new relationship with her fellow American.

"I had to give the dogs away," he said.

She'd almost forgotten she'd asked about them. "That's too bad. Still, it wouldn't be easy to be on the lam with two dogs, never mind ones as large as they were."

"Samkevich shouldn't have sent you here," Janssen said tightly. "We should have met somewhere else."

"That would have had its own risks."

Vlad Samkevich, a Russian who lived in London, was a well-known arms dealer who also had an international warrant out for his arrest. But he wasn't as rich or as desperate as Janssen, and Libby needed someone who was both.

Janssen stared at the tourists talking loudly to one another in Dutch. "Samkevich says you've done work for him. You look like a child. How old are you?"

"Thirty-six."

"You look younger."

It wasn't a compliment. She was small and wiry, and although her very short hair was prematurely gray, it still hadn't added years to her appearance. It was her size and her cute face that made people think she was younger—always *too* young.

"I can do the job, Mr. Janssen," she said. "Just give me your list."

"I'll need you to prove yourself."

She was prepared. "I already have."

He glanced sideways at her. "How?"

"I killed Vladimir Samkevich before I left London two days ago."

No reaction from Janssen. Not shock, not respect, not anger.

Libby responded in kind and kept her mix of satisfaction and fear to herself. What if she'd guessed wrong? But she knew she hadn't. The man next to her had no more feeling for the Russian than she did. "Samkevich wasn't your friend. The authorities don't have solid evidence on you. You were as much a victim in May as anyone else. You didn't shoot the two marshals in Central Park or have the Dunnemores kidnapped in Amsterdam. Your guy had his own agenda."

Janssen made a little noise at her mention of Stuart and Betsy Dunnemore, parents of one of the wounded marshals, friends of John Wesley Poe, the current U.S. president. Libby wasn't sure she should have brought them up. Janssen had fancied himself in love with Betsy, his former college classmate, and tried to manipulate her into interceding on his behalf with Poe.

He'd thought Betsy would dump her elderly diplomat husband and marry him.

But Libby understood what it was to have unrealistic dreams, dreams everyone else thought were insane—not that most people gave a damn about anyone else's hopes and dreams. Nick Janssen didn't. He'd wanted a presidential pardon and let it be known he'd pay for one. He didn't care who got hurt in the process. His blindness to the aspirations of others had backfired on him as well.

When he didn't speak, she went on. "You had a guy use you in May for his own ends. The two men you sent to the States to clean up after him could have been a problem, too, but they're dead. They can't testify against you. They were two of your most trusted bodyguards, but who's to say they wouldn't have turned on you?"

"What does any of that have to do with Samkevich?"

"*He* could testify against you. The authorities were closing in on him. He knew it. He'd have cut a deal in a heartbeat, given them you in exchange for a lighter sentence."

Janssen thought a moment. "You're right, of course."

She hid her relief. "I don't want payment for him."

"His body—"

"He won't be discovered for a few more days."

"You're a very cold woman, Miss Smith."

She tried not to bristle, but she wasn't cold. Not at all. "I'm good at what I do."

"This is a nice town," he said absently. "I could have stayed here for a long time. I was on an island off the coast of Scotland for two months. Did you know that?"

"No," she lied.

He seemed to like that, having one over her. "The food was terrible. Here . . ." He gave a wistful sigh. "I have other safe houses."

"Of course."

"I want to see my mother's grave." His words were soft and yet toneless, as if he'd said them so many times they'd lost their meaning, become an unattainable fantasy. "It's within walking distance of where I grew up in northern Virginia. She died last winter."

Libby squirmed. She'd gone to her father's grave once, just so she could spit on it. "I'm sorry. Do you have your list?"

He looked at her again. "Yes. You really are very cold." But he fished a white index card out of his shirt pocket and passed it to her. "Ten names. A hundred thousand dollars for each."

She tucked the card into her canvas bag. "Excellent."

"You didn't look at any of the names."

"There's time for that. I'll need a deposit of a hundred thousand dollars wired into my account."

He nodded. "I'll take care of it. Should I be arrested—"

"I'll work faster and expect a bonus. Double."

"That's two million dollars."

"You rich tycoons." Libby smiled, hoisting her canvas bag higher onto her shoulder. "Always so good at math."

She slid smoothly to her feet, noticing that Janssen didn't so much as glance at her breasts straining against her tank top.

Wrapped up in his own problems, she supposed.

She glanced at her watch. Four-fifteen. What to do with herself the rest of the day?

"I want this all to be over," he said quietly.

"It will be. Patience."

"The bonus?"

She'd started to move away from the bench, but his words—his cool tone—forced her to turn back.

"Any bonus would be paid only upon my release." His eyes, a frosty blue, held her in place. "I wouldn't want you to get any ideas."

"Of course. I understand."

She did, too.

She understood that one or two million—whichever amount Janssen ended up paying her—was a miniscule amount to him. And it wouldn't satisfy her. She was finished being a bit player, a hired gun, an anonymous force in a larger game.

She wanted it all, and Nick Janssen was her vehicle for getting it.

You have no fellow feeling, do you?

The words came out of nowhere. The jolt of memory. Philip Spencer might have been perched on the branch of a nearby linden tree, speaking to her from the dead.

Her heart pounded, and she actually glanced around her, just to make sure he hadn't somehow materialized in her shadow.

He'd tried to save her from herself.

Leaving Janssen on the bench, Libby hurried away. Glancing around, she noticed a balding man in a rumpled suit break off from the boat tour queue and walk down the street.

A prickly sensation crawled up her back. *Something's wrong.*

She walked into a small café and sat at a table inside, with her back to the wall so that she could see out the open front.

The balding man had disappeared.

She had good instincts. She was a superior shooter. But she wasn't trained at surveillance, countersurveillance, any of those tricks of the trade. Mostly, she got along by guts and a willingness to take risks—and the unexpectedness of being a petite woman in her midthirties who killed people for pay.

It was possible she was wrong.

She bit into the small cookie that came with her coffee.

Five minutes later, Nick Janssen got up from the bench and stretched.

He walked to a fence overlooking the narrow waterway.

Ten minutes kicked by. He seemed transfixed. Libby drank her coffee. *Something isn't right.*

Janssen turned and started toward the street. The Dutch police pounced.

An *Arrestatieteam,* their version of a SWAT team. They moved fast, intercepting their target, giving him orders in English, getting handcuffs on him.

Libby joined the onlookers at the outdoor tables.

There was no sign of the balding man. Was he a police officer?

Had he seen her on the bench with Janssen?

Janssen went quietly. He wasn't a fighter. He relied on others to do his fighting for him.

And his killing.

Libby paid for her coffee, wondering if he'd blame her for his arrest.

There was very little she could do if he did.

In the meantime, she had a job to do.

Ten names to memorize. Ten people to kill.

Two

Equal light, level sight.

Falling back on the basics, Rob Dunnemore aimed his .40-caliber Glock and emptied it into the silhouette twenty-five yards away.

Four months ago, he'd been the target. Alive, not a paper silhouette.

Even with ear protection, he could hear the shots echo across the indoor range. He didn't flinch. He was soaked with sweat under his Kevlar vest. He'd popped off a couple of boxes of ammo and felt the burn in his shoulders and back, another reminder that he was out of practice.

He racked back, then made sure he'd counted his shots right and hadn't left a round in the chamber. He didn't want to ruin his practice by putting a bullet in his foot. Shooting was a perishable skill, and he was rusty—he hadn't done this much in one outing since he'd taken a round to his gut in Central Park almost four months ago.

He'd almost bled to death. He'd lost his spleen. Lying in his hospital bed, helpless, he'd nearly lost his family.

Those hadn't been good days.

Shrugging off his goggles and ear protection, he could smell the smoke from the powder and the spent ammunition. His hold on his Glock was tighter than it needed to be. A death grip, like a damn rookie's.

He made sure his gun was clear and safe, then set it on the wood counter in front of him and reeled in his target.

Thirteen in center mass, one a clear miss.

Not bad. Just a hair off a hundred percent.

The rest was a mind game that had nothing to do with technical proficiency.

The door behind him creaked open. "Don't shoot," Juliet Longstreet said in her usual cheeky manner. "It's just me."

But Rob could tell from her expression that something was up with his fellow deputy U.S. Marshal, and he unclipped his target, loosened his vest. "Hey, Longstreet."

She nodded to his target. "How'd you do?"

He showed her.

She whistled. "You'll be back on the street in no time, taking down bad guys."

Her heart wasn't in her words. Something had definitely happened. "Juliet—"

"Nick Janssen's been arrested," she said quickly.

"Where?"

"Some town in Holland. A Dutch SWAT team picked him up on a tip to our embassy there."

"When?"

"A couple hours ago."

Rob pushed back an image of a young Nick Janssen in his mother's college yearbook and studied Longstreet. They'd been an item for a while, splitting up well before the shooting in May. Juliet had her own demons from those difficult days—she'd nearly become one of Janssen's victims herself.

"You okay?" he asked.

"Yeah. It brings it all back, that's all. About time we got the bastard."

"Any word on extradition?"

"Legal eagles are already on it. The Dutch say they have enough to charge him with Char Brooker's murder. If we can't do better than that—" She shrugged, then gave a dry smile. "It's not as if he succeeded in killing any of us over here."

"Not for lack of trying."

Juliet's eyes seemed to flatten. "Yeah, well. The two goons he sent over here to find out what was going on are dead."

And she and a former Special Forces officer—dead army captain Charlene Brooker's husband—had found the bodies. A lunatic out of the Dunnemore past had believed he could use his knowledge of their relationship with President Poe to extract a pardon for Nick Janssen and earn millions for his efforts.

The story, with all its complexities and intricacies, had been fodder for the media for weeks.

"News of the arrest public yet?" Rob asked, keeping his own emotions in check.

Juliet shook her head. "You and I are getting a heads-up before reporters get the bit in their teeth and start calling."

"For what? To ask us how we feel now that Nick Janssen's in custody?"

"Pretty much."

"I'm not talking to any reporters."

"Me, neither."

The shooting range was curiously quiet. Rob still could smell the smoke from his practice. He shoved a full magazine into his Glock, aware of Juliet watching him. "Want to shoot a few rounds?" he asked her.

"I'm a better shot than you."

"Always the ambitious one."

She smiled, not taking offense where she would have six months ago. "Just stating the facts, Dunnemore. Let me get some ear protection and goggles. It's too goddamn hot to wear a vest—"

"Wear a vest, Juliet."

She waved a hand. "Yeah, I guess I'd better, given my luck these days."

"I suppose we should be relieved now that Janssen's in custody."

"I suppose. So why do I feel like another damn shoe's about to drop? I'm not that paranoid."

Rob had no answer.

Whether it was instinct or post-trauma stress at work he just knew he shared her sense of dread.

By the time Maggie dragged herself back up to her small apartment it was after midnight. Without hesitation, Dutch police had followed up on her anonymous tip and arrested Nick Janssen without incident. They had no idea who her "friend" was. Neither did she. She was hungry again and heated up leftover Indonesian fried rice, which she ate standing up, pacing, too wired and uneasy yet to settle down.

Her gaze landed on a picture of her father on a sailboat in south Florida. Smiling. She remembered how his eyes would crinkle when he smiled. He'd worked as a consultant for small businesses, mostly in eastern Europe and Russia—supposedly. Maggie had had her doubts, more so since his death. Little things didn't add up. She suspected he'd played some kind of role in the multifaceted world of intelligence—one that he couldn't talk about even to his DS-agent daughter. As the sharp edges of her grief had worn down, her questions had become more focused, but answers weren't any easier to come by. She hated the idea that she might have to learn to live with her questions.

But her father had always been a fairly remote figure to her. Even when she was growing up, he was never around. Her mother finally couldn't take his long absences anymore, and they'd divorced when Maggie was in high school. He hadn't changed his ways. He couldn't. She understood that part. She had that same sense of wanderlust.

"Well, Pop," she said, dipping her wooden spoon into her pan of spicy vegetables and rice, "we got the bad guy today."

She didn't know if he'd ever really approved of her career in diplomatic security. He'd seemed okay with her political science degree in college, then her first job at the State Department. She'd hoped her decision to become a DS officer and the prospect of a foreign service career might have intrigued him, but he'd remained outside her life, not disinterested but not a part of it.

The DS special agent in charge of her field office had given her the news of her father's death himself.

Philip Spencer had simply been in the wrong place at the wrong time.

Except Maggie hadn't believed it. Still didn't. Czech authorities, U.S. authorities—she wasn't getting the whole story. She'd pushed and bucked and bitten off heads, and everywhere, from everyone, she got the same line.

Shot by bank robbers who then got away. *Bullshit.*

There were no witnesses. Newspapers, even in Prague, barely covered the story. And the reaction she got from investigators—American and Czech—amounted to stonewalling. But she'd finally backed off. What was the point in sticking her neck out for a man she'd seen maybe a half-dozen times in the five years before his death?

Maggie dumped out the rest of her fried rice and ran cold water into the pan, leaving it until morning.

No one—not the Dutch authorities, not anyone at the American embassy—was celebrating Nick Janssen's arrest. As pleased as they were with having him in custody, they all knew his tentacles were far-reaching. There was a lot of work yet to be done.

The media were all over the story. The

embassy's public affairs officers as well as the FBI and USMS people back in Washington were fielding questions. Janssen's attorneys had descended, screaming and hollering. News of Maggie's anonymous tip was out.

On her way to bed, she noticed that her solitary plant, an orchid she'd bought in deference to the collective Dutch green thumb, looked dead. It was supposed to be a hardy variety that she'd have a difficult time killing, but she'd killed it in less than three weeks.

She took it to the sink, doused it with water and left it next to her soaking leftovers pan. Maybe it'd revive by morning.

She rolled her eyes. Who was she kidding? The thing was *dead.* To hope otherwise wasn't optimism—it was refusing to face reality.

And if nothing else, Maggie thought, she was a woman determined to face reality.

Libby Smith left her window open in her room at her small hotel around the corner from where Dutch police had picked up Nick Janssen. It was brazen of her. A risk. But there was no reason for authorities to investigate hotel guests. Even if they did, they'd never suspect her of being anything but what she was: an American antiques dealer, a woman looking for off-the-beaten-track bargains.

What if they had him under surveillance and saw you on the bench with him?

If they caught up with her and asked about it, she'd say she'd stopped to rest her feet and they'd chatted for a few minutes about the sights.

She couldn't seem to get cool.

She lay naked atop the cotton duvet and noticed the sheen of her sweat in the light from the street. She could hear the traffic, the sound of music playing somewhere not too far off, the voices of people under her window, out enjoying the warm summer night.

The hundred-thousand deposit had been wired into her account. Janssen must have prearranged the transfer.

Libby had never made such money.

And it was just the beginning.

She'd memorized Janssen's list of targets and burned it, flushing the ashes down her toilet.

Knowing his enemies—and eliminating

them—would help her to understand his network and, in time, replace him.

His arrest was inevitable, just a bit earlier than she'd hoped for. Some Dutch Goody Two-shoes must have recognized him and called the police.

The balding man—who was he? Closing her eyes, Libby breathed deeply and tried not to feel as if she were suffocating, told herself the balding man didn't matter. Only her plan did, her next target. The thrill of her work had satisfied her in the beginning. Now she wanted more.

Money.

Power.

She smiled to herself, relaxing, feeling in control at last.

Three

Nate Winter came home to find secret service agents crawling all over his house, a reminder of just how much his life had changed in the past four months.

His fiancée, Sarah Dunnemore, was on the back porch having peach cobbler with President John Wesley Poe, who regarded her as the daughter he'd never had. Being together brought out their Southern accents.

Nate had a feeling he knew why Poe was there.

Nick Janssen.

The rich, murdering bastard was finally in custody.

It was hot even on the shaded porch, but the two Tennesseans didn't seem to mind. While looking for a home of their own in northern Virginia, Nate and Sarah were living in a corner of an 1850s historic house she was researching and getting ready to open to the public. Supposedly it was haunted by both Abraham Lincoln and Robert E. Lee. Poe liked to joke that he wished he could ask both men for advice. But Sarah, a historical archaeologist, was serious about her ghosts.

Before they'd met, Nate had been a senior deputy U.S. Marshal dedicated to catching fugitives and not much else.

He was still a marshal, he was still dedicated to his work—but now he could come home to Sarah, ghosts, peach cobbler and the occasional presidential visit.

"Mr. President," Nate said, "it's good to see you."

Poe, already on his feet, put out his hand, and the two men shook. "It's good to see you, too, Nate. Sarah's ruining my diet with her peach cobbler."

Nate had helped her pick the peaches from one of the trees in the old house's sprawling yard, knowing she expected to make jam one evening. The cobbler meant she was upset, because otherwise she'd still be up to her elbows in the hundred-year-old dump she'd found out back and was in the process of excavating. When she was upset, she dug out family recipes, usually ones involving a lot of butter.

Her gray eyes connected with Nate's for a split second, enough to tell him that Poe's visit hadn't been her idea. She had on cropped jeans and a tank top, barefoot even for peach cobbler with the president.

As welcome as it was, Janssen's arrest had brought back the trauma of her ordeal last spring. Her twin brother badly injured in a sniper-style attack in Central Park, a killer on the loose in Night's Landing, the Dunnemore family's Tennessee home, their refuge. John Wesley Poe happened to have grown up next door.

Sarah was fair-haired and beautiful, and Nate—tall, lean, impatient—hated for those dark days to prey on her again. But he'd learned that Sarah Dunnemore wasn't an ivory tower intellectual who wanted to remain aloof from life. She dove in, sometimes without looking.

"I stopped by to see how Sarah had

taken the news of the Janssen arrest," Poe said. "And Rob. I wondered how he was doing."

"I haven't talked to him yet," Sarah said. "I called my parents a little while ago—they're fine."

"I tried to reach Rob on his cell phone earlier," Nate said. "He didn't answer. I left a message."

"How is he recuperating from his injuries?" Poe asked.

Sarah dabbed at the ice cream melting onto her cobbler. "He's doing well, but he's frustrated because his recovery took longer than he expected. At least he's back to his triathlon training."

Swimming, running, biking. From all accounts, Rob was as fit now as he'd been before the shooting. But he'd endured a weeks-long media barrage. Now the whole world knew that he'd graduated from Georgetown and spoke seven languages, that he and his twin sister were like the son and daughter President Poe had never had. Rob often came off in media reports as a silver-spoon, Southern frat boy, but nothing about him was that simple.

"Is he back on the street?" Poe asked.

Nate shook his head. "Not yet."

The president sighed heavily. "I worry about him."

Which, Nate knew, Rob would hate. Sarah knew it, too, but she nodded with understanding. "It's hard not to worry."

"Janssen's arrest will fire up the media again. I hate to see him go through *that*. They'll rehash everything that happened in May." Poe winced. "They'll be calling you, too, Sarah. And your parents."

"The marshals have sent someone to Night's Landing in case it gets crazy. If any reporters show up here, I can handle them." She smiled and licked her spoon. "I'll have Bobby Lee or Abe talk to them."

Nate could see Poe forcing himself to relax. "I never know when you're serious—"

"*Every* resident of this house since 1875 swears the two of them are haunting the place. I take that seriously." She rose, calmer now herself, and grabbed her bowl. "Are you going to eat your cobbler, Wes? Because if not, I'll take it into the house before the flies get to it. There's no wasting fresh peach cobbler around here."

That elicited a real smile. "Can I take it with me?"

She beamed. A Ph.D. with academic credits up and down both arms, and she loved getting compliments for her cooking. "I'll go wrap it up."

When he heard the screen door shut, Wes breathed out, any hint of a smile gone. "Nate—I hope you'll tell Rob he can call me anytime. I'll make sure he's put through right away."

"He knows that, Mr. President."

The older man nodded. "I'd like to think so. I'd like to think that now that our families' relationship is common knowledge—" He seemed to fight for the right words. "That it won't ruin his life."

Nate had no idea what to say.

A secret service agent stood on the bottom step of the porch.

Time for Poe to leave.

He glanced at the screen door. "You and Sarah are good for each other. After you're married—" He shook his head. "Well, never mind."

Nate thought he understood what Poe was getting at. "We'll want you to be a part of our lives, Mr. President. Both of us."

He sighed. "Thank you."

"Rob—"

"Rob's a different story. He always has been."

After Poe left with his entourage of secret service and staffers—and his peach cobbler—Nate found Sarah in the kitchen, flipping through her grandmother's recipes. Given the array of ingredients on the table, she was looking for something that involved both cream of mushroom soup and mayonnaise. He slipped his arms around her. "I don't think my arteries can take whatever it is you're about to whip up."

She shoved the cans aside. "I'm missing an ingredient, anyway."

"Dare I ask what?"

"Water chestnuts."

He let his hands move up her midriff toward her breasts. "Do you think Abe and Bobby Lee would object if we made love this early in the evening?"

"If I think about them watching us—"

"I don't know, it could be fun. A foursome—"

She elbowed him in the gut, registering her disapproval, and he laughed, sweeping her up off her feet, getting her away from her cans and her kitchen. He figured he could ease her stress in other ways.

*   *   *

Rob rolled out of bed at six in his first-floor Brooklyn apartment, pulled on shorts and a T-shirt and headed out for his morning paper. He'd ignored all messages from reporters on his voice mail when he got home last night.

A woman in biking shorts was on his doorstep. "Deputy Dunnemore? My name's Patty. I'd like to talk to you about the arrest of Nicholas Janssen yesterday in the Netherlands."

No last name, no credentials. A freelancer. She looked young enough to be a journalism student. She was sweating and panting, indicating she'd pedaled a ways to get to him, which at least meant she didn't live nearby.

Rob picked up his paper and noticed Janssen's arrest had made the front page. No surprise.

Patty frowned when he didn't respond. "Have you and President Poe talked about the arrest?"

Her eyes fell to where his scar was under his shirt. The whole damned world knew the details of his injury. There'd been diagrams of the path of the bullet on TV. Doctors had discussed his prognosis, his recovery, how people could live normal lives without a spleen.

"It's a nice morning for a bike ride," he said. "See you, Patty."

He didn't like shutting the door in her face, but his other options—for example, talking to her—were even less appealing. When he got back up to his apartment, he looked out his living room door and caught her giving him the finger from her bike.

A pro.

No way would he get a bike ride in himself. Or a run. Or even a swim at the Y. There'd be more reporters to deal with. He'd been shot and his family nearly destroyed because of their connection to the president. For months the media had hounded him.

Now Janssen was in Dutch custody.

Due to an anonymous tip to a diplomatic security agent three weeks on the job.

Something about it didn't sit right with Rob. He took a shower, got dressed and headed for work, contemplating the unlikelihood of what had gone down across the Atlantic.

He managed to sneak past a throng of reporters outside the federal building where the Southeastern District Office of the U.S. Marshals Service was located. When he got to his desk, a stack of messages, all from reporters, was waiting for him.

Reporters and a day of desk work. He swore to himself and dumped all the messages in the trash.

Mike Rivera stood in his office doorway and jerked a thumb at Rob to join him. Rob doubted it was because the chief deputy wanted to put him back on the street. A heavyset man in his early fifties with bulldog features that his wife seemed to adore, Rivera was well respected but not a soft touch. He wouldn't like having reporters crawling all over his office and harassing one of his deputies.

"Talk to me," he said. "Who've you heard from?"

Rob sat in a spongy plastic chair. "A lot of reporters. I haven't talked to any of them. There's not much to say."

"We can issue a statement. It probably won't do much good while the feeding frenzy's on, but we can try. Do you want to be available for interviews, issue a statement yourself or anything?"

"No."

"Didn't think so."

"I want to do my damn job."

Rivera's eyes flashed. "Yeah, well, you're going to need to lie low for a couple of days until the dust settles on this Janssen arrest."

"I've been laying low since May."

"You've been recovering from a goddamn bullet wound that nearly killed you—"

"It didn't kill me." Rob kept his voice calm. "I'm fit for duty. I don't want anyone coddling me."

"Who the hell's coddling you? You don't want to move too fast, get in over your head—"

"What, with a computer?"

"With another asshole with a gun."

Rob didn't respond. He hadn't had a chance in May. He'd dragged Nate down to Central Park to see the tulips—they'd never live that one down—and gotten shot. No warning, no way to fight back. They'd walked into the park and come out on stretchers.

Rivera sat forward, his chair squeaking loudly. "Why do you look so thin?" he asked, making it sound like an accusation.

"I'm back into my triathlon training. I can pass any test you want to throw at me—"

"Yeah, okay. Don't drop and do push-ups here in my office. You nailed your fitness for duty assessment. I know that. It's your head I worry about."

"I've done everything I've been asked to do, all the desensitizing and reprogramming or whatever it's called. Time for you all to stop walking on eggshells around me."

Rivera grunted. "Today isn't a good day to tell me you're just a regular deputy trying to do his job."

His chair squeaked again when he leaned back, bugging the hell out of Rob. Not a good sign, probably, that a noisy chair irritated him. "I want to get out of here, at least for a few days. Let the dust settle."

"Will you go down to Tennessee?"

"The Hague."

Rivera stood and turned to his grime-encrusted window. "Christ, Dunnemore. You don't make my life easy, do you?"

Rob smiled. "Not my job, Chief. Less chance of anyone getting misquoted or harassed if I'm out of the country."

"So go to Ireland."

"Nick Janssen's not in custody in Ireland.

The DS agent who got tipped off about where to find him isn't in Ireland."

"You're serious, aren't you?"

Still in his plastic chair, Rob shrugged. "Sure, why not? I can check with our people in the Netherlands, see where things stand now that the Dutch have Janssen. A Dutch judge is considering our request to interview him. We don't want anything slipping through the cracks."

Rivera shifted from the window and held up a hand. "I get your point. What says a Dunnemore showing up in Holland won't fire up reporters there?"

"Nothing. Janssen's arrest is a public reminder of my family's connections to President Poe. There's not much I can do about that. But the media will be looking for me in New York, not The Hague."

"You want to do this thing?"

"I can be on a flight out of Kennedy tonight."

"Listen, Rob, if this is personal—"

"Of course it's personal." Rob stood, feeling the August heat even in the air-conditioned room. "Janssen put out word that he'd pay for a presidential pardon. He tried to get under my mother's skin. Ultimately, he's the one responsible for everything that happened in May—"

"It was a bad time."

"Then there's Charlene Brooker. The Dutch are charging Janssen with ordering her murder in Amsterdam last year. We're all still scrambling to unravel his network."

"None of that is why you're going to Holland."

Rob shrugged. "Maybe not."

"You want to know who gave that DS agent the tip."

"Don't you?"

Rivera pulled out his chair and plopped down with a loud, obnoxious groan of metal. "Hell." He looked up at Rob. "Bring me back some Dutch gin."

"Mike—"

"Just a little bottle. I don't drink as much as I used to."

Rob knew he'd won. There was nothing to do now except figure out which flight to take, dig out his passport and pack.

Four

Maggie stared at her boss in disbelief. "Why me?"

George Bremmerton regarded her with a reasonable measure of sympathy from the other side of her desk, but she knew he wasn't about to change his mind. "Because he requested you."

"Why would Rob Dunnemore request me?"

"Because you made the Janssen arrest happen."

"I got an e-mail tip and made a phone call. That was the extent of it." She sat back in her chair. "I can't get out of this?"

"Not unless you find a way to get run over by a bus."

"Great," Maggie said without enthusiasm. "You know Dunnemore's a rich frat-boy type playing marshal until he decides to start living off his trust fund, don't you?"

Bremmerton almost smiled. He was in his late forties and one of the most respected regional security officers ever, a very serious-minded man who was nonetheless getting a kick out of her predicament. "I met his parents last winter. They're not rich."

"Rich people never think they're rich. And they're friends with President Poe. They don't need to be rich."

"Are you whining, Spencer?"

She groaned. "Yes, I'm whining. How long is Dunnemore staying?"

"Not my problem."

Which meant it was her problem. Maggie had seen pictures of Rob Dunnemore. He was fair and very good-looking, more rugged than she'd expected—or particularly wanted to admit at the moment, since she preferred to think of him in terms of stereotypes.

People said he had gray eyes, but she hadn't really noticed.

"When's he getting here?" she asked.

"Half an hour."

"I like the big warning I get."

Bremmerton shrugged. "I just found out myself."

"You have his flight information?"

He handed her a printout. "Don't treat him like a VIP. He's a federal agent. He's here on business."

"Marshal business? Or President Poe business?"

"Don't go there, Maggie. Dunnemore's main reason for being here is to see you. He's not even being very subtle about it."

Since Bremmerton had more than two decades of foreign assignments behind him and she had three weeks, Maggie trusted his instincts. She was fortunate to be working with him. He'd gone to Nairobi in the aftermath of the American embassy bombing that had killed scores there. From all accounts, he'd been a steady presence amid tragedy and fear. It wasn't a surprise to anyone who knew him or his reputation. No task within the realm of diplomatic security was too big or too small for him to tackle, which, along with his mix of competence and genuine decency, had earned him widespread respect and admiration. He also managed to have a relatively normal family life, with his speech-therapist wife with him in The Hague and two kids in college in the Midwest.

Maggie had worked hard to gain George Bremmerton's confidence in her three weeks at the embassy and didn't take it for granted.

If he wanted her to baby-sit President Poe's marshal pal, that was what she'd do.

"I guess I should get going," she said.

"His twin sister's getting married in a few weeks to the marshal who got shot with him in Central Park." Bremmerton shrugged at his own non sequitur. "It'll give you something to talk about. She's an archaeologist. Sarah."

"He's going to want to talk about Nick Janssen."

Given the small size of the Netherlands, Schiphol was almost exclusively an international airport—a very busy one—but Maggie had no trouble finding Rob Dunnemore. She recognized him from all the pictures she'd seen of him since the Central Park attack.

He was even more good-looking in person. Tall, very fit. Lightly tanned. He had on a dark suit that had come through the long flight virtually without wrinkles.

His eyes were, indeed, gray.

She introduced herself. "Can I carry something?"

"No, thank you, I've got everything."

She'd expected more of a Southern accent. He had a small carry-on suitcase that she hoped meant he didn't plan a long stay.

But as he observed her, she sensed an air of danger about him that took her aback. She quickly told herself she'd imagined it. It was just something she'd assumed because she knew he'd nearly been killed in the line of duty four months ago.

"Decent flight?" she asked, leading him out to her car.

"Uneventful."

"That's the way I like it. I always feel as if I've come out of the dryer after a long flight. Did you sleep?"

"I'm fine, Agent Spencer."

But cranky, she thought. "Please, call me Maggie."

He didn't seem too excited about riding in her red Mini. She unlocked the passenger door. "SUVs don't work that well in Holland with all the narrow streets and teeny-tiny parking spaces."

"The Mini's no problem. It's yours?"

For the first time, she detected his Southern accent. She nodded. "It's cute, isn't it?"

She thought he might have smiled.

"Jet lag's a killer," she said when she got in behind the wheel. "My father used to swear by drinking a gallon of water on the plane and not eating a bite. I thought he was exaggerating, but he meant it. A whole gallon of water."

"I ate everything that was offered."

Maggie smiled. "That's what I do."

Dunnemore stared out his window most of the drive back to The Hague. She didn't bug him. It was still before dawn his time. His body wanted to be in bed, asleep.

"I'll drop you off at your hotel," she said. "You can get settled, and I'll come fetch you when you want—"

"I can make it to the embassy on my own."

So it was going to be that way. He wanted control. No suggestions from her. She shrugged. "Fine by me."

He sighed. "I'm sorry. I didn't mean to

sound surly. Thank you for trekking me around."

"You asked for me. My boss gave the order."

"I asked if I could talk with you. I didn't mean—"

"It doesn't matter." She smiled over at him. "You've got me for the duration of your visit, Deputy."

When they arrived at his hotel, he turned down her offer to make sure his room was ready. He'd see to it. He was definitely independent. Self-sufficient. Not one who played well with others. Maggie hoped it wouldn't become a problem. She didn't want to bump heads with Rob Dunnemore, friend of the president.

Thomas Kopac intercepted her when she got back to the embassy. "Rumor has it you're escorting President Poe's—"

"You shouldn't be listening to rumors."

"Rob Dunnemore. He's here?"

"He's freshening up at his hotel. He's a marshal. We're not supposed to think of him as Poe's surrogate son."

Kopac grinned. "Says who?"

"Says me. Anything I can do for you? Or

do I get to do a little work before Dunnemore gets here?"

"Nothing you can do for me, Special Agent Spencer." He leaned in toward her, adding in an amused conspiratorial whisper, "I'll be in my office if you need a place to scream. It's in the bowels of the building. No one'll hear you."

"Very funny."

He laughed. "I thought so."

When she got back to her desk, Maggie checked her e-mail, hoping for another tip, something that would force Bremmerton to find someone else to stick Rob Dunnemore with. The guy put her nerve endings on edge. It wasn't the Poe connection, she decided. It was the gray eyes.

But there was nothing.

Her mobile phone rang, almost as if it knew she was looking for distractions.

A private number.

"Maggie Spencer—"

"St. John's Cathedral is the finest example of Gothic architecture in the Netherlands."

The voice was male, the accent East Coast American, and the words had her sitting up straight. St. John's was in 's-Hertogenbosch, the same city where Dutch police had picked up Nick Janssen yesterday.

"Who is this?"

"I'll be there tomorrow afternoon. It's important that we talk."

"I understand, but I need more information—"

"Just trust your instincts."

"My instincts tell me this is a crank call."

She thought she heard the start of a laugh. "I doubt that. Do people still call you Magster? Your father did when you were small, didn't he?"

Magster.

Her stomach flip-flopped, but she warned herself that using her childhood name could just be a good guess, a way to manipulate her. It didn't mean he knew anything about her father's death. She couldn't let herself think it was anything more.

"Who are you? I need a name."

It was as if she hadn't spoken. "Come alone. If you don't, I'll disappear, and you'll have missed an important opportunity."

"An opportunity for what?"

But he was gone, the connection dead.

A meeting. Was the guy out of his mind? He must have prepared every word in advance. Of *course* her father called her Magster. What father with a daughter named Maggie didn't?

Some days she couldn't believe it'd been eighteen months since his murder; other days, it was as if her father was more a dream than anything else, lost in a fog of memories and lost possibilities.

Had the caller known him?

Maggie felt a sudden rush of tears that she immediately fought back, impatient with herself.

But Rob Dunnemore materialized behind her, startling her with his good looks. The ends of his fair hair were still damp from his shower. He hadn't wasted any time in getting cleaned up and settled in.

She smiled quickly, hoping there was no sign of even one damn tear in her eyes. "Have a seat, Deputy. We can get started."

"Bad day?"

"What? Oh." She made herself smile. "No, not yet."

He didn't seem to believe her. "That's good."

Maggie wished she'd indulged in chocolate sprinkles that morning, because it was going to be a very long day.

Magster.

She'd figure out what to do about her anonymous caller when she didn't have Deputy Dunnemore's gray eyes on her.

Wide awake despite his overnight flight and long day, Rob sat on a wooden chair at a small table in his room on the top floor of his hotel, a renovated eighteenth-century building. It had low, slanted ceilings and no air-conditioning, but it wasn't a hot night, at least by middle Tennessee standards.

He heard laughter through his open window and looked down four floors at a young couple standing under a linden tree, its branches carefully trained.

Rob turned away from the scene.

His eyes were heavy, scratchy, from fatigue and jet lag.

Maggie Spencer had walked with him back to his hotel, turning down a quick after-work drink.

A woman with things on her mind, Special Agent Spencer.

He'd gone into the dark, quiet bar by himself, but in a few minutes another man joined him, introducing himself as Tom

Kopac, an embassy employee. Maggie's friend.

They'd had a beer together. It was clear word had gotten out that the wounded marshal from the Janssen mess in May—the marshal who was friends with the president—was in town and Maggie was stuck with him.

Kopac had decided to check him out.

Their conversation was cordial but superficial. Rob had smiled at the older man. "Maggie's a DS agent. She protects you. You don't protect her."

"She's also a friend."

After Kopac left, Rob had a spicy, meat-filled *kroket* with mustard, then went up to his room.

Why the hell was Kopac suspicious of him when Spencer was the one who had received the damn anonymous tip about Janssen? Not even an hour afterward, he was under arrest. Tips like that didn't happen often, even with minor nonviolent fugitives, never mind with violent fugitives with international warrants out on them.

Was it someone wanting to collect the reward for information leading to Janssen's arrest?

No one had come forward.

Rob put aside his questions and picked up the phone, dialing his future brother-in-law's office in Arlington.

"What do we know about the DS agent who got the Janssen tip? Maggie Spencer." Rob didn't mention her rich red hair, her turquoise eyes, her creamy skin, and chastised himself for his gut-punched reaction to her. "She's gritting her teeth, but she's not complaining about getting saddled with me. At least not to my face."

"Her name's familiar," Nate said.

"Because she's the one who got the Janssen tip—"

"No, it's something else."

"You want to see what you can find out?"

"Sure."

"She's fetching me up in the morning and carting me to the town where Janssen was picked up."

"Her idea?"

"She's finding things to do with me."

The alternative meanings of what he said struck him like a junior high student. *Jet lag.*

"I'm not touching that," Nate said with a chuckle. "I'll check her out, let you know if I find out anything. Has she given you any idea of who she thinks gave her the tip?"

"She's not a talker—she's not easy to read."

"All right. I'll see what I can do. Isn't it midnight there?"

"Just about."

"Go to bed. Take a sleeping pill."

"I don't want to oversleep and miss my field trip."

Then again, Spencer was probably the type to throw a brick through his window to wake him up.

"I'll tell Sarah you called," Nate said.

"And the president?"

Silence.

"He wanted to know how I reacted to Janssen's arrest, didn't he?"

"It's not that simple—"

"It never is with Wes. Yeah. Say hi to Sarah for me."

When he hung up, Rob glanced down at the street and saw that the laughing couple was gone. The street seemed empty, almost too quiet. He lay atop his bed in his shorts. No shirt, no shoes. He'd visited his parents in Holland in April, when Nick Janssen was just wanted for failing to appear in court to face tax evasion charges. He'd made a move on Rob's mother, and Rob hadn't even known it.

So much had happened since then.

But his parents were back in Night's Landing, permanently, and his father, in his late seventies, was finally easing up on his schedule. His mother seemed more at peace than she had in many weeks. Neither had wanted Rob to go back to work after the shooting—they hadn't wanted him to become a marshal in the first place.

"Should have called them before you left New York," he said to the ceiling. But he hadn't talked to them at all since Janssen's arrest.

He let his eyes close, pushing back an image of Night's Landing and the old log house his grandfather had built, thinking instead about Maggie Spencer and Tom Kopac and what it was about the diplomatic security agent that bothered him.

Five

Maggie pulled up to Rob's hotel in her Mini at eight. She didn't know what else to do except drag him to 's-Hertogenbosch with her.

He greeted her with a charming smile and two espressos and folded himself into her small car without complaint, handing her one of the espressos. "What is it, about two hours to 's-Hertogenbosch?"

He pronounced the full name of the southern city the same way her Dutch friends did—flawlessly. It translated as "the duke's forest" and was typically shortened to Den Bosch, which Maggie could pronounce easily enough. "Should be," she said, pulling out onto the street.

As he sipped his espresso, Rob dug out a pocket map and checked their route. "Den Bosch was founded in the twelfth century by Hendrik I of Brabant."

"Ah."

"Biggest attraction there is Sint Jan's Kathedraal."

Maggie didn't let herself react to his use of the Dutch name for St. John's Cathedral, where she was supposed to meet her anonymous caller, her ulterior motive for going to Den Bosch on a warm Saturday morning. "You've been reading tourist brochures, I see."

"We might need something to do after we look at the spot where the Dutch police picked up Janssen. Do you know the address of his safe house?"

She nodded. "We could go there, too."

"Maybe it has window boxes."

His sarcasm was barely detectable, which, Maggie decided, only made him more dangerous. She'd underestimated him. Dismissed him as not serious, indulged in stereotypes because she hadn't wanted to deal with him—she'd had better things to do than take care of a deputy marshal who counted among his friends the U.S. president. But Deputy Dunnemore was proving himself to be a much more complicated case than she'd anticipated.

She got onto the motorway, the traffic relatively light on a Saturday morning. "If you don't want to go to Den Bosch, I can drop you off somewhere else."

"I'm into the idea now. Have you seen many sights since you've been here?"

She reached for her espresso and took too big a sip, nearly burning her mouth, then shook her head, putting the coffee back in the cup holder. "I've only been here three weeks. I haven't had much time. I vary my run just so I can see more of the streets in The Hague." She made herself smile through her tension. She didn't like hiding her real purpose for going to Den Bosch from him. "I could get into castles."

"All work, no play," Rob said, looking up from his map. "Does that describe you, Maggie?"

"I don't know. I'm not that introspective."

"Interesting, since you're the new kid, that you should be the one to get the tip on where to find our guy Janssen."

"Yes, isn't it?"

"Where were you before here?"

"Chicago."

"And you grew up in . . ."

"South Florida, for the most part. We moved around a lot before my parents were divorced."

"They still live there?"

"My mother does." She left it at that.

But Rob persisted. "Your father?"

"He died a year and a half ago."

"I'm sorry." No hesitation, no awkwardness. He had the social graces down pat, when he wanted to use them. "Any theory why Janssen was in Den Bosch?"

She shook her head, reminding herself that Rob's family had nearly all been killed because of Nick Janssen and she should cut him some slack. But he wasn't going to change the subject, obviously. He'd keep grilling her about Janssen and Den Bosch and the tip until she put a stop to it. She didn't know if he was suspicious of her because of the tip or just tenacious—or both.

"Why do you think the marshals sent you here?" she asked casually. "Given your personal connection to Janssen—"

"No one sent me. I asked to come here."

It wasn't the answer she'd expected. "They let you?"

Janssen's arrest stirred up the media. "I had a lot of reporters on my tail. This way I'm out of sight, out of mind."

"Or out of sight and they'll all want to know why and show up here next?"

He shrugged. "I don't think so. Have you had many reporters contact you?"

"Not directly. A few have contacted Public Affairs."

"I guess it's not nearly as interesting to have an international fugitive arrested as a presidential connection exposed."

She tried more of the espresso. Rob had done fine yesterday at the embassy. He was good at small talk, at ease with people. His connection to President Poe made people eager to meet him and be on their best behavior, but in the end, Maggie thought, it hadn't made that big a difference. The guy was likable. The mistake, she suspected, was to assume that translated into being a soft touch.

He again consulted his map. "Janssen was picked up on a canal?"

"The Binnendieze. I wasn't sure of what it was, either. It's a shallow river, but it looks and feels like a canal. Den Bosch is located in a triangle where the Aa and the Dommel join to form the Dieze River, which eventually runs into the Maas."

"Ah. So I see on the map."

"Water's a big deal in the Netherlands. About a third of the country's below sea level. We tend to think in terms of the North Sea, but river flooding is a concern, too."

"Binnendieze—does that mean 'little Dieze'?"

"Aren't you the one who speaks all the languages?"

He finished his espresso without answering.

"I heard it was seven," Maggie persisted.

"Well, one of them isn't Dutch."

She laughed. "*Binnen* means inner, or inside. It's the section of the Dieze that runs within Den Bosch's original city walls—it's sort of a natural moat. They've cleaned it up and run boat tours on it these days."

"Bet it used to be the town sewer."

"That's what I understand. The tour's unusual because it takes you *under* the city, actually under people's houses. For safety reasons, centuries ago, people could only build inside the city walls. When they ran out of room, they started building over the waterway."

"Very clever."

"It sounds like a fascinating tour, doesn't it?"

"Better than the cathedral, if you ask me."

Maggie got off the A2 motorway and drove toward the city center, Rob pointing out a stunning fountain featuring a gold dragon in the middle of a roundabout. Remembering directions she'd gotten from a Dutch police inspector, who hadn't questioned her reasons for asking, she found her way to the boat-tour entrance and parked nearby.

It was a pleasantly warm morning under a clear Dutch-blue sky, a perfect day to play tourist—except that wasn't why she and Rob were there, Maggie reminded herself as they walked along a shaded street. The narrow, shallow waterway flowed next to them, below street level. Steps led down to a small dock for the boats, a crowd gathering for the next tour.

"Janssen had two dogs," Rob said, stopping along the open black-iron fence above the waterway. "Rhodesian ridgebacks."

"Big dogs."

"Do we know what happened to them?"

"They weren't with him when he was arrested. I doubt he had them with him when he took off in May."

"How long do we think he was in Den Bosch before you got the tip?"

From his tone, Maggie knew he didn't expect her to have an answer. "Not long, but that's not a guess at this point. Den Bosch strikes me as an unlikely place for the leader of an international criminal network to turn up. It's possible he—"

She stopped. *Who was that?* A man in front of a café just down the street . . . balding, rumpled. Tom Kopac?

Rob was instantly alert. "What is it?"

"I think I recognize someone. Hold on."

Maggie started toward the café, but Tom had disappeared. She pushed past the outdoor tables, where a few tourists were enjoying coffee, and checked inside, her eyes quickly adjusting after being in the bright sun.

Nothing.

Had she mistaken someone else for Tom?

No. She was positive it'd been him.

He must have continued past the café or cut down another street.

She headed back outside and scanned the scene.

Rob stood behind her. "What's going on?"

"A colleague at the embassy is here. Maybe he's like us, just checking out where Janssen was picked up."

"Did he work the case?"

She shook her head. "No. But he's a good guy. A friend."

"What's his name?"

"Kopac. Tom Kopac. He works in economic relations."

Rob frowned at her. "He came by my hotel last night."

"Tom did? Why?"

"Checking me out. Are you two—"

"No."

She thought she detected a flicker of amusement at her forceful answer. "You DS agents are the expert drivers. Could he have followed us out here?"

"It's not like I'm on a secret mission or driving around the secretary of state. I wasn't paying that close attention, but I doubt—" She realized she sounded very serious and deliberately lightened up. "I'm sure he didn't follow us."

"Did he see you just now?"

"You mean, was he running away from me? I don't know."

At the same time, they noticed a change in the crowd at the entrance to the boat tour. A sudden tension, gasps.

Screams.

Maggie and Rob charged back down the street, heading for a half-dozen people who were standing at the open fence, pointing into the water. A woman was screaming.

"Een man . . ."

A man.

Maggie picked out another word. *Gevallen . . .* Fallen. Fell.

"A man's fallen into the river," Rob said tightly.

There were more screams, excited words in Dutch that all ran together to Maggie's untrained ear.

Rob obviously spoke enough languages that he was able to make out the basics. "They think he's dead."

"Not Tom—"

She didn't know why she said his name. When they got to the fence and looked down at the river, they could see the body of a man floating facedown in the shallow water, drifting downstream.

The balding head, the stocky build, the rumpled clothes.

"Hell," Rob breathed. "It's him. Kopac."

Maggie turned away and took in a breath, pushing back a rush of emotion, then forced herself to look again at Tom's body.

Blood.

His head . . .

The images she was seeing came together, registered. He'd been shot at the base of his neck, the bullet going upward into his brain.

Tom. My God.

There was almost no hope he was alive.

Rob pounded down the stairs to the waterway, and Maggie jumped after him, a man yelling to them in Dutch. From the tone of his voice, she knew he was worried about them.

She understood his fear. "A shooter. Rob, if there's a shooter—"

But another look at Tom confirmed, at least in Maggie's mind, it hadn't been a sniper attack. There was no one hiding on a rooftop—or in the bushes, as the gunman who'd shot Rob had done in Central Park four months ago.

From what she could see, Tom had been shot up close and personal. She felt a sense of revulsion, anger and grief, even as she forced herself to pull back from her emotions and focus on the problem at hand.

Rob pushed out to the edge of the dock. "Someone will have called the police by now."

As he spoke, Maggie heard sirens. Neither she nor Rob had authority as law enforcement officers in the Netherlands. Given the circumstances, they weren't even armed.

But they had to make sure there was nothing they could do for Tom.

Rob knelt down and grabbed Tom's arm. His body was snagged on a support post, and Maggie helped, taking hold of Tom's belt. His skin was warm, water pouring off his clothes as they managed to get him up onto the platform.

He was dead. He'd probably died instantly.

"I just saw him," Maggie said. "It wasn't, what, even five minutes ago? The killer can't have gotten far. Someone must have seen something, someone—"

Rob glanced up at the frightened and horrified people along the fence. "At least we know one of us didn't kill him."

Maggie nodded. At least they knew that much, if not a damn thing else. Like why Tom was here. If he'd spotted her, heard her. If he'd taken off because he didn't want to talk to her.

If he'd known his killer.

And if his killer had anything to do with the American fugitive who'd been picked up in Den Bosch two days ago.

"Come on," Rob said. "The Den Bosch police are going to want to talk to us."

A dead American in their small city?

The local police most certainly would want to talk to the two U.S. federal agents who'd pulled him out of the river.

"He was the kind of guy who got home-sick for Krispy Kreme doughnuts," Maggie said, realizing her front was soaked with river water.

"A nice guy," Rob said.

"A very nice guy."

*   *   *

It was four o'clock before Rob and his DS escort left the police station, their clothes finally dry, every question asked of them answered. Maggie pushed ahead on the narrow, sunny street. "I need to walk," she said.

Rob didn't object. It was a hot, still afternoon. The city seemed quiet, almost as if it were mourning the violence that had taken place there a few hours ago.

An exhaustive search hadn't produced a single lead on Thomas Kopac's killer so far.

No one saw anything. No one heard anything.

Except for Maggie Spencer.

Rob said nothing as he walked alongside her. She seemed preoccupied. Not, he thought, that she was an easy woman to read.

Various Dutch and American authorities had swarmed the Den Bosch police station, including the FBI and Regional Security Officer George Bremmerton, Maggie's immediate boss. All of them grilled both her and Rob about what they'd seen that morning, what Maggie had talked about with Kopac in recent days, why he'd shown up at Rob's hotel last night.

Although she knew Tom Kopac well enough to consider him her first real friend since she'd arrived in the country, Maggie had been straightforward and professional with her answers. She'd also had her own questions, namely, if there was anything about Tom Kopac that she hadn't been told.

Rob had that same question himself.

Den Bosch police were trying to locate people who'd been in the vicinity of the boat tour that morning, interviewing the café's wait staff and manager—anyone who might have seen the American who'd turned up in the Binnendieze. Maggie's sighting of Kopac and the subsequent commotion along the river pinpointed the approximate time he'd been killed.

Apparently someone had walked up to him, shot him and disappeared.

Not an easy feat to pull off.

The brutal, calculated murder of an American diplomat had taken Dutch and U.S. authorities by complete surprise. They had Nick Janssen in custody. The killing was supposed to stop.

"Another American in trouble on Dutch soil," Maggie said as she and Rob walked across the street to Den Bosch's market square, crowded with booths and shoppers. She was obviously spent, taken aback by Kopac's death, the loss of a friend. "The second American murdered in less than a year."

"Nick Janssen ordered Charlene Brooker's murder," Rob said unnecessarily.

"No one had a clue that she was on to him. He was still a fairly low-priority tax evader then."

"Has there been any sign of Ethan Brooker since Janssen's arrest?" Rob asked.

After his wife's death, Ethan, an army Special Forces officer, had made finding her killer his personal mission. It'd taken him to Tennessee, where he'd posed as the Dunnemores' property manager. After helping Sarah Dunnemore, Nate Winter and Juliet Longstreet stop their Central Park shooter—a loose cannon with a crazy scheme of his own—Brooker had simply disappeared.

When things exploded in Night's Landing, Rob was still recovering from his gunshot wound in his New York hospital.

"It's not as if Brooker's kept the embassy informed of his whereabouts," Maggie said.

"Could he have given you the tip on where to find Janssen?"

"I don't know. I suppose it's possible. But nothing suggests he's anything but one of the good guys—he couldn't have killed Tom." Her voice cracked, and she turned away, fixed her gaze on a nearby food booth. *"Damn."*

"Are you going to be all right?" Rob asked.

She nodded. "I'd like to offer up a prayer."

A prayer? "Okay."

She lifted her chin, squinting against the late afternoon sun. "It'll only take twenty minutes or so. Do you mind?"

"No, of course not."

She smiled faintly. "You can try the fresh herring. It's a Dutch favorite."

"It's raw."

"Yes, but it's good. You salt it, then more or less drop it down your throat as if you were a seal. I like it. The tradition is to chase it with a shot of *genever.* Dutch gin."

"I'll take the gin without the herring."

Her turquoise eyes went distant again. "Twenty minutes."

Rob nodded. "I'll be here."

He saw her relief, as if she'd expected she'd have to fight him for a few minutes on her own. She started through the square, the strong afternoon sun lightening her deep red hair.

Normally he was good at reading people, a combination of training, experience and instinct. But Maggie wasn't easy to read.

Still, as he winced at the lineup of raw herring on ice, all his alarm bells were going off.

Special Agent Spencer had something up her sleeve.

"Prayer, my ass," he said under his breath, deciding he'd try raw herring another day.

Six

St. John's Cathedral was cool and dark, a sharp contrast to the afternoon heat and sunlight on the streets outside. Its massive interior seemed quiet for a summer Saturday. Maggie suspected word of the brutal murder of an American had prompted at least some tourists to change their plans.

Tom . . . I'm so sorry.

Why didn't you answer me when I called you?

She wanted to believe he hadn't heard her, but, as she'd told the Dutch and American investigators, she didn't know for sure one way or the other.

She tried not to think of his easy manner, his smile. With physical effort, she pushed back the personal regrets—the grief—she had for the death of a new friend and focused on the job she had to do.

Could Tom have been the caller who wanted to meet with her? Had he disguised his voice and played on her father's death to lure her to Den Bosch?

Why?

But that made no sense.

She hadn't mentioned the call to anyone. It was a long shot that the lead was legitimate, and there was no reason to believe it had anything to do with Tom's death. The Dutch police would probably be irritated with her for withholding any information, but Maggie had no evidence it had been anything but a crank call.

She hadn't told her boss or the FBI about the strange call, either, or, certainly, Rob Dunnemore.

If it'd been Tom, there'd be no meeting.

If it was a nut, either there'd be no meeting or he'd show up and she'd find out that he was crazy soon enough.

If it was a legitimate informant, she'd get

what she could out of him and proceed from there.

She felt the uneven stone flooring under her feet. *And if it's whoever shot Tom in the back of the head?*

Then, Maggie thought, she'd kick herself for not having opened her mouth.

And she'd deal with it.

Bringing Rob along for extra security wouldn't have worked. If her caller was still at the cathedral, he'd realize she wasn't alone—and Dunnemore would have quickly figured out she wasn't there just to pray.

Maggie made her way along the outer aisle of the huge cathedral, aware of shadows and the silence. People were buried here. For eight hundred years, people had worshiped in this place. Its thirteenth-century tower and some of its interior were Romanesque in style, but its more ornate Gothic features from later expansion and rebuilding dominated.

Brochure in hand, Maggie pretended she was a tourist, peeking at the baptistery and the Passion altar, checking out the seven chapels that ringed the cavernous interior, staring up at the medieval figures of saints and the religious reliefs depicting the life of

Christ and John the Baptist. There were enormous flying buttresses, and beautiful stained-glass windows let in just a thin filter of light.

She could feel the weight of the centuries, the inevitable flow of history, and thought about how much the world outside the cathedral's thick walls had changed.

She pictured Tom's body in the Binnendieze and wondered how many deaths its waters had seen. Conquerors had come and gone. Liberators, wars, floods, people. Maggie was aware of her own impermanence. Perhaps that was part of the purpose of such a place, part of why it endured.

A few people here and there were kneeling in silent prayer, as if to remind her the cathedral was a house of worship.

Most of the pews in the center nave were empty. Maggie made her way into one near the outermost aisle, with a good view of the major entrance and exit. When she sat down, she felt chilled, suddenly isolated and very tired. *Tom.*

A white-haired man worked his way into the pew and sat next to her.

Five aisles, dozens of pews. He picked hers.

She could smell the stale cigarette smoke that clung to him. Glancing out of the corner of her eye, she saw his yellow-tipped fingernails and the blue veins bulging in the skinny hand on his thigh.

He didn't kneel or pull out rosary beads.

Hell. It's him, Maggie thought.

"Where's your marshal friend?" he asked.

His East Coast prep school accent didn't fit with his down-and-out appearance. "I don't have a lot of time," she said, not giving him a direct answer. "I need to know who you are. Your name. Why you sought me out. Why Den Bosch. Start now."

She spoke in a whisper, but her urgent tone—and her skepticism—didn't seem to bother him. "My name is William Raleigh," he said. "I was in the foreign service once."

Oh, God. A nutcase. Some threadbare old guy who thought he was a spy or a diplomat. "For the U.S.?"

"Yes. Then I went out on my own. My specialty is economics." He smiled. "As much as it's anyone's specialty."

Although he sounded lucid, Maggie knew he could just be playing the part, trying to persuade her that he was the real thing. "I was never any good at economics."

"No one is, even the experts. It's just that the experts know it and the rest of us hope it's not true."

There was a hint of humor and irony in his whispered words, but Maggie wasn't willing to bet yet whether he was legit or a mentally ill drifter determined to reel her in to his delusions. "Mr. Raleigh, I need to know what this is all about."

He faced the front of the cathedral, not looking at her. "I've had an interesting life. I'm an economist. I've traveled all over the world, doing what I could to bring fairness and prosperity to others, first in my work as a foreign service officer, then as an economic consultant. That sounds lofty, but I don't mean it to. I did what I could. I think that's what we all do, don't you?"

"No."

He smiled. "So young to be a cynic."

"It hasn't been a good day."

"No, it hasn't. I'm sorry about your friend."

Then he knew about Tom. Of course, Den Bosch was a small city, and news traveled quickly.

"I've met everyone from small-time war-lords to the last five U.S. presidents," the man next to her said. "Not the current one yet. Poe."

Yet. Maggie wondered if Raleigh had brought up Poe's name deliberately, if he knew the marshal with her was Rob Dunne-more. Was Rob's connection to President Poe, ultimately, what this meeting was all about?

She shifted in the pew, studying Raleigh. He wasn't much taller than she was, and he was thin, dressed in a blue madras shirt that must have seen him through at least one of his decades of supposed travels. She noticed that he'd let the hem out of his khaki pants, as if they'd shrunk in the dryer.

Maggie checked for drool and dried fried egg or something on his shirt, and hated herself for doing it.

His belt wasn't pulled too tight or hanging too loose.

His fly was zipped.

He had on sports sandals, a definite sur-prise. No socks.

He smiled faintly at her. "Do I look dotty?"

"Let's just say you don't look like a retired economist. How old are you?"

"Not as old as I look."

"What kind of economist are you, the kind for or against tax cuts?"

He gave a small laugh. "That's a very American question."

"I'm a very American diplomatic security agent. Come on, Mr. Raleigh. Who are you, really?"

His eyes, a pale grayish blue, focused on her a moment, emanating a warmth and affection—a familiarity—that made Maggie edge away from him.

"My father . . ."

She didn't know if she'd spoken aloud.

"What about your father, Maggie?"

Her chest tightened, and she turned abruptly from him and stared up toward the pulpit. She had to stay focused, on task. She couldn't lose control.

"Did you know him?" she asked.

"I can't say I knew him well. We ran into each other in Prague a few weeks before his death. He told me about his DS agent daughter. He was so proud of you. He called you his Magster." Raleigh's tone was formal and very correct, almost without emotion, incongruent with his tattered appearance. "I believe it's fate that our paths crossed."

"Fate or bullshit."

He didn't respond.

"Thomas Kopac—"

"I had nothing to do with his death. It's a terrible shame. I know he befriended you."

Maggie noticed red veins in Raleigh's eyes, bulging veins in his nose. A drinker. "That wouldn't be hard for you to find out. It's not as if we kept our friendship a secret."

"No doubt." Raleigh went very still next to Maggie, staring down at the bony hand on his thigh. "So many of the people I've met in my day were forgettable. Shallow, venal, selfish, arrogant—I don't want to remember them in my retirement. Others weren't. They were the best. They had honor and integrity. Not all of them went on to live to an old age the way I undoubtedly will, if only because I'm destined to be the one to remember what they were." He didn't raise his voice or ramble. "I'm often haunted by the good people I couldn't save."

Jesus.

"Who are you talking about? Why am I here?"

He inhaled through his nose. "I can feel the presence of the dead here, can't you? Eighteen months. It doesn't seem that long ago—"

"If you're using my father's death to try to manipulate me, it won't work. If you were responsible in some way for what happened to him—"

"He wouldn't have wanted me to put you in danger."

"I have a job to do. I intend to do it to the best of my abilities. That's not up to you."

"It wasn't up to him, either." Raleigh's tone lost its moroseness, became firmer, more serious. "He knew you were like him. You're capable of breaking a few dishes, Maggie."

"I'm a professional—"

"You're a self-starter, an independent thinker. And, yes, a professional. You won't cross the line. But you'll put a toe over it." His tone had lightened, but only momentarily. "You can't tell anyone about me, Maggie. No one. That's very important for your own safety. You have good instincts. Trust them."

"I didn't know Tom Kopac was about to be killed this morning."

"I didn't say you were clairvoyant."

"If you have any information, I can take you to the American embassy and we can talk there." Unless he was already familiar to everyone there—*good old Bill Raleigh, yeah, that head case.*

But he was very convincing. "That won't be necessary."

Maggie knew she'd lost him, that he was wrapping up, but she persisted. "I need more to go on."

His movements unhurried, he carefully, deliberately, stood. She noticed he had a walking stick with him, the retractable kind that hikers use. He turned to her. "There's an inn in Ravenkill, New York. The Old Stone Hollow. I don't know if it's of any significance. Perhaps it's just a pretty country inn."

"An inn? What—"

"It's good to meet you in person, Agent Spencer," Raleigh said, easing out of the pew. "Your marshal friend is here. He's not one to underestimate, is he? I'll be in touch if I have anything else for you."

Maggie whipped around in the pew, but she didn't see Rob.

A trick. Damn.

She jumped up, but Raleigh—or whoever he was—had darted into the outer aisle, moving faster than she'd thought him capable of. He kicked over a kneeler and it landed on her ankle, slowing her down as she went after him. Every fiber of her being told her that he was someone she could trust, but her common sense—her training and experience—warned her not to let herself get sucked into his story all the way.

She wouldn't be the first law enforcement officer to get taken in by a delusional alcoholic.

"Mr. Raleigh," she whispered, "please wait. Rob's not here. You have to give me more. This inn—"

Ignoring her, he picked up his pace. Maggie didn't know what she was supposed to do if she caught up with him. Tackle him and drag him to the Den Bosch police? Shove him in her Mini and drive him to the American embassy? She wasn't armed. She had no arrest authority in the Netherlands.

She heard someone mumbling a prayer in a nearby chapel, then the far-off moan of a door, the echo of footsteps. Her hands were clammy, her fingers stiff as if they'd been in the cold.

"Raleigh!"

She let her voice go above a whisper.

A woman spun around in a pew and glared at her.

He wasn't stopping.

If she tried to tackle him, Maggie figured he'd whack her with his walking stick. He'd make a scene. He'd play the crazy old drunk being attacked by a religious zealot. He'd scream for help, scaring the hell out of the few stragglers in the cathedral, and run.

Trust your instincts.

He disappeared, hiding in one of the thousand nooks and crannies of the massive cathedral, stealing out an exit.

Maybe he'd just gone up in smoke.

Maybe she'd imagined him.

Ravenkill, New York.

Maggie had never heard of it or the Old Stone Hollow Inn.

"Little unsteady on your feet there, Agent Spencer?"

Dunnemore. He didn't bother to speak in a whisper. Maggie recognized his Southern accent even before she swung around and saw him coming through a pew from another aisle.

Obviously he'd been in the cathedral long enough to have seen her trip on the kneeler.

That meant he'd also seen her chase William Raleigh.

"Just a little," she said with an edge of sarcasm. "Have I been longer than twenty minutes?"

"I don't know. I gave you a two-minute head start before I came after you." He stood very close to her, not much charming about his manner right now. "The raw herring wasn't that appealing."

She flexed her ankle, easing out any stiffness. "I should have remembered you track people for a living."

"Probably should have. Who was the old man?"

"William the Conqueror."

He held his suit jacket over his shoulder with one finger, his shirtsleeves rolled up. He hadn't had a particularly good day, either. Maggie felt herself softening as he looked her up and down. "You hurt?" he asked.

She shook her head, wondering if he might be exaggerating his accent just to throw her off balance. "How did you find me?"

"You said you were off to pray. This is the biggest church in the whole damn country. I figured it was a good place to start."

"You shouldn't swear in here."

"You're right. We can go outside, and I'll swear out there." His eyes—they were a dark gray in the dim light of the cathedral—fixed on her. "And you can tell me about the old guy in the madras shirt."

They found a table in the shade at an uncrowded café near the market square. "Get two of whatever you're ordering," Maggie said. "I'm not picky. I don't even know if I can eat."

Rob ordered two bowls of the soup of the day, which seemed to involve chicken, and coffee for himself, a Heineken for Maggie. He'd do the driving back to The Hague.

Their waiter brought the drinks first. Maggie touched a finger to the foam of her beer. She'd had a miserable day, and she looked more shaken than she'd want to admit, worse now that she'd finished with the investigators and the questions—and now that whatever her mission at the cathedral had been was over.

"The old guy looked like he planned to take you out with that walking stick," Rob said.

"For all I know, he thought it was tipped with ricin."

"Is that a joke?"

She sighed. "An attempt at a joke."

Rob lifted his small coffee cup. "I'd say cheers, but it wouldn't sound right today."

"I suppose not." She picked up her beer, hesitating, as if pushing back an intrusive thought, before taking a sip. "It's been a long week. Nothing about it's been normal."

Including having him thrust upon her, Rob thought, drinking some of his coffee. It was very strong, but he figured a jolt of caffeine wouldn't hurt. He was hot from chasing after Maggie, negotiating the narrow, unfamiliar city streets in the late August heat. "Your rendezvous with the old guy at St. John's. That's why we're in Den Bosch today?"

Maggie stared at the disappearing foam on her beer. "I shouldn't drink—"

"Go ahead. I'm sticking to coffee. I'll drive." He smiled, trying to take some of the edge off her mood and maybe his own. "It's okay. I can handle a Mini."

She raised her eyes from her drink. "I know what it must have looked like back there. Just forget about it, okay?"

"Not okay. The old guy's an informant?"

"A wanna-be, I think."

"Any relation to Kopac?"

"I don't know that much about him."

Rob sat back in his chair. "That's an evasive answer."

"Maybe it's a polite way to tell you—" She stopped herself. "Never mind. It's been a lousy day for you, too."

But she obviously wanted to tell him what happened in St. John's was none of his damned business. "Better to evade than to lie outright. Okay. I get that. You don't know anything about me except that I'm a marshal, I was shot four months ago and my family knows the president." He shrugged. "I wouldn't trust me, either."

"It's not a question of trust."

Then what else was it? But he didn't ask. "This guy's contacted you before?"

"First time."

"What'd he do, call, e-mail, send a carrier

pigeon? Come on. Throw me a bone. Let me think you're starting to trust me a little."

She didn't smile. "He called."

"When?"

"Yesterday."

"So, after I got here."

Their soup arrived in heavy bowls. Cream of chicken and fresh vegetables. It was steaming and substantial, which, despite the heat, Rob welcomed.

Maggie shifted around in her chair. "I wouldn't make too much of this. The timing's bad, I know, but I'm not all that sure he's playing with a full deck." She picked up her beer with such force, some of it splashed out onto her hand. "It's quiet, don't you think? Especially for such a beautiful afternoon. People must be worried after this morning. I guess I don't blame them."

"They'll decide it's an American thing and go on with their lives. In Central Park in the spring, people decided it was a marshals thing. It helped them get past the idea of a sniper on the loose. Someone wasn't picking off people at random."

Maggie took a drink of her beer, then set down the glass and blew out a sigh. "Tom's family must know by now what happened to him. It's an awful experience to go through, having someone come to your house and tell you—well, you know what I mean."

"I called my sister from Central Park so she wouldn't have to find out that way or, worse, see me on television."

"Did you know you were in bad shape?"

"I don't remember what I knew."

She looked away. "You didn't need what happened today."

"Maggie, I didn't come to the Netherlands to run away from anything. I can do my job."

"You're not back on the street," she said.

"That's not my decision to make. Look—"

She faced him again, her creamy skin less pale. "You should be. You didn't hesitate today. The shooter, Tom. You did fine."

He acknowledged her words with a nod. "I still want to know about this Scarlet Pimpernel character of yours."

This time, she smiled. "You marshals. Hound dogs on a scent."

Rob tried the soup, relished the normalcy of it. "Maybe I can help."

"That's nice of you to offer, but there's nothing for you to do."

Clever. It wasn't as if he could order her to come clean. He could badger her for answers, but he'd already seen her help pull a dead man out of a river, deal with the Dutch police and a nervous embassy and chase a white-haired old man. She'd hold her own against anything he threw at her and tell him exactly what she wanted him to know and not one word more.

This wasn't what he'd had in mind when he'd told Mike Rivera he wanted to go to the Netherlands.

"You saw the man with me at St. John's. My wanna-be informant. Did he look mentally stable to you?"

Rob shrugged. "Down on his luck, maybe. Lost his retirement, got a little daft. Could just be on a tight budget."

"I suppose." She picked up her spoon, held it in midair and sighed. "I shouldn't have wasted my time. I just ended up putting you on high alert, got you into tracking mode."

"Kopac's murder did that."

Her eyes shone, but she covered her

emotion by dipping her spoon into her soup.

"This guy," Rob said. "Does he have a name? Besides William the Conqueror."

"That was snotty of me. I apologize." She left it at that. "How long were you in the cathedral?"

"Obviously not long enough."

"Did you see anyone else, anyone who could have been with my guy?"

Rob remembered the scene when he'd walked into the cathedral, his eyes adjusting to the dim light, his sensibilities to the atmosphere. It was quiet, removed from the murder investigation outside its doors. When he spotted Maggie in a pew, at first he thought, guiltily, that she had, indeed, come there to pray.

Then he'd noticed the white-haired man sitting too close to her. In the next second, she was chasing after him.

"I should have followed your guy," Rob said. "But I didn't see anyone who might have been with him. Think he tipped you off about Janssen?"

"No. I'm sure he didn't. That message came by a free e-mail account. I doubt—" She stopped herself. "I shouldn't make assumptions. He just didn't strike me as someone who would know the where-abouts of an international fugitive."

"But he chose to meet you in Den Bosch, where Janssen was picked up."

"Probably for dramatic effect. He could have read about the arrest in the paper and decided to give me a call. You must know how it is with sources. I'm sympathetic to mental illness—I mean it. But it's not always that easy to sort out the cranks from the le-gitimate sources." She sighed. "I didn't ex-pect that part of this work, did you?"

Rob didn't answer right away. He'd dealt with his share of delusional would-be in-formants, from poor, illiterate drug addicts to highly educated society matrons. Getting sucked into one of their wild fantasies and acting on it was the nightmare of every law enforcement officer he knew. "Maggie—"

"I've told you what I can."

He could feel her tension and reached across the table, skimming his fingertips across the top of her hand. Her skin was cooler than it should have been on such a warm day. She didn't pull away, but touch-ing her was an instinctive gesture on his part and took them both by surprise.

She took a breath, looking down at her soup. "It's been a weird day. Surreal, almost."

"I'm not the prosecution or your boss." Rob tried to sound reassuring, not patronizing or irritated by her unwillingness to talk. Still, he could feel his own tension and fatigue clawing at him, and the caffeine had his mind going in a dozen different directions. "You don't have to tell me anything."

She was naturally very fair, with freckles across her cheeks—her appearance could have a tendency to make people not expect her to be an elite diplomatic security agent, not expect her to be as tough and competent as she was. She'd lost a friend today—an embassy employee—and it had to feel like a failure as well as a personal loss.

She raised her eyes, the turquoise, he noticed, softened with flecks of gold. "I know that. But thanks. It's a decent thing to say."

He sat back, letting go of her hand. "Eat your soup. You look like you're about to pass out."

"I never pass out."

But she ate more of her soup, although Rob could see it was an effort for her. She seemed far away again, caught up in something she didn't want to think about but couldn't stop focusing on. He noticed how drawn she looked, how closed off from him. It'd been that way at the police station. Even on a good day, getting anything out of Maggie Spencer wouldn't be easy.

"Want my opinion?" She looked up at Rob, more alert now, less distracted by whatever had her in its grip. "My guy picked Den Bosch and me because we've been in the news, and that's all there is to it."

But she wasn't willing to take the chance that she was wrong. Part of her believed her wanna-be snitch had access and information that could help her, Rob thought, or she wouldn't have stepped foot in St. John's. At the very least, she would have dismissed the guy she'd met there out of hand. Instead, she was thinking about whatever he'd told her, chewing on it, debating whether or not it made sense after all.

Rob finished off his soup. "I guess it would have been tough to frisk him there in the church—"

"Unless he had a gun strapped to his ankle, he wasn't armed."

"Going to tell the Dutch police about him?"

"Only if it's relevant to Tom Kopac's murder. Right now, I can't see that it is."

"I'll bet they'd like to decide that."

She ignored him, abandoning her soup. "We should get back. Sorry for the lousy day. Come on. Half a beer won't affect my driving." She got to her feet, more animated. "I'll pay—"

"No, I'll take care of it." Rob dropped some euro notes on the table, more than enough to cover their tab. "And I'll drive."

"Going to fight me for my car keys?"

An image of the two of them going at it popped into his head, but he stifled it, rising. He was taller than she was—not that she seemed to give a damn. "Sure."

That brought some color to her cheeks. "All right. You get to drive." She smiled brightly, unexpectedly, with a touch of self-deprecation. "*You* know President Poe. *Me*—I know a probable paranoid-schizophrenic old man who needs medical treatment, not the ear of a DS officer."

Rob narrowed his eyes on her. "This guy got to you."

"This entire day's gotten to me."

He had an urge to ease some of her emotional turmoil. He wanted her trust and almost asked her for it straight out. But why should she give it to him? They'd known each other for two days. She'd been stuck with him, the wounded marshal whose family was at the heart of the Janssen investigation.

Maybe it was the effects of pulling a dead man out of a Dutch waterway. He hadn't known Thomas Kopac, but, Rob thought as he followed Maggie out to the street, if he got to the point that murder was nothing to him, just another event in a day's work, he'd quit.

She glanced back at him, said nothing.

He took a sharp breath.

And maybe he should pull back from the effects of those turquoise eyes and that red hair and remember that she'd received the Janssen tip, that she had hidden motives for today's trip to Den Bosch.

Rob had less reason to trust her than she did him.

He had his own contacts.

He'd make a few calls and check out the old guy in the madras shirt himself, see what people knew.

Seven

Ethan Brooker stood next to a subdued William Raleigh on an arched bridge over the Binnendieze, the water dark and quiet with the fading sun. After the discovery of the American's body, boat tours had been canceled for the day.

"Ever do the boat tour?" Ethan asked.

"Once," the older man said, staring down at the canal-like river. "It's fascinating. You see things you never get to see on ordinary canal tours. The waterway runs behind buildings, not in front, and it literally takes you under the city. It's all very clean. You get an up-close view of the architecture of centuries-old buildings. There are many small surprises along the way. An unexpected window box or a pot of flowers, a statue. And it's so quiet." Raleigh glanced sideways at Ethan. "I take it you've never done the tour?"

"No, sir."

Raleigh looked tired. They hadn't expected Tom Kopac to turn up dead. Scooting out of St. John's before Spencer or Dunnemore pounced had taken some doing. Ethan had stood watch in the cathedral, in hiding, and gave Raleigh the high sign when the good marshal showed up. Dunnemore would have recognized Ethan. That meant Raleigh had to get away from the DS agent on his own. If it'd come to it, the old buzzard would have nailed her with his walking stick. It was more an affectation than a necessity, but it would have done the job.

Instead, Maggie Spencer had let him go.

Why? What had Raleigh told her? Their meeting was his idea.

It was to have followed a meeting with Tom Kopac.

"Did you tell Spencer that you and Kopac

were supposed to meet this morning, but he was shot to death before—"

"I didn't see how that would help."

"I don't know Dutch law—hell, I don't know U.S. law—but I'm guessing they could haul you in as a material witness."

"I have no information about the murder today."

"What did you tell Spencer?"

"I didn't have much time. She knows my name. That I knew her father."

Ethan turned to his side and leaned a hip against a stone support column of the old bridge. "She thinks he was killed by Czech bank robbers?" he asked. "Or does she know you're a suspect—"

"I'm not a suspect. Not in his murder."

"In fucking up something that led to his murder." Ethan didn't sugarcoat his words, although he and Raleigh had never discussed just how much Ethan had managed to find out in the short months of their acquaintance. "Spencer must not know or she wouldn't have let you go the way she did."

Raleigh didn't react. He was like that. He didn't act on emotion. Which was what made his contact with Maggie Spencer so weird—it was all emotion. That was the only explanation that made sense.

"Right now," Raleigh said, "it doesn't seem prudent or necessary to alert Maggie to all of our actions. I gave her a small mission."

"What small mission?"

"I'd like to keep that to myself for now."

The old man was getting testy. Ethan let it slide. He was thinking he should head for the American embassy and throw himself at their mercy for ever getting hooked up with this guy.

Raleigh pulled himself away from the fence. There was a slight tremble in his hand.

"You're not hitting the bottle, are you?" Ethan asked, and when Raleigh didn't answer, added, "People say you're a bottle-and-breakdown case."

"People say a lot of things. They don't know me." Raleigh glanced sideways at Ethan and smiled, not nicely. "You don't know me."

It was a fair point. "I want answers about my wife's death. All the answers. That's it. That's all I'm about."

"We're not about to take the law into our own hands," Raleigh said.

"I think we already have."

He regarded Ethan with paternal insight. "Is that what you think?"

"If I had a clue who killed Kopac, I'd be knocking on the door to the American embassy and asking them what the hell to do with what I knew."

"I don't have a clue, either, Major."

Major. Some months ago, Ethan had stopped thinking of himself as a West Point graduate, an army major who'd led covert special operations missions. In the past, he'd done his best to accomplish the mission tasked to him and his men.

His wife's death had changed all that.

Char.

The gut-wrenching anger, grief and guilt weren't there anymore. Just the determination to expose Nicholas Janssen as the person behind her death, and why. All of it, all the answers. Her actual killer—one of the two men Janssen had sent to the U.S. in May—was dead. Nick Janssen himself was behind bars.

It was a start.

Ethan hadn't seen Kopac's murder coming that morning. He'd have stopped it if he had. It had totally blindsided him.

He wasn't sure about William Raleigh.

"Tom Kopac was a good guy?" Ethan asked.

Raleigh didn't hesitate. "Yes."

"Raleigh . . ." Ethan turned away from the river. "You'd better be who and what I think you are."

Which was a spy. For what agency, even what country, Ethan couldn't be sure. But he'd spent a dozen years in the U.S. Special Forces and thought he could recognize an intelligence operative when he saw one. They'd met earlier in the summer when Ethan's personal mission of tracking down Nick Janssen and Raleigh's mission—unknown—had converged.

Unsettling stories about the supposed economist's drinking and mental health problems had reached Ethan, and he hoped he hadn't misplaced his trust. He didn't want to be duped by a delusional man haunted by his own wrongdoings, trying to dig his way back to some measure of self-respect.

"You're sure you shouldn't be in a home?"

Raleigh's eyes twinkled with sudden amusement, the kind of insight that made Ethan continue to work with him. "You are quite a direct man, Major Brooker. If you weren't, I fear I wouldn't have made it out of St. John's today."

"Spencer and the marshal never saw me. If they had—"

"You'd still have found a way out."

"I don't know about that." Ethan was a search-and-destroy specialist, not someone who hid from federal agents—they were all supposed to be on the same side. "I was just playing the hand dealt us back there."

"Yes."

Raleigh grew thoughtful, and Ethan could see he needed rest and a good meal—they both did. "Come on. I'll buy you dinner. Our American friends are on their way back to The Hague. We're not going to run into them."

"Would Rob Dunnemore have recognized you?"

"The feds weren't happy when I took off on them in May. I think they all had my picture tattooed on various body parts. Dunnemore was still recovering from the Central

Park attack, but I lied to his sister. Told her I was a gardener."

"In other words he'd recognize you. You and U.S. federal law enforcement—"

"We're square. They're not after me anymore."

"It's difficult for me to believe anyone would take you for a gardener," Raleigh said.

Ethan grinned. "Why not?"

They started off the bridge, the shadows long in the street with the waning light. "Our job is to keep more innocent people from being killed," Raleigh said abruptly, then glanced at Ethan in that holier-than-thou way he sometimes had, despite the ancient, worn shirt, let-out pants and veins in his nose. "No matter how great our will or noble our cause, neither of us has the power to change the past."

Ethan laid on his west Texas accent, a contrast to the erudite diplomat and economist who'd become his partner of convenience. "Sucks, doesn't it?"

"Yes, Major. It sucks very much."

Rob turned the Mini back over to Maggie at his hotel, waiting for her at the driver's door before handing over the keys. "Don't want to come in for a drink?"

She shook her head. "Thanks, no."

"You could dump your car at your place and come back."

"It's been a long day."

He smiled at her. "Dinner? A walk? Another bowl of soup?"

That seemed to penetrate her obvious preoccupation. She almost laughed. "You're very deceptive, Deputy Dunnemore. You have this easygoing facade, but underneath? Uh-uh. Not so easygoing at all. I'm going home and taking a shower and having a glass of wine."

"I'm not invited?"

"Like I said, underneath the Southern charm is a very dangerous man. See you tomorrow."

She slid behind the wheel.

Rob shut the door for her and leaned into the open window. "Maggie—"

"I'm fine. I'm sorry about today. I know it's not what you came here for."

Rob stepped back from the small car.

A shower and a glass of wine. Did he believe her?

He could understand her rationale for not

bringing up her clandestine meeting at St. John's Cathedral at the Den Bosch police station, before she even knew it would come off. But now that it had? Maggie had made no mention of going to the authorities.

Rob thought he could understand that rationale, too. If she planned to tell anyone, it'd be without him.

When he got to his room, he showered off the river smells, feeling the scar from his bullet wound under his fingers. Tom Kopac hadn't had a chance. His killer must have been standing next to him, unrecognized or a friend? An acquaintance Kopac had never suspected of murderous intent? Had he known, at the last second, what was happening to him?

Rob remembered almost nothing of the shooting in Central Park. The tulips. The miserable weather. So much of his life before and after the shooting was fuzzy, some of it gone forever, due to the trauma he'd endured—the loss of blood, the complications, the long recovery. For some reason, he vividly remembered the shock and determination on Nate Winter's face as he'd dragged Rob, injured only seconds earlier, to cover behind a rock outcropping.

But he couldn't be sure the memory was real, not something he'd pasted together from accounts and descriptions he'd heard and read after the fact.

He toweled off and put on shorts and a T-shirt, walking out into his room. His window was open, and he could hear a toddler squealing. When he glanced down at the street, he saw a towheaded little guy sitting in a child's seat secured to the handlebars of his father's bicycle. Neither wore a helmet. They pushed off, pedaling along on the quiet street on a pleasant summer evening.

Rob felt an urge to rent a bicycle and head off into the Dutch countryside for a few days, go up north to the polders and the lakes stolen from the North Sea. Who'd care? Just so long as no reporters followed him, no one would.

Pushing aside such thoughts, he sat at the small table next to the window and dialed his parents' number in Night's Landing. He pictured them on the porch of their log home, sipping iced tea punch, the air hot, hazy with the oppressive summer humidity. There was often a breeze on the

Cumberland River, and the porch was shaded by huge old oaks that beckoned family and friends to leave the comfort of their artificially cooled rooms.

His father answered, a man who'd traveled the world but never considered anywhere but Night's Landing home. "I didn't expect to hear from you," Stuart Dunnemore said. "Sarah told us you were in the Netherlands."

Rob felt a twinge of guilt, knowing he should have got word to his family himself. His father was almost eighty, and he liked to keep track of his only son. "I didn't get much notice that I was going." He hated the note of defensiveness in his voice. "I'm sorry I didn't call. How are you?"

"Just fine, son, just fine."

It was what he always said. "Mother?"

"She's in Nashville with friends, but she should be home for dinner."

His mother was twenty-two years his father's junior, a fact Nick Janssen had tried to twist to his favor—without success.

"The weather's nice here. What's it like there?"

His father, who'd grown up close to the land, loved to talk about the weather.

"We're expecting thunderstorms late to-night and tomorrow. It's been hot."

From the tone of their conversation, it was obvious he hadn't heard about the American killed in Den Bosch.

Rob's room suddenly seemed claustro-phobic, and he wished for a breeze; but the air was still, the street a few floors down quiet.

"Rob?"

"I'm okay. I wanted to tell you about something before you hear it elsewhere. An American foreign service officer was killed today in Den Bosch. A DS agent and I found him."

"Good God."

"We weren't in any danger." Which, of course, he didn't know for a fact. What if the killer had decided to put a bullet in the back of his head? Maggie's? But he kept his voice calm as he related what had hap-pened. "His name was Tom Kopac. You didn't know him from your time here, did—"

"No. No, I didn't know him. I doubt your mother did, either, but I'll ask her. Are you all right? How—"

"I'm okay. Nothing to worry about."

"Isn't Den Bosch where Nick Janssen was found?"

"That's right. We were there checking out the area."

"You don't think he had anything to do with what happened?"

Rob stared down at the empty street. "I don't know."

After reassuring his father that he was fine, he hung up, feeling guilty. His parents were still dealing with the aftermath of Conroy Fontaine and Nick Janssen's assault on the entire Dunnemore family in the spring.

I shouldn't have come here.

But Rob dismissed the thought before it could take root. His father would have chosen a different profession for his only son. The shooting in the spring and the murder in Den Bosch today would only add to his conviction that Rob didn't belong in the Marshals Service.

He dialed Nate's cell phone. He didn't want his sister picking up their home phone.

"Rob. Where the hell are you? I heard about what happened."

"I'm safe and sound in my hotel room,

about to head down to the bar for a stiff drink. My sister knows?"

"Yes."

"She's—"

"She wants to get on a plane and fly to Amsterdam tonight. You know she does."

The twin thing, as Nate liked to say.

"Do you want to talk to her?" he asked.

Rob tried to smile. "Why do you think I called your cell phone and not that haunted house you're living in?"

"That's not why. You've never been afraid to talk to Sarah. You aren't now. What's up?"

Rob pushed back from the window. "I need information. Maggie Spencer and Tom Kopac. What do you know about them?"

A half beat's silence. "Why?"

"Kopac befriended Spencer when she got here. No romance, according to both of them. But it's an odd pairing, even for a platonic relationship. I just want to be sure I'm not missing something."

"Talk to me, Rob."

The two of them had worked fugitive apprehensions in New York before the Central Park shooting and Nate's subsequent appointment to USMS headquarters. Rob didn't want to leave anything out. He had no intention of lying. At the same time, until he knew more, he didn't want to interfere in Maggie's business.

Nate, however, would sense that he wasn't getting everything.

"Maggie spotted Kopac minutes before he was killed," Rob said. "She called to him. Either he didn't hear her, or he pretended he didn't."

"Anyone with him?"

"She says she didn't see anyone."

"Any connection between Kopac and Janssen?" Nate asked.

"Not that I know of."

"I'll check on that, too."

Nate wasn't one to get carried away with speculation. Neither was Rob, although he had a thousand different scenarios and conspiracies and possibilities floating through his head, a distraction, perhaps, to stop him from thinking about Tom Kopac dead in the Binnendieze. But Kopac could have been killed today for reasons that had nothing to do with Nick Janssen—or Maggie Spencer.

"What's Sarah up to?" Rob asked finally, changing the subject.

"Planning the wedding of the century and negotiating with her ghosts. Sometimes I think she believes she really is talking to Abe and Bobby Lee."

"Are they talking back?"

Rob could feel Nate's grin. "I haven't asked."

After hanging up, Rob headed down to the hotel's café and sat at an outdoor table, where an accordionist was playing for spare change and accommodating tourists were laughing and clapping, some even dancing. He ordered a beer and watched the show, dispelling images of Kopac's body and Maggie's horror when she realized it was her friend in the Binnendieze, even as she sucked in her reaction and did her job.

As he drank his beer, Rob let a flashback of his first days back in Night's Landing after he was shot roll over him, not fighting it, but not diving into it. He'd been weak and dependant and guilt-ridden, angry at having missed clues that could have spared him and his family so much pain and suffering— that could have exposed Nick Janssen sooner. He remembered staring at his reflection in the mirror and making himself acknowledge that his life would never be the same again. That the shooting had changed him forever and there was no going back to the man he'd been before Central Park.

A fiddler joined the accordionist, then a singer, a plump woman in a ruffled skirt.

There was more laughter, more applause, but Rob had lost any sense that he was a part of the festivities. He left a few euros for the musicians and took his second beer up to his room.

After a simple meal at a nearby restaurant, Libby Smith retired to her room in a small tourist hotel in Brussels, a renovated mansion with antique furnishings and an oddly shaped bathroom. Unfortunately, it had only a shower; she'd have loved to have sunk into a hot tub.

It'd been a close call that morning.

The man she'd killed had known she was in Den Bosch. He'd known *where*.

His name was Tom Kopac. He'd come to Den Bosch to find her.

Why?

He was the balding man in the rumpled suit she'd seen on Thursday before the *Arrestatieteam* had swooped down on Jannsen.

Libby had a compulsion for checking out her surroundings. She'd recognized him early that morning at her hotel in Den Bosch, she'd heard him ask for her—by name—and she'd taken action.

Defensive action.

It was the man's own damn fault he was dead.

He was a diplomat, she'd learned later from news reports. An American. And he was friends, obviously, with Maggie Spencer, who was herself in Den Bosch for reasons unknown.

Philip Spencer's daughter.

After dealing with Kopac, Libby had checked out of her Den Bosch hotel, speaking with the desk clerk, in English, about driving to Belgium. She'd played the lonely solo American traveler wanting a chance to chat with someone. A normal conversation with a woman who had nothing to hide. The clerk, who spoke little English, gave no indication he realized the balding man who'd come in that morning was the American murdered steps away on the Binnendieze. Libby didn't bring up Kopac's name or ask what he'd told the clerk. She'd spotted Kopac when she came down from her room and overheard him ask for her by name. He obviously recognized her—or guessed who she was—and followed her when she ducked onto the street. His mistake. Minutes later, he was dead.

Lying atop her bedsheets, Libby noticed their lace edging and wondered if it was Belgian. Undoubtedly not. Too expensive for repeated washings, especially in a moderately priced hotel. She hadn't wanted to go rock bottom, though. As a woman traveling alone, that would have drawn attention—but she hadn't wanted to stay somewhere exclusive, either. Again, more attention.

If Maggie Spencer had spotted Kopac even a minute earlier, everything might have gone differently that morning.

"What if she becomes a problem?"

Libby spoke out loud, articulating her concern in a calm, focused voice that by itself steadied her.

She sighed. "Then you'll deal with her."

Just as she'd dealt with Miss Maggie's father.

And would have to deal with his friend Bill Raleigh sooner or later.

Her head throbbed. She blamed it on the sunlight during her drive to Brussels.

She'd booked an afternoon flight back to New York tomorrow. Soon, she'd be home, back in her bed in Ravenkill. That had its own set of problems, but they seemed to pale now against what she faced staying in Europe.

It was always the same, the restlessness and obsession after a killing. This time, she had acted out of necessity. She'd had no time to plan. Had she left behind clues, evidence, witnesses?

Should she have killed the desk clerk?

She shut her eyes, trying to rid herself of the repeated images of that morning. The American asking for her. Maggie Spencer calling him. He hadn't heard her. He'd been focused instead on his quarry.

"On me," Libby said quietly.

She wondered if she'd have acted differently if she'd known who he was. She'd motioned to him to join her along the river, and he'd come straight to her—which at least suggested he didn't know she was a hired killer. He must have seen her with Janssen on Thursday and somehow figured out who she was. Perhaps he'd followed her to her hotel, but she didn't think so. She assumed he wanted to talk to her about the now captured fugitive, but why? Kopac wasn't in law enforcement.

Libby had no choice but to put aside her questions. Tom Kopac was dead. He couldn't harm her from the grave.

She racked her brain for anyone who could have seen her with Kopac that morning and replayed every move she'd made in Den Bosch. If she'd screwed up, Nick Janssen would find someone else to do his killing, and *her* name would go onto his target list.

She squirmed in her bed, knowing sleep would elude her.

Maggie Spencer wasn't on Janssen's list, which didn't necessarily mean he wouldn't consider the DS agent a threat if he found out she'd been in Den Bosch that morning—with Rob Dunnemore. *He* was on the list. Libby wished she'd seen him in time to cross off his name. It was a missed opportunity, but she'd had her hands full dealing with Kopac and avoiding Maggie Spencer.

Janssen was in a Dutch jail. Janssen wouldn't like the idea of an American diplomat tailing her, never mind turning up dead.

But that, at least, bought her some time to get started on her work for him and, finally, deal with the blowback from Prague and what she'd done eighteen months ago.

Maggie unzipped her suitcase on her bed at midnight, trying to think what she should pack. She'd made a reservation over the Internet for three nights at the Old Stone Hollow Inn in Ravenkill, New York. She hadn't used a false name—she signed up as Maggie Spencer and gave her current address as The Hague, the Netherlands. She might not need to stay all three nights. Once she was convinced Raleigh's tip—or whatever it was—was off the mark, she'd leave. But she wanted to check out the inn and Raleigh's veracity herself. She owed her father that much if Raleigh indeed had tracked her down because she was Philip Spencer's daughter.

What did people wear for a stay at a country inn in the Hudson River Valley? Shorts, pants, shirts. Maybe a skirt. Underwear. Nightclothes. Her running shoes. According to the inn's Web site it had woodland trails where she could go for a run.

With any luck, this expedition would turn into a mini-vacation.

The inn looked like a nice place. A renovated upscale nineteenth-century farmhouse with pale green clapboards and white shutters. Sunflowers. Vegetable gardens and orchards. A path along Ravenkill Creek.

If it'd been a fleabag, Maggie thought, she might not have been so quick to go.

George Bremmerton had found her at her computer at the embassy, doing a search for information on William Raleigh. If he was an economist, he wasn't a very famous one. She couldn't locate a single speech, article, book or mention of him. But that didn't mean he'd lied about his identity.

She'd told Bremmerton she needed to take a few days off and let him think it was because of Tom's death.

"Planning to leave the country?" he'd asked.

"I'd like to go to New York. Someone else can keep an eye on Deputy Dunnemore. I think he'll understand, actually."

"You've only been here a few weeks. Homesick already?"

"It's not that . . . ."

"Then what is it?"

His eyes had bored into her, telling her he knew her story was, at best, incomplete.

"All right. I've got a guy who thinks he's a spy or something whispering in my ear." She remembered how Rob had called him her Scarlet Pimpernel, but William Raleigh wasn't nearly as romantic a figure as the fictional character. "He's not the source of the Janssen tip—"

"You're positive?"

"Fairly. I want to follow up some information he gave me."

Bremmerton had stiffened. "What kind of information?"

"Highly questionable." But, she thought, the e-mail that led to Janssen's arrest had sounded nutty, too, and yet it had turned out to be legitimate. "Give me a few days to find out for sure if there's anything to it."

Bremmerton had looked at her for a long time. "Is this personal or professional?"

"Both."

"I don't like that."

"Neither do I."

"Why not blow off this guy?"

"I can't. He could be a drunk or crazy, I don't know, but I feel like I have to check this out. I've typed up everything I've got and put it on your desk." She'd debated explaining further, then decided to leave it at that. "Let it just be me sticking my neck out."

"If you're going to work for me, I need your trust."

She'd kept her eyes on him. "That's a two-way street."

"A name, Maggie."

She'd looked away. "Raleigh. William Raleigh."

Bremmerton hadn't responded at first. Then, quietly, he'd taken in a breath, his decision to go along with her obviously made. "You're on an early flight?"

She'd nodded.

"I have a meeting first thing in the morning." His misgivings showed in his clipped words, his straight back, but his answer revealed he trusted her. "I'll read your report after the meeting gets out."

"Thank you."

He wasn't looking for thanks, though. "You get a whiff—one goddamn whiff—that you're not on a wild-goose chase after all, I want to know about it. First."

That Bremmerton had gone along with

her was a demonstration of his faith in her—and in his own judgment, his own instincts, not to mention his power and influence within diplomatic security. He had twenty years of experience and built-up goodwill on her.

Maggie pulled a pair of black pants out of a dresser drawer and tossed them in her suitcase.

If a head rolled because of her excursion, they both knew it'd be hers.

She grabbed a pair of jeans. Basically, she was packing what she owned. It wasn't as if she had a lot of wardrobe choices, and there was no time to go shopping. She'd need her weapon, too. She placed it beside the suitcase, to remind herself of the protocol she'd need to follow to take it on the flight.

She'd be on her way to Schiphol airport in the morning when Rob started looking for her. She hated to sneak out on him. He'd been decent to her that afternoon—suspicious, but decent, buying her a bowl of chicken soup, rubbing her hand.

And those eyes. She couldn't get over them. Gray with blue flecks, darker lashes than she'd have expected given his fair-haired good looks. Her own lashes were almost invisible without mascara.

"God, you *are* tired."

She almost banged her fingers shutting the drawer.

Her friendship with Tom would lend credibility to her cover story of needing a few days off.

"Cover story" at least sounded better than "lie."

It was after one before she finally collapsed into bed, the mix of crushing fatigue and grief and agitation reminding her of her first days of training, when becoming a DS agent was still not quite a dream come true and when everything she might see in her work—everything she might screw up— was still only theoretical.

When her father was alive, and she'd looked forward to meeting him on a level playing field.

Things change, she thought. Things always change.

Eight

Maggie dragged her suitcase out to the street at six, uncertain she wasn't acting precipitously, even less confident in William Raleigh and his "tip," now that she had some rest.

When she got to the curb, she found Rob half sitting on the hood of her Mini, drinking coffee, and she stopped abruptly. "What are you doing here?"

He smiled at her. "I guess we'd better get moving if we're going to make our flight. I thought I might have to pound on your door. Up late?"

"*Our* flight? How—"

"I'm good at what I do. I've never tracked a DS agent before."

She noticed that he had his carry-on bag with him. "You just got to the Netherlands. You're not even over your jet lag."

"Don't mind if I ride with you, do you? Or are you taking a cab?"

Her suitcase was upright next to her. He had her flight information. There was no way she could deny she was heading to the airport. "Cab. It should be here any second."

"Good. We can split the fare."

Her head felt pinched, tight. If she told Rob to get his own cab, she wouldn't be able to grill him about how he'd found out about her flight. And since he'd apparently already wrangled a ticket for himself, she'd only postpone having to deal with him.

He was getting on that plane with her.

"I thought you went back to your hotel and had a couple of drinks."

"I did."

"Someone gave me up. You must have made a few calls."

"Maybe I got a call or two myself."

Bremmerton? Had he sicced Rob on her?

Rob spoke amiably, as if he expected her

not to mind his interference. But Maggie had no intention of discussing her plans with him on the street, or at the airport, or on the flight. She peered down the narrow street. There was no sign of her taxi.

"You could be heading to New York on information from a man who needs psychiatric care," Rob said.

"I'm taking a few days off."

"Ah."

He didn't believe her, not even for a split second. That much was obvious. Not that she'd expected him to buy her story. She was just letting him know she wasn't playing by his rules.

Fortunately, the cab arrived. Rob grabbed both suitcases and dumped them in the trunk, then joined her in the back seat. The dark charcoal of his suit drew her attention to his eyes, a misty gray in the morning light.

"Where are you staying in New York?" he asked as the cab pulled out into the street.

Maggie decided to take a more direct approach. "I'm not telling you. You're suspicious enough as it is." Although not without cause, she thought with a minor stab of guilt. "Yesterday was a tough day. It must have rekindled bad memories for you. I'm sorry I dragged you to Den Bosch. I don't blame you for looking for excuses to get out of here."

He shrugged. "I didn't have to look far, did I?"

She gave him a long look. "You're going to bird-dog me until you're satisfied, aren't you? I don't need you snooping into my private life."

"I'm not so sure this trip of yours is personal. According to my sources, you don't have much of a private life. All work, no play."

"Did you stay up all night checking me out?"

"People say you're at the top of your game. You made the Chicago bust happen. You got the tip that took Nick Janssen down. Yesterday was tough, no doubt about it. But an officer even half as dedicated as you are wouldn't take off for a few days the morning after finding a friend dead. It just wouldn't happen."

"It *is* happening."

"You've been on the job here, what, three weeks?"

"About that."

He settled back in his seat, the cab on the motorway now, speeding east toward the airport. "No way are you taking a few days off, Maggie. No way."

She didn't take the bait and respond. If Ravenkill was a wild-goose chase, it was going to be *her* wild-goose chase. Until she knew what she was dealing with, she wanted as few people to know about her little adventure as possible.

It wasn't that far to the airport. Even if Rob had managed to get a seat on her flight, odds were it wouldn't be right next to her. She just had to endure the cab ride, then avoid him on the flight across the Atlantic and shake him when they arrived at JFK. She'd reserved a car rental. With a little luck, she'd be on her way to Ravenkill with Rob Dunnemore none the wiser.

Magster.

She told herself she'd have gone to Ravenkill and shut out the marshal next to her over the reasons for her trip even if William Raleigh hadn't mentioned her father, alluded to his death. Whether Raleigh had ever been to Prague—had ever met Philip Spencer, murdered American businessman—mattered, but it wasn't her only reason for heading to New York. She also owed Tom Kopac.

"Your mother's a painter in Boca Raton," Rob said. "Pretty good, too. She and your dad were divorced when you were in high school. He died eighteen months ago in Prague. Some story about bank robbers."

He didn't believe it, either. Did he know something she didn't? But Maggie forced herself not to respond.

"Must have been rough, losing him that way."

She took a breath. "It was. My family doesn't have the greatest luck. I've never assumed I'll be drinking lemonade in the shade and writing my memoirs at eighty."

"You just described my father." His tone was gentle, as if he didn't take his father's long life and good health for granted. "Why New York? Why not visit your mother?"

"It's hot in south Florida in August."

He drank the last of his coffee and crushed the cup in one hand. "I can't see you leaving town after yesterday. I can't see Bremmerton letting you leave. So this trip isn't without his blessing."

"Maybe it was his idea. Stress."

"Right."

Again that open, amiable disbelief. Maggie glanced over at him, wishing he wasn't so damn attractive. "Why are you leaving?" she asked him.

"Because you are."

Dumb question. "How did you find out?"

"I know people."

He was matter-of-fact, not smug. After yesterday, she couldn't blame him for checking her out. She'd hauled him to Den Bosch, on the pretense of seeing where Nick Janssen had been picked up, only to come upon a murder and a bizarre rendezvous with a man who was, at best, an eccentric.

That she'd let Raleigh go without a fight couldn't have helped Dunnemore's early impression of her.

"You're not going to give me your source?" she asked him.

"No, ma'am."

"You think that Southern charm's going to work on me, don't you?"

He smiled. "What Southern charm?"

"It'll only get you so far when you're sticking your nose into someone else's business. Is the source who finked me out someone you know because you're friends with President Poe, or someone you know because you're a marshal?"

"Could be someone who's worried about you and called me."

"I doubt that."

A very short list of names came to mind, any of whom could be charmed by the fair-haired U.S. Marshal.

When they reached the airport, Rob offered to carry her suitcase. Maggie refused, politely, trying not to let his easy manner and good looks get to her—or to go overboard in the opposite direction and be a witch. Either way, he won. She didn't need a well-connected marshal following her, especially when she was on her way to check out a dubious tip from a man anyone else might have dismissed as mentally ill. But William Raleigh had brought up her father, and he'd been in Den Bosch the same morning Tom Kopac had been killed. If she could be sure going to New York was smart, having Rob as a witness might be more appealing.

But she told herself it wasn't just a matter of sparing herself a little embarrassment. If this escapade blew up in her face, she didn't want Rob getting caught in the shock waves.

There it was, she thought. She was being altruistic.

"You can't tell anyone about me, Maggie. No one. That's very important for your own safety."

Histrionics. If she really thought safety was a serious concern, she'd have had more reason to let Rob in on Raleigh's tip, or at least given Bremmerton more details.

When they boarded the plane, it turned out Rob had the seat directly across the aisle from her.

For the next seven hours.

He'd probably planned it that way, Maggie thought. All feelings of altruism left her. If he wanted to interfere in her business and call in favors to find out what she was up to, fine. Let him. If he wanted to track her to Ravenkill, that was fine, too. His neck, his choice.

Trying to ignore him, she thought about Ravenkill. The Stone Hollow Inn's Web site had a picture of the room she'd reserved. It had forget-me-not wallpaper, a private bath and a view of a sunflower garden.

And it had a four-poster, queen-size bed.

Maggie felt a jolt of heat and awareness so powerful and unexpected she glanced across the aisle at Rob to see if he'd noticed. But as good as his sources were, he couldn't read minds. *Thank God.*

He gave her a half smile. "Long flight ahead of us."

A very long flight. She hoped she got a grip before they landed In New York.

Sitting across from Wes Poe at the White House was just about the last place Nate Winter wanted to be on a Sunday morning. But the visit was Sarah's idea, and he'd promised to go along with her. Slowly but surely, he was getting used to her relationship with the president.

Sarah sat forward on her chair across the dining room table from the president. Her honey-colored hair was pulled back simply, and she'd put on a sundress for her trip to Pennsylvania Avenue. She was happiest digging through musty diaries, old family attics and backyard dumps, piecing together the lives of ordinary people. But Nate knew it was a mistake to forget that Sarah, like her twin brother, had the blood of the Dunnemores of old running through her veins. They'd been loggers and riverboat workers, adventurers who'd worked hard and played harder, and too often died young.

"Rob's on his way back to New York," she said. "He didn't even have a chance to recover from jet lag before he turned around and flew back."

"It works that way sometimes," Poe said gently. He was dressed casually in a polo shirt and khakis. Evelyn, his wife, was out for the day. "I don't think Rob ever intended to stay that long."

Sarah hardly seemed to be listening to him. "You heard what happened yesterday? About the murder?"

He nodded. "It was a stroke of bad luck."

But she obviously suspected more than luck had been involved. "The DS agent with Rob knew the victim. He was a diplomat. He worked at the embassy."

Wes's expression gave away nothing. Nate had no idea what the president knew about Tom Kopac and Maggie Spencer—if anything. Sarah had pieced together her information from talking with her father, whom Rob had also called, and from news reports. Nate had kept his conversation

with Rob to himself and intended to continue to do so until he knew more himself.
Sarah would understand, but she wouldn't
like it.

"I don't have any information you don't
have, Sarah," Poe said gently. "I'm sorry."

"I'll call Rob when he gets in," she said
half under her breath. "I'm not sure why he
went to the Netherlands in the first place. I
know reporters must have been calling and
pounding on his door—I'm a little harder to
find, but I've had my share. And I know he's
been restless—"

"He'll find his way," Poe said. "You both
went through hell in the spring."

"Rob insists he's fine. He thinks he's
found his way. You and my father want him
to be a diplomat type, but it's not him. I
don't care how many languages he speaks.
He likes law enforcement."

"I have complete faith in him, Sarah. If
Rob wants to stay in the Marshals Service,
that's his choice. He can go far there. If
not—"

"The shooting's changed him." Sarah
looked away, her concern for her brother
not something she could hide, but she
shifted back to Poe. "I'm not sure anyone's

giving me the full story about what happened in Den Bosch."

Nate knew he hadn't. It hadn't occurred to him that her twin radar would go wild just with the information she had. He didn't have much more himself. He planned to make some calls once he got the hell out of the White House.

Poe didn't answer but kept his gaze on Sarah, as if he expected her to continue without hearing from him.

She frowned. "Wes?"

"Go on," he said.

"Is Maggie Spencer trouble?"

"In what way?"

"Any way."

"I don't know her," Poe said.

But Nate suspected the president knew that Maggie Spencer's father had been killed in Prague eighteen months ago under circumstances that just didn't add up. Nate had dug up that much himself. Whether the Prague murder and the Den Bosch murder yesterday were connected was anyone's guess, but toss in a DS agent, Nick Janssen and Rob's abrupt return to New York, and Nate had his questions, to say the least.

"Did you know Tom Kopac, the diplomat who was killed yesterday?" Sarah asked.

"No. I know very little about him. I expect to hear more today." Poe kept his tone steady. "His death is a tragedy. Our people in the Netherlands are doing everything possible to get to the bottom of what happened. Right now, I don't have any more details than you do."

Sarah swallowed visibly. "What about Nick Janssen? I know he's in jail, but he was arrested in Den Bosch. Could he be responsible somehow?"

Nate sat forward. "There's no evidence to suggest Kopac had anything to do with Janssen or his arrest. We don't know why he was in Den Bosch."

"Why was Rob there?" she asked sharply.

"Because Maggie Spencer took him to see where Janssen was picked up," Nate said.

Sarah spun around at Nate. "You've talked to him. When?"

Nate sighed. "Last night. He called on my cell phone."

Poe looked at Nate, then turned to Sarah, but she pushed back her chair. "You marshals," she said, not sounding that annoyed. "You all stick together. Was he okay?"

"It hadn't been a good day, but yes, he was okay."

"On the case?"

Nate nodded, not expanding.

Sarah frowned at him. "You're not going to tell me. Or you can't tell me. Okay, that's fine. It doesn't change what I already know." She glanced from Nate to the president, her expression one of resolve and deep concern. "Something's wrong."

"Sarah," Wes Poe said. "I know it's hard not to worry, to feel as if you're out of the loop."

"I *am* out of the loop. For good reasons or bad."

The president's eyes bored into her. "You were sitting on your porch in Night's Landing when out of the blue you got a call that Rob was shot. It's going to take a while for you not to go on high alert every time—"

"Every time he finds a dead man in a Dutch river?"

Only Sarah Dunnemore, Nate thought, could challenge Wes Poe like that. But Poe took it. "It would irritate the hell out of Rob if he could hear us now. You know it would."

"You're right about that." She blew out a breath. "I should let him do his job, right? Trust him. All that."

Poe smiled. "We all should."

She shot Nate a glance. "What did he want with you last night?"

"Just to check out Maggie Spencer and Tom Kopac."

"I could have figured that out myself. It's common sense. Why not tell me?"

But Nate knew she didn't expect an answer. On a gut level, she would already have it. She wasn't in law enforcement. She was a historical archaeologist working on a new project. And her brother had called Nate, not her.

"Rob knows better than to try to protect you," Wes said.

"He's protecting himself. He doesn't like for any of us to worry about him. He can take anything but that." She sighed again, no longer as frustrated. "Actually, I understand."

Poe quickly changed the subject, asking her about the wedding, then ushered her to the door, hugging her goodbye. He said

something innocuous about Night's Landing that brought a small spark of pleasure.

But when Sarah wasn't looking, Poe let
his eyes connect with Nate in a way that
communicated in no uncertain terms: they
needed to discuss Rob's DS agent, Maggie
Spencer.

Nine

Ethan Brooker caught up with Raleigh in Amsterdam's historic *Begijnhof,* an enclosed cluster of perfectly kept, very old houses built around a trim, green courtyard. It was open to tourists, although there weren't many on the humid Sunday afternoon, just a few stragglers wandering along the walkway, checking out the bright gardens and the lace-curtained windows.

But Ethan had never been much of a tourist. "Why can't we meet at a café?" he asked. "I walked by the entrance to this place three times before I found it. It's like its own separate world here."

"Do you know what the *Begijnhof* is?"

"Can't say I do."

"It's where the Beguines lived. They were an order of religious women who dedicated themselves to charitable work but didn't take monastic vows."

"Good for them."

"There's a *Begijnhof* in Breda as well. The Beguines died out around 1970."

Ethan couldn't drum up a lot of interest and didn't want to set himself up for one of Raleigh's history lectures. The guy couldn't put enough of a living together to buy himself decent clothes, and he might or might not have all his marbles, but he knew the history of a tucked-away Dutch courtyard.

Still, it was a pretty spot. Quiet, removed from the city's congested streets.

"It's strange, isn't it?" Raleigh ambled along, touristlike. "The work we do. Yours as a Special Forces officer, mine as an economic consultant privy to government workings, diplomatic communications. We're so tapped into what's going on in the world and yet, at the same time, isolated because of our knowledge and experience."

"I was all about accomplishing the mission."

Raleigh smiled faintly. He had on the same clothes as yesterday. "You still are, I believe."

Ethan changed the subject. "Spencer and Dunnemore got on an early flight this morning to New York."

Raleigh stopped in front of a black wooden house. "This is the oldest house in Amsterdam," he said, but his voice faltered—Ethan's news had surprised him. "It dates from around 1475. You'll note it's constructed of wood. Even then Amsterdam was a crowded city, and wood burns. After huge fires did enormous damage, wood construction was forbidden. I believe there are only two wooden houses in all of Amsterdam. The Dutch are a sensible people. They . . ." He abandoned any pretext of interest in the historic site. "New York?"

"Uh-huh."

"Then you must go."

"I've got a ticket for a morning flight. You?"

He shook his head. "I can't right now."

"Hook up with me when and if you get there. I'll need more information. What did you tell Spencer, Raleigh? It's time to talk. Why New York?"

"Ravenkill. That's where she's headed. She must be."

"It's a town?"

"Yes. It's on the Hudson River about an hour, perhaps a bit more, north of the city. I saw it—the name of an inn—" Raleigh couldn't seem to go on and stopped in front of an attractive, spotless brick house, frowning. "The Old Stone Hollow Inn."

Ethan stared at him. "What? An inn?"

"Tom Kopac had printed information about Ravenkill and the inn off the Internet. I saw it in his apartment when I confronted him about why he'd been asking questions in Prague about Maggie, her father." Raleigh paused again, almost as if he were talking to himself. "I still have friends. They told me he'd been making calls."

"When the hell did you see Kopac?"

Raleigh seemed momentarily confused, flustered. "Was it Friday? Yes, it must have been. It was after Janssen's arrest. I dropped in on Mr. Kopac before he went to work that morning. He wouldn't talk to me. We arranged to meet in Den Bosch the next day. Then I called Maggie."

"Christ, Raleigh. I should haul your ass to the embassy—"

He waved a hand irritably. "It would only waste time. The police must have searched Kopac's apartment by now. They must have the printout. If they don't—if someone cleaned out his apartment . . ." He was talking to himself, but stopped, shooting Ethan a distressed look. "Do you suppose she's gone to Ravenkill on her own? Maggie? I thought she'd do some checking. The Internet, friends, see what she could find out from her desk at the embassy."

Ethan felt the sun hot on the back of his neck. He wasn't fond of Amsterdam. His wife had died here, only blocks away from the quiet, isolated courtyard. "What did you tell Spencer back at the cathedral?"

"Very little. There was no time."

"You used her father's death to manipulate her, didn't you?"

No answer.

"Come on, Raleigh. You let her think this inn holds the secret to what really happened in Prague. You know goddamn well—"

"I never said it did—"

"It's what you intimated. It's what you

wanted her to think. That's why she got on that plane yesterday."

The older man pursed his thin lips as he moved along the walk, past a small church, in thoughtful, troubled silence.

Ethan knew he had to be merciless. "If you think you could have sent her into danger, she needs everything you have. *I* need it if you expect me to help her."

Raleigh shook his head, as if to counter something he was telling himself. "Agent Spencer's prepared to handle difficult and dangerous situations. I have nothing that would help her." He glanced at Ethan. "Or you."

"You're so used to manipulating people you don't even know anymore when you're doing it. You're using her—me—to clear your name. Was Kopac on to Philip Spencer's real killer? Is that what you think?"

"I don't know what to think. For all I know, Mr. Kopac had that printout because he was planning his next vacation. Yes, he gave me an excuse to make contact with Maggie." He gave Ethan a stubborn look. "I have my reasons for wanting to meet her."

"She's in the dark—"

"I don't have all the answers, Major

Brooker. I have more questions than anything else."

"That's not the point."

But Raleigh would know it wasn't. "Philip Spencer had an uncanny ability to make things happen. His instincts were flawless. His energy. His timing." Raleigh turned to Ethan, as if it would help convince the younger man of his certainty, his righteousness. But tears rose to his red-veined eyes. "I believe his daughter is the same way."

"Let's hope she's better at staying alive."

Rob walked with Maggie to her car-rental agency at JFK, the airport bustling on a hot Sunday afternoon. "It's an expensive cab ride to Brooklyn," he said. "So why don't you drop me off on your way to wherever it is you're going?"

Maggie got into line. "You're kidding, right?"

"No, ma'am."

"You're trying to talk me into giving you a ride."

It wasn't working very well. A seven-hour flight was enough to make him antsy by itself; seven hours on a plane, anchored across from Maggie, had about done him in. There were times he thought the flight attendants would read his mind and make him change seats.

He should have just told them he kept fantasizing about whisking the passenger across from him off to a quiet beach somewhere and watched how fast they moved his butt to another part of the plane.

Something about Maggie had gotten to him. He wasn't sure he wanted to know what it was, since it would probably only mean trouble. She was a federal agent on a questionable mission. He was determined to find out what that mission was. That didn't leave much room for quiet beaches.

"I'll drive to Brooklyn," he said. "Then you can go on your way from there."

She angled him a not unfriendly look. "You're not going to give up, are you?"

"Not until I see you lock your doors and drive off—"

"Okay, okay." She rolled her eyes, but she was smiling. "I'll give you a ride back to your place. Then you'll leave me alone, right?"

He didn't answer.

She glared at him. "Right?"

He shrugged. "If you want me to."

Twenty minutes later, she was swearing at the Long Island Expressway traffic in her little rented car. "I'm not used to SUVs and great big trucks," she muttered. "You'd be surprised how unused to them you can get in three weeks."

"I offered to drive. Sure you don't have the jitters? I noticed you ate a *stroopwafel* on the plane."

Mention of the syrup-filled Dutch cookies made her smile. "No jitters. I'd have offered you a bite—"

"Except you were pretending I wasn't there."

"Fat lot of good it did me. A break from Dutch goodies will do my waistline good." But she pulled her top lip under her teeth, holding back a sudden sigh of regret. "Tom teased me at the bakery the other day. Damn. I wish he'd heard me yesterday. I wish I'd at least seen something."

"You did what you could."

"It wasn't enough."

"There was no reason to suspect someone was about to kill him."

She'd let the speedometer creep up and eased off the gas, calming down. "I still have no idea why Tom was killed. Why he was there. Why he was targeted—if he *was* targeted."

Rob had done enough obsessive speculating of his own on the long flight. Maybe Kopac had provided the tip about Janssen, and Janssen had found out and had him killed. Maybe Kopac had stuck his nose where it didn't belong in some naive effort to impress Maggie Spencer and ended up in the path of one of Janssen's cohorts, and it got him killed.

Maybe he'd hooked up with Maggie's guy in the cathedral, and it got him killed.

Maybe he'd been in the wrong place at the wrong time in a quiet Dutch city that had a random killer on the loose.

Given Tom Kopac's solitary life and dedication to his embassy work, none of the scenarios felt right. He wasn't, as far as Rob knew, an intelligence, military or law enforcement officer. He was one of the countless career foreign service workers who kept U.S. embassies running all around the world.

"What will you tell your bosses about why you're back so soon?" Maggie asked.

"I'll see if anyone asks, first."

"Are you a hundred percent since the shooting?"

"Yes."

"But you're not back on the street," she said.

Rob admired her directness but didn't want to get into a discussion of his status. "Not yet. Mike Rivera, my chief deputy, isn't one to rush something like that."

"He's worried about post-traumatic stress disorder?"

"It's just the way he is."

"He must have heard about Tom's murder." Maggie gave Rob a dry, pointed look. "Are you concerned people are going to start thinking of you as a shit magnet or something?"

He didn't answer.

"Sorry. That was unfeeling. I'm not going to interfere with your business. Just like you're not going to interfere with mine. Right?"

"Apples and oranges."

She ignored him. "What if we get to your place and it's crawling with reporters?"

"I'll duck," he said mildly.

But his street was quiet on a hot August Sunday, with no one hanging out on his building's front stoop wanting to talk to him about anything, never mind Nick Janssen's arrest.

"Why don't you give me your cell phone number?" Maggie stared straight ahead, both hands gripping the wheel as if she was saying something she knew she had no business saying. "I can call you if I get into any trouble."

Rob jotted his number down on the back of the car rental agreement and handed it to her. "Anytime."

She smiled tentatively. "Thanks."

"Maggie—"

"A few days off," she said stubbornly, "probably wouldn't hurt you, either."

That was the end of it. She wasn't budging on telling him her real reasons for flying to New York—or where she was headed. Getting his cell phone number was as far as she was going. Since there was nothing else he could do, Rob grabbed his suitcase out of the car and thanked her for the ride.

When he got into his apartment, he could smell the milk he'd left on the counter, and his voice mail was full. Reporters and more reporters.

He called Nate. "Anything on Kopac or Spencer?"

"Nothing specific."

Something was in his tone. "What?"

"Your sister talked to Poe."

Christ. "That's not what I needed."

"Poe didn't say as much, but Spencer's name rang a bell with him. Her father was killed in Prague a year and a half ago. Got caught in a bank robbery." He paused. "Business consultant."

"Does Sarah know?"

"No."

"What kind of business consultant was the father?"

"The kind that travels a lot and talks to a lot of people."

"You think—"

"I'm just guessing."

Nate was just guessing that Maggie Spencer's father had been on the government payroll—a spook.

"Maggie?"

"A-plus DS agent."

Did her father—his death—have anything to do with her abrupt departure from the Netherlands? Rob had no idea. He could feel his frustration mounting. For all he knew, Maggie was worried her encounter in the cathedral would make her an A-minus DS agent.

His head felt squeezed. "She met an older guy in Den Bosch after we finished with the police. White hair, red nose. She won't even give me a name. I think he was the reason we went out there in the first place."

Nate was silent.

"She says she's here to take a few days off. Wouldn't tell me where she's staying. Thinks I'll be a pest, I guess."

"Is she out of control?"

Rob pictured her behind the wheel of her rental car and shook his head, as if reassuring himself. "No."

"Keep me posted," Nate said. "Here, your sister wants to say hello."

She came on the line. "Rob? Damn it, are you okay? What's going on?"

"I'm good, Sarah. You don't have to worry—"

"I do have to worry. You go to Holland and end up in the middle of a murder scene." Her tone softened. "I'm sorry it happened. It must have been awful. But

Rob—this isn't going to work if you tell Nate things that you don't tell me."

"He's my superior—"

"You don't report to him."

She had a point. "What did you and Wes talk about this morning?"

"You. Lately, that's all we talk about."

"Well, change the subject," he said testily. "You and Wes talking behind my back is worse than me talking to Nate behind your back."

His sister wasn't bothered by his mood. "That's not the way I look at it."

Rob grinned at her lack of remorse. "Of course not. Look, it wasn't pretty yesterday. Now we're all probably getting our knickers in a twist over nothing. Relax, okay? Enjoy playing in your old dump. Is it bearing fruit?"

"It's amazing. Totally. I couldn't be happier."

"That's great, Sarah," Rob said, meaning it. But when he hung up, his body didn't know what time it was, and his head was spinning with thoughts and possibilities, none of them worth a damn. He finally gave up on making sense of anything and pulled on his running clothes and headed out.

Maybe a five-mile run would help clear his mind.

Maggie put together her Glock while the lace curtains of her forget-me-not room billowed in the afternoon breeze. She couldn't relax. The Old Stone Hollow Inn was idyllic. Gorgeous. Sunflowers, dahlias, herbs, orchards. It was a perfect spot to rejuvenate.

So why had William Raleigh mentioned it to her in a clandestine meeting in a Dutch cathedral?

What did it have to do with her father, Tom Kopac, Nick Janssen? Any of them?

"Nothing," she muttered. "The guy needs a psychiatrist."

The inn was located at the end of a long gravel driveway flanked by an apple orchard and a cornfield that opened up into a beautiful yard of flower and herb gardens and huge shade trees, with stone paths and fences, cedar benches and screened gazebos. It all felt more remote than it was. The village of Ravenkill, with its antiques shops and attractive houses, was less than a mile down a country road.

Maggie could see the Hudson River from her bedroom window. According to her brochure, a smaller creek was just through the woods along the orchard and cornfield. She was in Ichabod Crane country. She could almost picture a headless horseman charging across the countryside and had the unsettling sense that anything could happen here.

But it had been that kind of week, she told herself, strapping on her holster. She slipped her Glock in place and put on a lightweight denim jacket that draped over it, then checked her reflection in the bathroom mirror.

Not good. She looked like her body thought it was the middle of the night.

She dabbed on some blush, not sure it helped, and headed downstairs.

The inn itself was a sprawling, elegant mid-nineteenth-century farmhouse with celadon-green clapboards and white trim. Any additions and renovations to the original structure were seamless. The cherry floors gleamed, and the tall windows sparkled. The downstairs rooms—a kitchen, dining room, living room, library, den and music room—were decorated with a mix of antiques and contemporary pieces, everything light, airy and comfortable-looking.

The owners, Andrew and Star Franconia, lived on the second floor of a picturesque red barn. An informal antiques shop on the first floor included everything from rusted farm tools to delicate tea sets. A separate outbuilding had sports equipment for guest use—cross-country skis, snowshoes, giant inner tubes, kayaks, canoes, mountain bikes. If nothing panned out, Maggie figured she'd have plenty of things to do before she headed back to The Hague.

She had a choice of eating inside or outside on the back porch and decided on the porch. A waiter led her to a small table covered with a white cloth, with an oversized hydrangea growing up over the balusters. She ordered iced tea and sat back in her chair, welcoming the clean, warm summer air.

The Franconias came over to introduce themselves. Andrew was in his early fifties, stocky and handsome, Star perhaps a few years younger, blond and very thin. They both were dressed casually, relaxed and friendly among their guests.

"I understand you're from the Netherlands," Andrew said.

"I work there, yes," Maggie said.

"Did you have a good flight?"

"No problems. Thanks for asking." She'd never been good at small talk. "It's a beautiful evening."

"It's been beautiful all weekend," Star said. "We were lucky. We had a full house. Weekdays tend to be lighter. It should be quiet while you're here."

Her husband cleared his throat, suddenly looking awkward. "Um—are you in law enforcement?"

As discreet as she was, he must have noticed that she was armed. Maggie sipped some of her iced tea. "I'm with the U.S. Diplomatic Security Service."

"I've never heard of them," Star said, obviously intrigued.

"A lot of people haven't."

Andrew bristled. His wife seemed to be getting on his nerves. "I don't want any trouble. I don't like guns."

"I certainly don't want any trouble, either," Maggie said, deciding to change the subject. "I was just looking over the menu. What do you recommend, anything in particular?"

"It's all good."

Star's cheeks reddened in embarrassment over her husband's curtness. "The lobster bisque is particularly wonderful tonight. I would think it would go down well after a long flight. Andrew and I often travel together on business—well, we used to. Now one of us tends to stay behind to keep an eye on things here." She smiled, as if making an effort to be cheerful. "A case of 'be careful of what you wish for.' We always wanted our own inn, and now we've got one."

"How long have you been open?"

"Almost two years. It's gone fast."

Andrew straightened, posturing for both women. "Enjoy your visit, Agent Spencer. Don't hesitate to let us know if there's anything you need."

"I appreciate that."

Once they left, Maggie ordered the lobster bisque and a salad made with greens from the inn's own gardens, although she wasn't that hungry. She supposed disguising her identity in Ravenkill would have been simpler, but perhaps not as effective—this way, she could stir the pot, see how people reacted to her presence.

But for all she knew, Ravenkill or the Old Stone Hollow Inn had been in the news recently, and Raleigh—drunk or delusional or both—had mixed it up with something he'd seen about her father or Nick Janssen or God only knew what and come up with some bizarre conspiracy theory.

Maggie finished her soup, surprised to find she was hungry after all. Then, because she was jet-lagged and the *stroopwafel* was a long time ago, she ordered the plum tart special for dessert. It arrived warm, topped with homemade vanilla ice cream. The smell alone was worth the price. She smiled to herself. So what if she was on a wild-goose chase?

After dinner, she took a walk along a stone path, puffs of white clouds high in the sky, the air still as dusk gathered, crows crying in the distance.

As she passed the barn, she could hear the Franconias arguing upstairs, their exact words muffled but the tone unmistakable. They'd lose business, Maggie thought, if they didn't get a rein on their marital tensions. Nobody wanted their country inn escape marred by the owners fighting.

She made her way upstairs to her room, hooking the chain on the door.

It wasn't even dark out yet. If she went to bed now, she'd be up before dawn.

She checked a small bookcase. *The Three Musketeers. The Complete Works of Jane Austen. Othello.*

Her bathroom amenities included a small bottle of bug repellant and a warning note about West Nile virus and Lyme disease.

Maggie doused herself, put on running clothes and headed back outside. A jog into the village and back would clear her head.

If not, at least she'd stand a better chance of getting to sleep.

Ten

Libby lifted a heavy tray of breakfast dishes and carried it into the kitchen of what had once been her family home and now was the Old Stone Hollow Inn. The affront was fresh again. It was always this way after she got back from a trip. The insult of her situation would be raw and biting, the reality of what her life had become something she had to get used to all over again. Yet she'd watched it coming for years. Even as a little girl, she'd seen this future for herself with a brutal clarity.

Death, poverty, betrayal, humiliation.

No way out but surrender.

Her parents were dead. Her father had squandered her future. She'd had to sell her childhood home in order to save it.

And everyone knew her sad story.

She set the tray on the granite counter. Jet lag brought her emotions that much closer to the surface. She'd be all right in a day or two. And she had work to do. Targets to assess.

Her father was the one who'd taught her to shoot, she thought bitterly, even as she smiled at Star Franconia. "Good morning. It looks as if you have a few guests, anyway, for early in the week."

Star tugged at an apron that was too long for her. "Thanks for bringing in the dishes, Libby. I haven't seen you in a few days. Did you have a good weekend?"

"Yes, thanks. I was checking leads on some wonderful new pieces."

"Were you?" Star picked through a colander of herbs in the sink. "You must be getting quite an inventory by now. Soon you'll open your own shop. You wait."

Star liked to consider herself Libby's mentor. Libby knew she was supposed to be grateful. But there'd have been no inn for the Franconias if she hadn't kept her father from selling it to developers years earlier, or burning it down in a drunken party or letting it become condemned.

"How was your weekend?" Libby asked.

"We were busy, but most guests left yesterday. We had one new one arrive. She's a diplomatic security agent, in fact. Isn't that interesting?"

Libby grabbed a chair and jerked it out from under the round table, sitting down before her knees could go out from under her. She made herself smile. "I don't believe I've ever met a diplomatic security agent. Aren't they supposed to be overseas?"

"She came from The Hague. She's staying for three nights. Isn't that wild? Having a federal agent here makes Andrew nervous, of course, but I think it's great." Star lifted a few dripping sprigs of orange mint from her colander and set them on paper towels. "I'm sure you'll get a chance to meet her."

Maggie Spencer.

Philip Spencer's daughter was in Raven-kill.

Libby fingered a saltshaker in the middle of the table. Her eyelids were heavy, and she felt as if she were stuck in a soupy fog, unable to move or think fast, clearly.

William Raleigh.

The DS agent's presence had to be his doing. Libby pushed away the saltshaker and gazed out the window at the sunshine and shade trees.

Raleigh had been nipping at her heels for months.

She had to deal with him. She'd known that, but could never seem to get him out in the open, to a place where she could kill him or win him over or do *something* to end this dance they'd been doing. She knew who he was. He didn't know who she was. She had the advantage. How hard could it be?

Damn hard.

"I think I'm going to need more mint," Star said. "Libby, would you mind?"

She eased to her feet, careful to hide her agitation—another perverse skill she had. "No, of course not."

The warm temperatures and the soft breeze in the shade helped restore Libby's equilibrium. Avoiding the stone paths, she made her way through the lush, clipped grass, remembered doing somersaults in the yard as a little girl, and came to the herb garden. It was Star's pride and joy, classically arranged and at its peak on the late August morning. The orange mint was in a separate bed to keep it from spreading.

Libby closed her eyes and smelled it. She felt her energy return. Her natural sense of hope and optimism.

Maggie Spencer, William Raleigh.

Her list of targets.

She'd rise to whatever challenges her job presented, just as she always did with every hardship she faced.

Rob headed to the USMS office in the morning because he didn't know what the hell else he was supposed to do. He could have taken the day off. Then he'd be climbing the damn walls for sure.

"When did you get back?" Mike Rivera asked, standing over Rob's desk.

"Yesterday."

"They kick you out, or you left on your own?"

"On my own."

"Finding a dead guy twenty-four hours after you land in the country—" Rivera sighed heavily, shaking his head. "Not good. I read the report. You and that DS agent could have had your heads blown off, too. You're okay?"

Rob nodded.

"The DS agent? Spencer?"

"We took the same flight to New York."

Rivera straightened. "What's she doing here?"

"Says she's taking a break."

"Where?"

"Wouldn't say. Rented a car and took off. She's not the most open type."

"She gets the Janssen tip. She drags you to this Dutch town where Janssen was hiding, and within a few minutes of your arrival, she spots this friend of hers from the embassy. Next thing, he ends up with a bullet in his head."

"Maggie didn't kill him. She couldn't have."

But Rivera didn't trust anyone. "You watched her every second?"

"Yes."

"So she decides, in the middle of all this, to fly to New York and take a break? Come on. You don't believe that. That's why you came back, isn't it?"

"I think she's following another lead, but I could be wrong."

Rob thought of Maggie's smile and that red hair, the gold-flecked turquoise eyes, and figured the effects of his whirlwind trip were to blame. His head was mushy. He felt like Maggie was two beats ahead of him. But he'd find her.

Rivera suggested something along those lines himself before stalking back to his office.

When Juliet Longstreet arrived in the office twenty minutes later, she had a similar reaction. Bad luck in the Netherlands. Not good to have Maggie Spencer on the loose given the circumstances. In her usual blunt fashion, Juliet added, "I think she's up to something. So do you."

"Federal agents get to take time off."

Juliet rolled her eyes. "Within a few hours of finding a body? The body of a *friend*?"

It was a fair point. It was a point Rob had made himself. "I'm on her," he said.

"But of course."

He was still contemplating just how he'd go about finding Maggie when he answered a call from a guy who identified himself as Andrew Franconia.

"My wife and I own an inn in Ravenkill, New York," Franconia said, sounding stressed and irritated. "We don't want any trouble."

"What can I do for you, Mr. Franconia?" Rob asked.

"Diplomatic security agents deal in passport and visa fraud, don't they? Are we under investigation?"

Rob sat forward. "Why are you asking me?"

"Don't be cagey, Deputy. You know goddamn well why. I've read the papers. You and a DS agent came upon a murder on Saturday in the Netherlands. I didn't make the connection at first, but I think it's awfully damn coincidental she shows up here—"

"Who?"

"Agent Spencer." Franconia gave a hiss of impatience. "I'm sorry, it's been a difficult morning. I knew something wasn't right yesterday when she arrived, and I did some checking. I read about the diplomat's murder. Kopac. I'm very sorry. It must have been terrible. But I have my own considerations."

"I understand," Rob said. "What's the name of your inn?"

"The Old Stone Hollow Inn. It's about a mile from the village. I'd feel better about having Agent Spencer here if she hadn't just been involved in two high-profile criminal events. She got the tip that led to Nick Janssen's arrest, too, as I'm sure you're aware."

"Mr. Franconia, I can't speak for Agent Spencer, but if you're concerned that you or your wife or your guests are in any danger—"

"It's not that. We just don't want any trouble. We run a quiet inn here, and we're law-abiding—" He broke off. "Christ, that sounds stupid to say. But we are. We're law-abiding citizens."

"What's Agent Spencer doing now?"

Franconia paused. "Taking a walk in the herb garden."

Hell, Rob thought. Maybe she *was* just taking a few days off to clear her head. He smiled into the phone. "That doesn't seem too suspicious, does it, Mr. Franconia?"

"No, I suppose not."

He sounded only slightly chastened. Rob decided to give him a little more to chew on. "I flew back with her yesterday. She told me she was taking some time off."

"Did you believe her?"

Not even a little, Rob thought. "No reason not to. Why did you call me?"

"It seemed the thing to do. I wasn't sure if you were still in the Netherlands. Thanks for your time."

After they disconnected, Rob didn't have a chance to stand up before the phone rang again. He picked up and identified himself.

"Andrew Franconia beat me to you, didn't he?" Maggie said, not sounding remorseful at all.

"You're scaring the hell out of him."

"Upsetting his applecart, maybe. He's not scared."

"What are you doing?"

"Right now? Looking at the sunflowers from my bedroom window. I just got in from a walk in the herb gardens. It's a beautiful day, Deputy. But I almost wish it was snowing. Then you'd be more likely to stay put in New York."

"Don't count on it."

Just a half beat's hesitation. "How long do I have before you get here?"

"Ninety minutes at the most, unless traffic's bad."

"Good," she said. "I won't tell you where

I'll be. You can find me. It'll be more fun for you that way."

He almost smiled. "I'll try the sunflowers first."

A click told him she'd hung up.

Rob stood in Rivera's office doorway. "She's in Ravenkill. It's on the Hudson."

"Ravenkill?" Rivera squeaked back in his chair. "My wife dragged me up there once to go antiquing. I thought I'd hang myself, but it's a cute village. Your DS agent into antiques?"

"No idea."

"Go up there," Rivera said. "Find out."

Maggie was sitting in a screened gazebo, amid summer roses and ivy, when Rob found her. He had on sunglasses that only made him look sexier, reminding her—as if she needed reminding—not to get ahead of herself around him.

"You haven't been here a full day," he said, "and you're already scaring the locals."

"They're more irritated than scared." She'd put on capri pants, a tank top and her denim jacket and wondered if he was thinking she looked sexy—or if he, too, was irritated with her. "At least they won't be calling the media. I figure the Franconias don't want reporters sniffing around here any more than I do."

"The old guy in St. John's sent you here?"

She angled a look up at him. "You cut to the chase, don't you? Have a seat. Enjoy the moment. You can smell the roses and listen to the birds twittering."

"I like birds," he said, but didn't sit down.

"The Franconias have bluebird houses set out on the edges of the fields and orchards. It's a different kind of life, isn't it?"

He shrugged. "I used to live this kind of life, except not this fancy."

"On the Cumberland River, you mean."

"That's right."

Next to President Poe's boyhood home. "There are snakes down there."

"Mostly you don't see them." He seemed to be laying on the Tennessee accent. "The snake you see first is always better than the snake you surprise."

Maggie smiled. "That could be my motto. Well, I didn't grow up in a country inn or on a Southern estate. We moved around a lot. Don't you want to sit?"

"I've been in the car for more than an hour, and I sat all day yesterday." The knotty cedar floor creaked as he moved toward her. "Nice spot."

"The inn's lovely. I only had a peek at Ravenkill. I'm not much on shopping, even if I lived here and didn't have to haul my purchases back to the Netherlands."

"First time here?"

"First time in the Hudson River Valley at all."

He was silent.

"I talked to George Bremmerton this morning," Maggie said. "Tom left the embassy early on Thursday. Right after lunch."

"The day Janssen was arrested."

"Tom was such a loner. No one knew where he went. He didn't say anything to anyone. He didn't leave a note." She paused, physically forcing herself not to picture him in the Binnendieze. "He came to work like normal on Friday. Then he shows up in Den Bosch on Saturday."

"But he had nothing to do with the Janssen case?"

She shook her head. "Not even remotely."

"Investigators will be all over him taking off early."

"He wasn't the type to take off, ever. He loved his work. He—"

"I know. I'm sorry."

"It can be a damn cruel world," she said tightly, leaving it at that.

"Bremmerton knows where you are?"

"Yes."

"But it wasn't his idea for you to come here," Rob said.

She burst to her feet. "Come on, let's have lunch. The food here is very good— lots of stuff from the garden. Makes me want to be careful where I step, in case it lands up in my salad."

"Maggie—"

"I don't know anything, Rob. Nothing worth knowing, anyway."

He followed her out of the gazebo and onto a stone path warmed by the midday sun. A tidy vegetable garden with carefully staked and marked plants sprawled to one side, with grapevines and gladiola in a half-dozen colors on the other. Maggie wondered what it'd be like to spend three days here on a romantic getaway, then pushed the thought far away. Men and romance

were not in her cards, at least for the immediate future. She needed to get her feet under her in her first foreign assignment.
Then, maybe, she could consider a relationship.

"No dogs?" Rob asked in that slow,
Southern way he had. "You'd think a country inn would have dogs. My granddaddy
had hounds. I never knew him. Died before I
was born. Some kind of logging accident.
We Dunnemores live long if we don't get
killed."

"My father was only fifty-seven when he
died."

The path widened, and Rob eased in next
to her. "What was he doing in Prague?"

"He was a business consultant. He traveled a lot. It finally drove him and my
mother apart."

"You joined diplomatic security because
of him?"

"Because I have the same sense of wanderlust, yes." She smiled suddenly, trying to
lift her mood. "As you can see—"

"Being here has nothing to do with wanderlust." He glanced at her, gave her one of
his half smiles. "Or with just lust, from what
I can see."

She could feel heat on the back of her neck. "What, you don't think I have a guy hiding in my room?"

"No, ma'am."

Since even the way he said *ma'am* got to her, Maggie decided she had low blood sugar on top of jet lag and mounted the steps to the back porch. She could hear the clicking of ice in glasses and smelled mint and charcoal, as if someone had been grilling. Three tables were filled. Breakfast was for guests only, but lunch and dinner were open to the public.

A slender woman cheerfully seated them at a small round table. "I may have gotten you in trouble, Agent Spencer," she whispered; despite her short gray hair, she couldn't have been more than in her midthirties. "Star and Andrew are in such la-la land, they might never have known about the shooting if I hadn't said anything. I saw it on the news."

"That's not your fault," Maggie said.

"I feel bad. They're under a lot of stress." She handed Rob and Maggie each a printout of the day's menu. "I understand the victim was a friend of yours."

"We'd only known each other three weeks, but, yes, Tom was a friend."

"What a shame. My name's Libby, by the way—Libby Smith."

"It's nice to meet you," Maggie said.

"You're smart to get away for a few days after such a tragedy. How'd you end up in Ravenkill? Do you have family here?"

Maggie shook out her napkin and placed it on her lap, noticing Rob eyeing her over the top of his menu, wanting answers himself. "No, no family here. It's just something I picked on a whim. I'm glad I did. It's beautiful."

"Well," Libby said, obviously not satisfied, "enjoy your stay. What can I get you two to drink?"

"Iced tea would be fine," Maggie said.

Rob smiled up from his menu. "Make that two, Miss Smith."

"Just Libby is fine. My family owned this place for generations." She grinned irreverently. "Star and Andrew saved it from a wrecking crane. I help out when I can. I live on the first floor in a little ell my dad used as his trash room. He had problems. Two iced teas it is."

When Libby withdrew to fetch their iced

tea, Maggie leaned over the table. "I think there's a subtext around here, don't you?"

"I'd say that's a fair guess, Agent Spencer."

She smiled. "At least you still have a sense of humor."

Libby returned with two glasses of tea with sprigs of orange mint, and Maggie, starving now, felt like ordering everything on the menu. She settled on the carrot-orange soup, the walnut-pear salad with goat cheese and the grilled salmon.

"The goat cheese is local," Libby said. "Star toasts it."

"Sounds wonderful."

Rob chose the chicken salad with grapes and pulled off his sunglasses after Libby left with their orders. "Nate Winter has my description of your old guy. Nate's my future brother-in-law, and a marshal. We're going to find out who your guy is."

"You're relentless, aren't you? I suppose it's a good quality in someone who catches fugitives for a living."

Maggie tilted back her iced tea and wished she could just keep drinking all afternoon and avoid those eyes. But she set the glass down, observing a middle-aged couple sharing a salad at another table.

Rob said nothing. He was, she suspected, trying to use silence to his advantage.

"He says his name is William Raleigh. He's a retired economist." She ran a finger down the frosty side of her glass. "He gave me the name of the inn. It was my decision to actually come here."

"Any contact with him before Saturday?"

"No."

"He had to have said something significant to make you go to the trouble of flying to New York at the last minute, giving me the slip—"

"He referred to my father and his death." She heard the sharpness in her tone but couldn't do anything about it now. "You saw him. He's down and out. He smelled like stale cigarettes and looked like he just finished a drinking binge."

"You think it could be a bad lead."

She tried to smile. "I've been to worse places on wild-goose chases. I have a four-poster bed in my room and forget-me-not wallpaper."

"Do you?"

"Damn it, Dunnemore—"

"You're the one who brought up beds and forget-me-nots."

"Do you even know what a forget-me-not is?"

"Flower." He grinned at her. "Bluish purple."

Andrew Franconia trotted up the porch steps and beelined for their table, saving Maggie from further talk of her bedroom. But he was annoyed. "I didn't mean for the marshals to come up here," he said through clenched teeth. He was sweating, in shorts and an orange polo shirt that was neatly tucked in. "You're Deputy Dunnemore, aren't you? I recognize you from the news—"

Rob got to his feet and shook hands politely, taking some of the steam out of Franconia's irritation. "Maggie and I are enjoying your inn," he said. "We just ordered lunch. Would you care to join us?"

"No, no, that's all right. Thank you. I was just—" He glanced around at the occupied tables, then lowered his voice. "It struck me that whoever murdered that diplomat on Saturday is still at large. If Agent Spencer is someone who protects diplomats—"

"I'm not here because of Tom Kopac's murder," Maggie said.

Andrew glanced at her. "But you made your reservation just hours afterward."

"It'd been a bad day." She kept her tone even. "Have you ever been to Den Bosch? Its full name is 's-Hertogenbosch. There's a lovely gothic cathedral there, and they do boat tours on the waterway—"

"No, I've never been there, but I've been to Holland, of course, many times. Star and I travel frequently in our work—well, we used to." His voice softened slightly, became less rat-tat. "It's harder for us both to get away now that we have the inn."

"You go on solo trips?" Maggie asked.

He narrowed his gaze on her. "Is this an interrogation?"

"A friendly conversation, Mr. Franconia."

"I'm sorry," he said in a half whisper. "I don't mean to be rude. Please, enjoy your lunch."

He couldn't get away fast enough.

"He embarrassed himself," Rob said. "You make him nervous."

"You don't help matters," Maggie said. "He knows marshals arrest people, but he's not sure what diplomatic security agents do. And he knows you're pals with the president. That'd make anyone nervous."

"Doesn't seem to affect you."

"Sure it does. I'm just better at containing my emotions."

Libby Smith returned with the carrot-orange soup, a dollop of sour cream melting in its center.

"I'm not that hungry anymore," Maggie said. "Maybe I should cancel the salmon."

"As you wish," Libby said, smiling. "Don't you just hate jet lag? I never know whether I'm supposed to eat, sleep or just be cranky."

Maggie laughed. "Some people would say I always know when to be cranky."

Libby laughed, too, but when she left, Rob picked the mint sprig out of his iced tea and set it on his place mat. "I want to know everything you know about your Sir Walter Raleigh character. Start to finish. When he contacted you, how, what he said, why St. John's, what happened there. All of it."

Maggie dipped her spoon into her soup. "Why should I tell you?"

"Because we're in this thing together."

"That's what I was trying to avoid—"

"Not that hard. If you'd wanted to disappear once you got to New York, you'd have figured out a way to do it." He nodded to her. "Go ahead. Eat your soup and talk to me."

Whether he meant to or not, he managed to sound rational and calm and reasonable—not dictatorial, not panicked, not annoyed. It was a skill, Maggie thought. If their positions were reversed, she'd never have pulled it off.

"It's William," she said. "Not Walter."

"He doesn't think he defeated the Spanish Armada?"

"As far as I know, no."

And she told Rob everything.

Start to finish. All of it.

Eleven

After lunch, they ran across Libby Smith folding cloth napkins at the dining room table, and she offered to show them around the place. "I'll give you the secret grand tour."

She had an eager but somewhat self-deprecating manner that Rob attributed to the awkwardness of being reduced, basically, to the live-in help in a house that had been in her family for generations. She pretended not to mind, that she loved what the Franconias had done to the place and appreciated having it off her hands. But it had to stick in her craw.

Before Rob could bow out of any tour, Maggie accepted for both of them. A minute later, they were standing on the front steps and Libby had them listening for sounds of the nearby creek.

"Its official name is the Raven Kill," she said. "*Kill* is an old-fashioned Dutch word for river or creek, but nobody knows that anymore. So, we generally say Ravenkill Creek. Technically it's redundant, but otherwise, who'd know what we were talking about? Do you speak Dutch, Agent Spencer, since you're assigned to the American embassy in The Hague?"

"I've picked up the grammar, and I know a few words."

"And you, Deputy," Libby said. "They say you speak eight or nine languages."

"Not quite that many," Rob said.

"It's such a gift. I can get along in French, but that's about it. Anyway, it used to be farmland right down to the creek. The woods are relatively recent. They've grown up in the past seventy years or so. The orchards and gardens are all my family's doing, revitalized, of course, by Andrew and Star."

"When did your family arrive in Raven-kill?" Maggie asked.

"Just before this house was built in 1846. There wasn't a lot of money until my great-grandfather's day in the early 1900s. My grandfather added on to the house and turned it into more of a country estate—a gentleman's farm—than a homestead." She trotted down the steps onto the front lawn. "Then my father squandered the family fortune. You know the old adage. First generation makes it, second generation spends it, third generation loses it. That about sums it up as far as the Smiths go."

Rob followed Maggie down the steps. "What was your great-grandfather's fortune in?" he asked.

"Investments. I don't know." Libby waved a hand, her tone cheerful and dismissive. "It doesn't matter now."

Rob noticed the grass was virtually without weeds. Everything about the Old Stone Hollow Inn was picture-perfect. "Your parents—"

"Dead. First my mother, then my father. They were both gone before I was out of college."

"When did you sell the property to the Franconias?" Maggie asked.

"Four years ago. It was that or the wrecking crane. I never thought I'd stay here, but Andrew and Star wanted someone on the premises during renovations and I didn't mind. It was fascinating, actually." She shrugged. "I just haven't left yet. I'm collecting antiques to open my own shop. Quality stuff. My father was a drunk, but he knew a bit about antiques and taught me. It's taking some time to pull the right pieces together. I do a little dealing, but it's not enough so that I can afford to strike out on my own."

"Are those your pieces in the barn?" Maggie asked.

Libby shook her head. "No, they're Andrew and Star's. They made their money in the antiques business. They think of themselves as sort of my mentors. Come on. I'll show you my pieces. They're on the tour."

She led them around to the side of the house, pointing out old rose bushes and lilacs, a sugar maple where her grandmother had once had a swing and a marble fairy statue that her grandfather had picked out because it so looked like her grandmother. She was still talking when she led them down a slope to a full-size cellar door.

"You *have* to see the wine cellar," she said, hefting the heavy door open. "My grandfather had it built almost a hundred years ago."

A switch just inside the door turned on a naked yellow lightbulb in the middle of a narrow hall. An old dehumidifier rumbled against one wall. Maggie sneezed. "Dust sensitivity," she said, sneezing again.

"You can't keep the dust out of here," Libby said. "The original cellar is all stone. Can you imagine? They built it one big old rock at a time. There was a dirt floor, but it got paved over with concrete. This part's newer, but, still, there's just not much that can be done about the dust."

Rob nodded to an arched wooden door. "Is that the wine cellar?"

Libby smiled. "Good guess. Doesn't it remind you of a Vincent Price movie? Alas, no bats and vampires down here."

She pulled open the door, which was heavy for her. The room was small and windowless, naturally cool, its concrete walls lined with mostly empty wooden wine racks. Only a few dust-encrusted bottles re-

mained. Libby pulled on a string, and another naked yellow lightbulb came on.

"It gives a lot of people the creeps to be
down here, but not me," she said. "During
the winter and bad weather, I'd hide in here
with a book. Of course, my father cleaned
out any last remaining bottles of wine. Andrew talks about actually using it again, but
he's very picky about temperature and humidity controls."

"What's through that door?" Maggie
asked, pointing to a more ordinary door in
the corner of the small room.

"Storage. It's interesting to see a house
from the inside, don't you think? But maybe
I'm just a frustrated architect. My antiques
room is just up the hall."

They returned to the hall, passing a battered wooden canoe and broken paddles.
"Are these some of your antiques?" Maggie
asked.

"Junk. Andrew thinks he can restore the
canoe. I don't."

"Was it in your family?"

"Everything down here was in my family."

Rob didn't think the canoe had much
hope. "Are the Franconias originally from
Ravenkill?" he asked.

"Poughkeepsie," Libby said, tackling a combination lock on another door. In a few seconds, she had it unlocked and the door pushed open. "Voilà."

The room was stacked nearly floor to ceiling with old furniture and crates of glass pieces. Another dehumidifier rumbled and rattled in a corner. Rob noticed desks, tables, chairs, dressers, sofas, cupboards and bookcases, but he couldn't place any value or determine the origin of any of them.

Libby sighed proudly. "I know it all looks like dusty old junk to most people, but I can see how it'll all fit into a shop in the village. I even know which one I want."

"Do you specialize in a particular country or era?" Maggie asked, peering at the eclectic jumble of pieces.

"I just buy what I like. I spend a lot of time and money traveling to find things, keep track of all the documentation. There's a lot to it."

More, Rob was certain, than he wanted to know.

But the cellar tour ended, and they made their way up the back stairs to a small laundry and supply room, then continued their tour through the main rooms of the first floor. Libby pointed to the door to the ell where she had her minisuite. "It's very cute," she said.

"Anyone else live here full-time?" Rob asked.

Libby shook her head. "Just the Franconias and me."

"Do they have any children?"

"Two grown daughters. I'm sure they'll end up inheriting the place." She spoke without apparent bitterness. "Andrew and Star are such planners. I'm more spontaneous—which is probably why I don't have a husband, kids or much money."

She pointed out several items the Franconias had ended up buying from her, never mind their own expertise in antiques. An early twentieth-century sofa, a Victorian piano stool, an 1840s quilt. "I'd dreamed for so long of what this place could look like," Libby said. "It was easy to come up with the perfect pieces."

They headed upstairs, where she took them through unoccupied guest rooms and sitting rooms, pausing at a hall window with a breathtaking view of the Hudson River. They were near the narrows, Libby explained, where the famous river forced its way between the Appalachians and was at its deepest and most treacherous.

She turned away from the window. "I never thought I'd have to give up this view."

They returned to the main floor and wandered out to the back porch. Libby put her hands on her hips and breathed in the summer air as if to counter all the dust and the nostalgic memories stirred up on her tour.

Rob dredged up something to say. "It's humid. Maybe we'll get rain." God, he thought, he sounded like his father, talking about the weather. "Think it'll storm?"

"A forty-percent chance of thunderstorms, according to the latest weather report," Libby said. "I should pick the beans before one hits. Thanks for indulging me."

"Our pleasure," Maggie said.

"That's very gracious of you to say." Libby gave an irreverent smile. "I've never shown the place to a couple of feds. Enjoy the rest of the afternoon."

She set off happily down the driveway.

"Either it doesn't kill her that she lost the place to a brittle couple she doesn't like that much," Rob said, "or she's good at hiding it."

"Maybe she knows that without the Franconias the gardens and orchards would be a golf course by now."

He shrugged. "The golf course might have kept the fairy statue."

Rob said he wanted to check in with Mike Rivera, and they ended up in Maggie's room. He didn't comment on the four-poster bed or the forget-me-not wallpaper. Maggie ducked into her bathroom while he made his call and checked her face for dust and smudges after crawling around the inn's cellar.

Libby Smith. Andrew and Star Franconia.

A country inn.

Antiques.

It wasn't a lot to go on.

"It's not *anything* to go on," Maggie said to herself, then rejoined Rob in the bed-room.

He'd finished with his conversation and stood at her window. "Juliet Longstreet thinks Ethan Brooker must have had some-thing to do with the Janssen tip."

"Brooker? We don't have any indication he was even in the Netherlands last week, never mind on Janssen's heels. I doubt he'd have bothered with a tip."

"He wouldn't have killed Janssen—"

"I didn't mean that. I meant he'd have grabbed Janssen himself and hauled him to the police station. He wouldn't have risked an anonymous e-mail tip. I could have not gotten it in time, I could have ignored it, the Dutch SWAT team could have missed Janssen. Brooker doesn't sound the sort to take that kind of chance."

"Maybe he had a contingency plan if the tip didn't work out."

"Possible. Does Deputy Longstreet trust him?"

"She doesn't trust anyone."

Maggie hesitated, remembering what she'd read about Rob and Longstreet. "You two—"

She didn't have to go further. Rob shook his head. "Long and well over."

"I don't even know why I asked."

"Because you're curious," he said. "You want to know."

She licked her lips, her mouth suddenly dry. "Why would I want to know?"

"Because you want to dismiss me as some stereotype—"

"The well-connected Southern frat boy who speaks five languages—"

"Seven."

"And who's friends with the president and is a guest at diplomatic receptions, not just the protection—"

"I can be the protection, too. But, yes. That sums up the stereotype you want to lay on me to keep from getting too close—"

"Rob, you *are* a well-connected Southern frat boy who speaks seven languages."

He smiled. "I never joined a fraternity. And it doesn't matter. You like me, anyway."

"I suppose one shouldn't mistake charm for a lack of confidence—"

"No, one shouldn't."

He spoke with an ease and natural humor that somehow only underlined the edge to him, the air of danger that had nothing to do with posturing and everything to do with self-assurance and purpose.

He'd had a hell of a year, Maggie reminded herself. He'd been shot. His family had nearly been destroyed. He'd had a long recovery that, in some ways, was probably still ongoing.

A little flirtation and attraction that she could keep under control she could handle. But they were fast passing that point.

"Your father's a diplomat," she said.

"The first in the family. My ancestors were riverboat workers and brawlers. Most of them probably looked like Southern frat boys, too."

"Okay. So I won't pigeonhole you."

"It'd be smarter not to. Less likely you'll get in over your head."

"How would I—"

"By thinking I'm something I'm not. Like not interested in redheaded DS agents who have clandestine meetings in Dutch cathedrals and a penchant for trouble—"

"I don't always have that penchant. Only this week."

He touched her hair. "You're not that easy to draw out, are you, Maggie?"

The way he said her name. She shut her eyes a moment to collect herself. "Christ, Rob. I'm supposed to be checking out this inn."

"You did check it out. You had a tour of the cellar and you saw the fairy statue and the view of the Hudson."

His voice was so quiet, and he was standing close enough to her that she could feel his hips, the brush of his chest against her. He let his hand linger on her arm. Even as she warned herself against the impulse,

Maggie leaned into him, and he dropped his hand to her waist, gently turning her into him. She thought he whispered her name. She could feel the warm air, moist and heavy with the increasing humidity.

"Rob . . . it's okay, it's . . ." She smiled, raising her mouth to his, answering the unspoken question. "Yes."

Their kiss started out tentative, but that didn't last. Maggie opened her mouth, eager to taste him, let him explore her. He lowered an arm to her hips and pulled her against him. She felt the tight, strong muscles in his shoulders and back, the tautness of his hips as her hands skimmed over him, everything about him suddenly firing her senses.

He lifted her onto him, and she could feel that he was as aroused as she was, as if their close proximity to each other since he'd arrived in Holland—together with the violence and chases and diversions—had built up, erupting now with more intensity than either of them could have anticipated.

He skimmed his thumbs over her breasts, eliciting a soft moan from her that had nothing to do with fatigue or jet lag. It would be so easy just to fall into bed with him. Her pretty four-poster was right there, a few feet way, in the path of the afternoon breeze.

But they broke apart as suddenly as they'd come together. A timer might have gone off, or an alarm reminding them of who they were and what they were about.

Rob backed up a step, exhaling as he ran a hand through his hair. "I didn't expect that to happen."

Maggie took in a ragged breath. "Ha."

He grinned at her. "Okay, I didn't expect it to happen the way it did. I've been thinking it might sooner or later, but—" He smiled at her, not even breathing hard. "I don't want to get you fired."

"Trust me, Bremmerton can find more reasons to fire me than sneaking a kiss with a good-looking marshal."

His expression turned serious. "Maggie—"

She didn't let him draw her out. Just stick to the facts. "You must need to get back to New York. Did you tell Chief Rivera everything?"

Rob pulled open the door to the hall. "He doesn't know you're a redhead with the most beautiful turquoise eyes—"

"That charm again."

He laughed. "It's a killer, isn't it?"

They walked downstairs, past the view that Libby Smith had said she loved so much. When they reached the back porch, Maggie felt the carrot-orange soup burning up her throat. "You're going to look into William Raleigh, aren't you?"

"Discreetly, but yes."

"Let me know—"

"Of course." There was no sarcasm in his tone. "Bremmerton?"

Maggie thought a moment. "I think he knows more than he's saying, but I can't be more specific than that."

Rob sighed. "Fair enough. You've got my cell phone number. You know the number at the office. Call. I can be back up here in less than an hour if I break the speed limits."

She walked with him to his car.

He winked at her. "I'd kiss you goodbye—"

"We've given the locals enough to talk about, don't you think?"

After he left, Maggie felt the afternoon humidity in the air. There was no breeze. She heard bees in the dahlias and a crow far off in the distance, but no birds, it seemed, nearby.

Libby waved from the vegetable garden, but kept to her task which seemed to be picking loose leaf lettuce. Maggie continued on to the back porch, where Star Franconia was cleaning tables and taking in short, quick gulps, as if she were trying to keep herself from crying. Maggie didn't disturb her and ducked inside.

There was no sign of Andrew in the garden, on the porch or inside.

Maggie had no idea what to do with herself. There was no evidence the Franconias or their staff or any of their guests were engaged in criminal wrongdoing.

Why had William Raleigh sent her here?

Who the hell was he?

When she and George Bremmerton had talked that morning, he'd all but vouched for Raleigh. That counted for something, even if he was being vague.

She headed back up to her room, telling herself that it was necessary, okay and actually quite smart of her to be in Ravenkill on her own.

Twelve

It was early evening when Ethan arrived at JFK.

He didn't know what'd happened to Raleigh. Probably wandering around Amsterdam, checking out the sights and talking to himself. Maybe hitting the bottle. Trying to talk himself out of a psych ward. Ethan was a decent judge of character, but the year since his wife's death had left him less certain about everything he'd once taken for granted.

He paid a fortune for a cab to take him to the Upper West Side building where Juliet Longstreet was borrowing an apartment from a friend who was off to Hollywood for six months.

Deputy Longstreet wouldn't be happy to see him. But he didn't have money for a New York hotel, and he'd be happy to see her.

He didn't know why.

He talked his way past the doorman. It wasn't that hard, which made him think she needed a new doorman. When he got up to her floor, her door was shut and locked up tight, and it occurred to him she could be on vacation.

But surely not Deputy Longstreet. It'd been just four months since two of Janssen's goons had dragged her off the street into their car with every intention of killing her. She'd escaped, jumping into oncoming traffic and getting a hell of a road rash on her upper thigh. Ethan'd seen the rash when it was still raw and bloody, because she'd also turned up in a limestone cave in Night's Landing, where he'd been posing as the Dunnemores' property manager.

She'd still be trying to prove to herself and all the other marshals that she had handled herself well back in May. She had—

she'd done great. But she wasn't going to take his word for it.

Ethan plopped down on the floor in front of Julia's door. He hadn't been at his best when they'd met, either. He'd been playing a good ol' boy from west Texas working as a property manager while he tried to make his mark in Nashville as a songwriter. He *had* written a few songs, all bad.

Juliet had come to Night's Landing already beat-to-shit by Janssen's goons. Then she and Ethan had found them dead at President Poe's childhood home.

Ethan was convinced Juliet had saved his life by giving him a chance to jump into the Cumberland River and escape certain death.

Then he got to save her life when he found her tied up, gagged and left in a cave on a vertical bluff above the Cumberland. Not that she saw it that way.

He'd done what he could to help and took off a little later the same day.

He hadn't seen Deputy Longstreet since.

He leaned back against the door and wondered if she'd cuff him when she saw him. Arrest him for something. Breaking and

entering. Harassing a federal agent. Annoy-
ing her.

The elevator dinged and she got off, blue
eyes on him, blond hair sticking out every
which way. She looked like August in New
York had gotten to her. Her arms were
loaded with, as far as Ethan could judge, a
bag of perlite, a flyswatter, a jug of organic
skim milk and a bag of Hershey's chocolate
nuggets.

She dropped it all and went for her gun.

"Jesus Christ, Longstreet," Ethan said,
not moving, "you have great reflexes. Unbe-
lievable. Where were you when I needed
you in Afghanistan?"

She didn't draw her weapon, just finally
stared at him, her stuff all over the floor.
"Brooker. Goddamn it. What are you doing
here?"

"Waiting for you. You're not a moment
too soon. Nature calls."

"I should arrest you—"

"You should not arrest me. I'm not
wanted for any crimes." He nodded to her
milk jug. "Look, it didn't break. Is that because it's organic?"

"It's because it's a good bottle." She had
a red spot on the V of exposed skin above

her shirt. Sunburn or emotion. "You skipped out on the scene of a double homicide."

"Ancient history. I've talked to the FBI and the marshals. We're square."

She pointed a finger at him. "I'm going to see to it nobody wants to talk to you. Understood?"

"If I can use your bathroom, I'll tell the FBI and the marshals everything I told them all over again."

"When did you talk to them?"

"Two days after I skipped out on the caves and the snakes and the fried apricot pies in Night's Landing. Didn't they tell you?"

She sighed. "Sort of. I wasn't sure I believed them."

"Figured they were coddling you? You know, about that bathroom . . . I wasn't kidding."

He thought she might have smiled. "All right, all right. Help me pick up this stuff. And if you're carrying, you'd better have the right paperwork. New York gun laws are very strict."

He knew all about New York gun laws. He wasn't armed, but that wasn't something he planned to tell her, federal agent or no federal agent. He picked up her perlite and the milk; she grabbed the chocolate and the fly-swatter.

"You've got something like sixty-five locks on that door," he said. "I'm pleading with you."

"You're not the pleading type."

Although she was armed, he expected he could get her keys off her. He had at least four inches on her, not to mention combat experience. But Juliet Longstreet was tough and he didn't want to fight her.

She unlocked her door, and he followed her into her apartment. She had on jeans and a tank top under a dark pink shirt that draped over her gun.

"How's the road rash?" Ethan asked her.

"Healed."

"Leave scars?"

"A few."

It'd been nasty, he remembered. "You look better than the last time I saw you."

"That's because I'm not beaten and bloodied."

He glanced around her living room, plants and fish tanks on every available surface. The place was small and probably way overpriced, even for New York.

She gestured toward a door up a short hall. "That's the bathroom."

"Going to get out your cuffs while I'm in there?"

"I might."

She wasn't softening.

He ducked into the bathroom. His reflection in the mirror above the pedestal sink wasn't reassuring. If he were Longstreet, he'd cuff him and haul him to the FBI just on looks alone.

She was leaning against the wall in the short hall, arms crossed on her chest, when he finished. He liked the direct way she looked at him. Not intimidated. "Where'd you come from?" she asked.

"West Point, by way of west Texas."

"Since then."

"Classified."

She rolled her eyes. "Since Tennessee in May. Where were you, say, last night?"

He ignored her question and studied her, wondering why he'd come here and not some flophouse of a hotel. He saw that the paleness and sunken eyes, the pained expression that had been there in May were gone. Her cheeks were pink, her skin lightly tanned. "The marshals wanted to know what you and I did in that cave."

"For God's sake, I was tied up—"

He grinned. "Like I said."

She cleared her throat, dropping her arms to her sides. "They wanted to know why I let you go."

"You didn't. You had to prioritize. It was more important to help Sarah Dunnemore and Nate Winter get your bad guy. I wasn't a threat."

"I'm calling the FBI and Chief Rivera—"

"Can we eat first? I haven't eaten all day."

"Brooker—" She kicked the wall with her heel. "What do you want?"

"Dinner. A night." He left her to chew on that while he walked back to her small kitchen, calling back to her over his shoulder. "How much you pay for this place?"

"Not nearly what I should."

"No air-conditioning, no view—"

She followed him and stood next to a counter. "No garbage disposal, either. But there's an elevator and a doorman."

"Doorman's useless. He let me in." Ethan pulled open her refrigerator and frowned at its limited contents. One Amstel Light, eggs, a head of lettuce. "There's nothing in here."

"Another thing about New York, you can get whatever you want delivered."

He shut the fridge door. "That works." He smiled at her. "You look like you want to frisk me, Deputy, and not for all the right reasons."

"It's Juliet," she said tightly. "I'm not dealing with you in any official capacity. You're a guest in my home."

"Now you're getting the idea."

"Don't you have a home of your own, somewhere?"

"No."

"The family ranch in west Texas—"

"My brother runs it. I could pitch a tent there if I wanted to."

"I checked out your ranch, Brooker. You could build a mall there."

He walked past her, back into the living room, and stood in front of one of her four fish tanks, bending down so that he was at eye level with a goldfish. "I had a goldfish once. Bought it at a fair. The bowl wasn't big enough, I guess, and it jumped out. The dog got it."

Juliet ran a hand through her short blond

curls, a gesture Ethan found very sexy. But it'd been a long couple of days—a long year. She blew out a sigh. "It'd be easier if you gave me a reason to cuff you, read you your rights and get you the hell out of my apartment."

"Wouldn't it, though."

"You heard about Nick Janssen's arrest in the Netherlands?"

"I did."

"That wasn't you who provided the tip on where to find him?"

He didn't want to encourage her to think he planned to tell her a damn thing. The more questions he answered, the more she'd ask. The camel's nose under the tent. He moved to another fish tank, then fingered one of her spider plants. "Pretty much into fish and plants, aren't you?"

"One fish led to another, one plant led to another. You know how it is."

"They look like a lot of work."

"An American diplomat was murdered Saturday morning in Den Bosch, the Dutch town where Janssen was picked up. Thomas Kopac. He worked at our embassy in The Hague."

Ethan didn't respond, instead walking

over to her cluttered table, where he started flipping through a stack of take-out menus. "You weren't kidding about the options. Any place you can get a burger?"

"Lots."

"Would that suit you? A burger, fries, salad?"

"You're avoiding my questions because you don't want to lie to a federal agent."

"I'm hungry and tired, Juliet. That's it."

She gave up. "A burger and salad. No fries. And you get the futon." She paused a beat, her gaze not as direct now. "I'm still checking with people."

But not right away, he realized. Not tonight.

An act of trust.

Ethan picked up the phone and handed it to her to call in their order. Her trust had to be a one-way street. At least for now. And tomorrow he had business to attend to that didn't involve any marshals, even one willing to feed him and put him up for the night.

Maggie waited until nightfall to call her mother, using her cell phone as she sat cross-legged on her bed. A passing shower had left the air moist and a bit cooler, the wind sucking her curtains against the wet screen.

If the light was just right, her mother wouldn't pick up the phone. At night, Maggie thought, her odds of reaching Cora Spencer, painter, were better.

She answered on the second ring.

"Hey, there," Maggie said. "It's me."

"Maggie! I'm so glad you called. I just got in from a walk. It's hotter than blue blazes here. How are you?"

"Doing fine. You haven't heard?"

A half beat's pause. "Heard what?"

Her mother didn't watch the news. If the world were ending, if a hurricane were bearing down on her, she would rely on a friend or neighbor to let her know. "Nothing. Never mind. You're doing okay?"

"Great. I'm working hard, teaching at the community college. Isn't it the middle of the night where you are?"

"I'm in New York," Maggie said.

"Oh. On business, I assume? Well, I know you've got an important job to do."

And she didn't want to know any of the details. She never asked questions. It wasn't that she didn't care—she was tired of caring, worn out from it. She wanted a quiet life with routines. She liked painting pretty pictures of gardens and beaches and flamingos and visiting with friends, talking about nothing more serious than whether there was a riptide or it was safe to swim in the warm water outside her apartment.

If she was a little self-absorbed these days, she was allowed. Or so Maggie told herself. Her mother had been married to a man with wanderlust and secrets, and her only child was the same. She'd figured out a way to have a life of her own and to let them—now just Maggie—have theirs.

"I was wondering," Maggie said, "did Dad ever mention Ravenkill, New York?"

"Not that I recall, no."

"The Old Stone Hollow Inn. Does that sound familiar?"

"No." She didn't ask why Maggie wanted to know.

Maggie unfolded her legs and stretched out on the bed, leaning back against fluffy pillows with lace-trimmed cases. "Do you ever recall meeting a man named William Raleigh?"

"I'm sure I haven't met him, no."

"He's in his midsixties, maybe late sixties.

White hair. Red-faced, probably from drinking—"

"Maggie, I don't know him. I'm sorry I can't help you. If he's a friend of your father's, I've put that part of my life behind me."

"I understand. Thanks."

Maggie knew there was nothing more to talk about. Her mother wouldn't ask questions. She didn't know about Tom Kopac and Nick Janssen. She'd listen if Maggie wanted to tell her, but the most basic information would suit her. Her daughter was fine. She was in New York or The Hague or wherever.

Her problems were her own, for her to solve.

Even before her father had wandered off from his marriage, Maggie had known that her mother wouldn't be there for her. She didn't mean not to be. She just wasn't.

But Cora Spencer didn't expect Maggie to be there for her in return, either. At her father's funeral, Maggie remembered, she and her mother had been more like two old friends who'd cared for him rather than mother and daughter.

After they hung up, Maggie wondered

what her mother would have done if she'd asked to spend a few days with her after pulling a new friend out of a Dutch river minutes after he'd been murdered.

It would have been fine. They'd have gone for walks and talked about her latest paintings.

Libby winced at the creaking sound the door made when she opened it.

It's past midnight. No one can hear you.

She ducked into the tiny, dark room and shut the door behind her before fumbling for the light string. She felt something on her neck and suppressed a shudder.

Cobwebs. The cellar was full of spiders.

Bats had got down here before, dropping between the walls. She'd screamed and screamed while one had flapped over her head when she was ten, but no one had heard her. Finally, exhausted, she'd pulled her shirt up over her head, believing that would keep the bat from getting tangled in her hair, and had crawled outside.

She caught the string, pulled on it and welcomed the dull light.

Her workroom.

It was barely eight square feet, its outer

wall part of the original stone foundation, but it contained everything she needed. Worktables. Her laptop. Boxes of ammunition. Her first pistol, a Smith & Wesson her father had given her for her fourteenth birthday. He'd instructed her in gun safety. At least in that respect, she thought, what she'd become wasn't his fault.

She had supplies. Her experiments. She was increasingly confident with what everyone knew now as IEDs. Improvised explosive devices. In other words, homemade bombs.

But she preferred her .22 Beretta, perfect for her tried-and-true tactic of surprising her prey and putting a bullet in the back of his skull before he knew she was someone to fear. It was simple, direct and effective.

Bombs were trickier. And messier.

She felt reassured checking her workroom, touching things, and her thoughts, in a frenzy all day, settled down.

Whatever their reasons for being in Ravenkill, Maggie Spencer and Rob Dunnemore knew nothing about her activities. If they did, Libby thought as she brushed more cobwebs off her arm, she'd be under arrest or at least have been taken in for questioning by now.

If William Raleigh had sent Philip Spencer's daughter here, why? What did Raleigh know? Where was he? What was he up to?

Libby opened the file she had on him on her laptop and recoiled at his face, those awful, knowing eyes. Her stomach muscles clamped down on her.

"You won't be the ruin of me."

Not another man, she thought. Not another drunk.

She'd kill him first, even if there was no money in it.

She closed the file and brought up the one on Philip Spencer. She touched his beautiful mouth and remembered the feel of his lips on hers, before he'd known what she was—before, she thought, she'd really even been what she was. He'd thought of her as an antiques dealer from upstate New York. He'd thought of her as a much younger woman he'd meant to resist.

He *had* resisted her. They'd had dinner a few times in Prague, but never slept together.

Their relationship felt like unfinished business, a bitter regret that Libby wished now she could go back and correct.

He was dead because of William Raleigh.

As she closed the file, she noticed how like her father Maggie Spencer looked.

Feeling better, Libby switched off the light and felt her way along the wall, creaking open the door, then tiptoed through the dark wine cellar and back upstairs to her room.

Thirteen

Maggie had apple-cinnamon muffins and fresh blueberries with water-buffalo yogurt on the back porch and found out from Star Franconia that there was only one other guest at the inn, who'd be leaving later in the day.

"You have the place to yourself," she said, heading down to the flower gardens with a pair of clippers in hand. "We have a full house starting on Thursday—it's a two-night minimum on weekends, which helps."

"But the inn's holding its own?" Maggie asked.

"Oh, I think so. We have to watch cash

flow, of course, but who doesn't? And we put a lot into renovations. Too much, according to Andrew, but it was better just to go ahead and do everything at once. You can't do renovations in stages when you're trying to run an inn. No one wants to wake up to the sound of power saws and hammers."

"I suppose not."

"What do you think you'll do today?"

Two more nights, Maggie thought. George Bremmerton would expect her to make progress or get back to The Hague, and she had the same expectation. But what was progress? Deciding Raleigh had pulled Ravenkill and the Old Stone Hollow Inn out of thin air?

"I thought I'd take a walk," she said.

"Have you been down to the creek? It's my favorite place to stroll. They say the sound of water somehow produces the same chemical changes in our brains as Prozac. It's a natural antidepressant." She caught herself, her very pale skin blushing easily. "Not that you're depressed, I mean."

"It's okay. I could use some positive energy."

Maggie returned to her room and

changed into shorts and trail shoes, noting how quiet the sprawling old house was. She debated calling Rob but decided it was better she didn't. There was no point in him getting any wrong ideas about her or their relationship. A kiss was one thing. Of the moment. Over and done with. But she was a DS agent posted overseas, and he was a U.S. Marshal posted in New York. End of story, as far as she was concerned.

Except, on another level, he felt like just the kind of man she'd always wanted— charming and sexy and not to be underestimated.

And carrying the baggage of being seriously wounded on the job.

A "mustn't touch," she thought, then warned herself that she was jumping the gun, to say the least. She and Rob had been through a trauma together. A tragedy. Tom's death must have stirred up everything Rob had gone through in the spring. A quick kiss when the opportunity had presented itself had been inevitable.

Maggie didn't want to make more of it than was there.

She scooted back downstairs out the front door, the air warm and a bit less humid than yesterday. But that wouldn't last. Thunderstorms were forecast again for later in the day and overnight.

Good, she thought. She'd sit through a storm or two, then head back to the Nether- lands and admit to Bremmerton that she'd grasped at a mentally ill man's fantasies be- cause he'd invoked her father's memory.

She'd have to admit her mistake to the marshals, too.

That didn't excite her.

She followed the stone path around to the back of the house past the fountains and the gardens, until it became a wide lane that led through an apple orchard, narrow- ing when it hit the woods. Soft ferns brushed against her bare legs. She breathed in the earthy smells and heard the rush of water below her, down a steep hill, through the birches, beeches and pines.

When she reached the creek, Maggie slowed her pace, the frenzy of the past week falling away. The coppery water was shallow, flowing over a gravel bottom strewn with rocks and boulders. The raging rapids that came with the early spring runoff had quieted, only a few treacherous stretches of white water now left in late summer.

She stood on a boulder jutting out over the river and listened to the gurgle of water tumbling over rocks, the rustle of leaves in the morning breeze. New York and its millions of people were just an hour or so to the south, but they might have been on another continent, another planet.

But then she stiffened, spotting something in the rocks and shade toward the middle of the river.

A flash of light.

Sun on metal.

Maggie jumped down from her boulder to the riverbank for a better view.

A leg. A running shoe.

Not again.

A body—a man—was caught on the rocks.

She ran into water up to her ankles. It was surprisingly cold, the current pushing at her, but she quickly climbed onto a large, flat rock, slippery from just the film of water that ran over it.

The man was on his back, his face out of the water. His torso had caught on a series of small, jagged rocks, but his lower half was bobbing in deeper water.

There was no obvious sign of injury.

Maggie splashed into the water up to her knees and nearly lost her balance in the current. She made her way to the jagged rocks, squatting down next to the man. He was unconscious, she thought, but not dead. Surely not dead.

She checked his airway.

He was breathing.

He had spots of blood on his neck and arms, and a tear in the shoulder of his black T-shirt.

Had he fallen? Slipped?

His skin was cool to the touch. She needed to get him out of the water, if possible, then find help.

He gave a small cough.

"It's all right," Maggie said, trying to sound reassuring. "I'm going to get help—"

"What're you doing here?"

His question was abrupt, antagonistic. His dark eyes focused on her, but she had no idea if he recognized her.

"Are you all right?" she asked.

She might not have spoken. He latched on to her wrist with one hand and, using it to anchor himself, stood up. Water streamed off his clothes and down his bare arms.

Maggie, rising next to him, noticed the raw, nasty lump on the back of his head and remembered that head injuries could make people belligerent, throw them off for a few minutes or even much longer.

"I must have slipped." His voice was ragged, and he didn't sound or look entirely coherent. He seemed to struggle to focus on her. "What are you doing here?"

"I'm staying at the inn. I was taking a walk."

The dark hair, the dark eyes. The black graphic tattoo.

The Texas drawl.

Ethan Brooker.

In that split second, Maggie recognized him and knew she was too late.

He stepped onto her toes and, with both hands, butted her in the chest. Even before she realized he'd moved, she was sprawling backward into the deep pool of water just past the jagged rocks.

Plunging to the bottom, she gulped in river water. Her arms raked across the gravel bottom. She got control of her sprawling, butt-first dive and burst up and out of the water, coughing and choking for air.

The water was up to her waist, the current slamming her against another rock. She grabbed it, then hoisted herself onto it.

"Brooker! You're hurt! You need a doctor!"

She heard nothing but the crows, the water and the wind.

Ethan Brooker was gone.

Hell.

She charged through the river to the bank, then ran, soaking wet, up the path.

He'd made it to the edge of the apple orchard before collapsing against an oak, still on his feet but breathing unevenly. And swearing.

She heard a crunching sound behind her and spun around.

William Raleigh stood under a pine tree. He had on a red madras shirt, another pair of threadbare khaki pants and his sport sandals, but he didn't smell as much of cigarettes in the open air.

Maggie stiffened. "What in hell—"

"What am I doing here?" He seemed at ease with having a half-conscious former

Special Forces officer slumped against a tree and a federal agent dripping wet. "Let me just say, Agent Spencer, that you are as thorough as I'd hoped you'd be. I expected you to make a few calls and check the Internet. Instead, you get on a plane first thing Sunday morning, and now here we are in Ravenkill."

"Brooker—"

"His injuries aren't my doing. I'm not sure they're anyone's doing. He probably slipped."

"That doesn't matter right now. He needs to get to a doctor. If he's not hurt, he's faking it well."

"I'm not faking a goddamn thing," Brooker said, using the tree trunk for support as he got to his feet. He looked at Raleigh. "My backpack's under another tree. Let's go."

Maggie shook her head. "Wait just a minute—"

Raleigh touched her hand. "Ethan's too miserable to talk right now. I'll take care of him and be in touch." He smiled, a twinkle in his pale eyes. "Go get dried off."

The breeze on her wet clothes and skin gave her a chill.

She looked at the two men, and she suspected they both knew fourteen ways to disarm her and tie her to a tree if she didn't cooperate, gun or no gun, training or no training. They'd simply done more dirty work than she had.

But if she'd meant to take either of them in, she'd have handled everything differently.

She nodded, knowing she was taking a risk. Breaking dishes, as Raleigh would have said. "Be in touch," she warned, then let the two men go.

"I just knocked your DS agent in the creek."

Rob braked halfway up the driveway to the Old Stone Hollow Inn. The voice on the other end of his cell phone was male with a Texas accent. "Who is this?"

"Redhead. Real pretty eyes. Armed."

Rob tensed. "Brooker?"

"It wasn't her fault. I thought she was on the attack. I hit my head on a rock or something—I don't remember."

"Where are you now?"

No answer.

Rob checked his cell phone readout. Private number. But Ethan Brooker had shown up at Longstreet's apartment last night. She'd just finished explaining the situation to Rivera before Rob headed north.

"Hell." It was Brooker again, sounding as if he were in pain. "My head's a mess. She hauled ass after me. Thought she might shoot me. She's on her way back to the inn. I don't think she's hurt, but you might want to go find her."

The connection ended. Rob jumped out of his car and ran across the driveway into the orchard, the tall grass almost up to his knees. There were Indian paintbrushes and black-eyed Susans in bloom, and the branches of the old trees were drooping with ripening apples. The ground was uneven, spotted with knobby apples that had already fallen, and he was suddenly aware of just how strange his life had gotten since he'd heard Maggie Spencer had received the tip that led to Nick Janssen's arrest.

What the hell was Ethan Brooker doing in Ravenkill?

But when Rob got to the woods, he found Maggie alone.

She was soaked, with bits of rotted leaves and mud splatters on her legs and puffy, pink scratches on her arms. And when she saw him, she swore under her breath.

"Where's Brooker?" Rob asked.

"On his way to the E.R., if he's smart. He's got a good goose egg on the back of his head." She brushed back a soaked lock of hair, a darker red when it was wet. "I found him unconscious in the creek."

"How did he get there?"

"Says he might have slipped." She didn't sound convinced. "When he came to, he was out of his head. He didn't know if I'd attacked him."

Rob observed her a moment, deciding she wasn't telling him everything. "So he dumped you in the river?"

"Correct. It's my own damn fault."

"Maggie—"

"He's a good guy, isn't he?"

"Yes."

"Then I'm glad I didn't shoot him." She coughed, spitting river scum into the grass. "God. What's in the Ravenkill? Anything toxic? I think I drank a gallon of it. It tastes like trout. Or maybe trout tastes like the Ravenkill."

Rob tried to smile. "I think Ravenkill trout was on yesterday's menu. Maggie—"

"Did Brooker call you?"

"Yes."

"He had your number?"

"I'm guessing he used Juliet Longstreet's cell phone and it's on her caller list."

"How—"

"He was at her place last night."

Maggie coughed again, not spitting this time. "They're an item?"

"She says not. She came home yesterday afternoon and found him sitting on her doorstep. She let him spend the night. He took off in the morning."

"With her cell phone?"

Rob shrugged. "He left a note."

"And Longstreet just let him—" But Maggie stopped herself, sighing. "But I did the same thing. I let him go."

"He must be persuasive."

"He didn't persuade me of anything." She wiped a drop of water off her nose. "I need to get on dry clothes."

Rob took a sharp breath. "You need to talk to me."

She nodded. "That, too."

"You're leaving something out. Brooker—"

"My guy from the cathedral was here," she said casually, flicking a glop of mud off her knee. "Raleigh."

Rob tensed, but she started toward the inn, then stopped suddenly and kicked off her wet running shoes.

"They're squishy," she said.

"Maggie—"

"George Bremmerton went to the hospital after Charlene Brooker was killed last fall and helped identify her. He thinks he should have done more to get answers to her murder. Pushed harder." She scooped up her shoes. "Ethan Brooker shouldn't have had to go off half-cocked to find his wife's murderer himself."

"Bremmerton didn't let you come here out of a sense of guilt."

"No, he didn't." She squinted back at Rob, the ends of her hair curling as water dripped onto her shoulder; her soaked cotton shirt clung to her. "Charlene Brooker was on to Nick Janssen before any of the rest of us. I can cut her husband some slack if I want to."

"About Raleigh. He and Brooker are hooked up?"

"Somehow. I don't have the details. Raleigh didn't hit Brooker on the head. Brooker says he doesn't remember what happened."

"Do you believe him?"

She squeezed water out of the end of one curl. "Right now, I don't know that I believe anyone. I'm damn lucky I didn't hit my head on a rock."

"Brooker would have grabbed you before you did. Even half out of his head."

"He's that good, is he?"

"Yes."

They came to the driveway, but Maggie stayed in the grass. "I'll meet you on the back porch. I'm in enough trouble with you marshals without dripping all over one of your cars."

Not that she was worried, Rob noticed. He watched her walk along the edge of the driveway, swinging her running shoes by their laces.

She was wobbly.

But, he thought, probably she wouldn't want him pointing that out right now.

Fourteen

Libby arranged fresh-cut asters in pottery vases at a long wooden counter in the inn's kitchen and tried to keep her hands from shaking with that familiar mix of fear, exertion and exhilaration.

If he wasn't such a damn bull of a man, Ethan Brooker would be dead.

Although he was on Janssen's target list, it was just as well the army officer was still alive. She'd be able to collect her hundred thousand dollars for his death, but there'd be a body to explain. That he'd survived his fall into the creek meant that she'd still have to deal with bereaved, out-of-control Major

Brooker—and the DS agent and her mar-shal friend would want to know what Brooker was doing in Ravenkill.

Libby stabbed a particularly tall red aster into the middle of a vase, pushing back her irritation with Star, who was sniffling and muttering to herself at the sink. "Star, please. What's wrong?"

"Maggie Spencer." Star gulped in a breath, her skinny shoulders hunched against her distress. "Did you see her? She came in just a little while ago. Something happened—"

"It looked to me as if she slipped and fell in the river."

"Why was she armed?"

"Because she's a federal law enforce-ment agent."

"But diplomatic security—"

"I know, I know." Yanking out the too-tall aster, Libby snipped another inch off its stem and tried to smile through her own tension. "It'd be easier if she were a florist. Which I clearly am not. Do these flowers look okay to you?"

Star sniffled again—it was maddening to Libby—and nodded. "They're lovely. It's hard to go wrong with asters. Aren't they so cheerful?"

Cheerful. Libby hadn't thought of them that way. She'd picked them upon her return from the creek, as a reason for her to have been outside, out of view. It wasn't as if she'd thought through any kind of alibi or even had anticipated needing one. As with Tom Kopac on Saturday, she'd had to think on her feet and take action.

Ethan Brooker was a problem. He'd been since his wife's death last fall.

A pity, Libby thought, that Nick Janssen hadn't hired her for that job. *And* the one in May. She'd have done far better than the men Janssen had sent. The fools had ended up dead themselves.

How had Brooker ended up in Ravenkill? Why?

He could be trailing Maggie Spencer, or he could have come here for the same reasons she had.

Whatever those reasons were.

This time when Libby jabbed the red aster into the vase, its stem bent. She tossed it aside, feeling her tension clawing at her. Star's whining didn't help.

Libby had prepared herself as best she

could for the inevitable questions she'd be asked if Brooker turned up dead. But how would she explain herself if the police checked into her whereabouts for the past week and discovered she'd been in the Netherlands? In particular, in 's-Hertogen-bosch?

Again, she thought, just as well Brooker wasn't lying dead in Ravenkill Creek.

Star sniffled again, loudly, and heaved a dramatic sigh. *"Oh, God."*

"Star, it's okay. Honestly. Nothing's happened on inn property."

Libby tried not to indulge in unnecessary emotion. She was confident, at least, that Brooker hadn't seen her. She'd spotted Maggie Spencer in the apple orchard and had followed her, then taken a different, faster route down to the river. She'd planned to get to a spot that intersected with the path the DS agent was on and wait for her, try to gauge what she was up to.

Instead, Libby had come upon Ethan Brooker, recognizing him instantly from the photos of him she had stored on her laptop.

The rush of water, even in late summer when the river was at its shallowest, must have prevented him from hearing her on the path above him. If he'd caught her, she'd have claimed she was picking wildflowers or off to dip her feet in the Ravenkill on a warm August morning. He'd have no idea who she was.

She didn't know whether she'd panicked or had simply attempted to seize the moment. She'd wanted Brooker dead. She knew that much.

She didn't have her Beretta and silencer with her, but she wouldn't have used it—if Ethan Brooker was going to die in Ravenkill, it had to look like an accident. She had to take her chances and at least disable him, impede him from doing whatever he was in Ravenkill to do.

She'd dismissed jumping him. He'd pick her off him like a bug.

Given her limited options, she'd tossed a pebble into the river in front of him, distracting him for a split second, and pelted him on the back of the head with a baseball-size rock.

He'd had the grace to fall, hitting another rock and landing in the shallow river. As beat up as he was, he'd managed to stagger to his feet, stumble around for a few seconds, then fall on his back in the water, halfway to the other bank.

Libby quickly recovered the rock she'd used to hit him, but before she could finish off Brooker, Maggie Spencer arrived.

Libby managed to slip away without being seen. She'd stayed within the woods and avoided open ground, then walked boldly through the cornfield back up to the asters.

Brooker must have also spotted the DS agent on her walk and planned to intercept her, find out what she was doing in Ravenkill, share notes. Something.

Should have left well enough alone, Libby thought.

"I'll put these out on the tables," she said, collecting up her half-dozen vases of brightly colored asters.

"Maggie Spencer's upstairs changing," Star said, her voice slightly stronger. "The marshal who was with her yesterday is out on the porch waiting for her."

"Does that make you nervous?"

"It all makes me nervous. Where's Andrew? Have you seen him?"

Libby shook her head. "Not this morning."

"I hope he—" Star pulled her upper and lower lips between her teeth, fighting back tears. Finally, she let out a breath and waved a hand. "Never mind."

God. Libby almost dropped the vases. Star thought that *Andrew* had done something?

Warning herself not to read too much into Star's dramatics, Libby exited to the porch, where, indeed, Deputy Dunnemore was sitting at an empty table. He really was even more good-looking than he was in all the pictures of him in the paper and on TV last spring.

Libby set five of the small vases on one table, then started distributing them one by one to other tables.

"You picked those flowers just now?" Dunnemore asked.

"Mmm. Pretty, aren't they?" She set another vase in the middle of a table, pretending to admire the splashes of pink, orange and red against the pale green and white decor. "I understand Agent Spencer had a mishap in the river. Do you know what happened?"

"More or less."

He left it at that. Did he know about

Brooker? Had Spencer told him? Of course—why wouldn't she? But why hadn't she called the police, or at least an ambulance? The only explanation Libby could think of was that Brooker wasn't seriously injured and had told her not to.

Where the hell was the army major now?

"The riverbank can be deceptive," Libby said. "I grew up here and I've made a few wrong steps myself."

Maggie Spencer came downstairs and breezed out onto the porch. She smelled faintly of the lilac soap Star had in all the rooms. Her hair was still damp from her shower, and she'd changed into long pants and a denim jacket.

Libby placed the final vase.

Too bad Spencer hadn't hit *her* head when Brooker pounced on her. Maybe he blamed her for how he'd ended up in the river?

My life's not that simple, Libby thought.

Dunnemore turned to her, his Southern charm, she thought, less in evidence than his marshal demeanor. "Nice talking with you, Ms. Smith."

"Same here, Deputy."

The two federal agents left, and Libby returned to the kitchen, realizing she wasn't shaking or nervous.

If anything, she was exhilarated.

With William Raleigh humming to himself two steps behind him, Ethan staggered out of the woods onto a gravel turnaround that marked the end of the road that led from the village to the inn. The creek, shallower and wider than farther downstream where Maggie Spencer had found him, sounded almost like the wind.

His entire body ached. His head felt like it might blow into a million pieces.

Fine with him, he decided. Maybe it'd end his misery.

"You can't remember anything?" Raleigh asked for at least the third time. "Are you sure?"

"No, I can't. Yes, I'm sure. I can't remember anything after I got to the river." He turned to the older man, pushing back a wave of pain and nausea, trying not to let Raleigh see just how injured he was. "Relax, okay? You look worse on a good day than I do on a bad one."

Raleigh didn't smile. "Do you need a doctor?"

"I just need some time for my head to clear."

He'd made off with Juliet's cell phone that morning before she woke up. It'd seemed like a good idea at the time. He'd headed to Grand Central Station and boarded a train north to Ravenkill. When he got off in the village, he followed the directions he'd memorized from the inn's Web site and walked the mile to the Old Stone Hollow Inn.

Something had distracted him before he got to the inn, but he couldn't remember what. Had he spotted Agent Spencer taking a jaunt through the woods? It was all a blur.

He'd dumped his backpack out of sight under a tree. For some reason, he could remember that. Next thing he knew, he was looking into Maggie Spencer's eyes and thinking she was trying to kill him.

He'd been out of his head, belligerent, paranoid. His reaction to her had been instinctive and defensive, but he'd known he hadn't wanted to hurt her. Some reptilian part of his brain must have recognized she wasn't a threat, because he remembered checking the water behind her to make sure it was deep enough to take her fall, that she wouldn't hit her head on rocks.

But he'd taken a risk, attacking a federal agent.

He hadn't gotten far before she'd caught up with him. That annoyed him. But if his fall wasn't an accident, he figured Spencer's arrival may have spooked his attacker and saved his life.

That didn't sit well with him, either.

"You have a car?" he asked.

Raleigh shrugged. "Not really."

"What do you mean, 'not really'? That was a yes or no question."

"It means no."

"So we have to walk? Are you up to it? Do you want me to use your cell phone to call a taxi?"

Ethan's head was spinning. "Then what? Even if I could get a taxi to take me, they'd kick me off the train. I stink now, and I'll stink worse when my clothes dry. Hell. I've got dead mosquitoes in my hair. Blood on my shirt." He didn't think he sounded all that coherent but kept going. "And you— you're not much better. You look like you should be sleeping under a bridge."

"Then it's just as well I arranged a ride for you."

"What?" Ethan felt fogged in, as if his vision were being pinched. "What ride?"

"Deputy Longstreet. She was on her way up here, anyway." A flicker of a smile. "On your case, I'd say."

"Fuck. I'm going to barf."

"Sit down. Try to relax." Raleigh half shoved him to the pavement and sighed. "You're a wreck. She can take you to the ER."

"I'll be fine." It was his mantra, Ethan decided. *I'll be fine.* He closed his eyes, hoping the nausea passed. "It wasn't you who dumped me in the river?"

"We're on the same side, Major."

"Right." Ethan didn't know if he sounded sarcastic and dubious or just half-dead. His stomach rolled over again, but he shut his eyes and went still, managing to keep the contents where they belonged. "Raleigh—"

But when he opened his eyes, the old man had disappeared, and a battered pickup with Vermont plates rattled to a stop in the turnaround.

Juliet Longstreet climbed out, armed and not real happy. "Oh, man. Look at you,

Brooker. Your friend, whoever he was, should have called an ambulance."

"I'll be fine."

The mantra again. He got on all fours, then onto his knees, then got one foot flat on the gravel ground. The river water and the New York bagel he'd picked up in Grand Central Station bubbled in his stomach, and his head throbbed. He heaved himself up, staggering toward the blond marshal with the blue eyes and the scowl.

She slipped a shoulder against him and took his weight, easing an arm around his middle. "What are you doing?" she asked, the softness of her voice catching him by surprise. "When are you going to give it up and get your life back?"

"Char . . ." He could see his wife's face, hear her voice, even as he leaned into Juliet and let her take more of his weight. She wasn't a small woman. He wouldn't crush her.

"I know. Come on. Let me help you."

"I don't need help."

"No, you hate needing help. There's a difference."

She tugged open the passenger door of her truck and maneuvered him up onto the seat. "Don't throw up in my truck. Understood?"

As weak as he was, he grinned at her. "How come I keep seeing you after I've ended up in a river?"

"Karma. Watch your foot, I'm shutting the door."

She locked him in, as if he might fall out or jump out on the interstate, and came around to the driver's seat. Her movements were stiff, and he could see she was, on the one hand, irritated with her situation and on the other hand, resigned to doing something she knew she shouldn't do.

She stuck the key in the ignition. "I want my phone back."

"Why'd you let me borrow it?"

"You didn't borrow it. You stole it. That's what I told Mike Rivera."

Ethan felt his eyes starting to close against his will. "You're full of shit, Longstreet. You were awake."

She made a face. "Look at you. Damn, Brooker. Are you done bleeding? I shouldn't get you to the E.R. and get that head looked at? Head injuries can be tricky."

"I just need clean clothes and a cigarette."

"There's no smoking in my truck."

"I only smoke when I'm in pain."

She shifted the truck into Reverse, checking her rearview mirror. "Why Raven-kill? Did you know Maggie Spencer was here? You must have."

Even as out of sorts as he was, he knew not to get into his reasons for being in Ravenkill with a U.S. Marshal. "My head hurts."

"How did it happen? The bump on the head."

"I told you. I fell into the river."

She braked hard, putting the truck into first gear as she glanced over at him. "Like Thomas Kopac?"

"Well, he had a .22 round in the back of his skull. I just hit a rock—"

"Or got banged on the head with one. Which is it?"

"I think I fell."

"You think? You don't know. Goddamn it, Brooker—"

"I've slept with your plants and fish." The contents of his stomach were oozing up his throat, and the pounding in his head hadn't even begun to let up. "We should be Ethan and Juliet to each other by now."

She had a white-knuckled grip on the steering wheel. "You rattled my brain showing up last night."

He smiled. "First piece of good news I've had today."

"You don't remember anything about what happened? Don't tell me you slipped. You *don't* slip. I saw you jump forty feet into the Cumberland River that day in Tennessee. You had a guy with a gun at your head, two dead guys at your feet—"

"At the point I jumped, the gun was at *your* head."

"God." She raked a hand through her short curls. "I don't trust you, Brooker."

"Ethan. And, yeah, you do."

She softened again, and he could see the tension going out of her shoulders, her blue eyes shining with a depth of compassion that he suspected she preferred to keep at bay. He saw it because he was that way himself. It was easier. Less chance of getting your heart ripped out of your chest.

She gulped in a breath and averted her gaze, as if looking at him would just make her fall apart. "Tell me what you want me to do."

He couldn't involve her in his mess. Raleigh, Kopac, Janssen. Ravenkill. Whatever they all amounted to, he wasn't sucking Juliet into it. He'd crossed lines, but he could—he didn't answer to anyone. She did.

"Relax, Juliet," he said. "I've hurt my head worse than this fixing my car. I'll be fine. I just need some time."

"You *are* hurt, then?"

"I don't remember what happened. Until I do—"

"You're not trusting anyone. You're not talking to anyone."

He let his silence be his response.

"Ethan . . ." She sighed. *"Damn."*

His stomach settled down. He wasn't going to vomit, but he couldn't keep his eyes open, felt his body sinking and his fatigue overtake him.

"You don't scare me," she said.

He tried to focus on her through his pain and exhaustion. "I don't want to scare you."

It was all he could manage, but he saw her look of shock and confusion before he closed his eyes again, unable to stop himself from drifting off.

"Sleep well, Major Brooker," she whispered. "You've come too far to get killed on us now."

He didn't have the strength even to open his eyes.

Char . . .

His wife was gone, her memory like a stab of heat and guilt.

He thought he heard Juliet sigh. Or maybe it was his dead wife's ghost, leaving him alone to sleep and dream.

Nate Winter would rather be on Cold Ridge where he grew up in the White Mountains, immersed in a thick fog and fierce wind, than more or less alone in a room with the President of the United States.

John Wesley Poe, however, never showed any sign he noticed Nate's discomfort or shared it. His focus was on his reasons for calling Nate to the White House.

They were in a sitting area, Poe on a wing chair, Nate on a love seat.

Nate was surprised at how quiet it was.

Poe shook his head. "Rob's got himself mixed up with Philip Spencer's daughter and William Raleigh. I can't believe it. It's like I saw this coming, knew it would get here, but couldn't admit it."

Nate shifted positions, trying to get comfortable on the love seat. "Mr. President?"

"They were a pair. Raleigh and Spencer. Before my time."

"Intelligence operatives?" Nate asked, guessing.

But Poe didn't give a direct answer. "Friends. Good friends. Spencer was killed eighteen months ago in Prague." He sighed. "It was before my time in office, not that it matters."

Poe's emotional involvement—his dread— was palpable, beyond what Nate could understand. "Philip Spencer was killed when he walked into the middle of a bank robbery—"

"That's the story."

"There was no bank robbery?"

"Oh, there was a bank robbery." Poe sank back into his chair, looking tired, a rarity for a man with his renowned stamina. "I don't know how much it had to do with what happened to Spencer. Raleigh wants his killer. Some people think he's responsible for Spencer's death—that he screwed up, plain and simple. He'd retired, supposedly. Went back to drinking. Again, supposedly. There are rumors he talked out of turn, bragged to the wrong person."

"So Raleigh's not only looking for a killer," Nate said. "He wants vindication."

"From what I understand, the man's a riddle. I'm not sure anyone really knows what he's up to. He could simply want to look after a friend's daughter, no matter how competent and skilled she is."

"Do you know where he is now?"

Poe shook his head. "I have no idea."

"Mr. President," Nate said, leaning forward, folding his hands over his knees as if somehow it would help him understand this man who meant so much to the Dunnemores, who was so much a part of their lives. "What's worrying you?"

He averted his eyes. "I've been waiting for this moment. It's like watching a drought in the west, knowing the fire season's coming and that there's nothing you can do. The conditions are there. They're perfect. All it takes is a dropped match, a lightning strike, a spark of a dragging muffler."

Poe sometimes had a metaphorical way of talking that he seemed to think drove home his point. He could spin a story— Sarah said it was a Night's Landing tradition, a skill born and developed on their quiet stretch of the Cumberland River. But Nate was from the Granite State, raised by a Vietnam vet uncle. He tended to be more direct. "Mr. President?"

"Rob's not going to stay in the Marshals Service."

There was nothing Nate could add. He knew what Poe said was true. He'd known it the minute he'd met Rob earlier in the year, when Rob had been assigned to the southeastern New York district. It wasn't that he didn't belong in the USMS. He just wasn't staying.

"He's suited to intelligence work. William Raleigh will reel him in, just as he reeled in Philip Spencer. And it scares me." Poe sighed heavily, no longer dancing around the truth about Raleigh and Spencer. "It scares the hell out of me."

"Because Rob's a Dunnemore," Nate said.

"Leola and Violet wanted me to stay in Night's Landing," Poe went on, referring to the two unmarried sisters who'd raised him. "They worried about me all the time, from the day I left home."

Orphaned at seven, Nate had faced different kinds of fears. "I think it comes with the turf."

"I know Rob can take care of himself. It's just—" He broke off. "Damn. He thinks his father and I don't believe in him, but that's not it. It's a visceral thing, Nate. This fear. I've never had a son of my own."

"Is anyone in touch with Raleigh? You could get him to back off—"

"No, I couldn't. Whether I could get in touch with him or not, I could never interfere that way."

"You wouldn't, you mean."

"That's right. I wouldn't."

"I respect that, Mr.—"

"Wes," he said, managing a ragged smile. "Just once can you call me Wes?"

"Maybe when you're out of office, Mr. President."

Poe rose, and Nate followed his lead, the Washington humidity noticeable even in the air-conditioned White House. "What's Sarah up to today?" the president asked.

Nate relaxed at mention of his future wife. "Digging in her dump."

"She'll know—"

"She already does. She denies there's a twin connection between her and Rob, but it's there. She knows he's in trouble. This Raleigh character—he's not drinking now?"

"There are rumors he had a mental break-down. But I'm told William Raleigh is one of the most clear-eyed people we have."

"He's back on the payroll?"

Poe didn't answer.

"Then you don't believe he got Philip Spencer killed," Nate said.

"No. I don't."

Poe sounded more presidential just then, less like a tortured friend.

When Nate got back to Arlington, he found Sarah on the back porch in a T-shirt and overalls, her dump-digging clothes. His sister Antonia, an E.R. doctor married to the junior senator from Massachusetts, was there with their new baby, Jill, a bald bundle of drool, gums and bright eyes.

Nate tried to get his head around how much their lives had changed in the past year. Antonia's, their sister Carine's, his own. They'd faced fear and stress and their own deepest desires, their toughest chal-lenges, and come out on the other side—strong, united, ready to tackle a new future.

The Night's Landing Dunnemores weren't anything like the Cold Ridge Winters, except for that one thing—they didn't seem to do anything the easy way.

Sarah had her honey-colored hair pulled back, and she frowned at him. "Rob," she said. "Something's up."

Nate turned to his sister. "Don't you medical types tell me there's no such thing as twin radar."

Antonia laughed, her baby laid across her lap, chubby bare legs kicking. "I stopped trying to tell you anything long before I became a 'medical type.' " She scooped up Jill, who smiled, looking more Callahan than Winter. "Say bye-bye to Uncle Nate. We'll see him another day. Right now, he's got to talk to Aunt Sarah."

Jill was barely two months old and didn't understand a word her mother told her, but she smiled and cooed all the way down the porch steps.

Sarah blew the baby kisses. "I could get into babies," she said without looking at Nate.

Six months ago—before Sarah—he would have choked at such talk. Now he just felt a little tight in the throat. But it wasn't a remark, he decided, that needed a comment from him. "I just came from the White House."

The baby out of sight, his fiancée shifted back to him. "You saw Wes?"

He nodded.

"You talked about Rob," she said confidently.

"It's a complicated situation."

"Meaning you're not going to give me the details." She smiled at him, giving him a knowing look. "You don't think I'd interfere in marshal business, do you?"

"You? Never."

"I haven't seen Rob since Janssen was arrested," Sarah said quietly, serious now. "Since the murder in Holland—"

"You know I'd never stop you from seeing your brother."

But she was suddenly tense, her smile gone. "I won't ask what Wes said."

Which just killed her, Nate knew.

She took a breath, let it out. "But Rob . . . If he's in over his head—"

"Rob can handle himself," he reminded her gently.

She squeezed her eyes shut a moment and nodded. "I know, I know. But if he's in the dark—if Wes knows something—"

"He won't be in the dark after I talk to him."

She relaxed visibly. "That's what I wanted to hear." She started for the porch door. "I finished up early and made fried apricot pies while Antonia and Jill and I visited."

Fried apricot pies were a Dunnemore family favorite, and a sure sign that Sarah was feeling the stress of whatever was going on with her brother.

"You cooked in this heat?"

That made her laugh. "It's not that hot."

When she pulled open the screen door, Nate noticed the small diamond on her finger, and it was as if he was seeing it for the first time. He'd given it to her on Cold Ridge.

In a few weeks, he and Sarah Dunnemore would be married.

Rob couldn't still be sneaking around with spies and DS agents then. He had to be at his sister's wedding.

Nate knew he had to do what he could to make that happen.

The rest was up to Rob.

Fifteen

Maggie drank unsweetened iced tea on a
bench in the village of Ravenkill, the afternoon heat and humidity having built up to
an uncomfortable level. She'd left Rob at
the inn. The walk had helped her work out
the kinks from her encounter with Brooker
and settle her mind.

The kinks were easier to deal with than
the mind.

Keeping his word, Raleigh had called her
at the inn and asked her to come to the village.

Alone.

She'd showered and changed by then,

getting her physical reaction to Rob more or less under control. They'd had lunch on the porch, and she'd told him exactly what had happened with Brooker and then with Raleigh.

But when Raleigh called, she hadn't told Rob she was off to the village to meet with the former economist, or whatever he was.

She'd said she needed some time alone.

Her bench was directly across from an upscale flower shop with an attractive sidewalk display of pots, cut flowers and birdhouses. On either side of it were antique shops, which dominated the small, pretty village.

She watched Raleigh come out of the too-cute restaurant where she'd bought her iced tea and cross the street, sitting down next to her with a huge iced coffee. "I didn't think the large would be *this* large," he said. "I've been away too long. I have to get used to American sizing."

"Mr. Raleigh—"

"You can call me William. Most people do. For some reason, I've never been a Bill or a Willie. Just William." He removed the plastic cap from his iced coffee and took a sip. "This is enough for a family of four."

"Where's Major Brooker?"

"Resting."

"Resting where?"

"That's for him to say."

Maggie rolled her eyes. "You two don't have to be so damn cagey—"

"Perhaps not," he said, taking another sip of his drink, "but we're used to it."

"How did you meet?"

"We were both on Nick Janssen's trail."

"I understand why Brooker would be looking for Janssen, but why would you?" She felt the humidity, which brought out the smells of the passing cars, the grass, some of the flowers in the display across the street. "Did he have something to do with my father's death?"

Raleigh lowered his drink and winced. "My calves are acting up. I could have used my walking stick today, tramping out in the woods. I left the bloody thing in Amsterdam. It's more a nuisance than anything else."

Maggie stared at him a moment. Beads of sweat had collected on his forehead and nose and seemed to make the sprinkle of brown spots across his cheeks stand out more.

"Are you CIA?" she asked him quietly.

"I'm just a tired old man, Maggie," he said.

"You're not that old. What, sixty?"

"Sixty-two." He smiled sideways at her. "Sixty. I like that. You know I look older. You're just too polite to say so."

She smiled in spite of herself. "No, you look as if you've had a hard life. There's a difference."

"Most of my hardships were self-inflicted." He sipped more of his iced coffee, but didn't seem to enjoy it. "I'd better restrain myself. Rest rooms in this quaint little village are difficult to come by."

"Why are you here?"

He focused on something across the street, avoiding her eye. "There's been another killing."

"Jesus. Who? Where—"

"London. Your colleagues in federal law enforcement will know soon, if they don't already. A Russian arms dealer named Vlad Samkevich turned up dead there late today. He'd been dead for some time. At least a few days."

Maggie recognized the name. Investigators believed Samkevich was one of Janssen's main suppliers of illegal small arms. Janssen never touched any of the illicit goods he moved around the world. He made deals happen. Already a rich man, he got richer from them.

"How?" Maggie asked.

"A .22 round to the back of the head."

Just like Tom Kopac.

"A neighbor found him." Raleigh made a face at his iced coffee. "How can anyone drink this much of anything? Well. I should talk. If it were whiskey—" He sighed with a sense of acceptance mixed with regret. "There's enough caffeine here to end any-one's jet lag, that's for sure."

Maggie's mind wasn't on iced coffee. George Bremmerton had told her that Jans-sen was refusing to cooperate with Dutch authorities. American investigators, in the process of getting permission from a Dutch judge, had yet to question him. His attor-neys had vowed to fight his extradition to the U.S. Nick Janssen's criminal friends and associates had to be wondering if he would give them up in exchange for another kind of deal, one with prosecutors instead of ex-tortionists, murderers, drug and arms traf-fickers.

Maybe they were all jockeying for the top position now that their deal-maker was in custody.

"Do we have a turf war on our hands?" Maggie asked. "Is that what you think? It doesn't explain Tom's death—"

"Perhaps it does."

"Are you suggesting he was working with Janssen? I don't believe it. Mr. Raleigh—William—if you know anything, now is the time to tell me."

He gave her a dry look. "I suppose I should remember that we're in the U.S. now. You have the powers of arrest here. And I see that you're armed. I'm not, in case you were wondering."

"I should take you in and let the FBI and the marshals grill you just for being here and knowing Major Brooker—never mind the rest of it, the kooky phone call, Den Bosch."

"Your instincts tell you to trust me."

"My instincts tell me you're manipulating me." She had an urge to fling the rest of her iced tea in the street and walk away from this man. Tom Kopac. Now this Samkevich. What the hell was going on? And her father.

Where did he fit in? "People say you're mentally ill, you know."

"Ah, yes. Of course they do." It didn't seem to bother him. "There are days I wish I were. I wish I could take a pill and discover that all the bad voices and images in my head were imaginary. There are days I wish I were delusional."

"Did you kill Tom Kopac and Vlad Samkevich?"

He set his drink on the bench next to him. "Maggie."

His tone. The lucid blue eyes on her.

"Hell," she said. "You believe we have an assassin at work. You *know*."

"A paid assassin, not someone who believes in any cause but money." He leaned back against the uncomfortable wooden bench, stretching out his bony legs, flexing his feet. "It's someone I've been tracking for eighteen months."

Eighteen months.

Maggie didn't breathe.

"I picked up where your father left off. But I'm the one who put him on the trail."

"How—" She paused, composing herself. "How do you know? Who the hell are you? Who was *he*?"

But Raleigh didn't answer her. "Nick Janssen must have hired our assassin. He must have had a contingency plan in the event of his capture. He wouldn't leave anything to chance. His arrest could only make him more dangerous. It's all or nothing for him now. He has no choice, in his view, but to be bold and ruthless."

"He'll eliminate any rivals who threaten his position, any friends who could turn against him."

"Anyone he blames for his current predicament could also be a target."

But Maggie reminded herself not to get sucked into Raleigh's sense of drama and to stick to what she knew—and to remember what she didn't know. Like whether or not the man sitting next to her was even in sound mental health. He could still be spinning wild fantasies and conspiracies.

"Why are you here?" she asked him pointedly.

"Tom Kopac and I were to meet in Den Bosch the morning he was killed."

"His idea or yours?"

"Mine. I heard through my contacts in Prague that he'd been asking questions about your father."

"My father? But why?"

"That's what I wanted to find out. I caught up with him at his apartment early Friday morning after Janssen's arrest. He was on his way to the embassy. We agreed to meet in Den Bosch the next day."

"Why Den Bosch?"

"Another unanswered question."

"Then it was Tom's idea," Maggie said.

Raleigh nodded. "I phoned you. I wanted to meet Mr. Kopac first—"

"Where?"

"The cathedral." But he anticipated her next question. "I don't know why he went to the river. Perhaps he was curious about where Janssen was arrested. His safe house was nearby. I'd planned to tell you everything I knew. Then he was killed, and there was your deputy marshal."

"Why Ravenkill?"

"I saw a printout on the inn at his apartment. It was in plain sight. I thought . . . well, I wanted to see your reaction when I mentioned it, for starters. I didn't know if it had anything to do with your father or his death, if it was significant at all. Perhaps a place you and your father went on vacation

when he was alive. Something of that nature."

"I'd never heard of it," Maggie said.

Raleigh cast her a steady glance. "Your
father never mentioned Mr. Kopac, I take it?
I didn't want to use his name. I wanted to
see your reaction to Ravenkill and the Old
Stone Hollow Inn first."

"No, you didn't. You knew for sure I'd
never let you out of that cathedral if you
mentioned Tom. And no, as far as I know he
and my father didn't know each other." The
air was still and very warm, and she hoped
for a rumble of thunder, a bolt of lightning—
anything to jump-start her brain. "Did you
leave the printout in Tom's apartment?"

"Yes. I left everything just as it was."

"Then presumably the police have it
now."

"Unless he tossed it," Raleigh said.

"George Bremmerton didn't mention it
when I spoke to him this morning. Maybe
the Dutch police are still sorting out what
they found and don't believe it has any significance—"

"It may not, Maggie. Major Brooker thinks
he probably slipped and fell in the river and
wasn't attacked."

"Is that what you believe?"

He shrugged. "What I believe hasn't mattered for a long time now. I'm not being morose or self-pitying. It's the truth. You're here in Ravenkill because of me. I'm here because of you. Major Brooker's here because of both of us."

"Janssen's in custody," Maggie said. "You'd think Brooker would call it quits and go do whatever comes next for him."

"I don't think he knows what that is."

"That's a hard way to live."

"I think it's how your new marshal friend is living, too." Raleigh returned the cap to his iced coffee and made a face. "Look, I've drunk it down just an inch and I'm swimming. What a waste."

"Take it with you. Where are you staying?"

"Me? Oh, here and there." He nodded at the shops across the street. "Tom Kopac was a serious antiques collector. He could have been planning a shopping trip to Ravenkill."

Maggie shook her head. "I doubt it. I didn't know him that well, but I understand he didn't take vacations, never mind shopping jaunts to the States. There are plenty of antique shops right in the Netherlands."

"Was your father interested in antiques?"

"No."

"Phil was a good man. Intelligent, interested in everything—he gobbled up information like no one I've ever known." Raleigh seemed to be talking to himself more than to Maggie. But he smiled suddenly at her. "Perhaps our Mr. Kopac had more than a friendly interest in you."

"I can't—" She faltered, picturing him in the Binnendieze. "Please don't. There was nothing romantic in our friendship."

"I'm sorry." Raleigh patted her knee, his hand cool from the massive iced-coffee cup. "I'm very sorry for all of this."

"Tom was just a good guy. Who the hell would walk up to him and put a bullet in his head?"

"He had secrets, Maggie. He didn't tell you he was asking questions about your father, did he?"

She didn't answer. There was no point. Raleigh already knew that she and Tom had talked about nothing more substantial, more important, than doughnuts.

"I know it's difficult," Raleigh said. "I remember early on, someone told me it doesn't get easier. It was a frightening thought to me at the time. I wanted it to get easier. I didn't want to have to suffer so much when someone I knew, someone I liked and admired—a friend—died. But now?" He sighed heavily, sweat dripping down the end of his red nose. "It's a comfort to know it doesn't get easier. That every loss still matters."

Maggie dumped out the last of her tea and melting ice in the grass. Her father was dead. Tom was dead. A Russian arms dealer was dead. She and William Raleigh and Ethan Brooker and Rob Dunnemore were all in Ravenkill. They all could be spinning their wheels in the picturesque little Hudson River Valley town.

"I was hoping if I ended up with egg all over my face over this excursion, it'd be with fewer witnesses," she said, her shirt sticking to her back in the crushing humidity. "This assassin could still be in London, picking out another victim."

Raleigh seemed rooted to the bench, his legs outstretched. "You know your father wasn't killed by bank robbers?"

"I'm fairly certain he wasn't just a business consultant, either. Do you know how he was killed? I was never told—"

"It was a .22 round to the heart."

"Your assassin?"

"I'm sure of it."

"Now you're sounding like a nut again." She squinted at him against the afternoon glare, realizing she was stiff from her dunking in the Ravenkill. "But you're not a nut or a drunk or a breakdown case, are you?"

He didn't answer.

Maggie watched a middle-aged woman pick up a pot of bright yellow mums, examine them with a skeptical frown, then shrug and take them inside the shop. *I should be buying mums.*

But she glanced again at the man next to her. "How can I believe a word you say?"

His pale eyes twinkled. "Magster. You must have been an adorable six-year-old. Freckles, turquoise eyes, red hair and skinned knees. Am I right?"

"It's not that hard. I still have freckles, turquoise eyes and red hair."

"And skinned knees. Brooker did that?"

"My own damn fault."

"Phil wanted to be a better father to you," Raleigh said softly, seriously. "I suspect when it's all said and done it's what most of us wish. That we'd done better by those we love."

"Listen, okay? I loved my father, and I miss him. I'll always miss him. But I'm not going to let emotion drive my decisions—"

He scoffed. "That's what we always tell ourselves, isn't it? It's ridiculous. Emotion drives most decisions. We just don't like to admit it."

The woman came out of the shop with her mums, smiling now, no regrets, no second thoughts about her choice. Even if her mums had bugs, Maggie thought, what was at stake? Throw them out, get new ones. A loss of a few dollars.

"So you believe the same person—your assassin—killed my father, Tom and Samkevich. Any proof, any leads we can use?"

"None."

"Brooker?"

"Solid, but he has nothing. We'd tracked Nick Janssen to his safe house in Den Bosch. Before we could confirm it, he was arrested."

"I should take you in—"

"If you do, the stress could cause a relapse of my alcoholism and mental illness." He smiled, almost looking handsome. "You don't want to be the laughingstock of the Diplomatic Security Service."

She scowled at him. "That's so lame."

He got stiffly to his feet, leaving his iced coffee on the bench. "Transparently half-hearted, isn't it? I've told you what I know, Maggie. Every tangible lead I've had on this assassin has evaporated. If I had more, I'd give it to you. I want to find whoever killed Tom Kopac and your father. Vlad Samkevich wasn't a good man, but his murder..." Raleigh shook his head. "That wasn't justice."

"I can stop you," Maggie said.

"Of course you can, Agent Spencer. I'm just an old drunk."

He crossed the street, smelled a bouquet of flowers and blew her a kiss.

And she let him go.

Just as he knew she would.

Rob arrived in the village in time to see Maggie's white-haired guy—William Raleigh—turn the corner and disappear up a side street.

She was picking up a huge drink cup off her bench.

"You're not going to chase him?" he asked her.

Shaking her head, she squinted at him. "Are you?"

"No."

"Why not?"

Through Nate, Wes Poe had just vouched for William Raleigh. But Rob shrugged. "Trust in your judgment?"

"Ha."

"You look hot." He smiled at her. "Very hot, in fact."

"As in I could use more iced tea?"

"As in however you want to take it."

"Did you walk?"

He nodded. "Felt good. I needed the time alone."

She winced at his sarcasm. "I'm sorry I lied, but it's just as well you don't get mixed up with this guy."

"Protecting me, are you?"

"Trying. So far, so good. You didn't get killed on Saturday in Den Bosch, and you didn't get killed today in Ravenkill Creek. Okay—who gave you the word that Raleigh's okay?"

"Sure about someone did, are you?"

"Otherwise you'd have gone after him. You got here in plenty of time. You saw him. Did your source also tell you about Vlad Samkevich?"

There was no use pretending he didn't know. "Yes. It was Nate, by the way. He called."

"The future brother-in-law. The marshal of marshals." She smiled. "I'd like to meet him someday. And your twin sister."

"You're changing the subject."

"I need a minute to clear my head."

"Let's walk."

She glanced in the direction Raleigh had just gone, wondering what he was up to—if she should change her mind and follow him after all. "I thought I heard a rumble of thunder a minute ago."

"The Franconias said storms are moving in from the west. They're a pair, those two. Stressed to the point of cracking. Libby Smith suspects they're overextended."

"Not enough to kill people for money, I hope."

Rob heard an edge in her tone. "Maggie?"

"Nothing. I'm not serious."

She started up the street, and Rob hesitated, noting the stiffness of her movements. It wasn't just the dunking in the creek. Raleigh had said something that rattled her. But she kept walking, not looking back, and Rob finally got moving and caught up with her.

"Your sister and Nate Winter are getting married in a couple weeks, right? Is President Poe coming to the wedding?"

"That's the plan."

They continued along the country road in the shade of huge old oaks and maples, squirrels chattering at them from overhanging branches. Rob had no illusions that Maggie's mind was on the scenery or the afternoon heat or even President Poe and his sister's wedding.

She kept her eyes pinned to the pavement in front of her. "It's President Poe's doing, isn't it? That Nate Winter got in touch with you about Raleigh."

"I really can't say. I don't know it for a fact." Which was true, as far as it went. He didn't need facts—he knew the information Nate had relayed had come from Wes. "You just let Raleigh go yourself. What did he tell you?"

"That we have an assassin at work who probably killed Tom and Samkevich. And my father."

She spoke briskly, as if she didn't want to dwell on the emotional impact of her words. She picked up her pace, but Rob had no trouble staying with her. He was taller, he was a runner, and he wasn't letting her get too far ahead of him.

"The part about my father could be bull-shit—"

"I don't think so."

She stopped abruptly. "Poe? Did he—"

"I haven't talked to President Poe."

"Goddamn it, quit dancing around in circles! What did Winter tell you? We are talking about my *father.*" But she put up both hands and shook her head, more at herself than Rob. "Never mind. Forget I said that."

"No one's taking you off this thing, Maggie. You're the one Raleigh will talk to." Rob felt an urge to take her hand, but she had her shoulders squared, her arms tight at her side. Untouchable. "I don't have any specifics about your father."

"He wasn't just a businessman," she said.

"Raleigh isn't just a retired economist, either."

"I knew," she said, almost to herself. "About my father. I've known for a long time. In my gut. He never said anything—he wouldn't. I think my mother was in the dark. But even as a kid, when he was away for long stretches, I'd make up spy stories about him."

"Kids' instincts can be amazing."

She kicked a pebble, sent it flying into a field on the side of the road. "Bank robbers in Prague. Jesus."

"Raleigh," Rob said. "What else did he tell you?"

He watched her bank back the emotion, pull herself out of the pain and grief she must have felt in the early days after she'd learned of her father's death. She gave him a quick smile. "He doesn't care for what's considered a 'large' drink nowadays."

Rob said nothing.

By the time they reached the end of the inn's driveway, she had repeated her conversation with her father's friend, her Scarlet Pimpernel from the Dutch cathedral.

When she finished, Rob could smell mint in the heavy air. The inn was just up ahead.

"That's it, huh? A printout of the Old Stone Hollow's Web site in Kopac's apartment?"

"That's it. There's no reason for him to hold back."

Unless everyone, including Wes Poe, was wrong, and it was William Raleigh who was out of control. Mentally ill after all. A drunk. Perhaps he was even their assassin.

A hawk swooped low over a small meadow of wildflowers. Maggie gave a small cry of pleasure, and Rob saw the shine of tears in her eyes and knew it was as much as he'd get. She was used to holding her emotions closely. She wouldn't tell him how much pain the talk of her father's secret life and of an assassin had caused her.

She didn't need to, Rob thought. He understood.

He slipped his hand into hers. "Let's pretend we really are on vacation. At least for a few minutes."

She leaned into him, just enough, just for a second. "I hope the humidity finally blows out of here tonight."

"What humidity?"

She squeezed his hand and even smiled. "My mother loves south Florida. The humidity never gets to her. She and I have a different kind of relationship, but we understand each other. She paints flamingos." Her smile broadened, and she had a bounce to her step. "You'll have to see them sometime."

"Flamingos," Rob said.

"The most amazing flamingos."

"How does a flamingo-painting mother end up with a spy husband and a federal-agent daughter?"

"I think that's what she wonders, too."

But Rob supposed it was no more bizarre than Leola and Violet Poe raising a president, or his own parents raising a marshal and an archaeologist.

The light was green on the horizon.

The storms would be rough tonight.

He decided to wait to tell Maggie that he wasn't going anywhere. He had his room at the inn, and he was staying.

Sixteen

She'd seen him.

It hadn't been her imagination.

William Raleigh was in Ravenkill.

Libby pushed back a fresh wave of panic and kept herself from puking on the dining room floor. Her father had passed out in this very spot countless times, except there'd been no English antiques and cottage colors in those days—just ratty old junk that he hadn't been able to pawn off to friends for extra cash.

She'd always wanted control. Always. She'd fought and clawed for it as a child— for just a few moments when she was in control, for a small space that was hers and hers alone.

Taking up shooting had helped.

Now, years later, she had the thrill of her quiet work as a hired killer. The ultimate control. Someone else's destiny in her hands. Her own destiny, since even the smallest mistake could be costly.

Philip Spencer had been a mistake.

She'd known he and Raleigh were friends. She should have killed them both. But she'd believed the stories about Raleigh's mental breakdown and his chronic drinking and assumed he wasn't a serious threat.

There'd been no money in Spencer's killing and would be none in Raleigh's.

Only survival, she thought. No sense of control, no thrill, no profit.

She hadn't become a killer because of her father.

He wasn't responsible for anything she'd become, good or bad. No credit, no blame. He'd squandered what should have been hers, and he'd provided her a miserable childhood. But she was free of him.

"Libby?" It was Star, coming in from the porch. "Have you seen Andrew?"

"No. I'm sorry."

She gave a little hiss of annoyance. "We're busy outside, and he takes off. Damn him!"

"I can help. What would you like me to do?"

"Keep the feds on the porch happy. God! I can't help it—they make me nervous. Why did they pick here?"

A good question. Now Ethan Brooker and William Raleigh were sneaking around. Libby tried not to look frozen and sick. "Because you and Andrew have done an incredible job and it's a beautiful place?"

Star caught herself, obviously embarrassed by her curt tone. "I didn't mean that the way it sounded."

"I understand—"

"I hate to ask you—"

"It's okay." Libby smiled. "I like the idea of 'keep the feds happy.' "

Star's relief was palpable. Libby stopped in the kitchen to wash her hands. Maggie Spencer. Rob Dunnemore. Ethan Brooker. Whether they knew it or not, they were all here because of Philip Spencer and William Raleigh.

Libby dried her hands, feeling less nauseous.

She wouldn't get a dime for killing Raleigh. He wasn't on Janssen's list—Janssen didn't even know he existed. She planned to keep it that way. If Janssen had known she had the CIA or whatever Raleigh was on her tail, he'd never have hired her.

She had to stay calm and make sure none of the loose ends in her life came back to haunt her. Otherwise, Janssen would fire her and hire someone else to do the job for him, and her name would get tacked onto his new hit list.

And she'd lose this one opportunity to gather her strength, then make her move and take over Nick Janssen's network. His months on the run had weakened him. He wasn't getting out of prison anytime soon. He'd left a void. Libby planned to fill it.

She had to seize the moment. There was no alternative. She wasn't going to spend the rest of her life living in a suite in a house that was no longer hers, collecting furniture, killing people here and there for extra cash—for the thrill of it. She wanted more.

Pasting an insipid smile on her face,

Libby headed out to the porch and the two federal agents who awaited her.

If Juliet drove any faster up Central Park West, the cops were going to pull her over. Then she'd not only have to explain her speed, Ethan thought, but him.

And her truck.

"Did this thing pass inspection?" he asked.

She glanced at him. "Good. You didn't die on me. I was getting worried. I hate having to explain corpses in my truck." She tapped the sticker on her windshield. "Vermont says my truck's fine."

"You must have an in with someone."

"Are you kidding? I have five brothers. They're all cops and landscapers. I don't get cut any slack. Besides, just because you Texans trade in your trucks every two seconds doesn't mean we Vermonters have to. We're thrifty."

"You're cheap."

She braked at an empty parking space, yellow cabs whizzing past her. Ethan tried to sit up. His head ached. Even his eyeballs were pulsing with pain. "You won't fit."

"If we were parking a Humvee in the

desert, I'd defer to your expertise," she said, looking over her shoulder as she backed up. "But since it's a truck I've been driving forever, and it's New York City, where I've been working for a few years now—"

"If you hit something, just don't hit it hard. I have a head injury."

She whipped the steering wheel around, maneuvering the truck into the space, which was, in fact, too small. But, undeterred, she inched backward, then forward, barely nudging the bumpers of the cars—both more expensive than her truck—in front and behind her.

"There." She turned off the ignition and pulled out her key. "Plenty of room."

Ethan grunted. "I'd let the air out of your tires if you parked that close to me."

She sighed at him. "Hell, Brooker, you look awful. Are you sure you don't want me to take you to the E.R.?"

He attempted a reassuring smile. "If I survived the ride down here, I can survive anything."

"How's your headache? Not severe, I hope?"

"It's fine."

"You don't have trouble staying awake, do you?"

"I did. I don't anymore. Juliet—"

"Double vision?"

He sighed. She was running down the list of trouble signs for head injuries. "No. No weakness in the extremities, no convulsions, no problem walking."

"We'll see about the walking part. I still think you should go to the E.R."

"Aren't you supposed to be at work?"

"Chief Rivera gave me the day off. A few days off, actually. I was supposed to go camping."

Ethan had met the chief deputy when the feds had questioned him after he took off in May and then came back. A tough guy. Loyal, but he expected loyalty in return. "You told him I showed up at your place?"

"I'm responsible for my own decisions."

"That's not what I asked."

"I told him. I didn't mention the call from your friend."

Raleigh. Ethan didn't want to think about him right now.

"You're going to talk to me, Major," Juliet said. "You're going to tell me everything."

"What if I have amnesia?"

She ignored him. "Can you carry your backpack?" But she peered at him again, then shook her head. "No, obviously you can't. Stupid question. I'll carry it. Wait, and I'll open the door for you."

She shoved her door open with her shoulder and jumped out, but Ethan didn't wait. His door was stiff and creaky, but he managed to push and kick it open, then climb out onto the sidewalk.

He reached into the jumpseat for his backpack, but the motion sent blood rushing into his head. His stomach turned over. He grabbed hold of the top of his seat and stood very still, waiting for his vision to clear and his nausea to abate.

"Don't pass out," Juliet said from behind him. "Damn. I'm taking you to the hospital—"

"No." He thought he spoke out loud but wasn't positive. "Just leave the backpack."

"You don't want to fool around with a head injury."

"I'm not."

She reached behind him and grabbed his backpack, hoisting it over one shoulder. "I should have searched this thing when I had you in my place last night."

She was right, but Ethan didn't say any-thing. He pried his fingers loose and stood up straight. He didn't throw up, didn't pass out. He shut the truck door and followed Juliet up the stairs to her building.

"You can still go camping," he said.

"I'd go crazy. Rivera thinks I'm experienc-ing post-trauma symptoms from Janssen's goons, the cave—"

"Are you?"

"No."

"That kind of thing can grab you from be-hind when you least expect it."

"I got debriefed or whatever they're call-ing it now. I passed the fitness-for-duty test." She stopped herself, glancing back at him. "Not that I have to explain myself to you. Where's my cell phone?"

He handed it to her.

"You're lucky you didn't wreck it with your antics today."

"Looks like Rob Dunnemore called you a few times on our way down here."

"How many?"

"I don't know. Maybe a hundred."

She checked the call history. "Six. That's like a hundred from anyone else. I'll call him when we get upstairs. You okay?"

"I'm okay."

Her doorman obviously remembered him from yesterday and gave him a dirty look, but Juliet smiled, as pretty a smile as Ethan had seen her give anyone yet. "This is Major Ethan Brooker," she said. "He's with me. He's had a bit of a mishap."

Ethan hated every second of the elevator ride up to her apartment.

She unlocked all her locks, and he fell onto the couch in front of a fish tank. He lay on his back and realized it wasn't just his head that was hurt. He'd done a job on his back, his shoulder, one hip.

"Who'd take care of the fish and the plants if you went camping?" he asked.

"Rivera said he would. Is your speech slurred?"

"I wish. It'd mean I'm drunk."

Juliet snorted. "If you were drunk, you'd be barfing as well as slurring your words."

"You're a hard woman, deputy."

"Keep talking. It's probably good for you. What can I get you? Beside whiskey. Beside anything alcoholic. Is there anything I can do for you?"

He raised an eyebrow and tried to give her the sexiest look he could.

She didn't budge. "Don't get any ideas, Brooker. Never mind the concussion, you smell like a swamp." She put her hands on her hips and sighed at him. "You're sure you don't remember what happened to you?"

"I fell into the Ravenkill."

"You and your rivers."

"This one had rocks."

"If you were attacked—"

"I can't say that I was or I wasn't." He squeezed his eyes shut, trying to push back the pain and bring forward any new details about that morning. But there was nothing. "It hurts to think."

"Well, then." She hesitated, then sighed again. "Just rest."

"Your couch . . ." He wondered if his words *were* slurred. "I'm a mess . . ."

"It's okay, Ethan."

Her tone had softened, and he thought her voice might have cracked. But he knew he wasn't in great shape.

"I'm one of the good guys," he mumbled.

"Yeah. I know you are."

After that, he just heard the gurgle of the fish tanks, and for the first time in days— maybe months—felt himself relax.

* * *

What Maggie knew about William Raleigh, now the marshals knew.

At least Rob did.

Sitting on the veranda over coffee and dessert, she saw a flicker of lightning somewhere across the Hudson. In a couple of seconds the thunder came, a long, low rumble. The green light, the still air and the unrelenting humidity were all signs of an impending storm.

"My sister had no intention of falling for Nate when we were shot in May. For anyone." Rob spoke quietly, aware of Maggie across the table. "She'd just finished a major project. She likes to say we Dunnemores are at our most dangerous when we're idle."

"You're not idle."

"I'm sitting here drinking cappuccino and eating plum tart—"

"That's now. A couple hours ago you were sneaking around after me. Before that, we had Ethan in the river. And before *that*—"

"I get your point. Sarah also says she and Nate fell for each other in a whoosh." Rob smiled, none of the blue in his eyes visible in the prestorm light. "A Ph.D. in archaeology, and that's her word. *Whoosh.*"

Maggie smiled, too. "I like it."

"All her fears and preconceptions about who she should end up with went out the window, right along with her common sense. My sister and a marshal."

"You're a marshal."

"I'm her brother."

"But her twin," Maggie said.

"You mean if I hadn't become a marshal, I would have become an archaeologist?"

"I don't know. Maybe. I can see you digging in ruins."

"Think more in terms of an old dump. That's where Sarah's been spending her time lately."

"Probably more productive than chasing me over hill and dale."

His gray eyes darkened, or maybe it was the light. "I don't know about that."

Maggie tried to ignore the flutter in the pit of her stomach. "You got hit hard in May, didn't you? Not just physically. Going through something like that . . . you must know in a way the rest of us don't how short life is and how much we're not in control, no matter how hard we try to be." She lifted her water glass and winced, self-conscious. "Listen to me. All philosophical. And I'm only drinking water."

"Getting dunked in a river must bring out the philosopher in you."

"I don't know what I was thinking, going up to Brooker like that—"

"You were thinking you'd help him."

"I'm glad he wasn't hurt any worse than he was. I wish we could have helped Tom—" She forced herself not to go that route and sipped some of her water, half tempted to dump it down her front. She was hot, restless, hyperaware of her surroundings. Of the man across the table from her. "It's been a weird few days. I'll say that."

Rob was spared answering when Andrew Franconia pounded up the porch steps and yanked out a chair at their table, sitting down without waiting for an invitation. "I heard on the news that some Russian with ties to Nicholas Janssen has turned up dead in London. Shot. Wasn't that guy you found in the Netherlands on Saturday shot? What the hell's going on?"

"You know as much as we do," Rob said.

"Bullshit."

Maggie set down her glass. "I know this kind of news is upsetting—"

"Don't patronize me. I don't care if you're both federal agents. I want to know what's going on."

"Fair enough." Maggie kept her voice steady, reassuring. "The Russian's name is Vladimir Samkevich. I don't know a great deal about him. He and the man Deputy Dunnemore and I found dead were both shot in a similar fashion, but it's far too early to make any connection between the two murders."

Andrew's mouth snapped shut, and he sat back in his chair, exhaling loudly. "I don't know how you do this work. I truly don't. The worse Star and I deal with is the occasional unpaid bill."

"Thomas Kopac and Philip Spencer," Maggie said without warning. "Do you know either name?"

Franconia frowned at her. "No. Why? Who are they?"

"Tom Kopac is the man who was killed on Saturday—"

"Jesus Christ! Why would I know him? Why would you even ask—"

"Philip Spencer is also dead. He was

killed eighteen months ago in Prague. He was my father."

"Is this personal?" Andrew asked tightly.

"I'm not sure I know the answer to that. I'd appreciate it if you could check your records and see if either name pops up."

His eyes were half-closed. "Do I need a lawyer?"

Rob was the one who answered. "It's a simple request, Mr. Franconia."

Star, who'd just walked onto the porch, rushed to the table, putting one hand on her husband's shoulder. "What's going on?"

He repeated what Maggie had said in terse, unemotional words, although there was still no color in his face. "Do you recognize the names Philip Spencer or Thomas Kopac?" he asked his wife.

"No," Star said, shaking her head. Her sundress, at least a size too big, hung loosely on her thin frame. She turned to Maggie. "No, I don't know either name. I can check our records. We have a mailing list, but we're not as computerized as we probably should be. We have some records on our antiques buyers, and more on our guests."

"How are reservations handled?" Maggie asked. "I filled out a form on your Web site."

"But it was just an e-mail," Star said. "Whoever's here takes the call or the e-mail and puts it in the book and provides a confirmation number. For instance, I received your e-mail reservation with your credit card information. I e-mailed you back with your confirmation number. It's fairly informal. We like that. It feels more personal."

"Can you check what you have on all your different customers?" Maggie asked. "People who've stayed here, people who've just eaten here, people who've just bought antiques?"

Star glanced at Rob, whom she seemed to think had some kind of veto power over Maggie, then nodded. "I'll check our records tonight and let you know what I find."

"It's very difficult on both Star and me having you here," Andrew said, looking directly at Maggie. "Frankly, I'm glad it's only for one more night."

Maggie managed a quick smile. "I don't blame you."

But he jumped up and spun on his heels,

heading off the porch without a backward glance even at his wife.

Star smoothed the folds of her too-big dress and kept her eyes lowered. "I apologize. We're stretched thin with this place. Our cash flow's improving, but . . ." She gave an embarrassed smile. "The stress sometimes gets to Andrew. We have a lot at stake, and if your presence here . . . If there's trouble—"

"You don't want the inn's reputation hurt," Maggie finished for her.

"No one needs that kind of publicity."

After Star withdrew, with less drama than her husband, Maggie abandoned the last of her coffee and plum tart and asked Rob if he'd like to join her for a walk before the storm hit.

They headed down the stone path, veering off into the sunflowers, like smiling faces in the fading daylight. Rob walked very close to her but they didn't touch. She breathed in the musty smell of the flowers and smiled. "Do you think sunflowers smell different in the evening? I think they might."

"I can't say I know what sunflowers smell like during the day."

"They're not very fragrant, are they?"

"Not very."

"You really are a dangerous man, Rob," she said quietly, surprising herself with her own words. "Other people might be fooled by the charm and the good looks and the education. I'm not." She turned to him, a giant sunflower taller than he was behind him. "Your future brother-in-law has a reputation as a hard-ass. I'll bet you're as big a hard-ass as he is."

"He's a hard-ass in a good way. His parents were killed in a mountain-climbing accident when he was seven. I think it made him less patient with BS at an earlier age than most of us."

"There's no easy age to lose a parent, but at seven? Both of them?" She shuddered. "I can't imagine."

"Maggie, your father—"

"I didn't know my father," she said. "Obviously."

"I have a feeling you're a lot like him. Not that easy to get to know. Self-contained. Dedicated to your work to a point that might shut out even the people you care about most."

"It's not an easy way to live, never mind whether or not it's fair to anyone else."

"We all have something. It's what we do with it that matters." He winked at her. "Now I'm being the philosopher."

"Rob . . ." She sighed. "Never mind."

He gave her a knowing look. "You see? Self-contained. We're attracted to each other. That's what you wanted to say, isn't it?"

"Maybe." She shot out of the sunflowers, onto the grassy lawn. "Doesn't this heat get to you?"

"Heat gets to me, but this isn't hot. Maggie—"

Thunder rumbled in the distance. Taking it as a sign—an excuse—Maggie laughed. "There you go. All we need now is to be struck by lightning."

"We should go inside."

Lightning flickered on the green, western horizon, and a breeze stirred. "Rob, I—" She spun around at him, determined to say her piece. "I can't fall for anyone right now. I've been in The Hague for just three weeks. I can't do that to myself. To you."

"Who're you trying to convince?" He touched a curl by her ear. "Your hair seems lighter since you got here. Maybe there's something in the river water."

"You're having—" She made herself go on. "You're having an effect on me."

"An effect?" He laughed quietly, letting his fingers slide down her throat and skim her breast as he dropped his hand. "What kind of effect?"

"More than one kind, I'm afraid."

"Good?"

"Depends on your point of view."

He stood up straight, his expression suddenly unreadable. "I'm spending the night here, Maggie."

Hell.

"You're not choking?"

"It's my training," she said dryly.

"That'll teach you to sneak off to clandestine meetings with Scarlet Pimpernel types. I reserved a room while you were gone."

"Rob . . . you're not making this any easier."

"I'm not, am I? I was just wondering if it was my job to make this easier for you—"

"Your eyes are the same color as the sky right now. Did you know that?"

He sighed. "You're not going to make this easier on me, either, are you?"

"Not a chance."

He let his lips brush across her forehead. "We should get inside before the storm hits. The way things have been going, we *will* get struck by lightning out here."

"I swear we already have and it's affected our thinking."

"Not mine. I know exactly what I'm about."

He spoke with that mix of charm and confidence that had thrown her off balance from the beginning. Maggie pushed back a reaction to him that was physical, emotional and probably not at all appropriate.

"So do you," he added.

But the wind picked up, smashing the sunflowers into each other. Lightning and thunder flashed and cracked at the same time, the air darker, the light greener. Maggie could hear the rushing sounds of the approaching rain, and she and Rob ducked into the cellar.

Libby Smith was in her antiques room, pencil in mouth and pad of paper in hand. "Hey, there. Is the storm on us?"

"Almost," Maggie said.

She seemed delighted. "I love a good thunderstorm. We used to lose power all

the time when I was a kid, but the Franconias put in a lightning rod. So boring." She
grinned, shoving the pencil behind her ear.
"I'm doing an inventory. It's so dull I could
scream. Anything I can do for you?"

Maggie shook her head. "We're fine,
thanks."

And when they got up to the second
floor, it was no surprise to her at all that Rob
ended up in her room.

He swept an arm around her waist and
found her mouth with his, the wind pounding the rain against her window, as if to call
attention to his urgency, make her stop pretending that it wasn't there.

She felt her breath catch. She tried to
speak but gave up.

"Maggie." He placed his hands on either
side of her face and held her within inches
of him. "I'm not just being opportunistic.
There's something about you—"

"About us. When we're together."

All her reserve and natural caution fell
away. He seemed to feel it happening and
kissed her again, even as he caught her up
in his arms.

Before she could get her breath again, he
was carrying her to her four-poster bed.

She'd never been carried to bed before.

They dispensed with guns and cuffs and holsters and clothes, coming together quietly, hungrily, as if it'd been a foregone conclusion from the moment he'd stepped off the plane in Amsterdam. His mouth found hers again and again, often before she had the presence of mind even to take a breath.

She didn't push back, didn't say no, just responded to the feel of him, the taste of him. His strength and obvious urgency took her by surprise. It was almost as if he'd been thinking about kissing her, sweeping his hands over her, since he'd first folded himself into her Mini.

It seemed like such a long time ago. Yet it'd only been days.

A whoosh . . .

His hands slid over her hips, coursed up her back, then cupped her breasts with a boldness that only fueled her own response.

"Maggie . . ." Rob smiled at her, rolling onto his back so that she was on top of him, straddling him. "Stop thinking."

"How did you know—"

"Because you think all the time."

She eased her palms up his abdomen,

skimmed the scar from his bullet wound. In the dim light, she could see it. The round from Conroy Fontaine's sniper rifle had torn apart Rob's insides, cost him massive amounts of blood, his spleen, almost his life. But the scar was deceptively small, neat, no indication of the pain and suffering he'd endured. He was tanned and hard and muscular now.

He moved against her, and Maggie fell onto his chest, stifling a moan against his neck, tasting him, feeling his hands all over her, and whether it was her driving them toward the inevitable or him, she didn't know, didn't care.

The wind must have shifted, because a chilly breeze and rain blew against her overheated back, as if enticing her to respond to him. And she did, her heart racing as she reached over and placed her palm against his heart. Even as good a shape as he was in, his pulse was racing.

"I must be out of mind," she said.

But there was no more waiting, no more pretending or denying. He eased on top of her, kissing her throat, taking a nipple into his mouth.

She moaned with a deep pleasure. "You're sure it's okay? I don't want to hurt you. . . ."

"You won't."

And he didn't wait. He thrust into her, filling her up. She cried out immediately, an aching need overwhelming her. She'd never wanted anyone as much as she did him, now.

He made love to her with total focus, as if he might not ever get another chance at it.

"Easy," Maggie breathed, feeling the weight of him on her, inside her. "If this is the first time since the shooting, I don't want you to kill yourself."

He looked down at her, his eyes shining in the near darkness. "I've almost died doing stupider things."

She urged him deeper into her, giving herself up to a release that came out of nowhere and overtook her, and he responded by pounding into her, letting her claw at his arms and forcing her orgasm to go on and on.

She was spent, couldn't move.

He gave her a little half smile. "I'm not done yet."

"Oh, God."

When he finally came, she came again, with him, shocking herself as she felt him shudder, then collapse next to her.

They were both slick with sweat, breathing hard.

The storm was on them now.

Maggie pulled on some clothes and sat on a club chair in the window, watching the storm.

She could feel Rob watching her.

"I don't think I can make it to my room," he said.

He could. He just didn't want to. Maggie rolled off her chair and went to him, smiling as she traced the perspiration on his taut abdomen. "I guess I'm not as repressed as you thought."

"As *you* thought, you mean."

When he sat up, she was struck again by how damn good-looking he was. But he was serious now, brushing a hand over her hair. She took a breath. "I won't have any regrets in the morning." She smiled at him, making sure she didn't avert her eyes. "Ever."

He kissed her on the forehead, the nose, the mouth, lingering there. "I could fall in

love with you," he whispered. "It wouldn't
be hard at all."

Then he gathered up his clothes, got
dressed and left her room without another
word.

Seventeen

Maggie came downstairs early, wishing she'd brought some *hagelslag* with her from the Netherlands. Chocolate sprinkles on buttered bread would go down well after the night she'd had.

She pictured Tom in the Dutch bakery, making his crack about Krispy Kreme doughnuts not even a week ago. They'd just become comfortable with each other, and now he was dead. The image of his smile quickly changed to that first glimpse she'd had of his body floating in the Binnendieze.

She never wanted to get used to murder. Not ever.

But last night with Rob wasn't about Tom's death, or William Raleigh and his bizarre ways, or about her father. It was about something else, although she couldn't quite pin down what, except that she had no regrets and wasn't embarrassed. And yet she didn't expect ever to repeat such a night. She felt certain Rob didn't, either.

As she touched the latch to the porch door, Maggie heard someone sobbing in the kitchen and backed up, peeking in the doorway.

Star stood at the sink in a baggy denim jumper with a white chef's apron tied around her waist. She was running water over a colander of blueberries, tears streaming down her face. "Oh, God," she whispered. "Oh, God."

"Mrs. Franconia?" Maggie stepped into the sun-washed room, the air crisp and clear now that last night's storm had pushed out the heat and humidity. "Star?"

She spun around, hands dripping. "Agent Spencer. I didn't realize you were awake." She reached behind her and switched off the water, then grabbed a dish towel and brushed at her tears with it. "I had a bad night. I'm sorry."

"It's okay."

"You're not here to take on my problems. You're here for a break." She spoke with bitter sarcasm and lowered her towel, scrunching it into one bony hand as she glared at Maggie. "But that's just a line you gave us, isn't it? You've lied to us from the beginning."

Maggie crossed the kitchen with its cheerful terra-cotta tile floor and blue pottery vase of sunflowers on a round oak table, a contrast to Star Franconia's troubled, sarcastic mood. "Why don't we sit down? You can tell me what's going on."

Star took in quick, shallow breaths, one after another, in danger of hyperventilating, but she stumbled to the table, in a corner of windows that overlooked more flowers. Sunlight shone on raindrops on vines and leaves. Maggie imagined going off with Rob for a long, romantic weekend in such a place, but that wasn't why she was here, nor was it why Rob was here. And Star knew it.

She had to have had her suspicions last night when Maggie had asked her to look up her father and Tom in any database the inn had. Staring out the window as if Maggie weren't there, Star got control of her breathing. But her hands shook, and she hugged herself, goose bumps on her bare arms. "I should have worn a sweater," she mumbled.

"It's a beautiful morning."

As if to corroborate Maggie's words, a cool breeze floated through the cracked window.

Star released several heavy sighs and gulps, until finally she pushed back her chair an inch or so and shot Maggie an angry, accusatory look. "You think my husband is involved with Nick Janssen, don't you?"

"Why do you say that?"

"You think he has something to do with your father's murder in Prague, with the murder of that diplomat in Holland and now this Russian in London." She shifted back to the view, the bones in her shoulders visible under her thin pink T-shirt. "That's why you're here. I know it is."

Remaining on her feet, Maggie tried not to let Star's emotions affect her. "We know Tom Kopac was killed on Saturday morning,

because I was there. Where was your husband over the weekend?"

"Andrew?You mean did he have time to
fly to Holland, kill your friend and fly back
again?" There was a hard, sarcastic edge to
her voice that Maggie understood but didn't
like. "He was here. But he could have hired
someone to do his dirty work for him. He
could have arranged for Mr. Kopac's murder, Mr. Samkevich's murder. That's what
you're thinking, isn't it?"

"You didn't answer my question."

Star flopped back in her chair, her arms
still crossed over her chest. "He was here.
We had a full house, remember? I told
you—"

"I remember." Maggie let her tone soften.
"Ever want to chuck it and sell the inn,
travel, go back to the life you had before
you got tied down here?"

"No. I don't." Tears, probably unwelcome,
welled in her eyes, and she struggled not to
cry. "Andrew, maybe. I'm more the home-
body."

"Where is he now?" Maggie asked.

"I have no idea. Where's your marshal
friend?"

"I haven't seen him yet this morning."

Maggie pulled out a chair and sat down, focusing her attention on the woman next to her. "Mrs. Franconia, what did you find out about the names I gave you last night?"

With a small cry, Star jumped up, ripped off her apron and flung it on the floor, then ran outside onto the porch.

Maggie followed her, birds twittering in the flowers and shrubs, everything clean and fresh in the bright morning sun. Libby Smith lifted screened covers and cloths from the breakfast laid out on a wooden buffet table. Steam rose from a tower of freshly baked muffins. Apple-cinnamon, Maggie thought.

"Coffee?" Star asked her abruptly.

"What? Sure. That'd be fine."

Libby, obviously aware that Star was very upset, held up a hand. "It's okay. I'll get it." She filled a white mug from a stainless-steel coffee urn. She had on jeans and a sweatshirt with a picture of the inn silk-screened across its front, more appropriate for the cool air than Star's T-shirt and jumper. "Deputy Dunnemore's up. He took a mug of coffee off to the gardens a little while ago. Star? Can I get you anything?"

Star shook her head, gulping in a breath,

and plunged down the steps onto the stone path.

"Maybe I should go with her," Libby said, handing Maggie the mug of coffee. "She looks like she's coming undone altogether. I know having you and Deputy Dunnemore here has bothered her. Fair or unfair, you guys make her nervous."

Maggie held the mug with both hands, appreciating its warmth. "I'll go talk to her."

"Um, cream and sugar?"

"This is fine, thanks."

The stones were still wet and slippery from last night's rain, the grass sparkling with dew, and Maggie fought a visceral urge to get away, leave Ravenkill, abandon her questions—her mission there—and just drive north along the Hudson River and see where she ended up.

She found Star on her hands and knees in front of the fairy statue, picking weeds from a bed of miniature dahlias and baby's breath. "The fairy's nose is chipped," she said. "Did you notice? Libby says her father whacked it with a wine bottle one night when he was drunk."

"Was she watching?"

"Oh, yes. She was ten or eleven at the

time. But it's a beautiful statue, isn't it? I think the chipped nose adds character."

Maggie nodded, trying to be conversational and resist the urge to pelt Star with questions. "It seems to belong here."

"That's what I think." Star rocked back against her heels, shaking mud off her fingers, a brown worm wriggling out of the dirt she'd disturbed. "It's too wet still to get anything done out here."

"The gardens here are something. I have only one lowly orchid."

"What kind?"

"I don't remember. It's supposed to be unkillable, but I think I killed it."

"Nothing's unkillable," she said sadly, then got to her feet, the front of her jumper from the knees down soaked. "I didn't find a reservation for either your father or Mr. Kopac."

Maggie nodded. "All right."

"But I did—" Star faltered, sniffling as if she couldn't go on. "I did for the army captain who was killed in Amsterdam last year."

"Charlene Brooker?"

"I remembered her name from all the news stories in the spring. I thought . . . I don't know what I thought. I guess the Dutch connection got me."

"Captain Brooker was here? Or did she just make a reservation and—"

"She stayed for two nights around this time last summer."

A month before Nicholas Janssen had her killed. Eight months before he went after a presidential pardon and the Dunnemore family was nearly wiped out.

"Janssen," Star said, her voice half-strangled. "He ordered her murder, didn't he? That's what they say. And he was captured last week—"

Maggie could see that Star was very pale, her thin hands purple as she hugged herself. "I've learned the hard way to try to avoid speculating. It's natural, but it doesn't get us anywhere. Do you remember Captain Brooker?"

Tears leaked out of Star's eyes, and she choked back a sob. "Oh, yes. She was alone. She said she was taking a break. Like you."

"What did she do while she was here?"

"Took walks. Rested.She had most meals here at the inn. We talked about antiques." Star brushed idly at her tears, the anger and bitterness gone out of her. "I know I read about her death, but I never made the connection between the army captain killed in Amsterdam and our former guest. Andrew couldn't have, either. He'd have said something. I know he would have."

Who was she trying to convince? Maggie touched Star's thin arm. "We should go back to the house. You've got goose bumps. You do need a sweater."

But Star didn't seem to hear her. "We read the news accounts this spring when the two marshals were shot in Central Park and that whole business with President Poe and the Dunnemores came out. . . ."

"I was in Chicago then," Maggie said. "I remember."

Star gave a weak smile and walked back to the stone path, then stopped abruptly, doubling over as she started to cry.

"Mrs. Franconia," Maggie said, standing behind her, "if there's more—"

"There is." She straightened, her cheeks red and blotchy from crying; the rest of her skin was deathly pale. "I wasn't going to tell you. I was going to pretend—" But she stopped herself. "Never mind."

"Pretend what?" Maggie prodded.

"That I didn't know. That it never happened."

"Star—"

"Your father never stayed here at the inn, but he bought a piece from us. It's in our records. A crystal vase."

Maggie forced herself to stay focused on what Star Franconia had to say. "Here? He bought the vase from you here in Ravenkill?"

She shook her head. "No. In Prague."

Star's entire body was convulsed in shivering, more, Maggie suspected, from fear and a realization of the importance of what she'd discovered than from the cold. Her lips were stretched thin, a purplish blue, her veins in her hands and wrists bulging against her pale skin.

Maggie shoved her mug of coffee at her. "Take a sip. It's nice and hot."

"I want to find Andrew."

"Were you in Prague? You and your husband?"

She nodded dully.

"When?"

"Three months before he was killed. How—" She tensed her muscles visibly, as if to stop herself from shivering. "How is that possible? Then Captain Brooker was here a month before *she* was killed? And now you . . . you and Deputy Dunnemore, just days after . . . after—" She brushed at tears that had dribbled into her mouth. "There's been so much death."

"Mrs. Franconia, I want you to go inside. I'll get Rob Dunnemore, and I'll find your husband. Okay? Come on."

"Your father," Star whispered. "I didn't connect the two of you. I doubt I would have if you hadn't asked me to look up his name. The sale wasn't that big a thing. Even if I'd remembered, I never would have guessed he had a daughter who's a federal agent. He was just this nice man who was interested in an antique crystal vase. Austrian. Libby was the one who found it."

Maggie held her elbow and got her to start walking. "Libby was in Prague with you?"

"We met her there. She was on her own buying trip. It was our last big travel extravaganza before we opened this place. We opened in the winter deliberately, to get our feet under us before our first summer season." But Star looked abruptly at Maggie and gave a small gasp. "You have your father's red hair. I didn't think of that until just now."

When they reached the porch, the muffins and fruit were covered again, and Libby Smith was gone. "Are there other guests at the inn?" Maggie asked. "You said it was quiet—"

"It was just you and Deputy Dunnemore last night. I think . . . I think that's for the best, don't you?"

"Probably."

Maggie escorted her inside and found a sweater on the back of a chair in the kitchen. She carefully folded it over Star's shoulders.

Star tried to smile. "You're very kind, Agent Spencer. I know you have a job to do. Your father—" She wiped more tears with her fingertips, her sensitive skin raw from the chilly air and her crying. "I can't imagine. That must be so awful. This has something to do with your father's death, doesn't it?"

"I can't answer that right now. Do you have any idea where your husband is?"

"He's not . . . he's not a killer, Agent Spencer."

"I just want to talk to him."

Her shoulders slumped, and she sank onto a chair at the table, fingering a sunflower in the blue pottery vase. "In the shop in the barn, I would guess. He wanted to work on some projects there today."

"Can I get you some coffee or tea, anything warm to drink?" Maggie asked.

She shook her head. "I can get something if I want it. I'll be fine. Andrew and I haven't discussed what I found out—what I remember about Captain Brooker and your father." She sniffled, slightly more composed. "You'll let me know when you find him?"

"I will."

When Maggie left, Star was looking forlorn but not as dramatically upset as she picked bits of yellow blossom off a sunflower and laid them neatly in a row in front of her.

Ethan saw the news of the Russian arms dealer's murder when he woke up on Juliet's couch and flipped on the television.

Samkevich.

So somebody had taken out the bastard.

Hell.

His bruises less painful this morning,

Ethan rolled off the couch and tried to find coffee in the small New York kitchen. He checked the cupboards, the refrigerator, the freezer. No coffee. It was just another reason to clear out.

He and Raleigh had tracked Samkevich to London, hoping he'd lead them to Nick Janssen—hoping they could turn both lying, murdering sons of a bitches over to authorities.

Now old Vlad was dead, and Nick was in the pokey.

Ethan gave up on his coffee hunt and ducked into the bathroom to get washed up. The lump on the back of his head had gone down, but it was an ugly mix of purple, red and smudgy-looking black. He had scrapes and bruises here and there, and his eyes were sunken and bloodshot.

If he'd been Juliet, he'd have left him by the Ravenkill.

If he'd been Agent Spencer, he'd have left him *in* the damn river.

But he was lucky in that way. Always had been.

Not Char.

He washed his face and brushed his teeth, then returned to the outer room. He picked up his backpack and headed out. He didn't feel bad at all about cutting out on his blond marshal friend. Juliet would likely thank him when she crawled out of bed and realized he'd cleared out. Less complicated that way.

When he got to the sidewalk, he considered stealing her truck. The thought of navigating the New York City public transportation system didn't sit well with him on a good day, never mind the morning after he'd tumbled into a rock-strewn creek. But if he went back upstairs and found Juliet awake, hair tousled, ripping apart the place because he'd slipped out on her, who the hell knew what'd happen?

He had work to do. He had to find Raleigh. He had to figure out what was going on with Samkevich, Kopac, Philip Spencer, Maggie Spencer. What the connection among them was. And what, if anything, it had to do with Char.

Halfway down the block, he realized he'd forgotten his toothbrush.

He gritted his teeth. Goddamn it. He wasn't going back up there.

He heard footsteps approaching him from behind. Fast steps. New Yorker steps.

"You damn ingrate," Juliet said calmly, easing in next to him. "You could have left me a note."

She had on a red flannel shirt over a ribbed tank top and what looked like men's boxer shorts. Unlaced running shoes on her feet. Her short hair was tousled just the way he'd pictured it.

"You didn't have any coffee," he said. "That put me over the edge."

"There's coffee. There's always coffee in my place."

"Where?"

"The Vermont cracker tin in the fridge."

"Now, why didn't I think of that?"

She hunched her shoulders. "It's cooled off, hasn't it? I can smell fall in the air. You want to tell me where you're going?"

"No." He glanced at her strong legs. "You lift weights?"

"Three times a week."

"Good. You can carry me if I pass out from all this walking."

"You're Special Forces, Brooker. You can take on an army even with the shit knocked out of you."

He remembered how he'd found her in the cave in the bluff along the Cumberland

River in Tennessee. Tied up, battered, worn out, keeping her eye out for snakes—and determined to help Sarah Dunnemore and Nate Winter no matter what condition she was in. Marshal Juliet. She'd tried to get his gun off him.

She sighed, as if she knew what she was about to say wasn't in her best interest. "There's a place we can stop for coffee on the way. Just give me two secs to put on some clothes."

"On the way where?"

"Ravenkill. That's where you're headed, isn't it?"

He didn't respond.

Her mouth was a straight, grim line. A cool breeze blew the ends of her short curls in every direction. "You were in the Netherlands last week. You flew in to New York on Monday."

"You searched my backpack," Ethan said.

"See? I learn from my mistakes."

"Juliet—"

"You're a very dangerous guy who can't come to terms with your wife's violent death." She spoke quietly, sincerely. "You blame yourself. You torture yourself with guilt and regrets."

"Thank you, Dr. Longstreet."

She ignored his sarcasm. "It'll destroy you if you don't get a grip."

He stopped dead on the sidewalk. She didn't flinch. He faced her squarely. "Here's the thing. I don't care."

"That would make you even more dangerous—if it were true."

"Don't fool yourself," he said, turning around and starting back toward her apartment.

"Where are you going?"

"I'm taking you up on your offer to drive me to Ravenkill." He glanced back at her, noticing she hadn't made a move to follow him. "I hate subways."

"As I recall, you aren't much on my truck, either."

She didn't have the keys on her, and he didn't want to go back up to her apartment with her. Speaking of dangerous, he thought. He leaned against the passenger door and pushed back the thready start of a headache, shutting his eyes against the bright hit of sunlight.

He remembered the cool water running under him yesterday in Ravenkill Creek.

The sun bearing down on him.

Before that, he remembered the sensation of falling, an out-of-control sprawl down the steep riverbank.

He'd hit a rock. More than one rock. He could feel the bruises on his hip and the small of his back, sharpening his memory.

He went very still against Juliet's truck. He kept his eyes shut but could hear the swish of New York's morning rush-hour traffic.

He could hear the sound behind him again, an intake of breath, as if someone were summoning the strength to—

"To hurl a fucking rock at me."

Had he spoken out loud?

Opening his eyes, he became aware of New Yorkers hurrying past him without making eye contact, which didn't necessarily mean he'd been talking to himself.

But he had it now. He remembered at least some of what had happened yesterday.

Someone had beaned him with a goddamn rock and sent him sprawling, not giving a rat's ass whether he broke into a million pieces or landed in the river and drowned.

It wasn't kids throwing rocks in the river for fun and hitting him by mistake. An accident. A kid might run off in a panic but wouldn't have taken that measured breath. Ethan was sure he hadn't made it up. He *remembered.*

It could have been anyone. Raleigh. Maggie Spencer. Rob Dunnemore. The couple who owned the inn. Another guest.

Ethan hadn't thought of any suspects at the time. He'd gone into survival mode, doing what he could to limit damage to his head and internal organs even as he knew he was going to lose consciousness.

He stood up from Juliet's truck. Either someone had deliberately hit him, or he'd just dreamed up the whole scenario and he'd simply lost his footing.

His marshal rescuer came out of her building, dressed and armed.

He didn't know how he'd kept his hands off her.

Rescuer. Juliet wouldn't see herself that way. He'd played on her good instincts— her natural desire to trust and help a former

army major who just wanted to find answers to his wife's murder.

Char. She'd want him to get on with his
life.

But how the hell could he be thinking
about taking Juliet Longstreet to bed when
he didn't have all the answers to Char's
death? When yesterday had raised fresh
questions?

He shook off his guilt and misgivings and
smiled at Juliet. "Ready to roll?"

"As ready as I'm going to be."

Ethan didn't ask her if she'd called her
chief deputy before she'd headed back
downstairs. Either way, she wouldn't want
to tell him.

And somehow he knew she hadn't, and
that she wouldn't want him to remind her
she should have.

They got into the truck and Juliet started
the engine with a rattle and roar. Ethan
rolled down his window and smelled the
soot and the cool late-summer air.

"You're taking a risk driving me to Ravenkill," he said.

"Hell, Brooker." She looked over at him
and grinned. "I took a risk not shooting you

on sight the day I met you on President Poe's front lawn."

Ethan didn't know if he'd tell her someone had tried to kill him yesterday.

But he might. They had at least an hour's drive ahead of them. There was time.

"That's all you marshals needed in May. One more body."

"Yeah," she said, screeching up the block. "It's all we need now, too. You're up to this drive?"

"Once you find me some coffee, I'll be up to anything."

She managed a smile. "That probably should worry me."

And he grinned back at her, as sexily as he could. "Probably should."

But she just made a hiss of mock disgust and reminded him she had five brothers.

Char had a younger sister who still hated him. So did her parents. None of them, Ethan thought, without reason.

Eighteen

Rob ran one finger through a thin film of dust on a rustic pine chest in the Franconias' antiques shop. They didn't rely on walk-in customers, which, he figured, was probably a good thing. There was no one to mind the store. A small sign urged shoppers to browse on their own and check at the inn if they needed help.

Trusting.

He'd knocked on the door to the Franconias' second-floor residence, but got no answer. On his way over to the barn, Star had waved to him from a tall blueberry bush. For all he knew, Andrew was off picking beans.

Maggie had to be up by now.

Rob shook off any thought of her and threaded his way through the furniture and glassware. His own place back in Brooklyn was a mix of hand-me-down furniture from friends and a few odd pieces he'd picked up out of necessity. He wasn't putting down roots in Brooklyn. Even in Night's Landing, his family had never been into antiques and fine furnishings—they bought what worked for the place, what was comfortable, what would last.

He supposed, by definition, antiques lasted.

He swore under his breath and stood on the wood ramp that led into the barn.

What the hell was he doing in Ravenkill?

The clear morning air, at least, provided a welcome contrast to the dust.

He'd gone to The Hague partly because of Nick Janssen's arrest, but it'd boiled down to reporters—to escaping the reverberations of his family's long friendship with John Wesley Poe. For the first time since the Central Park shooting, Rob was up against the full impact of his relationship with the president on his work as a marshal. They'd both treated their friendship with discretion, especially once Wes entered presidential politics.

But the anonymity they'd enjoyed was shattered now. Everyone knew he was President Poe's surrogate son. There was no changing it. It was a fact.

Nick Janssen's arrest had renewed public interest in the Poe-Janssen-Dunnemore connection. If it turned out Janssen had hired his own private assassin—someone who'd killed at least two people already— the media would have a feeding frenzy.

Because of Rob's injuries and Sarah's near death at the hands of a madman, their mother had been spared some of the ordeal of being hounded to explain her past, her connections to both the criminal master- mind now sitting in a Dutch jail and the self- made millionaire and dedicated public ser- vant now in the White House. Nick Janssen, Wes Poe and Betsy Dunnemore had all gone to Vanderbilt together. Thirty years later, Janssen had tried to use that connec- tion to get himself a pardon, a wild flight of fantasy that had resulted in violence, death and his own exposure as something more than a tax evader.

In a candid press conference not long after the foiled pardon-extortion scheme, President Poe had admitted he barely remembered Janssen, who'd transferred after his freshman year because of money problems.

Rob still had a hard time fathoming that his mother and Wes had been an item in college, their brief romance long in the past. Both were happy in their subsequent marriages. Wes and his wife hadn't let the tragedy of losing four babies rip them apart. Instead, they'd become even tighter.

The events of the past were facts none of them could escape, Rob thought.

He couldn't just turn the page on his own past and have it all be different.

As he walked back out to the stone path, Rob could see himself back in Night's Landing, sitting on the dock with Wes as they'd dangled their feet in the Cumberland and talked fishing and snakes and baseball.

Wes. Why couldn't you have stayed home and become a damn banker?

It was what the Poe sisters had wanted for the boy they'd found on their doorstep as a baby and raised. Roots, home, continuity, a simple life. Those were their values. Even Nashville was a long way from what

Leola and Violet knew. They were suspicious of politicians and ambition, rigid in their belief that all the good life Wes could ever want—all the contribution he needed to make—could be realized on their quiet stretch of the Cumberland River.

Yet, they'd have applauded his inauguration as president in January. They'd have dressed up and gone to the balls and had a grand time, because they'd come to understand, finally, that Wes was doing what he was meant to do.

When he went home to recuperate in May, Rob had paid more attention to the nuances of the relationships among his family and neighbors. For long weeks, he'd sat on the porch, taken the boat out on the river, explored the caves and sinkholes and trails of his home—and he'd tried to figure out what he'd missed by insisting that Night's Landing didn't matter to him. He'd never had the firm, clear connection to family and home that Sarah did. He didn't have her ability to whip up one of Granny Dunnemore's old casserole recipes and have it conjure up memory and meaning.

He saw Maggie coming toward him, the

sunlight on her red hair, and shook off the assault of introspection.

"Damn," he muttered. "No wonder Wes worries."

He suddenly wished he could whisk Agent Spencer away from Ravenkill and her own memories, her own questions and doubts.

"Have you seen Andrew Franconia?" she asked, squinting at him, all professional this morning. Only the hint of color in her cheeks, the way she didn't quite look him in the eye, told Rob that last night just might be on her mind.

He shook his head. "Maybe he's gone fishing. What're you up to?"

In a carefully neutral tone, she repeated her conversation with Star Franconia, describing Star's shattered state of mind, her recollections about Philip Spencer and Charlene Brooker. Rob knew Maggie had to be reeling from the information, but she kept her reactions to herself, under rigid control.

They continued on the path toward the inn. "I've never heard a hint that Char Brooker had anything to do with your father or William Raleigh, but that's not necessarily something I'd know. You? Do you think she could have worked on your father's murder case?"

Maggie gave a tight shake of the head. "No idea."

"What about your pal Raleigh?"

"Nothing."

"From what I gather from Nate, whatever the two of them did is closely held." Rob gestured back toward the Franconias' barn shop. "Did your father have an interest in antiques?"

"Not that I knew of. An Austrian crystal vase . . ." She looked skeptical. "It wasn't in his personal effects, not that I ever saw. Libby was the one who found the vase. We could ask her if she knows anything. Maybe he bought it as a gift—maybe it's got nothing to do with anything. He, Char Brooker and Tom Kopac could all have ended up sharing information on an antiques dealer and a beautiful Hudson River Valley inn. Then we got hold of bits and pieces and put them together all wrong."

"You believe in that kind of coincidence?"

She scowled. "It doesn't matter what I believe. My father—" But she broke off, refusing to go on. "Never mind. That doesn't matter, either."

There was the slightest edge to her voice, a hint of the anger she had to feel at having lost a father she'd never really had a chance to know. But she didn't want to face her resentment, her own guilt at missed opportunities—something Rob could understand.

He found himself accepting her natural reserve instead of trying to fix it. "Janssen thought my mother would leave my father when he got old. Then he'd be there. For all I know, it's still what he thinks. It's tough to know what goes on between two people, but I don't see my parents splitting up."

"My parents had been divorced for years when my father was killed." Maggie spoke quietly but not easily, without that urge to blurt out everything that Rob so often encountered. "But my mother still felt guilty. I think she believed his death was partly her fault."

"She's never said?"

"We don't have those kinds of talks. She didn't drive my father away. He had a bad case of wanderlust from as far back as I can remember. It wasn't a surprise to her. I guess she accepted it at first. But then, she just got sick of his long absences. I don't think she meant to."

"They say Charlene and Ethan Brooker spent less than a month together in the last two years of their marriage."

Maggie nodded. "Part of Brooker's drive to get all the answers to his wife's murder could be guilt. They drifted. He had his work, she had her work."

"She was killed and he wasn't there."

And she'd told everyone she was in Amsterdam on holiday, Rob recalled from his briefings. Alone.

"The Franconias' marriage is stressed," Maggie said. "For all we know, Char Brooker told my father they were a good source for a nice antique. Who knows? They got together, Libby Smith showed up in Prague. None of it could mean anything."

"People's relationships sometimes are complicated."

But Maggie wasn't touching that one. "Do we know where Major Brooker is?"

Rob didn't push her. "Probably still with Longstreet. The FBI is going to want to talk to these guys. Raleigh and Brooker, the Franconias and Libby Smith. You."

She nodded. "I'll fill George Bremmerton

in when I get a chance. We need to find out if my father ever met Char Brooker—and Tom. My God. Tom was just a dedicated foreign service officer."

"Maggie—"

She held up a hand. "It's okay. I just have to accept this awful sense of impotence, that I could have and should have done more. What happened on Saturday—" She turned away, as if she needed to make herself look at the flowers and the morning sun instead of whatever images were flooding her mind. "I want whoever killed Tom caught. I want to make sure nobody else dies."

Rob touched her shoulder, remembered the feel of her skin under his hands last night. "I'll find Andrew. Then I'll call Chief Rivera and let him know what's going on."

"Can you reach Deputy Longstreet and have her sit on Brooker?"

Rob smiled. "I imagine she's not letting him out of her sight."

"I'll find Libby and hang on to her and Star." Maggie paused, her expression serious, the raw emotion of just a minute ago gone now. "We need to find Raleigh, too. I doubt he's told me everything."

Rob decided this wasn't the time to agree with her. They split up at the porch steps, Maggie heading back inside while he veered off to check around outside for the inn's co-owner.

A quick look into the vegetable and herb gardens turned up nothing.

Nobody at the fairy statue or in the gazebo.

But when he reached the side of the house, Rob saw that the cellar door was ajar and eased down the slope to it, the grass slippery from last night's rain. He had to put his shoulder into the effort to push the door open wider, its rusted hinges creaking from lack of use. He wasn't exactly making a stealthy entrance.

"Ms. Smith?" he called. "Mr. Franconia? Anyone down here?"

His eyes had to adjust after being out in the bright sun. The cellar was cool, dark and damp. He felt along the wall for a light switch, trying to remember what kind of light had been in the hall.

But he heard a moan and turned sharply.

In the dim light, he made out the silhouette of a man in the wine cellar, sunk against the wooden shelves and racks, the door wide open.

Rob recognized the white hair. "Raleigh— Christ." He shot into the small room and grabbed hold of the older man's shoulders, realized how brittle and nearly weightless he was as he helped lower him to the floor. "What happened? What the hell are you doing down here?"

Raleigh was trembling badly, sucking in quick breaths as if to ward off pain. "Tom was on to something." His eyes flickered with something like grim amusement. "All roads lead to Ravenkill."

"Are you drunk? Hurt?"

"Not drunk. Someone . . . I took a punch of some kind to the kidneys."

He was clearly dehydrated, possibly hypoglycemic. Rob placed the back of his hand against the old spy's forehead; he had a slight fever. "Whose side are you on, Raleigh?"

"Phil's side. Char Brooker's. I failed them both. I put them together. I should have known they'd become targets." He coughed, moaning in agony, but it just seemed to irritate him. He swore viciously, then took a second to calm himself. "I didn't pull the trigger, but I'm responsible for their deaths. I used and manipulated them. Now I'm using and manipulating Maggie. It's a never-ending cycle. She doesn't know about Char and her father."

"They were lovers?"

"No, not that. On a similar mission."

The man needed medical attention. "Hang on." Rob got one of Raleigh's arms around his neck and half dragged, half carried him out to the hall. "Let's get you to a doctor."

"Leave me," he mumbled. "Leave me to die."

"Not my style."

"Bastard. I deserve it."

"That's not my call. Have you seen Libby Smith? Is she down here?"

"Her room—" Raleigh coughed, a wet, nasty sound, but there was no sign of blood on his mouth, anywhere. With any luck, he wasn't suffering from internal bleeding. He pointed toward the wine cellar. "She has a workroom."

He couldn't go on. Drawing his weapon, Rob returned to the dank wine cellar. "Ms. Smith?"

Behind him, the door slammed shut, and he heard the loud thunk of a lock twisting.

"Raleigh!"

But there was no answer, and Rob swore and kicked the door as hard as he could.

No luck. It didn't budge.

He was locked inside.

Swearing at himself, he swung his hands in the dark and caught the string to a light-bulb, pulling on it. A dull yellow light came on, but didn't reach the corners.

But he could see well enough to make out Andrew Franconia flopped against a small barrel on the outer wall, near a closed door to what had to be the adjoining work-room Raleigh had spoken about.

Rob approached Franconia cautiously, squatting next to him and placing two fingers on his carotid artery. A faint rhythmic beat said he was alive.

"Mr. Franconia?"

His eyes opened, barely focusing. "If you're here to kill me, get it done."

"I'm not here to kill anyone."

It was true, as far as it went.

Franconia tried to lick his lips, but he was only semiconscious and in obvious pain. Although his face was unmarred, his hands were shaking, his polo shirt soiled and askew, his pants muddied.

"Hang on," Rob said, rising. He checked the office door. Locked. "Libby? Are you in there?"

But there was no response, and he returned to Franconia, who'd managed to sit up a bit more.

"Can you talk?" Rob asked. "Tell me what happened."

Franconia couldn't seem to concentrate. "My wife—Star—"

"Maggie Spencer's with her. Do you know how long you've been in here?"

"Minutes. I don't know. There was a man. . . ."

"White hair? Looks like an old drunk?"

His eyes flickered. "Yes."

"Did he do this to you?"

A feeble smile. "Christ, I hope not."

Rob didn't blame the guy for wanting his assailant to be tougher-looking and appreciated his humor under stress.

"I—I was hit from behind," Andrew went on. "It felt like a baseball bat."

Someone had been busy. Star? Libby? Had Raleigh pulled a fast one and faked an injury? But Rob didn't believe Raleigh had locked him in the wine cellar or taken a baseball bat to Andrew Franconia. Someone had been hiding, waiting for the right moment to pounce.

Andrew was very pale, shivering now.

Rob noticed a handful of dusty wine bottles in the racks. "I wonder if the wine in these bottles is any good."

His host coughed and moaned, tears of pain more than anguish streaming down his face.

The man needed a doctor.

"Well," Rob said, "wine or no wine, I don't intend to stay locked up for long."

When Maggie reached the kitchen, she found the colander of blueberries in the sink and a radio on, tuned to news on a public station. But there was no Star. The radio hadn't been on earlier—she must have returned to the kitchen and turned it on, perhaps to settle her nerves, beat back her worries and racing thoughts.

Where was she now?

Maggie checked Libby Smith's first-floor suite, knocking softly on the door. "Libby? It's Maggie Spencer. Are you in there?"

But there was no answer. The door was locked.

It was as if the sprawling house had suddenly spit out all its people. Star and Andrew weren't around. Libby wasn't around. There were no other guests. As she returned to the kitchen, Maggie noticed that her footsteps echoed on the wood floor, underscoring the emptiness of the place.

She decided to check the cellar, wondering if Libby was down there working on the inventory of her antiques. But the stairwell light wasn't on—not a promising sign.

As she started to shut the door, Maggie heard a sound from the cellar. Muffled, perhaps just a breeze catching a door.

Had someone left the outside cellar door open? Gone out that way?

For all she knew, the inn had ghosts.

She switched on the light—the Franconias' renovations didn't extend to high-wattage bulbs and fancy stairwell lights—and ventured down the steep, old stairs.

The air was cooler, drier, and with the dehumidifier off, the silence was almost complete.

"Star? Libby?" Maggie called. "Anyone down here? Rob?"

No response.

She'd never been one for strange sounds in dark cellars.

She paused at the bottom of the steps, listening, but there was still no repeat of whatever she'd heard—or imagined—a few minutes ago.

It was a large cellar, with old parts and new parts and too many doors and nooks for her to remember the exact route of her informal tour with Libby and Rob. Maggie had been far more interested in the history of the house, how weird it had to be—despite her cheerfulness—for Libby to be relegated to a small suite and odd jobs in her childhood home. That she was pulling together an antiques business was a rationalization. It had to sting to have lost a home that had been in her family for well over a century.

She'd been in Prague.

She'd arranged for the Franconias to sell Maggie's father a vase a few months before he was killed.

She lived at the same inn Char Brooker had visited a month before her murder—the same inn Raleigh had found information about in Tom's apartment the day before *he* was murdered.

As she turned a corner, Maggie noticed an arc of light up ahead. Daylight, she thought. Then someone *had* left the outer door open.

"Anyone down here? Hello? It's Maggie Spencer."

Again there was no answer.

She continued toward the light, recalling that the outer door was near the old wine cellar. The door to Libby's storage room was unlocked, slightly ajar. Maggie pushed it open wider and realized a dim light was on inside. She moved past the tumble of pieces Libby had collected, then came to a long antique table neatly stacked with books, files and photo albums. An apple crate on the floor was filled with dust cloths, lemon oil, window cleaner and miscellaneous supplies.

One of the albums was opened to old black-and-white photographs, a series taken in front of the fairy fountain—before it had its nose smashed with a wine bottle. All the photos were of a handsome man who had to be Libby's grandfather. He looked rich, well dressed and content. If he could see his farm now, he'd probably be pleased it was as beautiful as it was, but shocked to find it in the hands of nonfamily members who'd saved it from certain destruction after his son's years of neglect.

Next to the album was a little stack of pieces of a color photograph that someone had taken scissors to and hacked into five irregular chunks. Maggie put the pieces together, like a puzzle.

The photo was of Libby Smith and a glassy-eyed wreck of a man, red-faced and clearly drunk—obviously her father. She couldn't have been more than seventeen, smiling, her arm around his waist, probably holding him up for their picture.

They stood in front of the fairy statue, as if to emphasize that the son wasn't at all like the father.

Drawing her weapon, Maggie wove through the precariously stacked antiques to a half-open door in the corner of the small, windowless room.

"Maggie . . ."

William Raleigh crawled on his hands and knees out from the cover of ladder-back chairs stacked on top of a low wooden filing cabinet, all of them encrusted with dust and shrouded with cobwebs.

Maggie dropped down and put her arm around his thin waist. "Raleigh? What the hell is going on? Here, let me help you. Are you hurt?"

Blood dribbled out of the corners of his mouth.

Jesus.

"Libby," Maggie said. "Where is she?"

"I don't know. She's—"

He slumped, semiconscious.

"Damn, Raleigh. Don't die on me. I'll get you to a doctor."

"Her room . . . It's all there. . . ."

As if he were summoning his last shreds of strength, he lifted a hand and pointed to the doorway behind him.

Was Libby in there?

"Hang on, okay?" Maggie said. "I'll be right back."

Gun in hand, she ducked through the open door into a suffocatingly tiny room, windowless, a naked bulb providing scant light.

Libby Smith—or someone—was using

this closetlike room as some kind of work-
space. There was a second door on the opposite wall—locked. Remembering her tour,
Maggie realized it must lead to the adjoining wine cellar.

A laptop was open, powered up on a
worktable. A small desk lamp shone
brightly on manila file folders neatly laid in a
row. Pictures were tacked to corkboard on
the wall above the table. Maggie scanned
them quickly, her grip tightening on her
Glock.

One was of Charlene Brooker, serious,
confident, in her army captain's uniform. A
Polaroid shot, taken here in Ravenkill.

There was Raleigh, smoking a cigarette
on a European street.

Vladimir Samkevich in London.

And her father, smiling, his eyes crinkling
in that familiar way. It was winter wherever
he was. He wore a parka, was hatless and
gloveless, but Maggie didn't delude herself
into thinking he'd been missing her mother
in Boca.

Had there been something between him
and Libby Smith?

Before Libby killed him, Maggie thought,

knowing she was right—she had Raleigh's assassin.

She quashed any emotional reaction and hit the space bar on the laptop.

On the screen was a picture of Rob with President John Wesley Poe on the Dunnemores' dock on the Cumberland River in Night's Landing, Tennessee. They were holding fishing poles and grinning at the camera, belying any pretense that they weren't that close. The picture had run in most of the world's newspapers in the spring.

Maggie quickly scanned the rest of the claustrophobic room.

Boxes of ammunition.

Pistols.

And bomb-building supplies. Wires, timers, cords, plaster.

Gunpowder. Lighter fluid. Paint thinner.

Did Libby Smith plan to kill Rob?

The president of the United States?

Below their picture were three more pictures.

Rob's parents, Betsy and Stuart Dunnemore. Sarah Dunnemore. Nate Winter.

Does she plan to kill them all?

Maggie left everything where it was and

returned to the storage room, kneeling next to Raleigh, who was still. "How long have you known Libby's your assassin?" she asked him.

He was a little more lucid, but still in obvious pain.

"An hour, maybe. Less. I'm sorry. I've been so stupid."

"An antiques dealer who travels the world. Attractive, educated." Maggie's voice was tight, controlled. "What a cover."

Raleigh tried to pull himself up, but gave up, wincing as he wiped his bloody mouth with the back of his hand. "Janssen hired her to eliminate anyone who could take over his network or who might cut a deal with prosecutors in exchange for information." He spoke haltingly, but his words were clear. "It's all in that horror of a room. You have to find her, Maggie. You have to stop her before she kills anyone else."

Maggie nodded and helped him into a sitting position. He had no strength left, his arms flopping aimlessly.

"Did Libby do this to you?"

"I don't know why she didn't—" He swallowed painfully. "Like Tom."

Maggie understood what he was trying to say. He didn't know why Libby hadn't put a bullet in the back of his head.

"She must not want you dead from a bullet wound. Where is she now? Do you have any idea?"

He shook his head.

Maggie put her arm around his waist and flopped his arm over her shoulder, getting to her feet with him. "She's operating from her own agenda."

"She wants to take over Janssen's network."

"Not satisfied being his paid killer, is she?"

His eyes closed, his skin grayish now as he sank against her. "Leave me, Magster. I'll slow you down."

"I'm not leaving you."

"She'll kill Brooker. Dunnemore." His voice was weak, and although he was coherent, he sounded as if he was babbling. "They're next. Rob's parents. His sister."

"I know. Come on. Let's just keep moving."

Raleigh clutched her sleeve as if he'd suddenly remembered something. "Rob is down here. Libby—I don't know what she did with him—"

Hell. "I'll take care of it."

He rallied enough to move with her at a half run; she didn't have to drag or carry him. When they reached the yard, he collapsed onto the grassy slope down to the cellar door.

"Go," he said. "Find her. . . ."

Maggie nodded and ran back inside, drawing her gun.

Just past Libby's storage room, a cracking sound—a hiss—stopped her. *What the hell?*

Libby. Her bomb-making ingredients.

Maggie dived for the floor even as the blast from the homemade bomb sent her sprawling.

As she hit the concrete floor, she smelled smoke and chemicals. She heard the distinctive sound of a fire spreading.

"Rob!" she called, scrambling to her feet. "Where are you?"

Smoke oozed out of the storage room. She couldn't risk going back the way she'd come.

She had only one choice. To go up and get out that way.

Covering her mouth with her shirt, she stayed low, under the smoke, and hoped she remembered the route back to the stairs.

Nineteen

Jarred by the explosion, Rob smelled smoke and grabbed Franconia, dragging him to the hall door. "We're crisps if we don't get out of here. Don't move, okay? I'm going to shoot the lock and get us out of here."

"My wife—"

"We'll find her."

Standing to one side of the door, Rob fired twice across his chest, shattering the lock, splintering the wood around it. He helped Franconia to his feet.

Andrew's eyes rolled back in his head. "Star thinks I love my work more than her—"

"Nah. She knows better."

He moaned in agony when Rob pulled him into the hall, but at least it shut him up. The cellar was filling up with smoke. He could hear the crackle of flames, lightbulbs breaking with the heat. Staying low, he hoisted Franconia over his shoulder and ran toward the outer door. When they reached fresh air, Rob kept moving, looking for a tree, a bench, a statue—cover was a necessity when a killer was blowing up things and beating the hell out of people.

Where was Raleigh?

Maggie?

Rob dumped Franconia onto the grass in the shade of a red maple.

It was a damn fine day. A beautiful spot.

Smoke was pouring out the cellar door.

Andrew, coughing and spitting, rolling in the grass in agony, finally noticed, finally let it sink in that his place was on fire. "Christ," he said. "Oh, Christ. Goddamnit. What—" But he coughed again, sobbing in pain.

Rob knew he had to think. "If Raleigh didn't lock us in the wine cellar, who the hell did? If he's a good guy and you're a good guy and Star's a good guy and Maggie's a good guy—" He stared down at Franconia. "I think your pal Libby wants us dead."

"I'm dying."

"You're not dying. You just feel like you're dying."

Rob scanned the immediate area and spotted Raleigh prone on the slope about five yards away, and ran to him. "Maggie," Rob said. "Where is she?"

But Raleigh couldn't answer, could barely move, and Rob swore. Libby Smith had already beaten the hell out of two men. If she found them, she'd have two hostages.

Rob couldn't leave Raleigh and Franconia for her.

Maggie was on her own.

Quashing any panic—any sense of exhilaration—Libby focused on the task at hand.

She had to get out of the house before she ended up dead herself.

She was almost there, almost to the porch door.

Her first-floor suite was on fire. She'd set a second explosive device there. The cellar had to be fully engaged now. Investigators would figure out it was arson—she didn't have the time, or even the skills, to make the fire look like an accident.

But she hadn't used bullets or poison to kill Dunnemore and Raleigh or Andrew if he ended up dead, too. He and Star were stretched thin financially and emotionally—investigators would suspect them first. By the time the authorities got around to her, Libby thought, she'd be gone, working her way down Nick Janssen's target list, solidifying her own position.

She had a contingency plan of her own. A new identity—a new life—waiting for her.

All she had to do was get out of the goddamn house before she collapsed of smoke inhalation.

Star seemed to materialize in front of her. *What?*

Her arms were flapping at her sides, and she was screaming incoherently. Libby managed to make out "my house" and "Andrew."

Libby shoved her back out onto the porch. "Go," she said. "Get to the barn. Call 911. *Hurry.* I'll find Andrew."

With any luck, he was dead in the wine cellar with Rob Dunnemore.

"I can't—"

But Libby kept moving forward, all but pushing Star, in a panic, sputtering, down the porch steps to the stone path, repeating her instructions. *Barn. 911. Barn. 911.* She'd be out of the way. She wouldn't suspect Libby of any involvement in the fire—which would further delay the police from looking in her direction.

When they reached the barn, Libby promised again to find Andrew. Star nodded, white-faced, in shock.

Libby left her.

And she ran, heading for Ravenkill Creek and freedom.

Ethan charged up a narrow path toward the apple orchard and the Old Stone Hollow Inn, Deputy Longstreet a step behind him with her Glock in hand. Not for the first time in the past twenty-four hours, he wished he hadn't been so scrupulous about getting her into trouble and had scored a couple of guns for himself.

They'd been on their way down to Ravenkill Creek when they'd heard something in the distance—a crack, a rumble. Whatever it was, it wasn't normal.

Then they'd seen the black smoke rising above the trees.

"Christ," Juliet had breathed next to him. "What the hell's going on?"

Now they were on their way to find out.

Ethan wasn't accustomed to sneaking around places that were as posh as Ravenkill. His old haunts at West Point were just across the Hudson, but he hadn't been back there in years.

He wasn't law enforcement. He was military.

Or he had been. He didn't know what the hell he was now. Wanted by the marshals, probably. Juliet had made calls on the way up to Ravenkill, explaining what she was up to.

A cloud of mosquitoes followed them into the orchard. Juliet didn't seem to notice. She went at a loping run, finally overtaking him. Ethan's head was pounding. Given his injuries, he supposed he might not be moving as fast as he thought he was.

He could smell the smoke now. The ground was soft, the grass wet against his lower legs. Up ahead, the Old Stone Hollow Inn was on fire.

With her free hand Juliet pulled out her

cell phone and, as she and Ethan ran toward the burning house, called for reinforcement.

Star ran around in circles in front of the barn like a two-year-old having a tantrum, her arms flapping at her sides as she screamed. She had her portable phone clutched in one hand. Maggie caught the frightened woman by both arms and held them still. "Star. Get hold of yourself and listen to me."

"Andrew—"

"He's safe. He's with Rob. I just saw them." And Raleigh, half-dead, she thought; she'd waved to Rob that she was okay and had gone to grab Star, in hysterics by the barn. "Did you call 911?"

"No. I can't. My phone—" She squeezed her eyes shut, then flung the phone to the ground. "It's *dead*."

If he could get through, Rob would have called for help by now, but Maggie wasn't sure how much he knew—if he'd figured out for himself or if Raleigh had managed to tell him that Libby was their killer. She squeezed gently on Star's arms. "Listen to me, Star. Libby—"

"She's gone." Crying, Star withdrew one hand from Maggie's grasp and waved toward the cornfield and the apple orchard. "Running—she's scared—"

No, Maggie thought. *She's getting away.*

"I need to go after her," Maggie said, dropping Star's other hand, trying to penetrate the woman's fear and panic. "I want you to go stay with Rob. He's getting your husband and another man away from the fire. He'll see you coming—you'll be fine. You can help him."

The frenetic pacing and flapping stopped, and Star stared at Maggie, expressionless. "The marshal?" She seemed to struggle to stay focused on what she was saying. "He has Andrew?"

"Yes." Maggie touched Star gently on the shoulder. "Tell Rob I've gone after Libby Smith. Tell him she's our assassin."

"What?"

But Maggie knew Star had understood her. "Can you do that for me?"

She nodded.

"Libby's going to try to kill more people. She has a long list. Tell Rob he needs to get his family into protective custody." Maggie paused a moment, but Star didn't switch back into panic mode. "I've got to go before Libby gets too far ahead of me."

"I can do this," she said.

Maggie tried to smile. "I know you can."

She waited as long as she could to make sure Star was okay as she staggered down the stone path toward her burning inn. Then, staying within the cover of the trees as best she could, Maggie went after Libby Smith.

Nate was at home preparing for a noon meeting when Mike Rivera called with the news from Ravenkill, giving it in an efficient staccato that nonetheless relayed his urgency in no uncertain terms.

"Libby Smith hasn't had time to get to New York, never mind D.C.," Rivera said. "We'll catch her. But I thought you'd want to know."

That he and his future wife and her family were targets of a hired killer? Yeah. He wanted to know. "Rob?"

"Alive, last we heard."

After Rivera hung up, Nate walked across the lawn in the hot sunshine to the small dump that Sarah had carefully marked off for her archaeological dig. Some days she worked with college and high school students, showing them how it was done, teaching them about the history found in mundane objects—but, thankfully, not today.

When she looked up at him from her pile of dirt, her face transformed from eager welcome to concern and dread. "Where's Rob?"

In hell, Nate thought.

But it wasn't what he told Rob's twin sister. "He's fine right now, but you need to come inside."

"I've got work—"

"It can wait."

She remained calm, brushing off her overalls as she stood up, but Nate knew the realization that her brother was in danger— that she, potentially, was in danger—had hit her.

"My parents?" she asked.

"Mike Rivera just told me that two deputies from the Nashville office are on the way to Night's Landing."

"Nick Janssen? He wants us all dead?"

Nate nodded, and she took his hand and walked back across the lawn with him.

* * *

Rob grabbed Star before she collapsed and got her to the shade of a huge maple, where he'd managed to drag both injured men, well clear of the burning house. The roof was engulfed now. It would be a total loss.

Star was shaking badly, her skin cold to the touch, but she clawed at Rob. "My husband—"

"He's hurt, but I think he'll be all right. Ambulance is on the way."

Rob released her, and she sank beside Andrew, lowering her head to his chest and sobbing. He tried to stroke her hair, but he didn't have the energy, his arm falling to his side.

Star looked up at Rob, her eyes wide and sunken with shock and fear. "Agent Spencer's gone after Libby. Toward Ravenkill Creek."

Rob acknowledged Star's words with a nod.

"You're not going after her?"

"I can't leave you all here alone."

Raleigh stirred. "Give me a goddamn gun," he mumbled. "Or a kitchen knife. I can do a lot of damage with a kitchen knife."

Rob had to give the old guy credit. "Maggie can handle herself."

"I should have known it was Libby. Crazy bitch." He moaned softly, his color better than it was. "In my younger days—"

"You managed to keep her from beating Andrew to death with her baseball bat."

"Then she turned her damn bat on me," Raleigh said with a bit more energy. "Beat the living daylights out of me."

From what Rob had pieced together from the mutterings of the two semiconscious men, Andrew had realized Libby hadn't been around over the weekend and had checked the cellar, where she spent a lot of time, discovering a treasure trove of incriminating evidence. He and Star had prided themselves on respecting Libby's privacy and the fact that the inn had been in her family for so long.

Rob heard the blare of sirens. Star jumped, startled, shaking hard.

Raleigh sat up, blood on the side of his mouth from a cut lip, not, Rob thought, internal injuries. "Go after Maggie," he told Rob. "Don't leave her to that woman. Libby would kill Maggie the same way she'd kill a cockroach. Without hesitation, without remorse. You know she would. It's how she killed Tom Kopac."

Rob was tempted, but he knew he wasn't leaving Raleigh and the Franconias until help got there. Then he spotted Juliet and Brooker on the stone path and signaled to them. They waved, picking up their pace as they pounded through a flower bed and ducked under a low-hanging branch, then joined him in the shade.

Rob quickly filled them in.

"It's your call, Dunnemore," Juliet said. "Do you want to go after your DS agent and assassin or shall I?"

"I'll go."

She managed a wink. "Thought so."

But first he turned to Brooker. "Talk to Raleigh. Your wife stayed here a month before she was killed."

Brooker had no visible reaction. "I'm going with you."

"Uh-uh," Juliet said. "You've got a concussion, Brooker, and Dunnemore here's a triathlete. You'll just slow him down."

But Rob was already on his way.

Maggie ran through tall ferns and brush in the woods below the orchard and cornfield.

There was no path. She could hear the creek just below her, tumbling over rocks, almost drowning out the sounds of the sirens of the onslaught of fire trucks, ambulances and police cars.

The riverbank was steep, covered in slippery pine mulch and exposed tree roots, but she made sure she didn't trip. She couldn't risk giving Libby any advantage.

When she reached the river, Maggie stayed within the cover of a white pine as she scanned the banks.

The water, deeper here, was high from last night's rain, crashing over a mix of rounded and jagged gray boulders, forming a stretch of whitewater rapids.

Libby stood on a rock, maybe a yard into the river.

"Drop your weapon," Maggie called from behind her tree, her Glock trained on the assassin. Tom's killer. Her father's killer. "Do it now."

Without a word, Libby released her Beretta and let it fall into the water.

What the hell was she up to? Maggie stayed where she was. "Keep your hands up where I can see them."

Libby smiled in her direction. "You won't kill me. You want your answers."

And she stepped off her rock into the river, as if she were walking over a threshold. When she hit the water feetfirst, she went under, her arms flailing, but the current was too strong and dragged her downstream, smashing her against a boulder.

Maggie ran down to the water's edge, Libby a couple of yards into the river. Blood flowed down the right side of her face. She tried to hold on to the rock, but lost her grip and fell back into the water, going under again. She managed to lurch up and wrap both arms around another rock, only her head above the rapids.

"Hang on," Maggie called to her. "You'll drown if you try anything else."

She heard a thrashing sound behind her. Rob identified himself as he emerged from the woods and joined her on the riverbank, nodding toward the struggling killer. "She was trying to get to the other side of the river?"

"Apparently. She hit her head on a rock. I don't know how long she can hold on—"

"I'll get her."

Maggie shook her head. "She gets

money for killing you. She doesn't get a dime for me. Motivation."

"Shoot her if she tries anything." Rob jumped onto a boulder that jutted above water a yard into the creek. "That'll take care of her motivation."

"I don't know if she has another weapon on her—"

"Well, if she lets go of her rock to get it, she'll drown. Then we won't have to worry about her trying to shoot me."

And Maggie would use deadly force if it was called for.

But when he got to Libby, she tried to scoot away from him. Rob gave her a chop to the carotid artery with the side of his hand, a move that would render her unconscious for five or ten seconds—enough time for him to pull her out of the water and toss her over his shoulder.

By the time he made his way back to the riverbank with her, she was conscious. He dumped her onto the ground just in time for her to vomit into a bed of brown pine needles.

She looked so small and helpless, Maggie thought. Yet Libby Smith was a woman who killed people for money.

Rob got Libby's arms behind her back, cuffed her and checked her for any other weapons, but there were none. She sat up, blood pouring from the gash on her right temple.

Maggie still hadn't lowered her own weapon.

Rob eyed her. "It's okay, Maggie. We're good."

But she stared at the woman who'd killed her father and couldn't make herself move. "Did my father know what you were before you shot him?"

"Yes," Libby said calmly. "I was in the nick of time. He'd have told Raleigh. He'd have betrayed me."

"Maggie," Rob said.

She ignored him. "You weren't lovers."

Libby smiled, blood from her head wound seeping into her mouth, between her teeth. "Almost."

"And Tom—"

"I saw him before the Dutch police arrested Janssen and recognized him the next day when he showed up in Den Bosch."

"You were in Den Bosch to get your list of victims from Janssen?"

"Not victims," she said. "Targets."

Rob took a step toward Maggie, his clothes soaked with river water, stained with Libby Smith's blood, perhaps William Raleigh's blood. "Maggie, she wants you to kill her. She knows the party's over. Maggie—"

She lowered her Glock. "I'm okay. I'm not like her. I don't kill for pleasure."

Libby glared at her. "Neither do I. I kill for money."

"You didn't get paid for my father. Or for Tom."

"That was self-defense."

In a few minutes the police descended. Rob, relaxing now, gave a mock shiver. "The water's a hell of a lot colder up here than it is down home," he said, laying on his Southern accent.

Maggie stared at Libby as the local cops took her away. "She didn't get to kill you. We stopped her. Finally."

"Yeah. We stopped her." When Maggie made a move to start back up the river-bank, Rob touched her cheek. "I didn't like it when I thought you were dead."

She tried to smile. "I didn't like it when I thought I was dead, either."

* * *

Chief Deputy Mike Rivera arrived at the Old Stone Hollow Inn not long after the ambulances had left. The local police had cordoned off the entire property as a crime scene—including the car, complete with a ticket to Washington, D.C., and a New York license in a new name, that Libby had stashed on the other side of Ravenkill Creek. She'd lived in Ravenkill all her life— she knew all the places to hide things.

"Smith wouldn't have succeeded in killing your sister," Rivera said, plopping down next to Rob on a bench in front of the blunt-nosed fairy statue. "Nate would have stopped her."

"Nate was on Libby's target list, too."

"Then Sarah would have stopped her. You Dunnemores are a resourceful lot."

"Vengeance. That's the only reason Nick Janssen put our names on his damn list."

"He's not one to let bygones be bygones," Rivera acknowledged. "But we've got him now. He'll stand trial for murder."

The acrid smell of the burned house hung in the summer air. Incongruously, Rob's gaze landed on a sunflower, untouched by the violence that had gone on around it that morning.

Firefighters were still inside, making sure they'd gotten out the last of the flames.

"House is a goner," Rivera said.

"Libby wanted it that way, more than she even realized. It was still burning when the paramedics loaded her into the ambulance. She started laughing."

"Creepy." Rivera feigned a shudder, as if he hadn't heard it all before—the excuses, the reasons, for killing and maiming and setting houses on fire. "The Franconias can rebuild. They're a mess, those two. Clinging to each other, sobbing like a couple of teenagers about how much they love each other. I guess they got their priorities screwed up for a while." Rivera shrugged. "Happens."

"Where's Maggie?" Rob asked.

Rivera let the barest smile escape. "Bitching out Brooker for letting Raleigh sneak out of here."

"Longstreet was the one with the gun."

"She says he got away when Andrew Franconia started coughing up blood and she went to help him."

It was bullshit, and both men knew it. If

Juliet Longstreet hadn't decided to let William Raleigh go, he'd still be there.

"She's a pain in the ass lately," Rivera said. "PTSD. But you're all right? You look cold to me."

"I had a change of clothes. It's gone up in flames."

Rivera grunted. "Whose room? Yours or the DS agent's?"

For the first time in hours, Rob let himself laugh. But he didn't answer Rivera's question, just walked with the chief deputy out past the sunflowers and the herbs, to where Maggie Spencer was standing with the sun on her hair. She was all alone, which wasn't, Rob decided, really the way she liked it. But it was what she was used to.

He'd have to convince her there was another way.

Twenty

Maggie arrived back in the Netherlands on Friday morning. George Bremmerton met her at Schiphol himself.

He eyed her as she dragged her suitcase behind her. "You don't look so good, Spencer. Any other luggage?"

She shook her head. She'd bought a few things to replace what she'd lost in the fire. Sarah Dunnemore, as beautiful as her twin brother was handsome, had flown to New York to check on her marshal brother and insisted on taking Maggie shopping in New York, somehow talking her into buying fuchsia shoes and a ridiculously expensive nightgown.

"Anything happen while I was in the air?" she asked, trying to stop thinking about the Dunnemores—but she'd been trying for hours.

"No." Bremmerton gave her a grudging smile. "Somehow we all managed with you out of commission for seven hours."

Her laugh sounded tired even to her.

"You got back here alive," her boss said. "That's what counts."

"I appreciate the thought, but Libby Smith kept meticulous records that all went up in smoke. I should have grabbed her laptop, at least."

"You did fine." He paused as they walked out to his car. "I'm just not sure I like having you come to William Raleigh's attention."

Maggie stopped. "Then you do know him."

He shrugged. "I know everyone."

As they continued to his car and she dumped her suitcase in his trunk, Maggie felt the same kind of uneasiness she'd felt the entire flight across the Atlantic—as if the other shoe was about to drop. As if Ravenkill was the beginning, not the end of what had been set into motion with the Janssen tip a week ago.

On their way to The Hague in the crush of Friday-morning traffic, Maggie sipped the last of the bottled water she'd had on the plane.

Finally she sank her head back against her seat and shut her eyes. "Raleigh told me he had contacts in Prague who notified him that Tom was asking questions about my father's death."

"Did he?"

She opened one eye and observed Bremmerton. "I don't think that's the whole story."

"Probably not."

"Goddamn it. There were no contacts in Prague who tipped him off." She had both eyes closed again but wasn't even close to relaxed. "It was you. You got in touch with him and told him to find out what Tom was up to."

But Bremmerton wasn't going any further. "You've had a hell of a week. You must be exhausted. Get some rest."

After he dropped her off at her apartment, Maggie unzipped her suitcase and dumped it out on her bed, wondering what had possessed her to buy pink shoes. Sarah Dunnemore's influence. She was so damn pretty, Maggie had felt compelled to go a little feminine.

But where the hell was she going to wear fuchsia sandals?

Her mind racing, Maggie checked her one orchid and was surprised to find it had revived in her absence. It was still alive after all.

She went down to the bakery and bought herself two soft white rolls and took them back up to her apartment. She had butter and *hagelslag.* She applied both liberally to one roll and sat in her tiny living room, thinking of Tom and Krispy Kreme dough-nuts and how and why he'd done what he'd done.

Ah, Tom.

He'd been to Den Bosch *before* Jans-sen's arrest. Libby had said she'd seen him there.

Had Tom e-mailed Maggie the tip about Janssen?

But why her? He knew everyone at the embassy—why not alert Bremmerton?

And why was Tom in Den Bosch in the first place?

Why had he chosen it for his Saturday meeting with Raleigh? Why go to the Binnendieze when they were meeting at the cathedral?

Maggie finished her bread and chocolate sprinkles and warned herself not to do serious thinking while she was jet-lagged and dehydrated from the long flight.

So she thought of Rob and his apartment in Brooklyn and how she'd stayed with him, and they'd made love. She wondered if he'd been thinking what she had—that it'd been a great fling, a temporary thing, of the moment . . . something they'd both needed and wanted and would look back on without regret.

But it wasn't what she *really* felt. It was what she told herself. She wanted to convince herself that she didn't care about Rob as much as she did.

After her lunch and shopping extravaganza with his twin sister, he took her to Central Park and showed her where he and Nate Winter had been shot four months ago.

Damn.

Adjusting to being back in The Hague, on her own, wasn't going to be that easy, Maggie thought, tearing open a dresser drawer. She pulled out fresh work clothes and peeled off her travel clothes, changed, then headed off into The Hague's picturesque streets.

How could anything be so right and so wrong at the same time as she and Rob were?

More serious thinking.

It wasn't to be done.

She remembered the excitement and energy she'd had in her first days in the Netherlands. Meeting legendary George Bremmerton. Tom.

Her serious mood wasn't going to abate and being at the embassy didn't help. After a couple of hours, George Bremmerton caught her and kicked her out.

She needed rest.

Time to calm her mind.

But even in the morning, after a solid night's sleep, two cups of coffee and more *hagelslag,* she couldn't push back the questions and the overwhelming sense that her life was at a crossroads.

She ducked into her Mini and drove out to Den Bosch on a Saturday morning as glorious as the one Tom Kopac had died on.

She parked in the shade and walked to the Binnendieze, stopping at the open fence and staring down at the shallow, ancient waterway. Tourists eagerly climbed onto the flat-bottomed boats, carrying on as usual, no matter that a coldly calculated murder had taken place here a week ago. But the killer had been caught. That, at least, had to provide them some reassurance—if even they were aware of the murdered diplomat, the solitary assassin.

"I bought us two tickets."

Maggie recognized the Southern accent, the mix of humor and charm in the male voice. She looked behind her, and for a moment thought the events of the past week—the emotions, the jet lag, the physical demands—had affected her mind.

Rob stood next to her along the fence. "You DS agents do tend to forget what we marshals are good at."

"Tracking fugitives. I'm not a fugitive. I'm—" She broke off and frowned at him. "How?"

"It wasn't easy. Yours isn't the only red

Mini in this country. I almost had my cab-driver follow an old woman and her dog."

She smiled. "You did not."

"Don't try to tell me you knew all along I was tailing you."

"I wouldn't want to bruise your marshal ego."

"You didn't know," he said. "Your mind's on figuring out what Tom Kopac was up to last Saturday."

She glanced at the river again and tried not to see Tom's body floating toward the dock, to hear the people screaming. "When did you get in?"

"This morning."

"So you haven't slept—"

Something sparked in his eyes. "I figure there's time for that. You want to see what we can do without alerting the Den Bosch police and getting them all pissed off?" He seemed relaxed, but Maggie knew he wasn't. He had the same questions she did. "Then we can do the boat tour."

She looked back down at the still water, longing, suddenly, for nothing more than normalcy in her life. But she'd rejected normalcy at every turn. And what was it, anyway? Her father had tried to discourage her

from a foreign service career not, she realized, because of the dedication and sacri-
fices and many rewards it offered her, but
because of the choices *he'd* made. He'd let
his work take over his life. He'd lost his family because of it.

Tom had never had a family.

But it didn't have to be that way. No one
was more dedicated to his work than
George Bremmerton, and he had a full, re-
warding family life.

Maggie winced at herself. How had her
mind gone off in *that* direction?

Because of Rob, she thought.

She shook off her rambling thoughts. "I
don't know if I can do the tour."

"I can always give the tickets away."

He needed a shave, but that only made
him sexier. And he wasn't armed—that had
to feel strange when he was standing yards
from a murder scene. Maggie moved away
from the fence. "I never saw Libby. I've replayed every moment of last Saturday a
hundred times. She must have acted fast
for us—for someone—not to have seen
her."

"She was brazen, that's for damn sure."

"But I can't see how she actually believed

she'd take over Janssen's network." Maggie sighed, listening to the tour boat on the river below them, the guide explaining, in Dutch, what they were seeing. "Presumably Libby was in Den Bosch to get her target list from Janssen, but when did she get here? And Tom—why was *he* here last Thursday?"

"Your father was on to Libby months ago. Maybe Kopac was on to her, too."

Maggie pointed down the street toward the café where she'd spotted Tom last week. "I wonder if that's where Tom was when Libby saw him before Janssen was arrested. It's not far from where the police picked him up. He could have been drinking coffee, spying on him—"

"You think he sent you the tip," Rob said.

"Who else?" She started walking toward the café. "I just don't understand why."

Rob fell in beside her, naturally, without any protectiveness or posturing—he had nothing to prove. "Libby must have stayed around here somewhere."

"Not with Janssen at his safe house. That would have been too provocative."

They found a small hotel around the corner from the café. It had its own café, a scatter of tables on the sidewalk. A good-looking kid of about twenty was working both the front desk and the café. He spoke halting English, but recognized the description of Libby Smith.

"She was here last week," he said, filling two small cups with strong espresso.

"Did you see another American—a man?" Maggie asked.

"He asked for her. Mrs. Smith. Like you."

The clerk seemed not to make any connection between his American and the American who'd ended up in the Binnendieze, never mind that Tom's picture must have been flashed on Dutch television and appeared in every Dutch newspaper.

Of course, Maggie thought, he could simply have decided not to get involved in a murder investigation if he didn't have to.

But he was struggling with his English to continue what he had to say, and Rob stepped in with his seven languages. In two seconds they were speaking French. Maggie, whose French was respectable but didn't roll off her tongue the way it did theirs, followed along haltingly.

The American had left a package at the

hotel Saturday morning and asked the clerk to hold on to it.

He delivered his two coffees, then came back and plucked the package from behind the counter. It was a large yellow envelope both clasped and taped shut, with no writing on the front or the back.

"I give to you?" he asked tentatively.

Maggie smiled at him and showed him her badge. "It's fine. Thank you."

He handed over the package. He didn't even seem that curious about its contents or why the American hadn't returned for it. Employing all his natural charm, Rob asked the young Dutchman if they could have coffee. He pointed them to a small outdoor table.

Maggie sat facing the sunlit street and placed the package on the table. "I don't know if I should open it."

"The desk clerk says Tom left it right after Libby came down from her room. He followed her out and never came back."

"Did she?"

"Yes, but he didn't give her the package. He was waiting for her to ask for it. Then she checked out."

"The police—"

"I asked. The kid says the police haven't talked to him."

The young clerk walked toward them with two cups and saucers.

"Did he know about Tom's murder?" Maggie asked.

"He's pretending it never occurred to him the package and the two Americans he saw here that morning had anything to do with it."

"It's understandable. I wanted to think Ravenkill had nothing to do with it. I'm sure he's nervous. Think he's calling the local police?"

Rob gave a small smile. "I would."

The clerk delivered the coffees and withdrew without a word.

Maggie tapped the package with her fingertips. "It could be argued Tom meant whatever's in here for me."

"It could be argued he meant it's evidence in a murder investigation."

"It's been sitting behind the desk here for a week. We don't even know for sure it's Tom's, never mind whether or not someone's tampered with it. What if it's tourist brochures on Den Bosch?"

"You're going to open it," Rob said.

"As our friend Raleigh says, sometimes you have to break the dishes."

"Finders keepers?"

She frowned at him. "What would you do?"

"Me? I'd have been into the thing by now."

Maggie peeled off the tape and unfastened the clasp, then carefully pulled out the contents of the envelope. There were four or five separate paper-clipped stacks of papers and photographs, she realized, all held together, in Tom's typical meticulous fashion, with a larger paper clip and a fat rubber band.

On top of the first batch was the printout of the Old Stone Hollow Inn's Web site home page. "No wonder the police didn't find it in his apartment," Maggie said, pulling off the rubber band and paper clip.

The rest of the paper-clipped stacks appeared to be in chronological order, beginning with two days after Maggie's arrival in The Hague.

It was a journal entry, handwritten on pedestrian yellow lined paper. Leave it to Tom not to trust a computer, she thought, her throat tightening, his precise, easy-to-read handwriting making her feel his presence, the loss of a good man. She scanned his words.

Maggie Spencer has no idea that her father and I were friends. We met ten years ago in South Asia and stayed in touch. As different as we were, we got along. He stopped by The Hague on his way to New York a few weeks before he was killed—he was flying out of Schiphol, said he was off to check out some antiques shop in Ravenkill, New York. I had the feeling a woman was involved.

"Maggie?"

She looked up from the paper and realized she had tears in her eyes. "I'm okay."

"We can pack up and head to the embassy—"

She shook her head. "Another minute. I won't read every word."

In that same matter-of-fact style, Tom explained how surprised he was to realize that her father's trip to the States hadn't included a visit with his daughter—it turned out to be their last opportunity to see each other. Shortly after he returned to Prague, he was killed. Tom had felt guilty for not tearing himself away from his work to attend his longtime friend's funeral.

He'd started asking questions. Researching his friend's death. At first, curiosity drove him. Then concern. Other entries detailed how he'd checked out Ravenkill and figured out that Philip Spencer had developed an apparent interest in antiques.

But Tom didn't believe it.

He found out about the Old Stone Hollow Inn and Libby Smith and the Franconias and put the word out to a few people he knew to alert him if their names popped up. He didn't identify his sources in his log. He indicated that he believed his friend Philip Spencer had gone to Ravenkill after Libby. Andrew and Star were in Prague—but that he'd never stayed at the inn. On Wednesday, the day before Nick Janssen's arrest, one of Tom's sources tipped him off that Libby had arrived in the Netherlands and was staying in Den Bosch.

Maggie made herself look up from her reading. Her steaming coffee was untouched at her elbow, but Rob was sipping his. "You're polite," she said. "You're not reading over my shoulder."

"Your hands are shaking."

"Just what I need then, sugar and caffeine." She tried to smile but couldn't pull it off, and he wasn't smiling, either. She pushed that first stack of papers across the table. "Here. Have at it."

But he kept his gaze on her. "Your father—"

"He had his own life. It was a good one. He made his choices."

"He didn't choose to be killed."

Maggie wasn't shocked at Rob's blunt words. They were what she needed. She picked up her coffee, took a sip and focused on the beautiful day. The cars, the bicyclists, fellow travelers stopping for coffee and a bite to eat.

"I don't think I could have done this right after his death," she said. "And Tom . . . he was killed because he and my father were friends."

"He was killed because a ruthless woman didn't want to be found out."

Rob's tone was kind without being patronizing or condescending. "He was a seasoned foreign service officer, Maggie. He knew the score."

"He came out to Den Bosch looking for an antiques dealer who might know something and found an international fugitive and a killer." She pulled off the paper clip and blank cover sheet to another stack. "Jesus."

She held up a photograph of Nick Janssen and Libby Smith together on a bench overlooking the Binnendieze.

Maggie read another of Tom's journal-type entries. Rob came around the table and stood over her reading along with her. "Tom thought Libby might be an undercover agent," she said almost to herself. "Someone my father worked with before his death."

"An intelligence operative posing as an antiques dealer," Rob said. "He was afraid of mucking things up."

"Poor Tom. He sent me the tip because he figured I'd handle it—I'd know if we really wanted the Dutch police to pick Janssen up, or if Libby was an undercover agent—"

"He didn't mention her in his e-mail."

"He wouldn't have risked it. He gave me

the chance to ignore it if he was stepping into something—if my father had stepped into something—"

"He wasn't just covering his own butt and trying not to compromise an investigation. He was protecting you."

Maggie quickly shoved the papers and photos back into the envelope.

Rob was still beside her. "That bothers you, doesn't it? Having someone looking after you."

"It's not what I'm used to, and look what happened—"

"Kopac knew your father had been murdered. He went into this thing with his eyes wide open, Maggie," Rob said softly. "Give him credit for that."

She reclasped the envelope. Tom had said he'd keep Janssen put for an hour—he must have planned to intercede if necessary, chat him up about the boat tour, or maybe Krispy Kremes. He'd given Maggie every opportunity to do her thing.

She'd called in George Bremmerton and set Janssen's arrest in motion.

Because of Tom, Nick Janssen and Libby Smith both were in custody.

Maggie didn't need to read the explanation of what Tom had done that Saturday. He had his package of information to give to William Raleigh, but he'd stopped at Libby's hotel just to reassure himself she wasn't an innocent caught up in events out of her control.

Maggie made herself focus on her surroundings. A young couple sat at a table in the sun, their bicycles nearby. Life in Den Bosch, back to normal. But it wasn't as if people were pretending a murder hadn't taken place there, or a notorious fugitive hadn't had a safe house on its pretty shaded streets—it wasn't callousness or denial that had the locals back on the Binnendieze.

Maybe there was just a desire to get out on a pretty summer day.

"I should have pushed for more answers months ago," she said.

Rob shook his head. "Don't do that to yourself."

His words were without bitterness, but Maggie felt their impact in her gut, knew he wasn't talking just about the past week. "You think you should have pushed harder to find out what was going on in the spring. That's what haunts you. Your mother, your sister—Janssen hates them now because he didn't get his pardon. Hell, Rob. You were almost killed yourself."

He didn't answer, and looked at him across the table, taking in the blue-flecked gray eyes, the fair hair, the good looks. They could mislead, make people think he'd never suffered, he'd never had problems and obstacles—and that he wasn't meant for the work he did.

He pushed aside his coffee. "I tell myself that all we can do is get up in the morning and do the best we can."

"Are there days you believe it?"

He smiled. "Some."

"Mistakes—" Maggie managed a quick smile. "I don't like making mistakes."

She nibbled on the cookie that came with her coffee, realizing she was neither hungry nor not hungry. Her body didn't know what time it was. And she could see her father, blue eyes crinkled as he laughed, as he promised her there'd be time—years and years—when he'd be in a rocking chair and they could spend all the time they wanted together.

"Did you really take a cab over here?" she asked Rob suddenly.

"What?"

And she had him. She knew she did. "Come on, Dunnemore. Who gave you a ride?"

He smiled mysteriously and got to his feet. "Let's go offer up a prayer."

A prayer . . .

St. John's.

William Raleigh.

They found the old spook with his arms sprawled over the back of a middle pew in the massive cathedral. He was cleaned up, dressed in neat olive-green pants and a navy polo shirt. He'd put on a pair of loafers, although Rob thought they looked tight. The man had dedicated his life to public service, secret battles, putting his own life and even the lives of the people he cared about at risk. Rob had no intention of judging him. Raleigh had endured private losses that he could share with very few people.

The death of Maggie's father was one of those losses.

She sat next to him, and Rob sat next to her. She still clutched Kopac's envelope.

"You and Rob were on the same flight back to Amsterdam?"

"Coincidentally, yes."

"I doubt there's much in your life that's a coincidence."

He glanced at her, his eyes no longer as pain-racked. "Or yours."

"Shouldn't you be in a hospital?"

"Nothing's wrong with me that several thousand milligrams of ibuprofen won't cure. Libby's probably wishing now that she'd killed me when she had the chance."

"She tried. She just didn't want to use bullets."

"Apparently her father was a self-centered, incorrigible drunk. It's a terrible way to grow up. He never got a grip on his alcoholism. But it's not the reason she became a killer."

"Are rumors of your drinking problems fact or fiction?" Maggie asked without judgment.

"A fiction, at least for the most part. But I knew how to play it. My own father was an alcoholic. He died in a bar fight when I was in my early twenties. There's no question his drinking had an effect on me. I just refuse to use it as an excuse."

"Raleigh—"

He smiled sideways at her. "William. Remember, it's not Bill, Will or Willie. We were a very correct family, despite my father's alcoholism. We all knew our lines. It's strange," he went on, turning away from Maggie. "No matter their failings, we always seem to say goodbye to our fathers too soon."

"My father's death wasn't your fault. Neither were his shortcomings as a father."

"I was on to Libby. I *knew* we had a new killer at work—someone both reckless and ruthless. Phil and I had tapped into the outer fringes of the Janssen network."

"Samkevich?"

Raleigh smiled, obviously pleased. "Very good. Yes, Samkevich. He gave Libby her first jobs."

"How long had she been at work at that point?"

"Months. No more than a year. Samkevich still was testing her."

"What about Charlene Brooker?"

He looked pained. "She was interested in Samkevich herself. She took the bit in her teeth after your father was killed. She focused on Samkevich and Janssen. I focused on our emerging assassin." He paused, letting his arms drop from the back of the pew. "It was a difficult time. We had very little to go on. In essence, we were stumbling around in the dark."

Rob remembered that Captain Brooker had told everyone she was going to Amsterdam for a vacation, not to track Nick Janssen. But he was staying out of this conversation, sensing where it might lead.

"How did Char Brooker end up in Ravenkill? Did she discover that my father had been there?"

"I'm not positive, but I don't think so. I didn't know, either. It looks as if she'd discovered a connection between Libby and Vlad Samkevich and was checking it out—"

"One doesn't expect to find a paid killer in such a beautiful spot as Ravenkill, New York," Maggie cut in. "She was there a month before she was killed. But it was Janssen who ordered her murder and hired one of his men to do the job—not Libby."

"Things must have unraveled quickly for Captain Brooker." Raleigh sighed heavily, his regret palpable. "I wish I'd had half the instincts she or your father had."

But Philip Spencer and Charlene Brooker

were dead, Rob thought; William Raleigh was in a Dutch cathedral, trying to learn to live with his mistakes.

"American investigators have permission now to interview Janssen in prison," Rob said. "He's crying foul over Libby's arrest. There's no such thing as assassin-client privilege. But she's not talking."

"She might as well talk," Raleigh said. "Janssen will find a way to have her killed no matter what she does. Why not tell her story?"

"Why not tell yours?" Maggie asked him quietly.

He gave her a dry smile. "Write my memoirs in my retirement?"

She smiled in return.

"Nick Janssen wants to see where his mother was buried," Raleigh went on. "She died last winter while he was on the lam. He wants to put flowers on her grave. It's something we can use."

Rob felt his stomach twist, and Maggie arched an eyebrow at her father's friend. "We?"

Raleigh shrugged. "The collective we're-all-in-this-together we."

"Right," she said dubiously.

"You're born to do this work, Maggie." The old spook faced the front of the cathedral and didn't look at her. "Your father knew it. Your mother knows it."

"My mother . . ." But Maggie didn't go on.

"She has more courage than you know. It takes courage to paint, to express yourself that way and put it out there for others to see and comment on. She found a way to live with who Phil was, who you are."

"She and my father were divorced."

"But he was still a part of her life."

Rob wondered if he should go for a walk, but Maggie seemed to sense his awkwardness—in restlessness—and took his hand. "I like my work in diplomatic security," she said.

"Rob likes his work in the Marshals Service." Raleigh turned and looked across Maggie at him. "Don't you, Rob?"

"Yes."

Raleigh inhaled through his nose and rose stiffly, the lingering pain of his injuries obvious. However much he wanted to pretend otherwise, he had suffered at the hands of the assassin he'd chased for months. "It's quite a cathedral, isn't it? It makes me wonder what would be here today if people over the centuries hadn't stepped up and done what they could." He glanced down at Rob and Maggie. "You'll find your way out of here?"

"No problem," Rob said. "You okay? Not going to collapse on us?"

"Libby's more efficient with her Beretta than with her baseball bat, but she still managed to bruise the hell out of me." He withdrew a bottle of ibuprofen from his pants pocket and rattled it, smiling. "I'm due another dose. I'll see you two around."

Rob would bet on it.

Maggie watched Raleigh make his way out of the pew into the aisle. "He'll go on awhile longer," she said, "but it won't be forever."

"I think a part of him wanted to die the other day."

"With his boots on." But she shifted to Rob, her hand still on his. "I suppose you want a ride back to your hotel?"

Suddenly he thought of her in his bed in his apartment in Brooklyn, pictured her in

the early-morning light. "I don't have a hotel."

She squeezed his hand. "Good."

A week after his escapade in Ravenkill,
Ethan showed up in northern Virginia for
fried apricot pies, prune cake or whatever
Sarah Dunnemore might have cooked up.
They'd shared a tough time in Night's Landing in the spring, and he'd cut out on her
when she'd been injured. Paramedics had
been on their way, but Ethan had never felt
entirely right about his conduct that day.

Sarah forgave him and showed him
around the historic Virginia house and her
archaeological dig—which he figured out
was an old dump—and served him pecan
pie on her shaded porch.

But he should have remembered she was
on her way to being married to a marshal
and was pals with the president, because
he soon found himself in the back of a black
sedan with tinted windows. Nate Winter
and an unsmiling woman in a dark skirt and
blazer were up front.

They secretly escorted him into a windowless room in a nondescript government
building somewhere in the suburbs.

Presently, John Wesley Poe joined them.

The unsmiling woman did the talking. "An American contractor has been kidnapped in Colombia by a team of Colombians and American mercenaries."

"And how is this my problem?" Ethan asked.

"You can identify the kidnapped American."

He leaned back in his chair, aware of Poe and Winter studying him, as if this was a test. "Can't you identify him?"

"Actually," the woman said, "no."

The other two registered no visible reaction to what the woman, who had yet to identify herself, had said. "What's your name?" Ethan asked her.

"I'm sorry. Mia O'Farrell. Dr. Mia O'Farrell."

She had long, straight dark hair pulled back off her face and probably wasn't more than thirty-five. "Doctor of what?"

"That's irrelevant."

"You made a point of telling me your name's *Dr.* Mia O'Farrell. I figured it was for a reason."

She kept her gaze steady on him. "No reason."

"Sure there is. You're trying to establish authority over me and get me to go fetch this American out of the clutches of whoever's got him."

"The American is important to us for reasons of national security," she said, not withering under his scrutiny.

"His name?"

O'Farrell didn't answer right away. Winter was staring at his hands, and Ethan knew if it was the marshal's call to make, he'd give the name.

But it was Poe, finally, who spoke. "This is a voluntary mission."

Ethan knew what that meant. "So its chances of success are slim to none."

Poe stood up and came around the table, clapping a hand on Ethan's shoulder. "It's voluntary," the president said, "but I could order you to do it. Technically, Major Brooker, I'm still your commander in chief."

Ethan scratched the side of his mouth. "Problems with my paperwork?"

"Serious problems."

"I was never good with paperwork."

Winter almost smiled. Dr. O'Farrell didn't come close.

Poe squeezed Ethan's shoulder. "I need an answer, Major."

Ethan thought of Juliet. Strange that he didn't think of Char. He'd been a guilt-ridden, grieving widower for months. But he'd done the best he could by her memory. He'd pushed and prodded and hounded, and at last he had answers. Vlad Samkevich was dead. Nick Janssen and Libby Smith were in prison. And Char had been on to all of them.

Now he had to find out who he was again.

"Yes, Mr. President, I accept the mission."

Twenty-One

Nate Winter and Sarah Dunnemore were married on a warm, overcast mid-September day in the sprawling yard of the Dunnemore family home in Night's Landing, Tennessee.

They were as beautiful and happy a couple as Maggie had ever seen, but a mosquito bit her and she thought she saw a snake.

It was her first trip back to the States since Ravenkill, which all, somehow, was becoming less a raw, open wound. Libby Smith was out of the hospital and had been denied bail as she faced prosecution. The media coverage had died down. Maggie had attended the memorial service for Tom Kopac at the embassy in The Hague, meeting friends who knew him better than she had and missed him terribly. But they'd laughed about his love of Krispy Kreme doughnuts, and they'd celebrated his life.

She walked out onto the dock that jutted out into the Cumberland River and kicked off her shoes, the fuchsia-colored ones she'd bought with Sarah in New York. The heels caught in the dock's many cracks and gaps.

She heard laughter and storytelling up toward the porch. Tents had been set up, tables spread with cobblers and fried apricot pies and casseroles and fancy hors d'oeuvres. Maggie hoped she hadn't been rude and stupid in accepting Nate and Sarah's invitation. Rob had stayed in The Hague with her for five days. They'd gone bicycle riding and sightseeing, and they'd finally done the Binnendieze boat tour—and they'd gone back to the Rijksmuseum, where Nick Janssen had approached Rob's mother back in April, trying to worm his way into her good graces.

Maggie remembered with a rush of

warmth how she and Rob had made love, but it didn't change the difficult logistics of their long-distance relationship.

Rob's parents were intelligent and gracious, and Nate had whispered to Maggie his theory that Betsy and Stuart Dunnemore really were wizards, making her laugh. The Winters were there: Nate's E.R. doctor sister, Antonia; his pregnant nature photographer sister, Carine; the crusty uncle who'd raised them after their parents had died on Cold Ridge. Antonia had her senator husband and their baby with her, but Carine's husband, an air force pararescueman, couldn't be there, since he'd been deployed overseas since early summer. Taking his absence in stride, Carine had tried to get a picture of Maggie's snake.

Gus Winter, the uncle, came alone, too. There was talk that he'd been seeing an ex-hippie named Moon Solaire, but she'd moved on to northern Maine and that was pretty much over. He was in his early fifties, a Vietnam vet and a mountain climber with the same build as his marshal nephew.

Maggie knew that Rob liked the Winters and was relieved his sister had married into such a tight-knit family. But Maggie had no trouble distinguishing the Cold Ridge Winters from the Night's Landing Dunnemores.

Juliet Longstreet didn't attend the wedding but apparently had sent the newly married couple a gallon of pure Vermont maple syrup.

Ethan Brooker had given them a song he'd written during his brief stay in Night's Landing.

John Wesley Poe joined Maggie on the dock. Secret Service agents were on the river, upstream and downstream. "You should dip your feet in the water," he said. "It's still warm this time of year."

"I don't know. Snakes—"

"The snakes will leave you alone."

"I like how you don't deny they're there."

"Well, they might be," he said, laying on his middle Tennessee accent, "or they might not be. But they don't have much interest in biting your feet. Trust me."

She had no idea what to say to him, but Rob, in his black tux, walked out onto the dock with them. Poe seemed to tense up, as if he might say or do something wrong, but Rob smiled at him. "Sarah's thrilled you came. Thanks for making it happen."

"My pleasure. I know it's a fuss to have me here—"

"We wouldn't have wanted it any other way."

It seemed to be enough for Poe. He relaxed, smiling at Maggie. "I'll leave you two alone. There's just one thing." He paused, but any awkwardness was gone now. Turning to Rob, he spoke. "I'm told William Raleigh has excellent instincts."

Rob smiled, but Maggie could sense his dread about what Wes Poe was about to say. "It's hard for me not to think of him as a head case."

"He wanted people to think that. It gave him room to maneuver. Agent Spencer?"

"Please call me Maggie." She'd never talked to a president before, but found Poe easy to be around, more so than she'd expected. "My father and Mr. Raleigh were friends. That gives him an edge in my mind."

"He says your father was one of the best."

Even with her security clearances as a DS agent, the details of whatever her father had done as an intelligence operative weren't for her to know. "I'm sure my father

would have said the same about Mr. Raleigh."

The corners of Poe's mouth twitched in
amusement. "He'll want you to call him
William."

She smiled back at the president. "Yes.
He's not a Bill, Will or Willie."

"He says we need people with your tal-
ent, your courage, your ethics." Turning to
Rob, Poe continued. "Maggie's *and* yours."

If Rob was taken aback, he didn't show it.
He shook his head. "Everyone knows who I
am."

"Because of me," Poe said. "Raleigh believes it can be an advantage. He was a bit
notorious after the death of Maggie's father—there were rumors Raleigh had
screwed up and dived into a bottle. He
looks like a heavy drinker. He used that to
his advantage and was able to sneak
around after Libby Smith and hook up with
Ethan Brooker without anyone realizing he
was up to anything."

Feeling as if the conversation was taking
a personal turn and not wanting to intrude,
Maggie sat on the dock and dipped her feet
in the Cumberland, snakes or no snakes. As
Poe had promised, the water was warm.

"Whatever you decide," the president said, still addressing Rob, "I want you to know you have my blessing."

"Do I?"

"I've known you wouldn't stay in the Marshals Service. I think all of us have always known."

Maggie glanced at Rob, who hadn't shifted his position; he was stiff, unbending, and she realized he'd been down this road before. He'd bucked a man who had become president. But the shooting in the spring—how close Nick Janssen had come to destroying his family—had given Rob pause. He didn't want to worry them. At the same time, he was who he was—which John Wesley Poe saw now and wanted to encourage.

"Sarah? My parents?" Rob shook his head again. "I won't have their blessing."

"You have options, Rob. Consider them all." Poe himself looked stiff now, as if he expected Rob to throw his support back in his face. "That goes for Maggie as well. Both of you."

"You're making assumptions about us—"

Poe smiled then, his eyes twinkling. "I don't know about that."

Maggie had to look away. The logistics of her relationship with Rob were difficult enough. If she chose to let Raleigh suck her into another line of work and Rob didn't want to follow her? Then what?

She kicked her feet in the slow-moving river, feeling the undercurrents of her own life tugging at her.

Rob didn't respond to Poe's comment, and the president sighed audibly. "Two years," he said. "If you and Maggie give us two years, then you can go back to doing whatever you want to do."

"What if Maggie doesn't want—"

"She does," Poe said. "Bremmerton, Raleigh—they insist she does."

She placed her hands behind her on the old dock and leaned back, looking up at the two men. "Maybe Rob and I need to talk, Mr. President."

"Of course." Poe looked at her, then at Rob. "We need you two. *I* need you."

He started off the dock, but Rob raked a hand through his hair and gave a small grunt of frustration. "Wes . . . Jesus. I didn't expect any of this. Thank you." When Poe turned back to him, Rob smiled at his old friend. "Thank you for everything."

Poe nodded without comment, and he left, Secret Service agents falling in around him.

Maggie focused on the murky water. She could hear someone singing, people laughing up on the porch. Rob sat down next to her, handsome—sexy—in his black tux. "Is the tux rented?" she asked. "Because if it is, I won't throw you in the river. Damn. Why didn't you tell me Poe was going to be here?"

He shrugged. "It was a given that he was invited."

"I'm not used to having chitchats with the president, never mind deep conversations."

But Rob, she realized, was used to staying true to himself, even in the face of great authority. He'd bucked two very different but powerful forces in his life—his own father, a quiet, brilliant man, and Wes Poe, a self-made millionaire, Tennessee governor and now president, to become a marshal.

He took off his shoes and socks and rolled up his pant legs to his knees. "My mother bought me this tux for Wes's inaugural balls and parties after he was elected president. She thinks all men should own a tux."

"I ended up with fuchsia shoes because of your sister."

"You'd never know Sarah's happiest in her dump-digging clothes and my mother wears sensible shoes."

"They're both very smart," Maggie said.

"That they are." He dipped his feet into the water and ran his toes along her foot, raising warm goose bumps all over her. "They want to turn us into spooks, Maggie."

She angled him a look. "George Bremmerton warned me more or less, before I headed here."

"He knows everything and everyone, doesn't he?"

"Except Wes Poe. He says they've never met."

"Not yet, maybe. So this conversation wasn't a complete surprise for you?"

She gave him a knowing look. "It wasn't for you, either. You saw this coming."

He gazed out at the river and its limestone bluffs, the familiar scenes of his childhood. Night's Landing was home for him in a way no place ever would be for Maggie. Accepting Wes Poe's offer—his *challenge*—to serve wasn't the leap for her that it was for Rob. He patted her thigh. "Maggie, Maggie."

"I've complicated your life, haven't I? You never thought you'd get mixed up with the slightly repressed DS agent daughter of a murdered spy."

"Your mother paints flamingos. I never thought I'd fall for a woman whose mother paints flamingos."

"I gave one to Sarah and Nate for a wedding gift."

But Rob kissed her forehead and whispered, "Tell me you ever imagined yourself falling for someone who's practically family to the President of the United States."

"The Southern frat-boy stuff was weird enough for me."

He slipped his arm around her and pulled her close. "I want our children to come here and catch snakes and explore the caves, Maggie. I want them to go fishing and cook up fried pies and casseroles with Sarah and drink tea punch on the porch with my parents."

"That sounds perfect to me."

"I'm in love with you." He said it softly, so that only she could hear it. "What they're asking us to do—I'll say no if it means losing you."

"Here we are talking about kids when we haven't even . . . Rob, are you asking me to marry you?"

"I am. Two years as a couple of secret agents or whatever it is Wes, Raleigh and Bremmerton have cooked up for us. Then the rest is forever. What do you say?"

Maggie smiled. "I say yes."

For Brig. Stiner Gimbel
From Commander Philip DuVal

With affection!

Phil

11/15/97

MILITARY UNIFORMS IN AMERICA
VOLUME IV

THE MODERN ERA — FROM 1868

The Seal of the Company of Military Historians commemorates the founding of the United States Army. On June 14, 1775, the Continental Congress resolved "That six companies of expert riflemen be immediately raised in Pennsylvania, two in Maryland, and two in Virginia." These ". . . remarkably stout and hardy men, many of them exceeding six feet in height, clad in hunting shirts and armed with a rifle-barreled gun, a tomahawk . . . and a long knife . . ." were the first United States Regulars.

MILITARY UNIFORMS IN AMERICA
VOLUME IV

THE MODERN ERA — FROM 1868

The Company of Military Historians

John R. Elting and Michael McAfee, Editors

PRESIDIO PRESS

Since its founding in 1949, the Company of Military Historians has produced its *Military Uniforms in America* print series. Its more than 584 plates and their accompanying texts represent the work of many members of the Company whose voluntary research and artistic skill have made this series possible. Contributors to this volume include:

Artists

David C. Abbott

John C. Andrews

Walter H. Bradford

Jose M. Bueno

Donald A. Burgess

Milton Caniff

Frederick T. Chapman

Peter F. Copeland

R. Darby Erd

Joseph Hefter

Ralph Heinz

Don Hoseney

James S. Hutchins

Raymond S. Johnson

James T. Jones

Harry C. Larter, Jr.

Edwin S. Lewis

H. Charles McBarron, Jr.

John H. Magruder, III

Eric I. Manders

Robert J. Marrion

Donna Neary

Frederic E. Ray, Jr.

John P. Severin

Ronald E. Spicer

Barry E. Thompson

Frederick P. Todd

Authors

David C. Abbott

John C. Andrews

Orton Begner

Dale E. Biever

Harrison K. Bird, Jr.

Walter H. Bradford

Jose M. Bueno

Donald A. Burgess

Milton Caniff

Frederick T. Chapman

Gordon S. Chappell

Wayne A. Colwell

Peter F. Copeland

John R. Elting

R. Darby Erd

William K. Emerson

Benis M. Frank

Anthony M. Gero

Bert Goodrich

James Gregg, Jr.

Albert W. Haarmann

Alfred Hahn

Joseph Hefter

Ralph Heinz

Don Hoseney

James S. Hutchins

Raymond S. Johnson

Edward S. Jones

James T. Jones

Harry C. Larter, Jr.

Edwin S. Lewis

Eric I. Manders

Robert J. Marrion

H. Charles McBarron, Jr.

Fitzhugh McMaster

John H. Magruder, III

Philip G. Maples

Robert E. Mulligan

Donna Neary

Irwin C. Nye

Ernest J. Owen

Hayes Otoupalik

Kenneth H. Powers

Frederic E. Ray, Jr.

John P. Severin

James P. Simpson

George A. Snook

Ronald E. Spicer

Roger D. Sturcke

Jack L. Summers

D. Lyle Thoburn

Barry E. Thompson

James C. Tily

Frederick P. Todd

Roger Willock

Michael J. Winey

Published by Presidio Press
31 Pamaron Way, Novato, CA 94949

Library of Congress Cataloging-in-Publication Data
(Revised for vol. 4)

Military uniforms in America.

   Vols. 3-4 edited by John R. Elting and Michael J.
McAfee.
   Vols. 3-4 published in Novato, Calif.
   Includes bibliographical references and indexes.
   Contents: v. [1] The era of the American Revolution,
1755-1795 — v. 2. Years of growth, 1796-1851 — [etc.]
— vol. 4. The modern era, from 1868.
   1. Uniforms, Military — History.   2. United
States — Armed Forces — Uniforms — History.
I. Elting, John Robert.   II. McAfee, Michael J.
III. Company of Military Historians.

UC480.C6   1974   355.1'4'0973   74-21513
ISBN 0-89141-292-1 (v. 4)

Table of Contents

Preface

With the Civil War's ending, the United States faced the tasks of reconstructing its federal union, completing the conquest of its western territories, and reestablishing its international status. The first, being a matter of practical politics, was accomplished in comparatively short order; the second was muddled, and the third largely ignored. Our mighty armies and fleets dwindled into tiny collections of military antiquities; an Army that took unnecessary losses in its Indian campaigns because it seldom could muster strength enough to overawe hostile tribes without a fight, and a Navy considerably inferior to Chile's.

That same sad story has been repeated after all our major wars. The post-1918 Army lived on World War I's leavings of weapons, uniforms, and equipment, until the beginning of World War II. American troops went into Korea in 1950 armed and equipped with obsolescent, often malfunctioning World War II hand-me-downs. And it remains highly uncertain whether the present administration's attempt to make up for the post-Vietnam neglect of our Armed Forces can be maintained.

This problem has been compounded by the accelerating changes in weaponry that began in the mid-nineteenth century with the rapid industrialization of the Western World. The Civil War was the last one in which wooden warships and regiments of raw volunteers, armed alike with simple, easily produced weapons, could preserve the United States. Our first foreign war since 1815 came in 1898. Fortunately, our enemy was merely the ramshackle Kingdom of Spain, and the Danish-designed Krag-Jorgensen rifle and an assortment of new steel warships saw us through. Our subsequent suppression of the Philippine Insurrection and our border squabblings with Mexico were little more than extensions of our Indian Wars. World War I jerked us momentarily once again into the international arena, from which we escaped as soon as possible. In 1939, the U.S. Army did not have one combat-ready unit. Since then our history has been one of wars and rumors of wars.

Like the preceding three volumes of our series, the fourth volume of *Military Uniforms in America* contains sixty-four color plates and texts portraying military organizations that served in North America during 1868-1985, or North American organizations that served overseas during that same period. These have been selected for both historic importance and artistic merit from the more than 584 plates published by the Company of Military Historians since its founding in 1949. When necessary, the original plates and texts have been revised to include information discovered since their publication. Consequently, they are the most accurate and authoritative descriptions available today, based on up-to-date research by internationally recognized scholars.

These books, however, are far more than a collection of pictures. Though not intended as definitive military history, they contain information on military organization, uniforms, weapons, equipage, logistics, and campaigns that no other known military history of North America can equal. In this volume, plates and texts together recreate the soldiers, sailors, marines and airmen who served the United States in both peace and war, from the dusty trooper of the 1870's to today's Green Berets, and also their allies and their enemies.

Each subsection of this volume opens with a listing of the wars and major operations waged during the years it covers. Within the subsections organizations are arranged in the order: U.S. Army, State troops, U.S. Navy, U.S. Marine Corps, U.S. Air Force, Foreign troops. U.S. Army organizations are listed numerically within the categories of infantry, artillery, cavalry/armor, and other arms and services including the various transformations of the Army Air Service. State troops are listed alphabetically. All plates are dated. At the end of each text is the name of the artist who prepared the accompanying plate, followed by the name(s) of the author, or authors.

Besides their long-suffering wives, the Editors thank Company Administrator Major Wm. R. Reid and his secretary Ruth N. Weaver for their efficient logistical support and emergency typing of mangled drafts, and Governor William J. Kane for his assistance. Especially we thank Adele Horwitz and the staff at Presidio Press for patience, encouragement, and full cooperation.

John R. Elting
Michael J. McAfee

Cornwall-on-Hudson
December, 1986.

Introduction

The Regular Army which moved out after the Civil War to complete the winning of the West, and to preserve law and order in the former Confederate states, was hard put to maintain an imposing appearance. Having doubled its own pay, Congress felt the need for economy in the other branches of the United States government; also, the quartermaster depots held vast stores of leftover Civil War uniforms. Unfortunately, much of this clothing had been manufactured hurriedly out of low-grade materials with little attention to fit or appearance. Officers complained that it seemed to be designed solely for potbellied or goose-necked men; that the shoes and boots would fit only flat or splay-footed soldiers; and that everything frequently wore out well ahead of schedule.

As the Regulars had learned before the Civil War, the issue uniform was not particularly suited for campaigning in the Far West. Officers and men reclothed and re-equipped themselves with scant concern for uniform regulations, or even uniformity. Home made "thimble belts" replaced the rattling Ordnance cartridge boxes, leather britches and moccasins the regulation trousers and boots. Soldiers spent their own scant pay for comfortable slouch hats rather than wear the various unsuitable types of headgear developed by the swivel-chair warriors of the Quartermaster Department. Pursuing Apaches through Arizona's blistering tangles of mesas and canyons, they might strip to their drawers and undershirts.

This prolonged campaigning finally convinced even Congress and quartermasters that the Army's standard blue wool uniform would not suffice for all climates and all seasons. During the 1870's, troops in the northern states finally were equipped with buffalo-hide overcoats and leggings and muskrat-skin caps and gloves. By the 1880's, British-style sun helmets and white duck uniforms were regulation wear in the South.

Until 1872, American uniforms had been greatly influenced by French military styles. However, after France's defeat in the Franco-Prussian War (1870-1871), the United States adopted a version of Prussian style in its 1872 and 1881 dress uniforms, undoubtedly the showiest American Regulars ever have worn. Infantry and other foot troops paraded in spiked helmets; mounted troops flaunted plumes of the distinctive colors of their arms and services.

For campaigning in Cuba and Puerto Rico, the Quartermaster began supplying uniforms of drab-colored cotton cloth in imitation of the khaki field uniforms worn by British troops in tropic areas. It was a good deal of a struggle, the first uniforms being poorly made and of a variety of brownish shades. Later modifications would make them into smart and serviceable summer and tropical dress. Meanwhile, worldwide experience with powerful, long-range "magazine rifles" firing smokeless powder ammunition had emphasized the need for less conspicuous uniforms. In 1902 the United States replaced the blue wool service uniform with one of olive drab wool — the famous "OD."

It was an effective shade, if expensive to produce because of the variety of colors woven into it. (That same year the British adopted a somewhat similar "service drab" shade; the German Army did not don its famous "field gray" until 1910.) Brass buttons and insignia were replaced by bronze; boots, shoes, and leather equipment became brown instead of black. Dress uniforms, trimmed with the distinctive branch colors, were still blue, but their cut was considerably simplified, much to the relief of many impecunious officers. The proud helmets were replaced by squatty little visored caps that lacked any military aspect whatever.

The following years brought more changes: the familiar slouch hat with its fore-and-aft crease gave way to a stiff-brimmed OD "campaign hat" with the four quarters of its crown dimpled into a "Montana peak." (Enlisted men's hat brims rapidly took on definitely individual shapes, simply from their daily usage; you frequently could recognize another man from your outfit in dim light by the shape of his hat.) In 1910, the long-suffering infantry were crammed into "pegged" riding britches, which looked smart, but bound the leg. As an additional insult they were given "wrap leggings" (also called "spiral puttees") that had no virtue whatever except the fact they were easy to manufacture and therefore cheap. The blouse — whether khaki, OD, or blue — had a snug "choker" collar, which had to be carefully fitted, but was comforting in cold weather.

World War I changed more than the map of Europe. Enlisted men's dress blues vanished (more because of Congressional stinginess than any valid military reason), though some soldiers might buy them out of their own pockets for off-duty wear. Officers adopted the more dashing British styles, to include trench coats and the Sam Browne belt. By 1925 this copying of British dress included the change to a blouse with a civilian-style collar, which in turn necessitated the use of that especially useless and unmilitary item, the necktie. Washington's chairborne heroes had great difficulty in deciding whether it should be black, tan, or green, and whether the now-visible shirt should be white or tan. Officers' blouses gradually became more of a forest green, and their trousers or riding britches passed into shades of gray or beige, known as "pinks." In fact, during the late 1920s and the 1930s, officers' service uniforms tended to take on some of the free and easy aspect of the frontier Army a half century before. This was especially true of mounted units, in most of which you suited yourself as to your boots and britches. In winter, non-regulation sweaters or sheepskin vests could be worn under the short overcoats. (If higher authority were persnickety, you wore them under your OD shirt.) Regimental drill teams improvised special uniforms; one showhorse field artillery battery dyed OD caps and blouses bright-red and bleached OD britches white. Enlisted men might have special britches made up from old overcoats (Cavalry favored them sewn with yellow silk thread). Shirt collars and cuffs would be reinforced by an overall diamond-pattern stitching with OD thread to keep them smartly stiff.

Army aviation units always had required special flight uniforms; in the late 1930s the activation of armor and airborne divisions required new types of clothing. Britches gave way to straight-leg trousers; Sam Browne belts and riding boots vanished, along with the campaign hat. The World War I "overseas cap" (now somewhat better tailored) returned. Combat boots — and paratroopers' jump boots — replaced leggings. More gradually, suitable uniforms were designed for arctic and jungle service. One excellent new uniform item, the short "Ike jacket," was soon abolished — it did not look well on well-padded rear echelon types, and it required less material than the standard blouse, which deeply troubled patriotic Congressmen from states producing woolen cloth. There also was the problem of finding sufficiently attractive uniforms for the Armed Forces' increasing numbers of women.

Following World War II, the OD uniform was replaced by "Army green," in both winter and summer weights. With this, the Army's leather changed back from brown to black. Fatigue uniforms were increasingly used for training and combat; their development, including the camouflage patterns used today, deserves serious study. At the same time a universal type of dress blue uniform was revived for honor guards and bands.

American uniforms continue to evolve, sometimes to the puzzlement of old soldiers. Army shirts are now a pale, pale green; sweaters are now regulation wear; officers have odd-looking black raincoats that suggest a convocation of undertakers. Higher authority is troubling itself over the tendency of Armored Cavalry officers to wear spurs with dress blues. We trust that this same authority remains ignorant of the fact that artillery officers are wearing red socks.

Though the photographer had an increasing share in recording the evolution of American uniforms during this period, his equipment was not suitable for covering the action of the Indian Wars. This was done by artists such as Frederic Remington, who drew what he saw, and Charles Schreyvogel, who created authoritative-seeming paintings out of his imagination. Charles M. Russell did a few pictures of soldiers, and there were fairly competent minor artists such as Rufus F. Zogbaum and Thure Thulstrup. Their work continued through the Spanish-American War — the contrast between the clean-cut soldiers in their sketches and the stubble-faced scarecrows photographers recorded is sometimes obvious. By World War I the artist was definitely giving way to the photographer.

The plates in this volume have been produced through the entire history of the Company of Military Historians, from 1949 to the present. In sad consequence, a number of the artists who contributed to it — Frederick T. Chapman, Joseph Hefter, Harry C. Larter, John H. Magruder, Barry F. Thompson, and Frederick P. Todd — are now dead. This book, and the three previous volumes of this series, are their memorial.

Among the living contributors, first place again must go to H. Charles McBarron, dean of American military artists and authority on American uniforms. Ray Johnson, Darby Erd, Walter H. Bradford, and David Abbott are new artists who have shouldered the responsibility for maintaining the high quality of the Company's art work. Eric I. Manders not only serves the Company as an artist, but also in the difficult position of Graphics Editor for *Military Uniforms in America*. Donna Neary has achieved distinction as a painter of U.S. Marine Corps and English uniforms; Jose M. Bueno is the acknowledged authority on Spanish military dress. James T. Jones, Ronald E. Spicer, and Clyde Risley all are known for their meticulous work on military subjects, as is our retired London "bobby," Robert J. Marrion.

Unfortunately, the list of authors and co-authors who contributed to this volume is too long for individual recognition. All of them have done invaluable research and writing.

The fourth volume of *Military Uniforms in America* continues the Company of Military Historians' effort to foster public knowledge of and interest in the military history of the United States. We offer it in honor of this nation's fighting men who — despite the periods of public neglect, derision, and even hostility that this volume covers — have steadfastly done their duty.

John R. Elting
Michael J. McAfee

Cornwall-on-Hudson, New York
December, 1986.

THE INDIAN WARS, 1868-1892

*Campaigns against the Cheyenne, Arapahoe, Kiowa,
and Comanche Indians*

Modoc War

Campaigns against the Apache Indians

*Campaigns against the Northern Cheyenne
and Sioux Indians*

Nez Perce War

Bannock War

Campaign against the Ute Indians

War with Korea, 1871

7th U.S. Cavalry Regiment, 1876

We see in this plate some officers and men of the 7th U.S. Cavalry Regiment in the year which brought the outfit its greatest tragedy and its greatest fame — the year of the Little Big Horn battle.[1]

The corporal in the plate is a messenger from another company (troop), and it is his horse that stands just behind him and the captain. The corporal does not wear a carbine sling; instead he has strapped his carbine to the saddle by means of a leather loop atop the pommel. This method was practiced by some companies of the Seventh in the field during the mid 1870s. Other company commanders in the regiment forbade the device on the grounds that it was injurious to both weapon and saddle.

The corporal's light gray hat is of his own purchase. He wears a "hickory" shirt and an altered version of the obsolete nine-button frock coat, which the quartermasters were still issuing in an effort to use up the existing stock. The drawing of this coat is based on a first-rate photo made in 1877.

A short time ago National Park Service workers, excavating along the line of rifle pits on Reno Hill at the Custer Battlefield National Monument, came across the skeletons of several Seventh troopers, killed during the siege and buried there in unmarked graves. With one of the skeletons were nine brass buttons, evenly spaced from throat to waist and each bearing the letter "I" within the shield on the eagle's breast; even the hook and eye at the collar were found, right in place.[2]

The corporal's improvised cartridge belt represents one of the several methods used to carry pistol cartridges — here by means of a pendant loop, sometimes worn on the left side, sometimes on the right. The men's trousers are of the sky blue kersey mixture with canvas saddlepiece.

The captain's hat is a straw in one of the styles shown in contemporary photographs. He has on a regulation sack coat, trimmed with black braid. The lieutenant wears a regulation wide-brimmed folding hat ("the outrageous black hat") of genuine felt with its brim edged with black tape. The drawing is based upon an existing sample, once the property of Captain F. W. Benteen. All these items show the considerable latitude allowed in field dress, especially in the case of officers. Some preferred buckskins for campaign.

The navy blue shirt is based on one which belonged to General Custer himself and is now in Memorial Hall, Old Deerfield, Massachusetts. Such shirts were trimmed in many ways but the Custer shirt, judging from contemporary photographs of cavalry officers, is quite typical. I have indicated crossed sabers and the numeral "7," worked in silk, on the points of the collar, using a photograph as guide. The knife scabbard on the lieutenant's belt is of an Indian pattern and is decorated with brass tacks.

The first sergeant wears a wool felt issue campaign hat, black, with a very wide brim. It was equipped with hooks and eyes so that the brim could be worn hooked up. Judging from photographs, however, it was more usual to leave the brim drooping. His shirt is the old gray issue of the period.

The nose bag on the horse behind the captain is shown hanging from an off side pommel ring where it was often carried. One trooper in the background is adjusting his cinch with its blue woolen "buckle" girth, still regulation. He also has on a straw hat. The guidon bearer to the right, a sergeant, wears a navy blue shirt, then being issued on occasions along with the gray.

The picture does not show a particular company of the regiment. Each company did keep all its horses of a particular color, however, and most officers rode horses of the same color as their men. Trumpeters' mounts were gray in all companies.

James S. Hutchins

---

[1]See the author's "The Cavalry Campaign Outfit at the Little Big Horn," in *Military Collector & Historian*, VII, 91-101.
[2]This could have been a pleated M1872 blouse.

First Sergeant, Lieutenant, Captain and Corporal in field service clothing

7th U.S. Cavalry Regiment, 1876

10th U.S. Cavalry Regiment, 1896

In 1866 an "Act to Increase and Fix the Military Establishment of the United States," provided "that to the six regiments of cavalry now in service, there shall be added four regiments, two of which shall be composed of colored men." These latter two became the 9th and 10th Regiments of Cavalry of the Regular Army.[1]

Colonel B. H. Grierson was appointed to command the 10th Cavalry and, with one other officer, constituted the initial muster roll which bore the entry "Recruits required 1092." By July of 1867 the regiment mustered eight companies with an aggregate strength of 25 officers and 702 men. By October of the same year the regiment mustered its full complement of field and staff and twelve companies.[2]

As originally organized, the companies (designation changed to "troop" in 1881) were mounted as follows: A, B, C, D, E, G, I, and K, all bays; F, grays; H, blacks; L, sorrels (chestnuts); and M, mixed. The field and staff were also "mixed," while troop trumpeters, color party, and, when organized, the band were mounted on grays. Shortly after the Spanish-American War the mounts for the color party were changed to blacks which the regiment felt to be more in keeping with their name, "Buffalo Soldiers." Most of this information was obtained from Colonel T. A. Roberts and Colonel J. C. King, both U.S.A. Ret. Both officers served for many years with the Tenth.

The national standard had "10th Regiment U.S. Cavalry" embroidered in yellow silk block letters on the center (red) stripe. The regimental standard differed from the later pattern of 19 March 1890 in the bends of the upper and lower scrolls, in the foliated trim of the latter, in the details of the plumage and talons of the eagle, and in that the 1887 pattern included the word "regiment" on the lower scroll whereas that of 1890 did not.[3]

With the exception of the carbine sling (model 1874), the horse equipments and cavalry accoutrements shown were those adopted in 1885 pursuant to the recommendations of the Cavalry Equipment Board of 1884.[4] Some articles recommended by the boards of 1872 and 1874 survived the test of field service to the satisfaction of the cavalry arm and were continued unchanged. These included the gray saddle blanket with a yellow six-inch "US" in the center and three-inch yellow stripes, three inches from the ends.[5] The belt plate was still the model 1872 pattern (3.5 inches x 2.2 inches), a raised "US" within a raised oval and raised edges. The McKeever cartridge box, formerly experimental, was now standard, "only one box being worn by each trooper." The minor details of the bridle, such as buckles, width of straps, and the rosette with raised center and interlocking letters "USA," were unchanged.

Improvements adopted included the following: the Shoemaker bit with raised brass "US" bosses was standard; the McClellan saddle was built on a slightly thinner tree; the hooded stirrups were wider (five-and-one-half inches) and deeper (four-and-one-half inches); the girth was made of braided hair instead of blue webbing; the saber slings (fourteen inches and twenty-eight inches long) were riveted to modified Stuart attachments (single-slotted brass plates with suspension hooks and a spring catch); the pistol holster, worn on the right hip, would carry the Colt or the Schofield-Smith and Wesson revolver; the saber knot was fifteen-and-one-half inches long and its discarded tassel had been restored.

Halters and halter ties were not used at dress formations, but the thirty-inch coat straps could not be removed from the saddle (a leather "stop" was riveted ten inches from the buckle end) and were looped, wrapped, and buckled in the last hole.[6]

The arms were the revolver, the Model 1860 Cavalry saber, and the Model 1873 or Model 1884 Springfield carbine.

The buffalo "on a wreath of the colors" was adopted as the crest of the regimental coat of arms in recognition of the name "Buffalo Soldiers" bestowed by the Indians. Apparently this name was first used in the early 1870s during the Tenth's long (twenty years) service in the Southwest.[7] The regiment was reorganized in 1950 as the 510th Tank Battalion.

Harry C. Larter, Jr.

[1] Major Edward L. N. Glass, *The History of the Tenth Cavalry, 1866-1921*, Tucson, Arizona, 1921, 11.

[2] *Ibid.*, 13f.

[3] Specifications No. 286, QMG, 1890-1893, canceling those of 7 July 1886.

[4] General orders 73, AGO, 1 July 1885. See also General Orders 60, AGO, 1872, and "Report of Cav. Equip. Board 1874," published as Ordnance Memo in 1874.

[5] A different method of folding the saddle blanket brings the yellow stripe across the back and just under the rear of the saddle bars instead of along the lower edge on the off side as it was previously used.

[6] Colonel T. A. Roberts, to author.

[7] Glass, *op. cit.*, 19. Colonel Fairfax Downey, in his *Indian Fighting Army* (25), attributes the name to "their woolly hair and shaggy hide coats they wore on winter campaigns." The latter were actually made of buffalo hides.

10th U.S. Cavalry Regiment, 1896

Captain Crawford's Battalion of Apache Scouts, 1885-1886

The battalion of Apache Scouts commanded by Captain Emmett Crawford, 3rd Cavalry, was one of two such units organized by Brigadier General George Crook in the fall of 1885. The two units were to attempt to return a large group of Chiricahua and Warm Spring Apaches led by Geronimo to the reservation from which they had escaped the previous May. General Crook decided to employ Indians to catch Indians. Two companies of fifty Apache scouts each were enlisted at Fort Apache for a period of six months and placed under First Lieutenant M. P. Maus, 1st Infantry and Second Lieutenant W. E. Shipp, 10th Cavalry. These hundred White Mountain and Chiricahua Apaches were carefully chosen because they were mountain Indians familiar with the haunts of the hostiles, or "broncos." Surprise being absolutely necessary, other tribes and soldiers were excluded as lacking the skill and endurance required to outwit Geronimo's vigilant band.

Such names as Cooney, Cuso, Dutchy, Wassil, Kate-kahn, Chi-kiz-in, Nah-wah-zhe-tah, Good-e-na-ha, Loco, and Josh appeared on the muster rolls. Cooney and Cuso were short big-chested men with almost unlimited power of endurance; in their savage way they were honest and loyal as men could be and were splendid scouts. Dutchy was a known murderer, brutal and mean, but in many ways a valuable scout. Nah-wah-zhe-tah, or "Nosey," was a "great medicine man," which means that he was doctor, preacher, conjurer, and prophet all in one. Dressed in an old alpaca coat, ornamented with a pair of shoulder straps and a pair of cavalry officer's trousers much too long for his short legs, his first appearance was hardly in keeping with his solemn character and functions. He may have been something of a humbug, yet his influence was exercised for good and rendered the task of governing the wild scouts much easier. A Chiricahua, Noche by name, was sergeant major and performed the duties of leading guide and scout. This Indian had the unqualified admiration of his officers.

No attempt was made to give the Apaches the appearance of Regulars. The soldier's blouse, cotton drawers, a waist cloth (or breech clout), moccasins, and a red headband completed their normal uniform. Beneath their blouses, they wore collarless shirts of the type designed to have a detachable collar. These may have been Army issue or the "trade goods" variety. The former were white, while the latter might have been plain or enhanced by colored polka dots or stripes. When approaching hostiles, the Indian scouts frequently turned their blouses inside out so the grey linings might serve as camouflage; in action the blouse was apt to be discarded altogether. "Nosey" carried a sacred buckskin over his shoulder and before the scouts made contact with the hostiles, a medicine dance was held at which the Indians kneeled before the buckskin, kissing it as their weapons were blessed.

On the march, the Indians thoroughly understood their duties. The officers exercised a general supervision over their work, but no attempt was made to interfere. It appears that the officers and scouts could understand one another for ordinary purposes. In important talks, however, one of the white chiefs of scouts, Horn, interpreted from English to Spanish, and an old Mexican named Concepcion who had once been held captive by Apaches translated from Spanish to Apache.

Because the Indians tended to eat all their rations at once if they were issued in advance, the principal duty of the two white scouts was to supervise the daily issuance of rations. Upon making camp, the Apaches cooked their own food and established whatever security precautions were necessary without any direction from the officers. Each morning they would be ready to start before sunrise and, if circumstances permitted, they would scatter on foot in hunting parties, followed by the officers afoot or mounted on mules.

Three pack trains of forty-five mules each supported the expedition.[1]

Edwin S. Lewis
John H. Magruder, III

[1]This account is based upon two principal sources: Lieutenant W. E. Shipp, "Captain Crawford's Last Expedition," *Journal of the U.S. Cavalry Association,* 5(1892):343-361 and "A Campaign Against the Apaches" (Captain Maus' Narrative), *Personal Recollections & Observations of Gen. Nelson A. Miles,* New York, 1897, 450-471.

Apache Scouts   Company Officer   Sergeant Major of Scouts   White Scout

Captain Crawford's Battalion of Apache Scouts, 1885-6

United States Scouts, Campaign Uniform, 1890

This plate describes the scouts' guidons and undress uniform, as prescribed, along with the full-dress uniform, in Paragraph 6 of Circular No. 10, Headquarters of the Army, dated 11 August 1890.

Two guidons were specified:

> For occasions of ceremony: To be cut square, three feet five inches fly, two feet three inches on the lance; to be made of scarlet silk, trimmed with one and one-half inches long white silk fringe, in the center and on both sides of the guidon two crossed arrows, in the upper intersection the words (in semicircle) U.S. SCOUTS, the arrows to be made of white silk held in place by a needle work embroidery of appropriate width, letters to be embroidery, arrows eighteen inches in length, letters two inches, in the lower intersection of the arrows there should be the letter of the troop and the name of the department to which it belongs.
>
> Service guidon: Similar in every respect to the foregoing except that it shall be made of bunting and other suitable material, to be used on drills, marches, campaigns and all other service other than occasions of ceremony.

The service guidon is shown here.

Indian scouts were enlisted for six-month periods and while in service received the pay of cavalrymen. They also received an additional allowance of forty cents per day if they furnished their own horse and horse equipment. Their undress uniform was the same as that of the Regular cavalry, with the exceptions discussed below.

The overcoat was probably the unique article of clothing issued to the United States Scouts:

> To be made of Irish frieze, or imitation of that material of some dark color, to be cut ulster shape, large and full enough to cover all accoutrements; to reach within ten inches of the ground; to be closed in front with two rows of brass buttons; to be slit well up in the rear to admit the seat in the saddle; to be provided with warm hood of same material as the coat, lined with black Italian cloth, or other suitable material, made to button around the neck, under the collar, and large enough to cover the head; to be worn at night and in inclement weather; and each hip to have a horizontal slit covered with a flap, this for access to the revolver and ammunition. The coat to be lined throughout.

The dark blue shirt was the same as that issued to all enlisted men in the Army, with the exception of its collar, which was made deeper — two inches wide at the back and three and one-half inches at the front — to hold a neck handkerchief.

The hat ornament, shown here enlarged for detail, was "to be made of nickel or some white metal, three inches in length, the letters U.S.S. in the upper intersection." The hat cord was of white worsted cord with one strand of scarlet interwoven, terminating in a white worsted slide and two white tassels at the front. Chevrons were of white cloth piped with scarlet.

The mounted scout in the background is wearing the "canvas cap" as officially designated in specifications adopted 17 April 1884 for all troops:

> Material: To be made of six-ounce cotton duck, dyed brown, lined with light blanket cloth next to the duck, and with light colored cotton jean in the inside; to have two buttons on the cape to button at the throat, and one, vest size, brown "lasting" button on the top for finish. The visor and edges bound with three-quarter inch brown cotton tape.
>
> Style: Scull cap with extension, forming a cape reaching to the shoulders and meeting in front, covering the throat, and buttoning together with two buttons. A visor of the same material bound with three-quarter inch brown cotton tape sewed on the forehead (to be worn up or down as desired) and having hook and eye to fasten it when turned up.

In 1886, specifications were adopted improving the canvas cap by substituting scarlet wool flannel lining for the original cotton jean lining, thus making the cap still warmer.[1]

Many Indians continued to use their personal items after enlisting in the United States Scouts. The kneeling scout prefers moccasins and leggings to heavy cavalry boots; hanging from his waist is a quirt, such as was commonly used by Plains Indians. The scout wearing the five-button blouse carried his "Green River" knife with its brass-tack-decorated sheath under his cartridge belt. Hair wrappings of flannel or trade cloth were worn by Indians who kept their hair long. The mounted scout in the background must have believed that the warmth of his buffalo robe could not be given up when he enlisted in the white man's army.

This plate was prepared with the generous aid of Members John Hooper, Joe Shornak, and Don Heckaman; Company Fellows Gerald C. Stowe and J. Duncan Campbell; also Marvin Kivett of The Nebraska State Historical Society, and the Office of the Chief of Military History.

Don Hoseney

[1]Captain John F. Rodgers, Military Storekeeper, *Report of Operations of the Clothing Supply Branch for the Year Ending 30 June 1886*, QMG, 15 September 1886.

Service Guidon   *Campaign Uniform*   *Hat Ornament*

United States Scouts, 1890

5th Battalion (Colored), Connecticut National Guard, 1884-1890

The period of 1866 to 1890 saw the opportunities for black Americans to participate in both the Regular Army and the various state militias limited to segregated or separate but equal military units. In 1879, the state of Connecticut authorized the formation of an "Independent Battalion (Colored)" consisting of four companies, using the "Wilkins Battalion" as the nucleus of the new battalion.[1] On 26 February 1880, the Independent Battalion was redesignated the 5th Battalion (Colored), Connecticut National Guard.[2] In 1890, the battalion was reduced to two companies, Company A becoming the First Separate Company and Company B the Second Separate Company.[3] The Second was disbanded in 1896 and the First around 1899, although it was later revived in the early 1900s and was called into federal service for World War I on 3 July 1917.[4]

Between 1884 and 1886, the Connecticut National Guard standardized its uniforms along federal lines. By using the 1884 Connecticut regulations as a basis, plus photographs of the First and Second Separate Companies in the collection of the New Haven Afro-American Society, we were able to reconstruct the uniforms shown. Various reports of the Connecticut Adjutant General on the 5th Battalion from 1884 to 1890, along with photographs of other Connecticut National Guard units in this period were used to substantiate certain details.[5]

The basic dress uniform for enlisted men was "substantially the same color, cut and trimmings as the U.S. Army Uniform . . . and the new U.S. regulation helmet. . . ."[6] The 1884 Connecticut regulations called for a nine-button dark blue basque coat, single breasted with five-inch cuff slashes and four-inch collar tabs of white. The piping down the front of the coat, on the bottom of the collar, on the shoulder straps, skirt flaps, and belt loops was also white. Trousers were sky blue with a one-inch white cloth stripe for all ranks. Belts and shoes were black. White gloves were worn in full dress. Hat cords were called for in the 1884 regulations but at present it is not clear if the battalion was ever supplied with these cords.

The fatigue coat for enlisted men was a five-button dark blue blouse with shoulder straps having no piping. The forage cap was a plain dark blue chasseur patterned cap with the letter of the company, in white metal, on top and the number of the battalion, in gilt metal, over the visor.

McKeever accoutrements were used in the 1880s and into the early 1890s.[7] During this period, the 5th Battalion was armed with the Peabody rifle.[8]

The full-dress uniform for captains and lieutenants was a dark blue, double-breasted coat with seven buttons in each row and plain cuffs. Shoulder knots were of gold cord, Russian pattern, with white cloth pads embroidered with rank badges. Trousers were sky blue with a one-and-one-half-inch-wide white welted stripe on each leg. The sword belt was of four gold stripes interwoven with white on black enameled leather. The belt plate was of U.S. pattern. The U.S. pattern staff sword was carried in a nickel scabbard with a gold lace sword knot and tassel.

The officer's undress coat was a five-button sack coat with falling collar and shoulder straps. The forage cap was of chasseur pattern with gold embroidered crossed rifles on a dark blue background with the number of the battalion in silver over the visor.

The officer's overcoat was double-breasted and of dark blue material with black braid on the breast and braided rank knots on the sleeve. Officers wore their sword belt under the overcoat with their scabbard outside by means of a slit in the overcoat. Enlisted men's overcoats were single-breasted and of sky blue cloth with the cape lined with scarlet.

The authors wish to thank the New Haven Afro-American Society, Mr. E. Saunders, and President and Mrs. H. Bishop of the New Haven Colony Historical Society for their assistance on this plate.

Barry E. Thompson
Philip G. Maples
Anthony Gero

[1] "An Act Concerning the National Guard," approved 21 March 1879, *Annual Report of the Adjutant General of the State of Connecticut*, Hartford: Wiley, Waterman & Eaton, 1880, 79, 377-378; *Annual Report of the Adjutant General of the State of Connecticut*, New Hartford: N. H. Tuttle, 1881, 5, 22.

[2] General Order No. 2, 26 February 1880, A.G. *Report, State of Connecticut*, New Hartford: N. H. Tuttle, Printer, 1881, 82.

[3] General Order No. 5, 1 March 1890, A.G. *Report, State of Connecticut*, Hartford: Fowler & Mitler, 1891, 130.

[4] A.G. *Report, State of Connecticut*, Hartford: Case, Lockwood & Brainard Company, 1896, 59; Williams, Charles H., *Sidelights of Negro Soldiers*, Boston: Brimmer Company, 1923, 231; F. I. Scott, *Scott's Official History of the American Negro in the World War*, Special Assistant to the Secretary of War, 1919, 33.

[5] Uniform of the Connecticut National Guard, Article XXX, Regulations C.N.G., 1884, (General Order No. 18, A.G.O., Connecticut 1886), copy in the author's collection. Although the Connecticut uniform was "substantially" the same as the U.S. pattern, there were minor differences, as illustrated in this plate.

[6] A.G. *Report, State of Connecticut*, Hartford: Case, Lockwood & Brainard, 1887, 10-11.

[7] A.G. *Report, State of Connecticut, 1891*, 78 and A.G. *Report, State of Connecticut, 1894*, 112.

[8] A.G. *Report, State of Connecticut, 1885*, 4-5.

Corporal   Captain   First Sergeant   Private
Full Dress   Overcoat, Forage Cap   Fatigue Uniform

5th Battalion (Colored), Connecticut National Guard 1884-1890

10th Infantry Regiment, New York National Guard, 1870-1880

The 10th Infantry, NYSM, was organized in Albany, New York, on 29 December 1860, although its field and staff officers were not appointed until 27 May 1862. After President Lincoln's second call for troops, Ira W. Ainsworth, captain of one of its companies, was promoted to colonel and given orders on 21 September 1862 to recruit the 10th to full war strength. On 21 November, with its ranks filled with residents of Albany County, the regiment was mustered into federal service as the 177th New York Volunteer Infantry, a nine-month regiment.[1] It was mustered out of federal service on 10 September 1863 and resumed its role in the National Guard as the 10th Regiment Infantry, NGSNY.

The dress uniforms adopted by the majority of the units of the National Guard of New York during the 1870s consisted of a tailcoat with three rows of buttons on the breast (frequently connected by braid), with large fringed epaulets in the "state" pattern. The most popular headgear was the "Baker & McKenney cap" — a black felt kepi, bound with patent leather and bearing a brass cap plate and colored pompom. The uniform selected by and authorized for the 10th Regiment in 1870 is representative of this type:

BILL OF DRESS[2]

Privates: Coat of West Point Gray Cadet Cloth, single breasted dress coat, faced with black cloth bound with white cord, ornamented with three lozenges in black cloth on skirt and sleeve and two on each side of collar, also two extra rows of buttons on front of coat.

Epaulets: N.G. pattern full size, black cloth top and white worsted fringe.

Pants: Pants of same material as coat, with black stripes one inch wide edged with white cord.

Hat: N.G. Pattern as furnished by Baker & McKenney of black beaver felt, top and base bound with leather, with a front ornament representing the 19th Corps badge, centered with the numeral ten, blue and white pompom.

Equipment: Cross belts and waist belt of white West Point webbing, patent leather boxes and scabbards.

Officers Dress: Same as above with proper insignia of rank.

Not mentioned were white chevrons on black backgrounds, worn points down. One-inch New York State buttons were sewed inside each lozenge on the skirt; one-half inch buttons were worn on sleeve and collar lozenges. Crossbelt plates bore the numeral "10"; waistbelt plates bore company letters. All metal was yellow; all leather was black.

Several years later (the date or dates are not clear), it was decided that the officers and regimental NCOs would substitute a matching cadet gray frock coat for the tailcoat. We thus find four variations in dress from that of the privates and line NCOs.[3]

All officers now wore double-breasted coats with one-inch collars and four-inch cuffs of black velvet, not bound in white. On each cuff were one, two, or three gold-braid buttonholes with one-half inch buttons, according to rank. On each sleeve, the officers carried gold-braid knots of five loops and from one to five braids, according to rank. State pattern officers' swords were hung from state pattern gold-braid sword belts, with light blue backgrounds. Officers did not wear sashes. Those of company grade wore gold shoulder knots with black velvet centers inside the crescents, having the numeral "10" embroidered in gold. Field-grade officers used gold-fringed epaulets instead.

The officer wore a better version of the private's cap, the officer's cap having a white braid edging on the leather trim. Field-grade officers wore an eight inch white egret plume with a light blue feather base, while those of company grade wore cocks' feather plumes, white over light blue.

The regimental noncommissioned staff wore single-breasted frock coats with one inch collars and four inch cuffs of black worsted cloth, both bound in white. Three rows of nine one inch buttons were connected by black-braided buttonholes across their chests. Their state pattern NCO swords hung from white and buff leather sword belts, worn over crimson sashes tied left. They wore gold shoulder knots like the company-grade officers.

The right and left general guides wore this same frock coat but with black and white fringed epaulets like the line NCOs. They carried NCO swords but did not wear sashes. On nine and one-half inch pikes, they carried guidons of light blue silk (eighteen inches x twenty-two inches) bearing a "10" painted in gold.

Knapsacks of black rubberized canvas were worn in the field, with a blanket rolled on top. The numeral "10" was painted in white on its flap. The regiment carried cap-lock Springfield rifle muskets during the first two years or so of this period; thereafter it used the .50 caliber Remington rifle.

The regiment served in the Spanish-American War and in the two World Wars. It exists today as the 210th Armor Battalion, NYARNG, in Albany.

H. Charles McBarron, Jr.
Robert E. Mulligan
Frederick P. Todd

[1]Major Clarence S. Martin, *Three Quarters of a Century with the Tenth Infantry, New York National Guard, 1860-1935*, Albany, N.Y., 1935.
[2]Special Orders No. 9, Gen'l HQ, S.N.Y., AGO, 22 January 1870.
[3]Information on these variant uniforms is based largely upon photographs, paintings by Brigadier General DeWitt Clinton Falls, and surviving uniforms.

Private General Guide Private Regimental Colonel
              Sergeant Major

**10th Infantry Regiment, National Guard
State of New York, 1870-1880**

69th Regiment, New York National Guard, New York, 1869-1884

This well-known Irish regiment of New York (now the 165th Infantry) was organized on 12 October 1851. The actual date of adoption of the uniform depicted in the plate is not known, but Brigadier General DeWitt Clinton Falls gives 1869 as the year,[1] and an order for distinctive regimental uniform buttons was executed "in the latter part of the 1860's" by the Scovill Manufacturing Company of Waterbury, Connecticut.[2] Our best source of reference for this uniform is a hand-tinted photograph from the collection of Anne S. K. Brown. It was taken in 1882 at the request of the Count de Rochambeau, head of the French delegation to the Yorktown Centennial. Photographs of the officers and enlisted men of various National Guard regiments that paraded at Yorktown were forwarded to him at Paris, to illustrate a work on the army and militia of the United States. From an Inspector General's report of the Sixty-Ninth for the year 1879 additional uniform details were found, and a contemporary photograph showing Company F in front of the Essex Market Armory was very valuable.

The uniform adopted about 1869 was similar in cut and color to the one worn from 1851 to 1858, with the exception of the tunic, which was dark blue instead of green. The green above the red for plume and pompom coloring was a tradition carried over from the pre-war uniform; its significance is quite obvious. This plus the wearing of brass shamrocks for collar insignia and a wreath of shamrocks on the uniform buttons were the only outward signs of the Celtic background of the Regiment.

In the Regimental museum can be found two examples of the white helmet depicted in the plate. One of these has been in possession of the Regiment for many years. The second helmet was presented recently to the Sixty-Ninth by the grandson of a former member, with the explanation that his grandfather wore it at the opening of the Brooklyn Bridge in May 1883. A third white helmet, in the possession of one of the authors, has "Dr. Ford" written on the inside lining — A. William Ford was commissioned a 1st lieutenant and assistant surgeon in August 1882.[3] From these dates it can be assumed that the white helmet was worn with this distinctive regimental uniform for a year or so before the uniform was discarded.

On the white helmet was worn the Irish wolfhound badge. This was a modified version of the regimental coat of arms, adopted when the Sixty-Ninth was first organized. The well-known character of the Irish wolfhound suggested the regimental motto: "Gentle when stroked, fierce when provoked." The Irish wolfhound has been the traditional mascot for years, and two giant specimens with green and gold blankets now parade behind the Regimental Colors in the annual Saint Patrick's Day Parade up New York's Fifth Avenue.

In 1869 the Sixty-Ninth had a total strength of 534 officers and men and numbered ten companies, lettered A to K.[4] The Regiment had its drill hall and headquarters in the Essex Market, on the lower east side of New York City in what was then a predominantly Irish neighborhood.

Each year, the most important day in the life of the Regiment was the 17th of March, the feast day of Ireland's Patron Saint. It began, as it still does, with a Mass in the cathedral and then the parade as military escort to the Irish Societies, a privilege and honor which is jealously guarded by the Sixty-Ninth.

In 1883 the strength of the Regiment was 660 officers and men, having reached a high of 780 three years before. Of its thirty-six regimental officers, we find that twenty-one called Ireland the land of their birth.

In 1884, the handsome and traditional uniform shown in the plate was discarded for the state regulation dress. Many of the other New York regiments did the same; hard as it was to sacrifice a distinctive uniform, the men were thereby saved a heavy burden of expense.

H. Charles McBarron, Jr.
Kenneth H. Powers

[1]Brigadier General DeWitt Clinton Falls, "Regimental Historical Notes," in *New York National Guardsman Magazine*, May 1928.
[2]Letter from E. H. Davis, Scovill Manufacturing Co., to K. H. Powers, 22 September 1954.
[3]A.G.N.Y., *Annual Report*, 1882.
[4]A.G.N.Y., *Annual Report*, 1869.

Private, Field Officer and Company Officer, Full Dress   *Sergeant, Summer Full Dress*

69th Regiment, National Guard, State of New York, c. 1869-1884

The First City Troop of Cleveland, Ohio 1877-1881

The great railroad strike of 1877 impressed a group of prominent civic, business, and military leaders of Cleveland with the need for a strong local militia. As a result, an independent company of cavalry, called "The First City Troop of Cleveland," was founded on October 10 of that year.

The official dress uniform adopted at the time of organization, and used continuously until World War II, was patterned after a hussar dress uniform of the Austrian army. A description of the officers' jacket, from the by-laws of the organization, reads as follows:

> . . . dark blue cloth, with skirt six to eight inches long, slashed on sides and rear, and bound with black silk braid three quarters inch wide; three rows of seven large gilt buttons on breast, connected by a facing of two rows of gold braid one-eighth of an inch wide, terminating on either side with clover-leaf knot and in front with a button loop; stand-up collar one inch high, with one small gilt button three inches from opening and connected therewith by two rows of gilt braid, terminating at button with small clover-leaf knot; at base of collar one strand of gold braid, with large clover-leaf knot in rear center; on cuff of each sleeve a single knot of three strands of gold braid. Double rows of gold braid extending from shoulder blades down the rear seams to the tail, terminating on either end with clover-leaf knot. Two gold frog buttons in the rear, at the intersection of the waist seam and braid.

Jackets for enlisted men followed the same pattern except that the trimmings were of yellow mohair cord, with the addition of shoulder knots of the same material. Trumpeters' jackets were scarlet instead of dark blue and lacked the black silk braid binding. Tight-fitting trousers of light blue cloth carried a yellow stripe down the outer seam, one and one-half inches wide for officers, one and one-fourth inches wide for noncommissioned officers, and one inch wide for troopers.

Dress headgear was a black bearskin busby mounted over a stiff leather frame. It was seven inches high, with the bottom edge an inch lower in the rear than in the front. The top was flat and covered by a scarlet busby bag, which hung over the right side to about an inch below the bottom of the busby and which was trimmed around the edge and down the center by a cord one-fourth inch in diameter (gold for officers and yellow for enlisted men).

The busby chin strap was leather, covered by a chain of flat brass links, and was attached to brass buttons on either side of the busby. A white horsehair plume five and one-half inches high, bound by a brass socket at the bottom, was fastened beneath a large yellow mohair button at the top front of the busby. Officers wore the same busby, with gold in place of yellow or brass. Officers' busby plumes were about ten inches high, and in addition to the brass socket they were bound by gold braid around the lower four inches of the plume.

A pillbox-type forage cap of dark blue, with a yellow band one and one-eighth inches wide (gold braid for officers) and a thin leather chin strap 3/16 inch wide, was an alternate dress headgear. When this cap was worn instead of the busby, a heavy yellow mohair braided cord with tassels was worn on the jacket, and was arranged in a fashion similar to that of the busby cords, in reverse. In the 1880s a white leather carbine sling was sometimes used in place of the black sling with cartouche box. During the same period, the standard cavalry helmet seems to have been used alternately in place of the busby, and the boots (or possibly leather leggings) rose above the knee in front, as shown in the figure on the right of the plate.

The horses were black, with the exception of the occasional use of a white or gray for trumpeters, and the outfit was commonly known as "The Black Horse Troop." When expanded into a squadron in 1925, Troop A continued to ride blacks, while Troop B was mounted on bays.

Rated as one of the outstanding cavalry units in the country, the enlisted personnel furnished a very high percentage of officers in national emergencies, with the result that the Troop usually formed the nucleus of the regiments to which it was assigned in wartime. It was admitted to the Ohio National Guard in 1887, and in 1895 officially dropped its original name and became "Troop A, Ohio National Guard." The original independent organization was continued throughout its history, and in 1925 it became "The First Cleveland Cavalry," while officially designated as Troop A and B, 107th Cavalry Regiment, Ohio National Guard.

The unit's federal service comprises: The Spanish-American War in the 1st Ohio Volunteer Cavalry, the Mexican border campaign in the 11th Provisional Cavalry, World War I in the 135th Field Artillery Regiment, and World War II in the 107th Cavalry Regiment (mechanized in 1942).

H. Charles McBarron, Jr.
D. Lyle Thoburn

Trooper, dress   Bugler, full dress

Officer, full dress   Trooper, full dress   Trooper, with helmet

1st City Troop of Cleveland, Ohio, 1877-1881

1st Infantry Regiment, Pennsylvania National Guard 1885-1898

Following the Civil War, Pennsylvania found herself possessed of a large body of veteran soldiers, many of whom were willing to continue the associations they had formed during the war. After a brief period, regiments and battalions began to form throughout the commonwealth, until by 1870 there was an unwieldy force of almost thirty of them. Then interest and attendance lagged, and when Pennsylvania was faced with the serious railway strikes of 1877, she had the mortification of seeing a handful of Regulars accomplish what her entire National Guard had been unable to do.[1]

The reaction came speedily. In 1878 Pennsylvania tightened her forces into a single compact division, carefully organized along U.S. Army lines. She made her ideal soldier the veteran volunteer of the Civil War and laid stress on rough field duty, practical mobilization, and marksmanship. Attendance was high but the tough work did not always attract the best class of recruit.

In no realm was the "Pennsylvania Plan" so obvious as in the uniforms of the officers and men. Not only were distinctive regimental dress uniforms abandoned for regulation U.S. Army clothing, but only the fatigue uniform was prescribed and, indeed, issued by the commonwealth. Repeatedly and almost defensively is it reiterated in official documents and regimental histories that ". . . the troops have no dress uniforms, and wear on all occasions the fatigue dress . . . all of excellent material."[2]

After a decade of drabness, the desire for dress uniforms was echoed by the Adjutant General. In 1888 he pointed out that the 1st and 3rd Regiments Infantry, the State Fencibles Battalion, and, of course, the 1st Troop Philadelphia City Cavalry possessed "handsome dress uniforms which were paid for out of private funds."[3] The other regiments of infantry, the two other cavalry troops, and the three batteries of light artillery still wore only fatigue dress.

We see the 1st Regiment as it appeared at about the time of this report. On duty with other troops it wore the state uniform, relieved only by white pants for street parade during warm weather.[4] The privates carry the U.S. model 1873, .45 caliber Springfield rifle, socket bayonet, black leather belts, and cartridge box of a special pattern. The rigid knapsack was of regimental pattern; above the knapsack sat a gray blanket recently adopted by the state as regulation. On the top of the forage cap is a keystone, red in color for the 1st Brigade. The other colors were white and blue, for the 2nd and 3rd Brigades.[5]

The two men in the foreground wear dress uniforms.[6] Coat, pants, and helmet were made of the same cloth: a bright medium blue. The black mohair braid differed in design between officers and men, as did the helmet plate. With some modification this dress uniform was worn from 1885 to 1911 or 1912. Being a staff officer, the lieutenant wears aiguillettes; field officers wore a gold lace baldric with full dress.

The 1st Regiment, born in the Civil War as the Gray Reserves of Philadelphia but with roots going back to the mid-18th century, was consolidated with the 13th Regiment to form the 109th Infantry of World War I. In 1921 it was reorganized as the 103rd Engineers.

Frederick T. Chapman
Frederick P. Todd

[1]Frederick P. Todd, "Our National Guard: An Introduction to its History," *Military Affairs*, V (1941), 158.

[2]Adjutant General of Pennsylvania, *Annual Report*, 1888, Harrisburg, Pa., 1889, Appendix A, 8.

[3]*Ibid.*, 8a.

[4]James W. Latta, *History of the First Regiment Infantry, National Guard of Pennsylvania (Gray Reserves)*, Philadelphia, 1912, 308-309; also lithographs of the Grant Funeral in New York, 8 August 1885, in which the Regiment paraded.

[5]*Report, op. cit.*, Appendix A, 7, 8.

[6]Data here is based on uniforms and photographs in the regimental armory.

Private, State Uniform

Field Officer, State Uniform

Private, Field Service

Regimental Staff Officer

Sergeant, Full Dress

Helmet Plate

1st Infantry Regiment, National Guard of Pennsylvania
1885-1898

Canadian Voyageurs, Nile Expedition, 1884-1885

In the early 1880s Egypt was in a state of chaos. Great Britain sent Major General C. G. Gordon ("Chinese Gordon") to Khartoum, ostensibly to look into the possibility of evacuating Egyptian forces from the province and leaving it to the rebels fighting under the command of a leader known as the Mahdi. Unfortunately for Gordon, the followers of the Mahdi soon surrounded Khartoum, and the general and his command were beseiged in the city.

A relief expedition, commanded by Lord Garnet Wolseley, was organized. Utilizing the experience he gained while leading the 1870 Red River Expedition in Canada, Wolseley decided to move his small army up the Nile by boat, and orders were placed in British dockyards for 800 thirty-two-foot whaleboats. Lord Wolseley, again drawing on his memories of the Red River campaign, requested that the British government recruit, in Canada, *voyageurs* capable of moving his river-borne army to the Sudan.

In a few weeks, 400 boatmen — probably a more accurate term, since by this date the early *voyageur* was a thing of the past — had been hired. The majority of the men were experienced lumber trade "shantymen" from the rivers of Quebec, Ontario, and Manitoba. Both major ethnic groups, French and English, were well-represented, and a goodly number of Indians were likewise engaged. The contingent was placed under the command of Brevet Lieutenant Colonel Frederick C. Denison, who in turn was aided by a staff of six officers, a sergeant, and eighteen foremen. Wolseley's choice of Canadian boatmen proved to be a wise one. These latter-day *voyageurs* performed yeoman service for the army both in ascending and descending the Nile. It was no fault of theirs that the expedition failed to succor Gordon in Khartoum.

None of the Canadian voyageurs was killed by enemy action in the campaign, but the Nile cataracts did claim six of their number, while ten more died of other causes during their term of service. The War Medal and the Khedive Star were awarded to the members of the contingent. Those boatmen present at the battle of Kirbekan received a battle clasp for their War Medal.

There was some uniformity to the contingent's appearance, at least in the beginning. It was common practice for Canadian woodsmen to get a free clothing issue, so, as part of each man's Nile Expedition contract, a clothing allowance was authorized.[1] At a meeting held 29 August 1884, organizers of the unit decided on the following kit: a dark gray smock and trousers, gray undershirt and drawers, a blue shirt or jersey, pair of beef moccasins, soft gray hat, gray blanket, towel, flannel belt, two pair of socks, tump line, and a canvas bag numbered for each man.[2] The flannel belts (believed to be a protection against cholera) were not available wholesale in Canada and it was asked that they be issued in Egypt.[3] Eighteen lighter suits of better quality were reserved for the foremen.[4] "Smock" was a lumberman's term for a Norfolk jacket, and both it and the trousers were of heavy tweed material.[5] Woolen underwear for men destined for Egypt may seem somewhat incongruous, but it was noted that such underclothing was worn by lumbermen in Canada during the hot season also.[6] Eyewitnesses in Egypt remarked that:

> . . . they look very slovenly in their suit of woolen tweed, half moccasins, and regulation white helmets, but strong, sturdy looking fellows they are, and when in their blue flannel shirts with sleeves tucked up, they look good enough for any boating requirements.[7]

The 'long moccasins' depicted on the central figure in the plate was modelled from prototypes existing in the National Museum of Canada and from a sketch that appeared in the *National Graphic* (London), 29 November 1884.

It was in the Egyptian campaigns of 1881-1882 and 1884-1885 that the color khaki came into general use by the British forces. Originating in India, khaki at this date varied considerably in shading from light brown to grayish-green. The captain in the plate is shown wearing a uniform typical for the campaign; khaki serge tunic, Bedford cloth breeches, blue puttees, and white helmet with pugri and brass curb-chain chin strap.[8] Since the boatmen remained nominally civilians throughout their service, only the officers were armed.

C. P. Stacey's excellent *Records of the Nile Voyageurs* was useful in providing background information for the text, while sketches that appeared in the *Illustrated London News* and *National Graphic* helped in compiling the plate.

Eric I. Manders
Wayne A. Colwell

[1] Public Archives of Canada (P.A.C.), G 19, vol 34., Letter, Melgund to Lansdown, 1 September 1884.
[2] P.A.C., G 19, vol 34. Notes of meeting 29 August 1884.
[3] P.A.C., G 19, vol 34. Letter, Melgund to Adj. General (London), 19 September 1884.
[4] P.A.C., G 19, vol 34, Minutes of meeting 8 September 1884.
[5] P.A.C. Minto Papers, microfilm. Letter, Melgund to Lansdowne, 1 September 1884.
[6] P.A.C., G 19, vol 34. Lansdowne report, 30 October 1884.
[7] *National Graphic* (London), 29 November 1884, 534.
[8] A. C. Whitehorne, "Khaki and Service Dress," *Journal of the Society of Army Historical Research*, XV, 182. The pugri (or "pugree") was the light cloth turban worn around the helmet.

Captain   Boatmen   Foreman

Canadian Voyageurs, Nile Expedition, 1884-1885

Canadian Volunteer Militia, Northwest Rebellion, 1885

In March 1885, armed violence erupted in the Canadian west when a band of Metis clashed with a force of Northwest Mounted Police and volunteers at Duck Lake. The government, realizing that the situation was beyond local police control, ordered the Volunteer Militia to mobilize.

A field force of some 5,000 militia, a handful of Regulars, and some irregular mounted scouts was rapidly assembled. Most of this force was transported 2,000 to 3,000 miles over the uncompleted Canadian Pacific Railroad and concentrated in three columns in southern Saskatchewan and Alberta. The columns swept northward in an approach march of more than 200 miles, which in each case led to contact and battle with a hostile force. The campaign ended with the pursuit of the scattered enemy into the lakes and swamps of northern Saskatchewan.[1]

By 1885 the government had assumed responsibility for the issue of clothing, and the Volunteer Militia achieved some uniformity in dress. The men were issued a tunic, trousers, greatcoat, and forage cap. Some items, including full-dress headware, leggings, and field service caps, were purchased by regiments. Boots, shirts, socks, underclothing, and personal small stores were the responsibility of the individual soldier. The regular troops were, of course, completely kitted through army stores.[2]

Officers were required to purchase their own clothing and a variety of fashionable undress uniforms was available for active service. This plate illustrates some of the orders of dress worn by officers during the campaign.

The officer of the Governor General's Body Guard, on the extreme left, wears a dark blue stable jacket with regimental pattern of piping on the cuffs, pockets, and front. The jacket is fastened with silver olivets.

The officer of the Queen's Own Rifles wears a dark green tunic, very similar to that of the men, and the wedge-shaped field service cap that was adopted and purchased for all rank of the regiment in 1882.[3] A belt with a single diagonal brace supports his sword.

Most of the field artillery were regulars, and the artillery officer is well prepared for active service with a light fawn-colored frock. He wears an unusual field service cap of very light grey — almost white — piped with blue and regulation blue pantaloons with broad scarlet stripes.

The next figure to the right is a lieutenant of the York and Simcoe Provisional Battalion in full dress. The entire unit wore the blue home pattern spike infantry helmet on service, as did some companies of the Midland Provisional Battalion. This was one of the very few times, if not the sole occasion, that this helmet was worn on campaign by any British or Colonial troops. This full dress was actually worn in the theatre of operations, but only on rare occasions.[4]

The officer of the 66th Fusiliers wears the blue patrol jacket and round peaked forage cap much favored by infantry officers for service dress. The jacket is trimmed with black braid and has four loops of black cord across the front. The leather belt with single cross strap supports his sword and pistol, and the bandolier holds ammunition for the Winchester rifle with which a number of officers armed themselves.[5]

By any standards, the Northwest Rebellion was a small affair. Yet it was significant in Canadian military history because it was the first campaign fought by Canadians without the assistance of regular British troops. The citizen soldiers of Canada had been asked to perform a complicated military operation under demanding climatic and geographic conditions. And they performed well. The Canadian militia had come of age.

Robert J. Marrion
J. L. Summers

[1] *Report upon the Suppression of the Rebellion on the North-West Territories by the Minister of Militia and Defense,* The Queen's Printer, Ottawa, 1886, Appendix I, "Special Report of the Major-General Commanding."

[2] E. J. Chambers, *The Royal Grenadiers, . . .* , Toronto, 1904, 41.

[3] E. J. Chambers, *The Queen's Own Rifles of Canada,* Toronto, 1901, 86.

[4] Original uniform, The Royal Canadian Regiment Museum, Wolseley Barracks, London, Ontario.

[5] Contemporary photographs, Canadian Army Museum Collection, Halifax Citadel.

Governor General's Body Guard
(undress—stable jacket)

2nd Queen's Own Rifles
(undress—frock)

York and Simcoe Provisional Battalion
(full dress)

Regiment of Canadian Artillery
(campaign dress)

66th Fusiliers
(undress—patrol jacket)

Canadian Volunteer Militia Northwest Rebellion, 1885

THE SMALL WARS, 1893-1916

Apache and Bannock Indian Disturbances

Spanish-American War

Philippine Insurrection

China Relief Expedition

Cuban Pacification

Mexican Border Troubles

Vera Cruz Expedition

Punitive Expedition into Mexico

15th U.S. Infantry Regiment, 1916

The color guard quickstepped to the *Fifteenth Infantry March* while, beyond the Tientsin Station, the world watched other soldiers. It was the summer of 1916.

Isonzo, Verdun, and the Somme were headlines. These and revolutionary Mexico held America's attention. The home folks read about the United States cavalry down by the Rio Grande. But the headlines and the Congressional debate over army augmentation meant nothing in North China, where the State Department had stuck an infantry regiment athwart the major communications to help keep the peace in a vital area where Japan was pushing all the time.[1]

In June, President of China Yuan Shih-K'ai died, and disorder degenerated into chaos. These conditions also meant little to the 15th Infantry, beyond explaining why they were there.[2]

The routine of garrison soldiering, parades, inspections, guard mount, and marksmanship was what mattered to the troops. Then along came the National Defense Act[3] of June 3, 1916, to make new work for the regiment. Infantry regiments were to form a headquarters company, a supply company, and a machine gun company without machine guns.

The 15th Infantry's years of isolation, in what was then the world's backyard, produced remarkably few modifications in its uniform and equipment. Old photographs show soldiers who might have stepped out of the Odgen uniform plates for this same period.[4] Some British influence, possibly introduced accidentally by English-trained and English-oriented native tailors, manifested itself occasionally, but the differences from stateside dress were largely those of quality: good tailoring of good materials cost comparatively little in China. With the honor and dignity of the United States to uphold before the world, the 15th Infantry dressed accordingly.

Privates detailed for military police in the summer wore custom-tailored cottons of the regiment's particular "golden" shade, hand-laundered without starch. Dull 1908-style bronze discs were pinned on the collar. No insignia was worn on the campaign hat. Many soldiers sported the 15th's unique, English-made, bright-metal buttons. To function as MPs, all they needed was a brassard and billy, since their duty was restricted to caring for their own people. (Foreign soldiers were not subject to Chinese courts or police.) The coloring of the MP brassard remains unknown.

A battalion sergeant major with time on his hands after *Retreat* would change into the army's last universal blues issue. Enlisted men wore a stand-up collar with a French-cuffed white shirt under blue and khaki blouses alike. Crossed rifles carrying a "15" and a "U.S." decorated the collars of the blue uniforms of all ranks. Enlisted men screwed the brass branch insignia to their visored caps.[5] Modern soldiers, brought up under the fetish of having all leather parts of their uniforms carefully matched, can only wonder at the use of the brown garrison belt with dress blues during this period. The privates and the battalion sergeant major were separated by nineteen lines of enlisted grades in 1916. After payday parade, a private drew about $23.60, less stoppages, and humped along with the squad "boy" making his bed and other "boys" shouldering the weights of fatigue and K.P. The battalion sergeant major made around $62.60, but his overhead usually was higher. The term for the attractive form it often took was "squaw."

On summer parade, the pith helmet was regulation. In the 15th, the chin strap was worn over the visor. Four 1916 photographs — color guard with Captain Bagby, two MPs before a beer parlor, Company G during inspection, and the Detachment of Mounted Orderlies — were primary sources for the plates on pages 27 and 29.

Frederick T. Chapman
Edward S. Jones
John R. Elting

[1] In 1912, when the Manchu boy-emperor abdicated, the U.S. had increased its Peking legation guard and ordered the 15th Infantry from Monterey, California, to Tientsin. In August 1914, the Japanese, with British support, seized the German concession at Tsingtao.
[2] The Protocols of 1901 permitted the U.S. to maintain a legation guard at Peking and station troops elsewhere to keep an open right-of-way to the coast.
[3] William A. Ganoe, *History of the United States Army*, New York: 1924, 456-458. This same act converted the 15th's 2nd Battalion, which had been left in the Philippines in 1912, into the cadre for the new 31st ("Thirsty-First") Infantry Regiment. The 15th reformed its 2nd Battalion at Tientsin.
[4] Henry A. Ogden, *Uniforms of the United States, Second Series*.
[5] Blues were optional purchase in the 1930s; the 15th all bought them.

Battalion Sergeant Major　　　*Military Police*

15th U.S. Infantry Regiment
Tientsin, China, 1916

15th U.S. Infantry Regiment, 1916

A specially selected company — not the color company — escorted the color guard from the colonel's office to the parade ground. The band, the color guard, and this select company then performed the ceremony. The 15th had no field music in 1916 because it had no company drummers. There were buglers, who doubled as wig-wag signalmen.

The escort captain's dangling saber knot was used when publishing orders, calling the roll, and discharging like duties, during which his saber dangled from his right wrist by the saber knot.

The regimental color pike was adorned with silver bands commemorating victories from Shiloh to Luzon. In the 15th, the American "hernia truss" sling was worn under the waist belt. Color sergeants marched "at the carry," the heel of the pike resting in the socket of the sling, their right hand grasping the pike at shoulder height.

Membership in the color guard was defined as follows:

> The color guard consists of two color sergeants, who are the color bearers, and two experienced privates selected by the colonel. The senior color sergeant carries the national color; the junior color sergeant carries the regimental color.[1]

The National Defense Act assigned the two color sergeants to headquarters company. Lineally, the noncommissioned ranking went: regimental sergeant major, battalion sergeant major, 1st sergeant, color sergeants, mess sergeant, supply sergeant, and on down, for a total of twenty lines. Insignia illustrating their jobs proclaimed their rank status. The color sergeant wore three chevrons above a star, alluding to the national color. The headquarters company first sergeant (who also was the regimental drum major) gloried in three chevrons above a lozenge resting on crossed drum major's batons. While these illustrative rank insignia represented the tail of a trend — the end came quickly after the August 1917 changes — the color sergeant's ribbons in this plate show the coming shape of things.[2]

In 1900, the Medal of Honor and the Treasury Life Saving Medals had been the three decorations worn. There were no campaign medals. Under Chief of Staff Adna R. Chafee, the Civil War veteran who led the Americans against Peking in 1900, the Certificate of Merit became a decoration on 11 January 1905. The first campaign medals were authorized on the same day in General Order 5. All in a lump came the Spanish War, Philippine Campaign, and China Campaign medals. The Philippine Congressional Medal followed on 29 June 1906, and then the Civil War and Indian Campaign medals in G.O. 12, 1907. Thus, the senior color sergeant wears a bar of four. In China, the 15th Infantry earned no medals. They simply kept the peace.

Frederick T. Chapman
Edward S. Jones
John R. Elting

[1] Par 763 and 778, *Manual of the Color*, IDR.
[2] Insignia of rank pieces, The Institute of Heraldry, Cameron Station, Alexandria, Virginia. The Army Mine Planter service retained illustrative insignia into the 1940s.

Private   *Color Sergeants*   *Private*   *Officer*

15th U.S. Infantry Regiment Color Guard, 1916

Porto Rico Provisional Infantry Regiment, 1901-1907

Following the surrender of Puerto Rico, the American authorities authorized the creation of a regiment of volunteer infantry from among its natives. On 24 March 1899 the Porto Rico Battalion was organized at San Juan. Next year an additional, mounted battalion was created and the two were combined to form the Porto Rico Regiment, Volunteer Infantry. On 1 July 1901 the corps was reorganized entirely as a dismounted unit with three battalions, placed on the Regular Army list, and given the designation Porto Rico Provisional Regiment of Infantry. After further changes the regiment, in 1920, became the 65th Infantry.[1] Since 1956 the regiment has been carried on the inactive roll of the Army.

During the early years of its life, the regiment was smartly turned out in a dress uniform which comprised a dark blue flannel blouse, long white cotton trousers, and white helmets. These helmets were high and quite full, but without chains, closely resembling in style the policeman's helmet of that day. Officers wore blue undress coats with this combination. Stiff white collars projected an inch and a half or more above the coat collars.

The uniforms in the plate are based upon photographs taken in San Juan in 1902. These pictures present several distinctive features. In this period Infantrymen wore white insignia — on chevrons, hat cords, and inside the officer's shoulder straps.[2] Chevrons on blouses were still the large size, which were authorized also for wear on the shirts. Russet leather shoes had been introduced with the khaki uniform, but black ones were still worn with the dress uniform.

For field uniform the Porto Rico Regiment wore a lightweight, khaki cotton or flannel shirt with cotton trousers, drab felt campaign hat, and brown cotton duck leggings. The men carried the Krag-Jorgensen magazine rifle, model 1898. By 1902 the canvas cartridge belt with the double loops had been introduced to hold the smaller cartridges. Apparently this belt was worn for dress purposes as well as field service.

Colonel Buchanan, the commanding officer, is shown on the left. His white linen cap was in the style authorized in 1900 for wear "during the warm season." No ornaments were allowed on the front; the cap cord for an officer of the line was silken, one-eighth inch in diameter, of the color of the arm of service. His undress coat of white duck or flannel was edged with white mohair braid. After 1900 it bore shoulder straps similar in style to those on the khaki blouse and had the same collar insignia. In his case the crossed rifles bear the letters "P.R." instead of a regimental number. "P.R." was worn on all insignia until the regiment was numbered in 1920.

Frederick P. Todd

---

[1]Dept. of the Army, *The Army Lineage Book — Vol. II: Infantry*, Washington, 1953, 253-254. The original, and incorrect, spelling "Porto" has been preserved in designations where it appeared that way.
[2]The pertinent dress regulations may be found in War Dept., *Regulations and Decisions Pertaining to the Uniform of the Army of the United States*, 1 May 1899; 31 May 1900; 6 August 1901.

Commanding Officer
White Undress Uniform

Private
Field Uniform

Officer and Corporal
Parade Uniform

Porto Rico Provisional Infantry Regiment, 1901-1907

Battery K, 1st U.S. Artillery Regiment, 1895-1898

This plate is based, in the main, upon three drawings by Frederic Remington of the men of Battery K during a practice march through New England in the summer of 1895.[1] The full dress at this time, it will be recalled, was a short blue coat and medium blue trousers, trimmed with scarlet, and a black felt helmet with brass fittings and scarlet horse or buffalo hair plume.[2] Here, however, we see the men in the more common uniforms of camp and garrison.

The officer wears the dark blue undress "sack coat" with black mohair braid, which was authorized for wear by all officers in 1895.[3] For twenty-five years after the Civil War, officers had worn a dark blue sack coat with five buttons and a roll collar for undress. In 1892 this had given way to an elaborately braided coat, similar to a model worn by the British army.[4] It had proved to be too elaborate and in 1895 was stripped of most of its braid to make the coat shown in the plate. This style was worn until after World War I.

The first sergeant wears the blue service uniform which had so long characterized the Army, while the guidon corporal has on a white canvas stable frock.[5] All of the artillerymen wear cork summer helmets, covered with white cotton drilling, which had been adopted in 1880.[6] The extent to which this helmet was actually worn is a matter of some mystery; it seems to have been a question of the whim of local commanders. Enlisted men had a small chin strap of white enameled leather, while officers wore the same brass chin straps as were used on the full dress helmet. The enlisted men's sabers are of the 1840 model which was worn until this side arm was abandoned by the field artillery about the time of World War I. The guidon corporal has put his gauntlets into his saber knot, holding them down against the tassel by means of the keeper — a favorite practice.

A word about the guidon. The model carried by the batteries of artillery came in both silk and bunting, of the same size and design. The bunting version showed in reverse the letters on its reverse. Such was and still is the practice with most guidons.[7]

The saddle leather is shown as black, but in 1897 experiments were made with russet leather horse equipment. Other elements of the horse furnishings are regulation.

The period of the plate terminates at 1898, for in that year the Regiment received khaki uniforms and much of the fatigue clothing illustrated became obsolete then or soon thereafter.

A light battery on war footing consisted of six guns and nine caissons with limbers for each, a combined battery wagon and field forge, and one relatively light artillery wagon. Five officers, one hundred and seventy-five enlisted men, and one hundred and forty-four horses made up the complete war complement. The standard light field gun was the 3.2-inch B. L. rifle model 1885 (modified).

In garrison, all individually mounted men and all drivers were armed with the saber. When in the field, sergeants of all grades were armed with the saber and revolver; lower ranks were armed with revolver and hunting knife. In horse batteries all cannoneers were individually mounted.

In addition to articles of uniform shown in the plate, each man was issued a light blue overcoat with scarlet-lined detachable cape, dark blue flannel shirts, campaign hat, canvas leggings, and black leather shoes.

Frederick P. Todd

[1] *Harper's Weekly*, 17 August 1895.
[2] See H. A. Ogden's plate XLII in the Quartermaster series.
[3] General Order 22, AGO, 12 April 1895; the effective date for its adoption was 1 July 1895.
[4] General Order 68, 29 September 1892.
[5] See H. A. Ogden's plate XLIV in the Quartermaster series, and QMGO Specifications, 12 March 1879 (no. 15).
[6] QMGO Specifications, 5 May 1880 (no. 2), and 5 August 1892 (no. 330).
[7] QMGO Specifications, 15 November 1895 (nos. 381 and 382).

Captain, Summer Undress
Uniform

1st Sergeant, Summer
Fatigue Dress

Corporal, Stable
Frock

Battery K, 1st U.S. Artillery, 1895-1898

Light Battery F, 5th U.S. Artillery Regiment, 1894-1896

The 5th Artillery of the Regular Army was the regiment organized in the early days of the Civil War to consist of twelve "batteries," the first time that term was used in the law. Until then "light company" had designated the field artillery portion of an artillery regiment.[1]

The Fifth was organized throughout as field artillery and all its batteries served as such during the Civil War. In 1865 all but F and G Batteries were dismounted; four years later G suffered the same fate but was restored to the status of a light battery in 1882. This remained the regimental organization until 1898, the other companies serving as coast artillery.

The uniforms shown in the plate are based on quartermaster specifications for 1890, which are basically the same as those prescribed in the Uniform Regulations of 1881.[2] The battery bugler with his distinctive musician's braiding is shown with the newly adopted short artillery bugle, trimmed with the twenty-one foot trumpet cord, loop-braided to form a shoulder sling.[3] Although specifications for the helmet cords for mounted troops stated that these were to be "loop plaited" so as to reach only to the upper edge of the chin strap in front and to within two inches of the lower edge of the helmet in rear,[4] contemporary photographs indicate that the chin strap or leather helmet band was frequently completely covered in front. This may have been due to stretching or due to alterations made to enhance the appearance of the helmet. The cords were secured by "tacking" with heavy thread to the body of the helmet at points about two inches above the chin strap line on each side of the loop.

When mounted full dress was worn indoors, and not under arms, the helmet was not worn but the helmet cords were. The free end, normally hooked to the helmet, was looped around a button high on the left — for enlisted men, to the left shoulder strap button; for officers, usually to the top left coat button.

The officer is shown with the special light reverse "P" guard saber authorized in 1872 for all mounted officers of artillery.[5] All mounted enlisted personnel carried the issue light artillery saber Model 1840 during ceremonies and other occasions when so ordered.[6] More frequently, and particularly during field service, the sabers of all but senior noncommissioned officers were carried on the ammunition chests or the limbers.[7]

The scarlet canvas saddle cloths, bound with black leather and with black leather regimental numerals were used over woven hair pads for full dress formations.[8] The normal padding for all other purposes was still the regulation scarlet wool saddle blanket with three-inch dark blue stripes three inches from the ends and a six-inch "US" in the center.

The harness, developed by the Light Artillery Boards of 1881-1884, was radically different from that used during the preceding forty or more years. Only the major innovations are cited here. These included: the adoption of adjustable steel snap collars,[9] simplification of the pole yoke and pole attachments, introduction of mogul springs into the draft linkage at the ends of the wheeler's trace chains,[10] the Shoemaker bit, and a completely new method of "hold back" by means of side straps from the breeching extending underneath to a martingale attached to the pole yoke. Finally, the special valise saddles for the off horses were dispensed with and the McClellan saddle, modified for artillery use, was used throughout.

The artillery McClellan differed from that used by the cavalry as follows: heavy D rings were riveted to the cantle and pommel arcs, sweat leathers or leg guards were added to the stirrup leathers, thongs were used instead of coat straps, and, for draft animals, the open-toed heavy brass artillery stirrups were retained.

Harry C. Larter, Jr.

[1]William E. Birkhimer, *Historical Sketch of the . . . Artillery, United States Army,* Wash., 1884, 69-75.

[2]QMGO, "Specifications for Clothing and Equipage," 1881-1896 (cumulative) specifically No. 299, 1890.

[3]*Ibid.,* No. 342, 24 April 1894; issued in addition to the "F" trumpet with "C" crook, required for all mounted troops by War Dept. General Order 12, 1882. Also specification No. 190, 1 June 1887.

[4]QMGO, "Specifications," No. 291, 23 May 1890.

[5]H. L. Peterson, *The American Sword, 1775-1945,* War Dept. General Order 121, 1893, 119-121.

[6]Peterson, *op. cit.,* 42-44.

[7]This practice was begun as early as the Mexican War in 1846, authorized at the discretion of the battery commander in 1861, and finally incorporated as "regulation" in 1873. See War Dept., *Artillery Tactics,* 1845, and later editions. Also see A. B. Dyer, *Hand Book of Light Artillery,* New York, 1898. In *Regulations* for 1873, par. 566, it states: "The sergeants, drivers, trumpeters, and guidons are armed with the saber; the cannoneers bear the saber belt only, their sabers being carried on the ammunition chests."

[8]Dyer, *op. cit.,* 154.

[9]*Ibid.,* 150-156, 435-447. Dyer gives an excellent description of the harness and particularly of the steel neck collar. When first introduced for artillery the steel collar was used on the wheelers only; a similar locking collar of padded leather with metal hames was used for lead and swing teams. As early as 1869 the saddles supplied to some batteries had fair leather seats (Dyer, *op. cit.,* 151) and by 1897 all troops and batteries had been issued at least six complete sets of horse equipment made entirely of "stuffed" fair leather (Evidence of Master Sgt. C. E. Kelley, U.S.A. Ret.).

[10]To reduce shock on the shoulders of the draft animals; similar devices had been in use for many years. See Francis Dwyer, *Seats and Saddles,* London (1886), part III, chapter III.

Battery Commander   *Caisson Wheelers and Driver*   *Bugler*

Light Battery F, 5th U.S. Artillery Regiment, Full Dress, 1894-1896

Light Battery G, 6th U.S. Artillery, Hotchkiss Mountain Gun Section, 1899

The Sixth Regiment of Artillery was established 8 March 1898. Its Light Battery G, consisting of six 3.2-inch field pieces and commanded by Captain Victor H. Bridgman, was detached in June and sent to the Philippines, where four 1.65-inch Hotchkiss mountain guns with pack mules were added. The battery was split up during the Panay campaign, with four 3.2-inch field pieces in Colonel Carpenter's column (since the other two 3.2s had been detached to Cebu prior to the start of the Panay campaign) while the four 1.65-inch pack guns became a part of General Hughes' column. The eight guns of these two columns succeeded in defending the columns' flanks while overcoming concentrations ahead of the advance. The infantry assigned to Hughes' and Carpenter's columns were the 18th and 19th Regiments of regular infantry and the 26th Regiment of Volunteers. Captain Bridgman received a citation for his battery's performance in this 400-mile campaign, which included thirty battles and engagements and culminated in the Battle of Jaro. In 1901, the battery's designation of G was changed to 13th Battery, Field Artillery, and in June 1907 to Battery E, 5th Field Artillery. As Battery E it served on the Mexican border in 1916 and in France in the 1st Division in 1917-1918. The battery was deactivated at Camp Bragg, N.C. in 1922.[1]

The officer shown is wearing a drab campaign hat with a gold and black hat cord, a khaki blouse with scarlet shoulder straps, khaki breeches, russet boots, and yellow metal spurs; on each shoulder strap is a yellow metal coat of arms of the U.S., one and one-half inches high but with no rank insignia since he is a 2nd lieutenant; on each side of the collar are yellow metal crossed cannon with a "6" in the upper vertex. Buttons are yellow metal, with a spread eagle having a shield with the letter A on its chest. Large buttons were used on the front of the blouse, with small size on the pocket flaps and at the end of the shoulder straps. He carries a pistol in a russet leather holster on a one-and-one-half-inch wide belt, with a 2-inch wide yellow metal belt plate with a silver wreath encircling the Arms of the United States.[2]

The quartermaster packer to the right holds a bull whip and is a civilian. As a former enlisted man who draws more pay for doing the same job, he wears semi-military clothing without a hat cord or other military insignia; he has a "quick-draw" holster and a belt with ammunition loops.[3] The enlisted men shown wear drab campaign hats with scarlet hat cords, dark blue flannel shirts, light blue kersey trousers, brown cotton duck leggings, and russet shoes; their weapons are slung Krags,

pistols, and even a bolo or so. The gunner, a corporal, is wearing scarlet chevrons on his shirt sleeves above the elbows, and, on his right arm below the chevron, a scarlet cloth projectile, one and one-half inches by three-fourths inch, point up, to signify a first-class gunner. His trousers have a one-half-inch wide scarlet stripe on the outside seam of each leg.[4]

The 1.65-inch Hotchkiss mountain gun was a breech-loading, rifled gun, without recoil and counter-recoil systems, weighing 241 pounds when assembled. It fired a 2-lb. fused projectile a maximum range of 3,500 yards. The gun broke down into loads for two mules; the barrel and wheels on the first, and trail and axle on the second. One or more ammunition mules each carried four wooden boxes; each box contained eighteen rounds and twenty primers, or a total of seventy-two rounds of fixed ammunition per mule. The gun crew consisted of a chief of section, a corporal, and five privates, with another private for each additional ammunition mule. The gunner, a corporal, commands the piece, sets the sights, points the gun, and oversees the ammunition supply. No. 1 mans the right wheel and its brake-rope, operates the breech, and fires the piece. No. 2 mans the left wheel and brake-rope, leads, and assists in pointing. No. 3 supplies ammunition to No. 2, while Nos. 4 and 5 attend the mules.

Tom Jones
Fitzhugh McMaster

[1]*Statutes at Large*, Volume 30, December 1897–March 1899 (GPO), 261; *Roster for Troops Serving in the Department of the Pacific and Eighth Army Corps*, Manila, June 1899, list ten batteries of the 6th Artillery in Luzon, including Light Batteries D and G; the other four batteries of the 6th were in the Hawaiian Islands, per General Order No. 50 of 17 March 1899; General Orders No. 36 and 37 of 1899 had added two batteries to all artillery regiments; Signal Corps Photograph #111 SC 114908, National Archives, of Battery G of the 6th Artillery in the Philippines in 1899 shows two Hotchkiss "pack guns," a few pack mules and a Filipino horse, some 20 enlisted men, and 2nd Lieutenant Richard Hugh McMaster. Diary of R. H. McMaster for 1898-1899, MS at South Carolina Library, U.S.C.; *Field Artillery Journal*, July–August 1974, 21; MC&H, XVIII, 20-21.

[2]*General Order* No. 3, 9 January 1899 and *Circular No. 24* of 28 September 1899; *General Order* No. 53 of 21 March 1899, *General Order.* (s) *30 and 51* of 9 May and 23 May 1898 as modified by *General Order No. 112* of 6 August 1898; *Regulations and Decisions Pertaining to the Uniform of the Army of the U.S.*, 3rd Edition, May 1899, 21-22. See also MC&H, XXXIII, 184-185.

[3]The quartermaster packer term was clarified by Company Fellows John R. Elting and Clyde A. Risley. The researcher had frequently heard the term used in his boyhood and always assumed that it was the rank or rating of an enlisted man.

[4]*General Order No. 128*, 10 July 1899, *C. No. 26*, 25 July 1898 authorizes chevrons for noncommissioned officers on dark blue flannel shirts; *Regulations*, Section 30 includes First Class Gunner insignia under chevrons along with Farrier, Saddler, etc.

Light Battery G, 6th U.S. Artillery
(Hotchkiss Mountain Gun Section), 1899

Signal Corps, U.S. Army, Full Dress, 1891-1902

The Signal Corps of the United States Army dates from 1863 and was in large part fathered by an army surgeon named Albert Myer. The first uniform of the corps was the cavalry uniform, with the addition of insignia consisting of crossed signal flags on forage caps and, after 1864, on jacket sleeves.[1] In 1872, when the cavalry went to plumed helmets for full dress, the Signal Corps continued to wear cavalry pattern clothing, but it was given a distinctive branch color of its own — orange — which prior to 1861 had been the dragoon branch color.

New uniform regulations adopted in 1889 dropped the full-dress uniform of the Signal Corps entirely, specifying instead a utilitarian uniform which was to be the same for dress and undress wear.[2] But two years' experience with this uniform (if the usual delay occurred in issuing it, it may never have been issued) convinced higher authority in the Army that the Signal Corps needed a new full-dress uniform, and General Orders No. 74 from the Adjutant General's Office, issued on 20 August 1891, prescribed a new full-dress blouse which was to be the Basque blouse, ". . . same as for cavalry, except that the facings shall be black piped with white and the pipings white." Signal Corps sergeants' trouser stripes were to be black, one inch wide, with no white piping. A "sergeant of the 1st class of the Signal Corps" was to wear chevrons of three bars and an arc of one bar, inclosing the crossed red and white signal flags and the burning torch; a "sergeant of the 2nd class of the Signal Corps" was to wear the same but without the arc. Service chevrons were to be black, the bars separated by white silk stitching, with the flags, torch, and their staffs embroidered in colored silk; dress chevrons were of gold lace on a black ground, with flags and flame embroidered in silk and the flag and torch staffs of gold.

This general order did not mention helmets, but they were already coverd in the paragraph of uniform regulations describing "Helmets for all Mounted Troops and for Band Musicians" which specified "Horsehair plume, and cords and bands of color according to arm of service." This meant that the enlisted men of the Signal Corps, always considered "mounted troops," were to wear with their new full-dress blouse, a helmet with black plume and black cord, bearing crossed flags and torch stamped from German silver as the overlay on

their staff corps helmet eagle, and stamped brass side buttons similarly bearing the crossed flags and torch. Signal Corps officers, however, were to revert to the feathered chapeau of the staff corps rather than to a dress helmet with gold cord and black plume.

Was this striking uniform ever worn, and if so for how long? A specimen of the dress blouse trimmed in black and white exists in the collections of the Smithsonian Institution. Black horsehair plumes and worsted helmet cords were manufactured, and surplus unissued specimens of these lie in many private collections today, proving that these components of the uniform were available. Similarly, the undress black Signal Corps chevrons are not uncommon in collections across the country; apparently they were unissued surplus. Yet H. A. Ogden, the noted military artist, who during the mid-1880s, the 1890s, and the early 1900s executed the army's official series of military prints illustrating the uniforms then worn, was depicting Signal Corps enlisted men wearing orange-trimmed dress uniforms as late as the Spanish-American War, seven years after the black-and-white-trimmed uniforms were prescribed. It seems likely that the orange-trimmed uniforms and helmets continued to be worn by at least some Signal Corps enlisted men during the 1890s due to surplus stocks still on hand or to the wearing of still serviceable orange-trimmed dress blouses by enlisted personnel. But it seems equally likely that by 1900 the black-trimmed uniforms were in common use in the Signal Corps, and that in some locations they may have been put to use not long after the 1891 regulation appeared. Whatever the extent of its actual use, this striking full-dress uniform was prescribed in U.S. Army uniform regulations from 20 August 1891 until 17 July 1902, and it may have survived several more years until the new styles of uniform ordered in 1902 could be manufactured and issued, and surplus stocks of old-pattern uniforms were depleted by issue and use.

H. Charles McBarron, Jr.
Gordon S. Chappell

[1] General Orders No. 36, WDSC, 1864; General Orders No. 88, AGO, 22 October 1868.
[2] Regulations For the Army of the United States, 1889, Washington, D.C.: G.P.O., 1889, Article LXXXVI, 209-210.

U.S. Army Signal Corps, 1891-1902

Philippines Constabulary, 1901-1906

Authorized in late 1901, the Philippines Constabulary took the field the next spring. War and insurrection had caused the economic and social collapse of much of the Philippine Islands. Technically, the Constabulary was a civil police force, which could be committed without declaration of martial law. Recruited from the martial peoples in each province, they were officered initially by American volunteers and, within a few years, an increasing number of Filipino veterans. Never numbering over 7,000 men for the entire Philippine archipelago, they took 1,029 casualties in their first five years of service — "Outnumbered, always; outfought, never!"

The first constabulary units were armed and uniformed with whatever was available. Their original field uniform was usually the general type shown by the second figure from the left of our plate: a wide-brimmed felt or straw hat with a red band one inch wide, gray cloth trousers, blue flannel shirt, and canvas leggings. Shoes might be leather or canvas, the latter frequently being hemp soled.

Concerning the Constabulary's initial uniform, a veteran officer delivered himself of definite opinions:[1]

> As a quasi-military organization, great care was taken to uniform the Insular Police[2] in some manner that would distinguish them from the Army. The material adopted was a soft, cottony fabric, steel-grey in color. *Camano* cloth, it was called.

Oddly enough, the *Handbook, Philippines Constabulary*, published in December 1901, which prescribed the design of this uniform in great detail, did not specify its color or material. With its red piping, the Camano uniform was better styled than the above quotation would suggest, but photographs show that the material easily became rumpled and wrinkled.

Constabulary insignia changed frequently, the general trend being toward Army standards. In the early years, noncommissioned officers wore their long, red-cloth chevrons below the elbow — one chevron for a corporal, two for a sergeant, three for a first sergeant. (In 1902, first sergeants were authorized to add a red disk below their chevrons.) A "wreathed monogram of the letters P. C." was to be worn on the front of the enlisted mens' caps. Plain "PC" insignia was worn on the collar. Buttons were brass, embossed "PC."

Officers' uniforms were identical, except in minor details. Cap insignia was a "small brass or gold eagle." Red shoulder straps carried the same eagle insignia on the cap, and the insignia of rank. When in garrison, officers were to wear white collars and cuffs "at all times." In the field, officers wore the campaign hat, flannel shirt, russet or canvas leggings, and "collars and cuffs to be worn or not at the option of the wearer." A gold hat cord with a red silk slide was to be worn on the left with the campaign hat.

All leather originally was to be "fair leather" (apparently tan). In 1904, both tan and black shoes were issued, but in 1905 "russet" became regulation. Off duty, officers and enlisted men were authorized white uniforms in regulation cut, less the red piping. In September 1906, khaki and white helmets were authorized for wear with uniforms of corresponding color, and experimentation with that vicious article, the wrap-around wool puttee, began. Khaki gradually replaced Camano cloth. Both were available for issue in 1904. The khaki flannel shirt replaced the blue flannel shirt about 1907.

Circular 20, Headquarters Philippines Constabulary, 18 August 1909, authorized officers "who are on duty with troops (raised among Mohammedan peoples of the southern islands) issued the fez" to wear with mess uniform. Photographs, however, suggest that it was worn "unofficially" with the garrison uniform years earlier.

On 12 September 1905, a new collar insignia was authorized: the "coat of arms of the government of the Philippines, less the crest and the scroll. . . ." This was cancelled in 1906; in 1907, a "new design" in gold was introduced, undoubtedly that shown at the top of this plate. It is, like the 1905 insignia, from the Philippines coat of arms, with the letters "PC" in silver superimposed. The officers' version is surmounted by an eagle.

The Constabulary went into action with whatever weapons it could scrape up, including smooth-bore muskets.[3] It was able, through captures, to outfit itself with Mauser, Remington, and Krag rifles. The constable at the left has a Krag, taken from a dead bandit who had acquired it from the U.S. Army. The sergeant at the left probably carries a Winchester shotgun — short-ranged, but extremely authoritative in ambush fighting. The decision to arm the Constabulary with nonregulation weapons worked in their favor in one case — they were issued the Colt caliber .45 revolver, then thought too heavy and clumsy for military use.

Information in this text comes in large part from Major Joseph M. Massaro. Company member Lieutenant Colonel Vorin E. Whan, Jr., likewise shook down the holdings of the United States Military Academy Library and made them available to the authors.

Frederick T. Chapman
John R. Elting

[1]Victor Hurley, *Jungle Patrol*.
[2]The Philippines Constabulary was frequently known by this title during its earlier years. The more familiar title, "Philippine Constabulary," was not adopted until 1911.
[3]Hurley, *op. cit.*, 65.

Always outnumbered, Never outfought

Private, 1901
(Provisional Uniform)

Third-Class Inspector, 1905
(Garrison Uniform)

First Sergeant, 1902-1904

Tribesman

Third-Class Inspector, 1902

Philippines Constabulary
1901-1906

Philippine Constabulary, 1912-1914

By 1907 the Philippines Constabulary had begun to take on an appearance much like that of the Philippine Scouts and the Regular Army. The gray uniforms had been replaced by khaki; the familiar blue flannel shirts must have been in their last "wear out" period and were being replaced by "khaki flannel." One thoroughly impractical item — khaki woolen spiral puttees — was introduced for field service.

Other adaptations, however, had demonstrated an appreciation of local conditions. Units recruited from tribes accustomed to going barefoot were allowed to authorize the "omission of the wearing of shoes in garrison"; and — although no approving regulation has yet been unearthed — the companies recruited from the "pagan" back country tribes, such as the Ifugao and Igorot, were allowed to retain their native dress from the shirttail down. (Existing black-and-white photographs indicate considerable variation in the design and coloring of their "G-strings.") The general cut of the uniform changed somewhat, the back of the blouse becoming plain, and its side seams being left open four inches at the bottom. Enlisted men were given a khaki cloth hat.

Officers' insignia underwent several changes, usually becoming simpler. When wearing field dress, officers were directed (in 1909) to wear the regulation constabulary ornaments on their collars and the insignia of rank "on the left breast above the center of the left pocket."

District directors were authorized to prescribe small brass buttons for their officers' shirts, providing "all officers in the same province will be dressed alike." That same year a mess dress (not shown) was authorized for officers. It consisted of a white mess jacket, a white, single-breasted vest, and either white or black trousers. A stripe (two for senior officers) of scarlet broadcloth decorated the outer seam of the black trousers.

Officers on duty with Mohammedan units, which were issued the fez, finally were given official sanction to wear that headgear. In 1910, the Constabulary officially adopted the cork helmet (which had been unofficially used at least since 1906), both in khaki and white.

In 1911 there were definite changes. The Philippines Constabulary became the Philippine Constabulary. The rank insignia of the U.S. Army was adopted for officers, with the note that "third lieutenants will wear the same insignia as second lieutenants." Army-style chevrons (sometimes called "small chevrons") appeared, placed between shoulder and elbow, instead of the original large chevrons worn just above the cuff. The official date of this changeover was November 1911, but the use of "small chevrons" with enlisted men's off-duty white uniforms had been approved in 1905. "Service chevrons," given for each reenlistment, were quarter-inch strips of red facing cloth on a khaki base, worn one-eighth of an inch apart around the upper end of the cuff.

The band's uniform was prescribed in Paragraph 687½ of the *Manual for the Philippine Constabulary*, dated 16 October 1913, being distinguished by a scarlet broadcloth stripe one and one-half inches in width on the outer seam of their trousers and a trefoil chevron just above the cuff.

The uniform regulations of 1911 provided for no particular change in dress. Officers in garrison might wear leather leggings in place of wool puttees, but they must wear straight white collars, to show about one-eighth of an inch above the blouse collar. Officers must wear campaign hats when their men were in khaki hats, and they must wear helmet and blouse in all formations when the enlisted men were so uniformed. About the only individual choice left officers was the type of gunbelt and holster worn in the field.

These 1911 uniform regulations are illustrated in a rare colored print, prepared by the Constabulary to illustrate nine examples of its uniforms. (See National Archives, Audio Visual Branch: No. 77-F-178-27-2.) These retain the distinctive red piping of the original gray uniforms. This print also shows that the enlisted men were then armed with the Krag-Jorgensen carbine.

The wear on the Constabulary's web cartridge belts seems to have fretted some economy-minded senior officers, producing (in 1908) this gem of quartermaster mentality:

b. The haversack will be so adjusted, if practicable, that the bottom of the haversack clears the top of the belt. In case the height of the soldier does not permit of this adjustment, he will carry no cartridges in his belt under his haversack.

Ronald E. Spicer
John R. Elting

Enlisted Man   Officer   Bandsman
      Garrison Uniform

Officer   Enlisted Men   Ifugao
      Campaign Uniform

Philippine Constabulary, 1912-1914

Panama Canal Zone Police, 1916

Construction of the Panama Canal required the importation of thousands of workmen from all parts of Europe, the United States, Colombia, and the West Indies — a heterogeneous collection needing strict and impartial policing. Also, the threat of tropical diseases, which had wrecked the earlier French attempt to build such a canal, made the enforcement of sanitary regulations imperative.

Accordingly, the Canal Zone Police were activated on 9 May 1904 by executive order of President Theodore Roosevelt. The original force had a high percentage of Panamanians and West Indies negroes, the intent being to form an equivalent of the Philippine Constabulary under white officers and noncommissioned officers, the latter being mostly former "Rough Riders."

This idea was a notable fiasco. White workmen would seldom tolerate arrest by policemen whose skins were darker than their own. The American element was "a band of 'bad men' from our ferocious Southwest."[1]

The force was reorganized. Pay was increased and the Panamanian contingent vanished. Regular Army lieutenants were detailed for duty as officers. A visitor in 1913 noted the results:

> The police force . . . was in command of a regular army officer. In 1913 it numbered 332 policemen, two inspectors, and a chief. Of the policemen 90 were negroes, all of whom had been in the West India constabulary or in West India regiments of the British Army. The white policemen had all served in the United States army, navy, or marine corps. The men are garbed in khaki; and look more like cavalrymen than police officers — indeed a stalwart, well-set-up body of a high order of intelligence and excellent carriage.[2]

Harry A. Franck also spoke proudly of this organization, stating that its members were far above the average in physical appearance, strictly disciplined, and noted for a high standard of honor and efficiency. White enlisted men were either NCOs or policemen first-class (originally private first-class). Nonwhite members were rated as policemen. One of the inspectors supervised the detective branch, which included Colombians, a Swede, a Greek, and a "Chinaman from Martinique." The police also had their "navy" — a steam launch on Gatun Lake.

Uniforms were khaki, usually made to order by the ubiquitous Chinese tailors, and they were worn starched. Cut and style were strictly Army. Buttons were yellow, with the initials "ZP." First-class policemen wore leather puttees and light gray campaign hats (termed "Texas hats") with extra wide brims; policemen had khaki-covered sun helmets and khaki leggings.[3] Noncommissioned officers' chevrons reportedly were yellow, but some photographs show them in the same khaki shade as the blouse.[4] A yellow stripe (possibly gold for officers) was worn around both forearms, just above the point of the cuff, for each two years' service. The top of the white shirt collar always showed above the stand-up collar of the khaki blouse — we must be degenerate offspring of a breed of men who wore such uniforms in the tropics! Gloves were optional. All leather was dark brown.

Officers wore the same uniform as the men. Their insignia of grade was the same size and design as their Army counterparts', but always of yellow metal. It was worn on both sides of the collar, approximately two inches in from the front.

The hat insignia of first-class policemen was of yellow metal with the initials "ZP" on two crossbars, encircled on sides and bottom by a laurel wreath. Policemen's helmets had a silver shield bearing the same initials.[5] Badges — worn centered above the left breast pocket — were of the same spread-eagle-topped design for both grades, but those of first-class policemen were gold, those of policemen silver.

Arms were "saps" (short, heavy clubs) and the .38 Colt revolver. The latter was worn under the blouse on the right side; if the tailor knew his business, the resulting bulge was imperceptible.

For mounted duty, the police used McClellan saddles with hooded stirrups. Saddle blankets were khaki-colored, bound with an edging of dark brown leather approximately one inch wide, and they had the initials "ZP" (also in leather) at their rear angle.[6]

Frederick T. Chapman
John R. Elting

[1] Harry A. Franck, *Zone Policeman 88*. New York, Century Company, 1913.

[2] Willis J. Abbot, *Panama and the Canal in Pictures and Prose*. New York, Syndicate Publishing Company, 1913, 356.

[3] Photographs show two patterns: one a heavy version of the first-class policeman's leather puttees (as shown in this plate), the other the old string-and-eyelet style.

[4] One photograph shows two NCOs with light-colored chevrons against a contrasting background, which may very well have been yellow.

[5] Besides the type shown, there was another — a simply shaped shield with "Canal Zone Police" and the policeman's number.

[6] The inspiration for this plate came from the artist's memories of the smart appearance of the Canal Zone Police when he passed through the Canal during World War I. Reference material was somewhat hard to procure, since the Canal Zone's present Police Division had no records of its own. It did, however, provide the name of Mr. Guy Johannes, the first chief to come up through the ranks to that position. Mr. Johannes furnished considerable information, and also put the author in contact with another former chief, Mr. A. O. Meyer. These two gentlemen, and Mrs. Beverly C. Williams, Chief Reference Librarian of the Canal Zone Library-Museum, provided most of the background material for this plate.

Captain

1st Class Policeman

Policeman

1st Class Policeman
(over 2 years service)

Panama Canal Zone Police, 1916

Company L, 6th Massachusetts Volunteer Infantry Regiment, 1898-1899

The fame of the "old" 6th Massachusetts Volunteer Infantry in the Civil War is well known; yet, equally as historic, but less known, is the fame of the state regiment which bore this title in 1898. Upon request of the federal government for volunteer regiments, Massachusetts began to organize the 6th Regiment from its National Guard forces in April 1898.[1] One of the companies which offered its services and was incorporated into the twelve-company structure of the 6th Regiment, was Company L of Boston. What makes this company of three officers and seventy-four enlisted men so important to the history of the Sixth is that Company L was composed entirely of Afro-Americans.[2]

After equipping itself, the Sixth was accepted into federal service, by companies, between 12 and 13 May 1898. The regiment was then ordered to Camp Alger, Virginia, and on 24 May it was mustered into the 2nd Brigade, 1st Division, which consisted of the 6th Massachusetts, the 6th Illinois, and the 8th Ohio. It was while at Camp Alger that the brigade commander, Brigadier General George A. Garretson, unsuccessfully tried to have Company L transferred to an all-black regiment. Despite Garretson's objections, Company L remained with the regiment. The resentment caused by this incident between Garretson and the regimental officers of the Sixth eventually led to the resignation of Colonel Charles F. Woodward, commander of the Sixth. Woodward resigned when the regiment was in Puerto Rico and was replaced by a regular army officer, Colonel Edmund Rice, a West Point graduate and Civil War veteran.

On 10 July 1898, the Sixth arrived off Santiago, Cuba to participate in the siege of that city, but the garrison capitulated before the Sixth could be landed. The regiment was then assigned to General Miles' invasion force for the capture of Puerto Rico. On 25 July the regiment landed at the harbor of Guanica, Puerto Rico with companies L and M being actively engaged with the enemy. As a result of this action, General Garretson, upon relinquishing command of his brigade on 1 September, officially cited the regiment for its "efficiency under fire. . . ."

After it helped clear the island of Spanish forces, the Sixth went on to garrison duties, one of which involved active campaigning against local bandits. On 21 October, the Sixth left the island for home. After arriving in Boston on 30 October, the Sixth paraded through the city streets and was officially disbanded on 21 January 1899. At the time of its arrival in Boston, regimental strength was 925 officers and men.

The uniforms illustrated are based upon photos of the Sixth and represent the actual style and cut of the clothing worn by the regiment.[3] The first field uniform worn by the enlisted men consisted of the five-button dark blue blouse with sky blue trousers, brown leggings, and felt campaign hat.[4] While in Puerto Rico, the Sixth received an issue of khaki clothing, but since we were unable to locate any photos of enlisted men of the Sixth in their khaki uniform, it has not been shown.

The officers' field uniforms, as shown in photos in Edwards' book, are clearly khaki uniforms with light blue cuffs, collars, and shoulder tabs.[5] There are, however, two interesting features of their uniforms which are clearly shown in the photos. One is the placement of the breast pockets which, contrary to federal style, are placed low upon the front of the coat. The other feature is the officer's belt plate. Although federal regulations call for an eagle-style plate, examination of the photos indicate that a U.S. lettered belt plate was worn by some officers of the Sixth.

The regiment was at first armed with the Springfield rifle but while in Puerto Rico, the Krag-Jorgenson rifle was issued. Regimental officers were armed with the U.S. pattern swords and .38 caliber pistols.

As to the style and types of regimental devices and markings worn on the uniforms and equipment of the Sixth, only those clearly shown in the photos we have seen are illustrated.

We are greatly indebted to Company Fellows Barry Thompson and Roger Sturcke, along with the Boston Historical Society and Mr. Robert E. Feeney of the Adjutant General's Office, Commonwealth of Massachusetts, for their assistance on this plate.

David C. Abbott
Anthony M. Gero

---

[1] All information on the Sixth was taken from these two sources unless otherwise noted: Lieutenant Frank E. Edwards, *The '98 Campaign of the 6th Regiment of Infantry, M.V.M.*, Little and Brown, Boston, 1899 and Charles W. Hall, (Ed.), *Regiments and Armories of Massachusetts*, W.W. Porter Company, Boston, 2 Vols., 1899.

[2] Although both of the above sources have valuable information on Company L, an interesting article, entitled "Company L, in the Spanish-American War" by Lieutenant Braxton, appeared in the *Colored American Magazine*, May 1900, Vol. I, No. I, 19-24.

[3] Edwards, *op. cit.*, and Hall, *op. cit.*

[4] From photos in Edwards' book, it seems that the Sixth wore the U.S. pattern undress cap when it left Massachusetts for Camp Alger, but sometime while there it received the felt campaign hat.

[5] Jacques N. Jacobsen, *Regulations and Notes for the Uniform of the Army of the United States, 1899*, Manor Publishing, N.Y., 1973.

First Lieutenant   Captain   Private   Corporal

Company L, 6th Massachusetts Volunteer Infantry Regiment
1898-1899

7th Infantry Regiment, National Guard, New York, 1900-1905

The years immediately following the Spanish-American War were years of marked transition in military dress and accoutrements. Nowhere are the changes illustrated more forcefully than in the types shown here. Still clinging to its traditional gray, the 7th Regiment in these years introduced field service innovations of several kinds. The result was an odd but not impractical medley which lasted until the adoption of the regulation state khaki uniform in 1906.

Up to 1900, despite several experiments, the fatigue and field uniforms remained essentially those the Seventh had worn since before the Civil War. In that year the famous gray jacket was replaced by the gray blouse shown in the plate. Officers were already wearing a dark blue coat with roll collar and patch pockets for fatigue, the blue continuing the tradition that officers be easily distinguished from the men. In 1900, too, a gray flannel shirt and a campaign hat were prescribed for wear at summer camp.[1]

The adjutant still wears his patent leather sabretache despite the fact it seems anachronistic with his wrap puttees, the latter introduced a few years before in the British army. Equally British are the short leather leggings worn by the enlisted men. For some fatigue formations the men wore their gray dress kepis; these years saw the last stand of this ancient article, worn since the 1850s.

The sergeant major and officer wear swords and the sergeant, armed with the U.S. rifle, model 1889, has the state regulation loop cartridge belt. This was the golden age of the bicycle and, naturally, one was standard equipment for an orderly. In these uniforms and accoutrements the Seventh served at the State Camp of Instruction at Peekskill, N.Y., and on maneuvers with another gray-clad outfit, the U.S. Corps of Cadets.

Frederick P. Todd

[1] DeWitt Clinton Falls, *History of the Seventh Regiment, 1889–1922,* New York, 1948, 44, 108.

Fatigue and Field Service Uniforms

Battalion Sergeant Major   Battalion Adjutant   Sergeant (in Shirt)   Orderly

7th Infantry Regiment, National Guard State of New York, 1900-1905

10th Pennsylvania Volunteer Infantry Regiment, 1898-1899

The success of Pennsylvania's militia organization following the Civil War can be attributed largely to the energy of one man, Governor John White Geary. During his tenure (from 1867 to 1873), he reactivated many old units, created new ones, and encouraged the employment of combat-experienced officers to bring the service to a high degree of efficiency.

The 10th Pennsylvania Infantry Regiment, coming from the southwestern part of the state, was organized originally as the First Provisional Battalion in 1872, and the next year, expanded into a full regiment.[1] Most of its companies could trace their lineage to Revolutionary days and one company, I, has in its possession the barrel of a bronze six-pounder captured from the British at the raising of the siege of Fort Meigs in 1813.

The adventures of the Tenth on its first overseas expedition remain one of the brightest spots of its history. It and the First Tennessee were the only volunteer units from east of the Mississippi. The Tenth was known as a "bob-tailed" regiment, i.e., it had but eight companies, organized into two battalions.[2] Following President McKinley's call for volunteers, the Tenth was mustered into federal service 12 May 1898 and less than a week later was on its way across the continent, bound for the Philippines as part of the VIII Army Corps commanded by General Wesley Merritt. It sailed into Manila Bay on the 17th of July.

Service in the Philippines lasted nearly a year and it is during this period that we see the men here depicted. Their dress and accoutrements reflect the medley of state and federal issue, of blue and khaki clothing, and of old and new weapons and tactics. Only some of the many combinations are shown; indeed, the Tenth also had a nonregulation all-white uniform, bought individually in Manila, which is not shown in the picture.

An entry in the diary of Private Jacob Detar of I Company well illustrates the mixed dress of the Regiment. Dated 23 April 1899, it reads: "Weather hot. Order for daily drill — brown undershirt, brown trowsers, leggins. Guard mount, Blue shirt, brown trowsers, *polished shoes*. Parade, Blue blouse, white trowsers, black shoes, &c. Gingham shirts still on hand. Have concluded the war is over."[3]

The sergeant on the left is a sniper and carries one of the twenty-five Krag-Jorgensen model 1892 rifles issued per company and used for sniper duty and night patrols. His belt is the double type fitted for the smaller cartridges. He wears a blue woolen shirt and khaki trousers. All veterans agree that these trousers faded badly after a couple of washings and soon became almost white.

The sergeant wears on his hat the insignia of the VIII Corps. His canteen carries the "NGP" of National Guard days; only the replacements who arrived well along in the campaign had canteens marked "U.S."

The next soldier has the Springfield .45-70 carried by the bulk of the men. His work shirt is of blue gingham and his trousers are the old style. On the front of his hat is the cross-rifles insignia; sometimes this was worn on the right side and sometimes it has "10" and "PENN" above and below the rifles.

The officer in the center has on a khaki uniform issued in the Philippines and, as a result, it has "USV" on the collar. The officer on the right wears the older field uniform with state collar insignia. He has, however, replaced his state cap insignia with a U.S. Army type; many of the officers wore the state cap device throughout the campaign.

It will be noticed that the soldiers wore no blanket rolls; they never did during their entire stay. Instead they carried only the poncho, which was folded and stuffed through the back of the Mills cartridge belt.

The regimental color is shown in the background. It was over six by six feet in size and bore the arms of Pennsylvania in the canton. It actually was carried in action, thus being one of the last American colors to come under direct fire.

The casualty report shows that fifteen men were killed in action, seventy were wounded, ten died of disease, and one man was reported missing.

Frederick T. Chapman
James Gregg, Jr.

[1] W. Packer Clarke, *History of the Militia and National Guard of Pennsylvania*, Harrisburg 1909, II, 150; Edward Martin, *History of the 28th Division in the World War*, Pittsburgh 1923, I, 371.

[2] *Annual Report* of the Adjutant-General of Pennsylvania for the Year 1898, Harrisburg 1900, 407-410. There are several accounts of the Regiment's Philippine experiences, notably in: Association of the 110th Infantry, *History of the 110th Infantry (10th Pa.)* . . . , Pittsburg 1920; *Official History of the Operations of the Tenth Pennsylvania Infantry, U.S. Volunteers, in the Campaign in the Philippine Islands*, Greensburg, Pa., 1950; special edition, *The Pittsburg Post*, 27 Aug. 1899. It is from illustrations in these and other histories and from descriptions furnished by Major General Edward Martin, the late Brigadier General Richard Coulter, Captain Richard D. Laird, the late Alex Eicher, Dan A. Dooley, and Harry P. Cope, all veterans, that this plate is based.

[3] "Diary of Jacob Detar," MS in possession of James Gregg, Jr.

Sergeant   *Private*   *Officers, Khaki and Blue Field Uniforms*

10th Pennsylvania Volunteer Infantry Regiment, 1898-1899

2nd Troop, Philadelphia City Cavalry, 1897-1941

Second Troop, Philadelphia City Cavalry was organized in 1776 soon after the 1st Troop had left Philadelphia for the field during the Revolutionary War. Since the 1st Troop took the name "Philadelphia Light Horse," the 2nd Troop adopted the name "Philadelphia Light Dragoons."[1]

However, the 2nd Troop possibly can trace its lineage back to the French and Indian War period, since some members who joined the ranks in 1776 had served with the Independent Troop of Horse of Philadelphia City in 1756.

After the Revolutionary War, the troop had the honor of escorting General George Washington, then President-elect Washington, through the city. It was at that time the name of the organization was changed to 2nd Troop of Philadelphia Light Horse. Soon after that, the troop formed part of the cavalry force called out to help suppress the Whiskey Insurrection in Western Pennsylvania.

During the War of 1812, 2nd Troop formed part of the 1st Pennsylvania Cavalry Regiment. After its return from federal service, the troop continued in active, performing escort duties and assisting in the suppression of local disorder. In 1824, it joined 1st Troop as escort to the Marquis de Lafayette on his triumphal tour of the United States.

At the outbreak of the war with Mexico, the troop enlisted almost to a man, for service with the Scott Legion. Soon after the Mexican War, interest in the troop waned, and its ranks began to thin. Organization was, however, maintained until the Civil War. By this time the troop could not muster enough men to enlist as a unit. Individual members enlisted in numerous Pennsylvania Cavalry regiments and fought gallantly through the four years of the conflict.

In 1896, a movement was projected to reorganize the 2nd Troop in Philadelphia, and in the fall of that year, a social organization was formed with that end in view. The first drill was held the following year, and the troop ranks were soon filled with many of the socially prominent men of the Philadelphia area. The troop was formally mustered into the National Guard of Pennsylvania on 4 June 1898.

The full-dress uniforms which the troop adopted were copied from those worn by the British 10th Hussars, and consisted of a scarlet hussar jacket with white braid, black fur busby with white plume and red busby-bag, blue stockingknit breeches with a broad red stripe, short cavalry boots, white leather baldric with cartridge box, gauntlets, and a saber belt of white leather, worn under the jacket. Collar ornaments and shoulder knots worn by officers were of gold; those of enlisted men were white. Trumpeters wore reversed colors for their tunics, that is, white with red trim.[2] The uniforms were purchased from Jacob Reeds' Sons for fifteen dollars.[3]

Sabers carried by the enlisted troopers were the model 1860 while officers' sabers were the officer's model 1872. These sabers were purchased from John Wanamaker for $4.50 including the belt. Saddles were the McClellan model and for dress a white sheepskin covered the saddle. Saddles and bridles were purchased from George de B. Keim & Co. of Philadelphia for $16.50 complete.[4]

It was in this strikingly handsome uniform that the troop performed escort and ceremonial duty for most of the dignitaries who visited Philadelphia.

The troop performed field duty during the anthracite coal strikes of 1902 and later during the Mexican Border Campaign of 1916. During World War I, the troop was assigned to Headquarters Company 53rd Field Artillery Brigade and saw service in France.

Returning to Philadelphia in 1919, the troop was reorganized the following year as Troop D, 1st Cavalry, Pennsylvania National Guard. On 1 June 1921, it was redesignated as Troop B, 103rd Cavalry, PNG.[5]

During the period between the two World Wars, 2nd Troop, Philadelphia City Cavalry, clung to its adopted name as a quasi-military-social organization, and at the same time it adhered to the more elaborate National Guard system of discipline and organization as a strictly military unit. The troop's annual training at the Pennsylvania National Guard encampment at Mt. Gretna proved to be a lark for the Philadelphia boys.

The troop's assignment in 1939 was changed from the 103rd Cavalry to the 104th Cavalry. Finally, on the eve of World War II, it was inducted into federal service once more as Battery B, 166th Field Artillery.

The colorful days of the society horse soldiers were over, and 2nd Troop as a handsomely uniformed, social-military organization did not survive World War II.

R. Darby Erd
Michael J. Winey

[1] Manuscript in the Archives of the Pennsylvania Historical & Museum Commission, Harrisburg, Pennsylvania, MG #237-2nd Troop, Philadelphia City Cavalry Collection, 1810-1941.

[2] _____, "Second Troop, Philadelphia City Cavalry," Our State Army and Navy, Philadelphia, Pennsylvania: Charles J. Hendler, Pub., Vol. II, No. 9, October 1899, 5. See also: Full Dress Uniform Regulations of the Second Troop, Philadelphia City Cavalry, Armory, Northwest Corner of 23rd and Chestnut Streets, Philadelphia, Pennsylvania, 1 September 1906.

[3] MSS-Archives of PHMC, op. cit.

[4] Ibid.

[5] Adjutant General's Office, Department of Military Affairs, Pennsylvania Military Regulations No. 80 (Histories and Records) Historical Outlines of Organizations, 1 March 1937, 60.

Captain	Trooper	Sergeant	Trooper	Trumpeter
Full Dress	*Dress with cape*	*Full Dress*	*Full Dress*	*Full Dress*

DARBY ERD

2nd Troop, Philadelphia City Cavalry, 1897-1941

U.S. Navy, Shore Party, 1917

The ceremonies for the transfer of the Danish West Indies to the United States took place on 31 March 1917. The United States was represented by officers and men of the United States Navy, under Commander Edwin T. Pollock.

The uniforms worn by officers and men of the United States Honor Guard for the ceremony in St. Thomas were as prescribed by the Navy's 1913 uniform regulations.[1]

Commander Pollock's uniform consisted of the special full-dress, double-breasted blue coat, blue trousers, cocked hat, and the full-dress sword and belt. The coat had an inch-and-a-half-wide strip of gold lace on the standing collar, and three half-inch strips of gold lace on the cuffs with a gold star above the lace. The trousers had an inch-and-a-half-wide strip of gold lace on the outer seams. The cocked hat for officers below flag rank had no lace on the outer rim but instead had strips of black silk. Grade was shown by a strip of gold lace over the cockade on the right side of the hat. For a commander, the lace was an inch and a half wide, like that on his collar. Grade was also indicated by devices on the epaulets. For a commander, there was a silver oak leaf on the frog, with the silver foul anchor above it on the strap. A commander's sword belt was the dress belt of black grain leather, faced with blue silk webbing on the outer side. The belt had seven gold stripes, 1/16 of an inch wide, woven into the silk webbing. All officers, except chaplains, carried identical swords and sword knots.

In warm locations, officers on duty with enlisted men ashore, under arms, wore the white undress uniform with leggings, high black shoes, and caps with white covers. An officer's grade was indicated by his shoulder insignia, which was the same as that on the sleeves of blue coats. For a lieutenant, the straps had two half-inch-wide strips of gold lace, with the star above them for officers of the line. The cap displayed the silver shield, topped by a silver spread eagle, mounted on two crossed gold foul anchors. Officers of the rank of lieutenant commander and below had plain black visors on their caps. When officers were with men ashore, officers wore swords with the black leather undress belts under the white coats.

Chief petty officers wore a white double-breasted sack coat with four medium-sized gilt buttons on each breast. The white coat was of the pattern prescribed for the blue coat, with no pocket flaps. A chief's rating was shown by a device on the upper sleeve — on the right sleeve of chiefs of the seaman branch and on the left sleeve for those of the artificer branch. The rating badge was made up of the class chevron with a spread eagle above the specialty mark. For a chief, the eagle was perched on an arc resting on the upper ends of the upper stripe of the chevron. The specialty mark of the quartermaster was, and still is, the ship's helm. For white uniforms, the sleeve marks were in blue cloth. The lower sleeve has stripes of blue cloth indicating the years of service, with one stripe for each four years. The visored cap had a white cover with a device, the letters "USN" in silver mounted on a slightly inclined gilt foul anchor. The chief was armed with a .45 automatic pistol hung from a cartridge belt, and he wore black shoes and khaki-colored leggings.

The enlisted men of the Honor Guard wore white dress uniforms. The dress jumpers had dark blue flannel collars and cuffs. The cuffs were trimmed with narrow white linen stripes — in the plate the enlisted man is wearing three stripes, which indicates a seaman first class. All enlisted men wore a white seaman's cap and black silk neckerchief. White trousers and black shoes were worn, with khaki leggings worn for duty with a landing force. The men of the Honor Guard were armed with rifles and had bayonets slung from their cartridge belts.

Bandsmen of the Navy wore white uniforms very different from those of other enlisted men. Under the 1913 order, bandsmen's white trousers were like those for chief petty officers, stewards, and officers' cooks. The white coat was patterned on the summer field coat of enlisted men of the Marine Corps, single-breasted with a standing collar. A metal device, the lyre, was worn on either side of the collar. Bandsmen also wore the lyre as a specialty mark on their left sleeve and as a cap badge. For the white uniform the device and rating badges were in blue.

H. Charles McBarron, Jr.
James C. Tily

[1]Uniform Regulations, United States Navy, Navy Department, 1913 (Revised, 15 January 1917, G.P.O. 1917).
(Some photographs of the ceremony in St. Thomas were secured from Denmark. Of great help were the Royal Navy Museum, Tøjhusmuseet, and the Royal Library.)

Chief Petty Officer   Lieutenant   Seaman   Commander Pollock   Bandman
Boatswain

U.S. Navy, Shore Party, 1917

U.S. Navy, Bandsmen, 1897

Although "musics" were part of the authorized complements of the first ships of the U.S. Navy built under the legislation of 27 March 1794, these musicians were marines, not seamen.[1] The first specific reference that musicians could be entered on the roles as such, and not carried as seamen or some other seagoing rating, is contained in the pay schedules listed in the Navy Register of 1838. The 1897 strength returns in the National Archives indicate one bandmaster, ten first-class musicians (eleven allowed), and eleven second-class musicians on the *Vermont,* and sixteen musicians, including one bandmaster serving with the cruiser *New York.* According to the "Register of Commissioned and Warrant Officers of the Navy of the United States to July 1, 1897," bandsmen were authorized the following ratings:

Rate	Grade
Bandmaster	Chief Petty Officer
1st Musician	Petty Officer 1st Class
1st Class Musician	Seaman 1st Class
2nd Class Musician ⎫ Bugler ⎭	Seaman 2nd Class

The first distinctive uniform for Navy bandsmen was described in the Uniform Regulations of 1886, approved 1 July 1885 by Secretary of the Navy W. C. Whitney. However, the succeeding alteration in dress, found in the 1897 regulations, prescribed a most colorful uniform which is the subject of this plate.[2]

The full-dress uniform for bandsmen consisted of "Dress coat; blue cloth or white trousers; helmet; shoulder knots and aiguillette; belt; gloves (and sword for bandmaster)." In undress, the uniform was "Undress coat; blue cloth or white trousers; blue undress cap, or cap and cap cover."

The full-dress scarlet coat was single-breasted, with eight large fire-gilt navy buttons and a standing collar. It was piped with white on the top and bottom of the collar, and on the front edge, bottom, and skirts. Yellow worsted lace, half an inch wide, banded the top of the collar. The pointed cuffs were trimmed with yellow lace, three-quarters of an inch wide, piped with white. While the shoulder knots of the bandmaster were gold cord, those of other bandsmen were white mohair braid. The same distinction was made in the aiguillettes, the bandmaster's being gold cord and white mohair for the rest. The spiked helmet was the same as that worn by the Marine Corps, but with the device of the Army on which a white metal lyre was superimposed. Dress trousers were of sky blue cloth, with a strip of inch-wide scarlet cloth on the outer seams for bandmasters, and a welt 3/16 of an inch wide for bandsmen. The bandmaster's sword was the same as that worn by field musicians of the Marine Corps, the 1840 model sword as carried by marine NCOs.

In undress, the dark indigo-blue coat was one-and-one-half inches shorter than the dress coat, with a single row of seven medium-sized buttons. On either side of the standing collar was a white lyre, the musicians' device. The coat was piped with scarlet flannel, one-eighth inch wide, down the front, along the bottom, around the base of the collar, on the edges of the shoulder straps, and on the top, bottom, and outer edges of the cuff straps. The undress chasseur cap was the same as worn by enlisted men of the Marine Corps, with the lyre as a cap device. Trousers were of blue cloth or white, depending on the season. Rates were indicated as in the rest of the Navy with petty officers' chevrons worn on the sleeve and the lyre serving as the distinguishing mark.

The overcoat was described by the uniform regulations as the "same as for enlisted men of the Marine Corps, except that navy fire-gilt buttons will be worn." The sky blue, double-breasted overcoat was lined with scarlet flannel and fitted with a detachable cape. On parade, the corners of the cape were turned back and hooked, showing the scarlet lining.

H. Charles McBarron, Jr.
James C. Tily

[1] Act of 27 March 1794, "To Provide a Naval Armament."
[2] *Regulations Governing the Uniforms of Commissioned Officers, Warrant Officers and Enlisted Men of the Navy of the United States,* approved 1 July 1897. Washington, GPO, 1897.

Bandmaster, Full Dress   Bandsman, Undress   Bandsman, Full Dress

U.S. Navy, Bandsmen, 1897

Naval Militia, Massachusetts and New York, 1888-1910

Although interest had been expressed during the post-Civil War years in creating naval militias, neither the federal government nor the states undertook funding of any units. In 1888 the state of Massachusetts decided to form the first naval militia unit.[1] By 1894, twenty-five other states had created such units, in great part due to a congressional act of 21 March 1891, which provided funds for state naval militias.

In the Spanish-American War, the naval militias served alongside the Regular Navy. By World War I, naval planners were counting on the militia for trained officers and men.

It is apparent that from the beginning naval militia uniforms tried to follow Regular Navy styles.[2] Our plate shows this, plus some variations which did occur in the early 1890s.

The lefthand figure of a Massachusetts officer is based on a photograph of Lieutenant Commander John Codman Soley. Soley wears the undress uniform with gold sleeve stripes. By 1897 the naval militias of both Massachusetts and New York had adopted the Regular Navy's practice of using gold sleeve stripes, instead of black, on their service dress.

The item of interest in Soley's dress is the cap. In the Regular Navy, officers above the rank of commander had gold embroidery lace (line officers) or flat gold lace (staff officers). Holding the rank of lieutenant commander, Soley is wearing lace above his station.

The next figure is based on photographs of seamen of the Massachusetts Naval Battalion in the 1890s. The photographs are from Hall's book.[3]

We have shown a bugler equipped for shore duty. He wears a dark blue jumper. From the photographs we cannot tell if there is any lettering on his seaman's cap, however. His Mill's belt plate bears the Massachusetts logo. The bugle cords are white.

The center figure is of Commander William B. Franklin, who commanded the 1st Battalion of New York Naval Militia from 1900 to 1909.[4] The photograph of Franklin in Minton's book shows him in the full-dress uniform of blue frock trimmed with gold lace.

The extreme righthand figure is of a N.Y.N.M. seaman in 1891. When first authorized in the state, the naval militia was called the "First Battalion Naval Reserve Artillery, S.N.Y." The Battalion consisted of four batteries with a total strength of fifteen officers and 190 enlisted seamen.

Photographs in Minton's book, dated 1891, show all seamen wearing white canvas jumpers and hats. On the front breast of each seaman's jumper is the lettering "NRASNY."

Our corpsman illustrates several items of dress different from those of the other seamen. The first is the Geneva cross worn on the left arm. The other feature is the naval cutlass of Civil War vintage worn on his belt, both of which are substantiated by photographs in Minton's work.

By an act of the state legislature dated 25 June 1892, the naval militia became known as the 1st Naval Battalion, and all batteries were redesignated as divisions. The emblem of the 1st Battalion was also illustrated in Minton, and we have shown it as pictured there. We assume its date of adoption can be no earlier than June of 1892.

Raymond S. Johnson
Anthony M. Gero
Roger S. Sturcke

[1]James Tily, *The Uniforms of the United States Navy*, New York, 1964. All factual data taken from this source unless otherwise noted.
[2]Naval Militia, General Orders No. 1, Adjutant General's Office, Albany, 31 January 1893. *Report of Adjutant General of State of New York, 1893*, I, 268-277. This order details all items of dress and establishes grades for N.Y.N.M.
[3]Charles W. Hall, *Regiments and Armories of Massachusetts*. Chapter IX, II, n.p., 1901.
[4]T. M. Minton, Lieutenant (JG) and Assistant Paymaster, 1st Battalion, NYNM, *History of the First Battalion, Naval Militia, New York, 1891 to 1911*, New York, 1911.

Lieutenant Commander and Seaman,
Massachusetts Naval Battalion

Commander, 1st Battalion,
New York Naval Militia

Seaman, 1st Battalion,
Naval Reserve Artillery, S.N.Y.

Naval Militia, Massachusetts and New York, 1888-1910

Cuban Volunteer Battalions, 1892-1898

The last thirty years of Spanish rule in Cuba, 1868-1898, were filled with native uprisings. In spite of reinforcements from Spain, the garrison of the 44th Antillas Infantry Regiment and the 17th Cuba and 18th Habana Rifle Battalions could not hold their own against the *mambí* insurgents, and the peninsular government had to form Cuban Volunteer Battalions to help uphold the Spanish flag. In time, practically every ablebodied Spaniard residing in Cuba saw service in this auxiliary force of some 80,000 men, who were organized, trained, and equipped like the regular infantry, cavalry, artillery, and engineers.[1] Two battalions formed a regiment; standard peacetime strength of a battalion with four active and one depot company was 404 officers and men, increased to 1,000 during wartime. Spain furnished arms and ammunition, but the volunteers bought their dress and equipment and frequently were paid by *abonaré* chits, to be cashed after the war.

The basic dress was the same for all branches and ranks of service. A straw hat of finer *jipijapa* for officers and coarser *yarey* for troops had a black patent-leather hatband with the red-yellow-red Spanish cockade held by a gold or silver loop for officers, yellow loop for cavalry, and green loop for infantry. Washable blouses and trousers were of white *rayadillo* cotton drilling with thin blue vertical stripes. Laced shoes, a raincoat in the wet season, grey blanket, white haversack, and black or brown leather belting with a variety of cartridge pouches comprised the scant general issue. Mounted units wore black boots or buffalo-hide leggings stitched to the trousers; foot units sometimes strapped short black leggings over trouser bottoms. Generally, no distinctive devices were used on campaign, but facings and rank insignia were worn in garrison: green collar, cuffs, and trouser-stripes, yellow piping and three yellow *sardinetas* (cuff flashes) for infantry; red collar, cuffs, and stripes for all others. Metal buttons and unit numbers within a hunter's horn on the collar were yellow for infantry, white for cavalry. Officers on duty wore metal gorgets and donned white gloves for full dress. Insignia of rank were: three half-inch stripes and large eight-point stars on cuffs for colonel, two for lieutenant colonel, one gold and one silver for major; these staff officers also carried canes. In addition, there were three quarter-inch-wide tapes and small six-point stars above the cuffs for captain, two for 1st lieutenant, one silver and one gold for 2nd lieutenant, a single tape and one star for ensign. Sergeants had three diagonal gold or silver stripes on the forearm, corporals the same in red worsted; a narrow red worsted chevron on the left arm from elbow to shoulder signified a buck private.[2] The same dress and insignia were also worn by Spanish troops in Puerto Rico and the Philippines.[3]

The standard Spanish army weapon at that time was the 1871 model single-shot, 1.31 mm long Remington rifle with a 62cm socket bayonet. This was the 1870 model, .50 caliber Remington Patent Breechloader originally manufactured at Springfield and widely used by foreign countries because of its strength, durability, and foolproof mechanical action. Cavalry troops carried carbines; artillery and engineers in addition were armed with broad machetes. The Remington was later replaced with the Spanish 1892 five-shot 7mm Mauser repeater, but in 1893 only one line regiment in Spain and one rifle battalion in Puerto Rico were experimentally issued the latter. Officers were armed with sabers or long machetes, and six-shot Lefaucheux revolvers.[4]

Jose M. Bueno
Joseph Hefter

[1]Letter, Villareal to Gomez, in Barado-Cusachs, *Nuestros Soldados*, Barcelona, 1909, 167-177.
[2]Uniform chart in *Reglamento para los Cuerpos Voluntarios de Cuba*, Havana, 1892.
[3]*Album Descriptivo del Ejército y la Armada de España*, Madrid 1894, 35-37, Plate 29.
[4]"Nuestro Material Moderno de Guerra," *Ilustración Española y Americana*, 1896, Vol. 38, 222-228.

Sapper
Campaign Dress

Lt. Colonel, Infantry
Duty Dress

Corporal, Cavalry

Infantryman
Garrison Dress

Cuban Volunteer Battalions, 1892-1898

Villistas, 1913

It is not generally known that the Mexican revolutionary troops, known as *Villistas*, or followers of Francisco Villa, grew out of a unit formed on U.S. soil between Nogales and El Paso. In 1912, "Pancho" Villa, who had joined Francisco Madero in a successful revolt against President Diaz in 1910, was serving as colonel of government irregulars under the command of Victoriano Huerta. Villa aroused Huerta's suspicions and was sentenced to death for insubordination. He was saved from the firing squad at the last moment by the intervention of President Madero and confined to a military prison. Villa escaped on Christmas Day, 1912 and crossed into the United States at Nogales, Arizona on 2 January 1913.[1] Here he was joined by nine of his former command, and with them, he returned to Mexico on 23 March 1913. In the short time between January and March, while safe behind the U.S. border, he had laid the groundwork for what was later to become the Division of the North, popularly known and feared as the Villistas.

Within a few months, the handful of men under Villa grew to a force of 18,000 combatants, two-thirds of them cavalry. From then on, until the force was dispersed by General Obregon at Celaya in 1915, the Villistas formed the most daring and picturesque division of the armies of the Mexican Revolution.[2]

The troops of Villa considered themselves armed citizenry and never wore any formal uniforms or insignia, yet their dress had striking characteristics that set them apart from all other divisions. Occasionally, some officer or sergeant pinned army stripes of rank around his cuffs, such as the mounted officer in this case who wears the insignia of a cavalry captain, three strips of silver lace over a bright red cloth background. Their most popular headgear was the broad-brimmed *sombrero jarano*, a tan or dark grey felt hat with conical crown, or the narrow-brimmed black, grey, or olive drab *sombrero tejano* similar to the U.S. "campaign" hat of World War I. A brown or tan ranch jacket or vest was worn over a white, olive drab, or golden-yellow shirt with a white or red neckerchief. Grey or brown riding pants were often covered with heavily buckled full-length brown leather chaps or leggings reaching to the thigh. Mexican-style ranch saddles were of natural russet leather. The laced stirrup hood, *estribo con tapadera y amarres*, is still used by Mexican ranchers and cowmen and was popular with mounted revolutionaries.

The principal weapon in Villa's forces was the standard Mexican 7mm Mauser army rifle or carbine, supplemented by revolvers in Western-style holsters. A variety of models of the Mauser rifle were in use in Mexico in 1913; the Mexican Mondragon, the Belgian, Spanish, and other styles designed between 1894 and 1903, different shapes and sizes but all based on the Spanish 1893 model Mauser. They varied considerably from the original German design but all had as their common feature, their 7mm caliber.

One to four cartridge bandoleers strapped across chest or waist became the trade mark of Villa's and other revolutionary troops. Belts with eight to ten pockets for five-cartridge clips alternated with those having double or single loops for individual cartridges. In 1903, in an attempt to improve army equipment, Mexican regular cavalry received bandoleers with eight buttoned pockets for cartridge clips, while the rurales and customs guards were issued bandoleers with loops. This government stock was captured by the rebels. When the demand for equipment grew with the revolution, large numbers of loop bandoleers were produced by local leather workers. The thirty-round folded cartridge cases were a discarded army model scorned by the rebels as well, who preferred the forty- to fifty-round chest and waist bandoleers.[3]

The troops were divided into brigades named after historical personalities such as Cuauhtemoc, Morelos, Juarez, Zaragoza and, of course, Villa. The early *Villistas* moved rapidly on horseback or in captured trains, relying on surprise attacks, ambushes, and feints, but also putting up desperate sustained battles when necessary. Written reports on their dress and equipment are scant, but eyewitnesses and photographs still exist to show clearly their types, dress, and general appearance. The figures in this plate are reconstructed from photographs of Villa and his followers shortly after they re-entered Mexico from the United States in 1913.

Joseph Hefter

[1]Personal notes by Luis Aguirre Benavides, Villa's private secretary.
[2]G. Casasola: "Historia Grafica de la Revolucion 1900-1940," Mexico 1940; Cuadernos, 4, 5 and 6, 451, 525, 653.
[3]Photographs in the possession of the Mexican Legion of Honor at the Defense Ministry, Mexico, D.F.

Villistas, 1913

Mexican 19th Infantry Battalion, 1914

On 21 and 22 April 1914, U.S. Marines landed at Vera Cruz harbor in Mexico and occupied the city. The seizure of Vera Cruz was the climax to a long series of disputes between the United States and the Huerta administration in Mexico. The latter had shown increasing indifference to the security of American lives and property. A series of "incidents" culminated with the arrest and mistreatment of an officer and boat's crew from the USS *Dolphin* while they were engaged in loading ship's stores at Tampico. They were finally released, but Mexican authorities refused to offer an apology.

The only organized Mexican military force in Vera Cruz was one undermanned company of the 19th Infantry Battalion which hightailed into the interior, pausing only to release the inmates of the local prisons — a rearguard tactic previously employed against Americans in Mexico City in 1847. The resulting looting, shooting, and riot appears in Mexican history as an epic of heroic patriotism against overwhelming odds.

At that time, the regular Mexican infantry was dressed in the 1912 model army uniform confirmed by the dress regulations of 1913.[1] Provincial garrisons, especially in the *Tierra Caliente* tropical belt, complied with these regulations only loosely. Mexico was then in the midst of a civil war, and neither discipline nor the supply service were of the type to guarantee correct uniforms and equipment.

The 1913 regulations provided both officers and men with a dark blue full-dress uniform, an olive green garrison and field uniform, and a white sailcloth dress for the hot country. The blue garrison uniform for officers consisted of a dark blue cap with black leather visor and chin strap, a blue-black coat with a row of seven buttons and four buttoned pockets, black epaulet loops with gold cord edging, a black cloth patch with gilt battalion number on collar, and blue-black trousers with a wide stripe at the seams. The infantry service color was rose madder (crimson) and appeared on the piping around the crown of the cap and the cuffs, on the cinch band of the cap, and on the collar, cuff patches, and trouser stripes. All buttons and emblems were gilt for infantry officers. A tricolor cockade with green center and red border appeared on the front of the cap. Rank was indicated by gold insignia (for a captain, three vertical bars,) on the cap band and epaulet loops, and by gold lace under the piping around the cuffs. While on duty, each infantry member wore a black leather pistol holster suspended from the left shoulder and a saber supported by a single chain from a yellow metal buckled black leather waistbelt. The sword knot was black leather with a small gold tassel.

The field uniform consisted of a cork helmet of the British colonial type covered with olive green canvas, the front visor lined in green, with a ventilator on top and a brown patent leather chinstrap. The service emblem, in this case an upright bugle over two crossed rifles for infantry, painted green, appeared on the front of the helmet, with the unit number above. The coat was olive green with five paste buttons, two buttoned breast pockets, turnover collar, and buttoned shoulder straps; the trousers were plain olive green. Officers wore brown leather leggings, while the man wore canvas gaiters. Open leather sandals over bare feet were worn by the rank and file for fatigue duty or on long marches. A dark gray overcoat and a gray-black blanket with wide black stripes eight inches from the edges were strapped down to the brown waterproof, leather-edged canvas knapsack together with a dark brown tent cloth. The blanket could also be carried rolled up over the left shoulder. All belts were of dark brown cowhide; the bayonet frog was at the left. A tin canteen, nested with a cup and two plates, was suspended at the right side from a leather strap. The standard firearm was the Mexican model of the 1898 German Mauser rifle and bayonet, with brown leather rifle sling. Under combat conditions, especially on the coast, the standard dress was either the cork helmet or an olive green cap combined with a white duck blouse, trousers, and gaiters. The Mexican soldier's habit of turning up trousers and underpants to the middle of the calf was noted in contemporary photographs.

The peculiar fringed chevrons, called *golpes*, on the bugler's sleeves are a distinctive device for all drummers and buglers in the Mexican army. They began to appear during the French occupation of Mexico, 1863-1867, and except for variations in color, remain in continuous use to this day. Rank insignia for 1914 noncoms were crimson silk lace around the cuffs and on the shoulder straps; three stripes for 1st sergeant, two for 2nd sergeant, one for corporal, and one on the left sleeve only for buck private.

A Mexican infantry battalion of the period consisted of four companies of 134 men and 10 officers each. Three of the companies were riflemen (*fusileros*), the other was a machine gun company.[2]

Joseph Hefter
John R. Elting

[1] *Reglamento de Uniformes para Generales, Jefes, Oficiales, Cadetes y Tropa del Ejerita Nacional*, Secretaria del Estrado y de Guerra y Marine, Mexico, 1913, with 115 color plates; reissued with errata corrections and 98 color plates in April 1914.

[2] *Ley Organica de Ejercito Nacional*, Secretaria de Guerra y Marine, Depto, del Estado Mayor, Decreto 225; Mexico, 1900.

First Sergeant Musician,
Field Dress

Captain,
Garrison Duty Dress

Private,
Marching Order

Second Sergeant,
Tropical Field Dress

Mexican 19th Infantry Battalion, 1914

West India Regiments, 1870-1900

This plate illustrates the radical changes in the uniforms of the West India regiments from those of the period 1800-1815.

On 1 October 1888, due to the Cardwell Reforms of 1881, the 1st and 2nd West India Regiments were consolidated into one unit designated "The West India Regiment." This new unit had two battalions of eight companies each, but with a single depot company.[1] Used primarily for colonial service in Africa, each battalion served a three-year tour of duty there while the other remained in the Caribbean area. By the 1880s the practice of enlisting native Africans had been discontinued; Jamaicans generally volunteered for the 1st Battalion while Barbadians went into the 2nd.[2] A third battalion was raised in 1897-1898.[3]

The precise date of adopting a Zouave dress for the West India regiments is unknown. Most sources agree it was around 1858-1859, although by 1863 the 5th West India Regiment was ordered clothed in Zouave dress with scarlet facings.[4] The inspiration for this change seems to have been Queen Victoria, who as early as 1853 expressed extreme interest in the French Zouaves.[5] By 1865 the prescribed issue was "a fez & two turbans, jacket, waistcoat, breeches, — dress and undress — leggings, gaiters, stockings & shoes, arms & accoutrements as line."[6]

This uniform was a red fez with a white turban; a scarlet sleeveless jacket with yellow braid; a sleeved white waistcoat with a chevron of the regimental facing color (till 1888); dark blue breeches with yellow piping; white gaiters and stockings in full dress, black otherwise.[7] According to plates in Ellis and photographs in the Institute of Jamaica, it seems that the 1st Regiment had seven laced loops on its jackets, while the 2nd had nine until it was consolidated with the 1st. Buttons and badges were of yellow metal, and a white belt was worn under the jacket. Sergeants did not wear sashes after 1877, and company sergeants major — who were Europeans — wore white helmets.[8] Until 1874, bandsmen wore jackets of the reverse colors of their regiments; the figure shown here is based on an illustration in Ellis. Upon consolidation, the facings and tassels were to be white, except that the band and drummers were to have yellow tassels. The facings of the 2nd Regiment were consequently changed from yellow to white.[9]

In the 1870s the regiments were armed with the Martini-Henry rifle and bayonet.[10] They appear to have carried this weapon through the 1880s and into the '90s, for the 2nd Battalion only received the new Lee-Metford in August 1894.[11]

A United States Quartermaster's report for 3 January 1898 serves to confirm the Zouave dress of the West Indian regiments, adding that such items as dark blue shirts, black ankle boots, and great coats (seldom used) were also issued to the enlisted men. White gloves, according to this report, were not issued.[12]

Sources covering the period 1859-1890 indicate that officers' uniforms were of the regular line pattern.[13] After 1877, officers wore a white helmet in place of a shako.[14] Chichester shows both the helmet and belt-plate worn in the 1890s. By that time officers wore no collar badge, and their lace was "gold bias and standard pattern." They were armed with standard infantry pattern swords.[15]

We wish to thank, for their help in preparing this plate, Company Fellows John R. Elting and Edward S. Milligan, the Institute of Jamaica and Ms. Marjorie Drake, and Mr. Peter Campbell of Barbados.

Barry E. Thompson
Anthony F. Gero

[1]J. E. Caulfield, A Hundred Years of the History of the Second West India Regiment, 1896, 193.

[2]A. B. Ellis, History of the First West India Regiment, 1885, 23. All information is from this source unless otherwise indicated.

[3]H. M. Chichester & B. Burges-Short, The Record & Badges of Every Regiment & Corps in the British Army, 1900, 882.

[4]G. Tylden, "The West India Regiments, 1795 to 1927 & from 1958," Journal of the Society for Army Historical Research, XL, 42-49. Also. R. Money Barnes, Military Uniforms of Britain and the Empire, London, 1960, 215.

[5]Tylden, op cit. Also, JSAHR, XXXI, 139.

[6]Tylden, op cit.

[7]Ibid. Facings of the West India regiments were: 1st white; 2nd, 3rd & 4th yellow; 5th green. From 1840 to 1870 the 3rd wore blue; in 1852 the 4th and 5th wore grass green and scarlet respectively.

[8]Ibid.

[9]Caulfield, op cit, 193-194.

[10]R. & C. Wilkinson-Latham, Infantry Uniforms, 1855-1835, 1970, 154-155.

[11]Caulfield, op cit, 203.

[12]Major F. von Schrader, QM, USV, memo dated 3 Jan 1899, Green Book of Uniform Regulations for Jan-May 1899, file 121944, Institute of Heraldry, Cameron Station, VA (located by Edward S. Milligan).

[13]Tylden, op cit; includes an illustration of an officer of the 2nd WIR, 1878, published in 1891. Also consulted: Barnes, op cit; Wilkinson-Latham, op cit; W. Y. Carman, British Military Uniforms from Contemporary Pictures, London, 1957.

[14]Tylden, op cit.

[15]Wilkinson-Latham, op cit.

Sergeant,
1st W.I. Regt.,
1874

Bandsman,
1st W.I. Regt.,
1874

Lieutenant,
2nd W.I. Regt.,
1878

Private,
The W.I. Regt.,
1890

**West India Regiments (Dress Uniforms),
circa 1870-1900**

THE WORLD WARS, 1917-1945

World War I

Occupation of Germany

Expedition to Northern Russia

Expedition to Siberia

Nicaraguan Intervention

Intervention in Haiti

World War II

15th U.S. Infantry Regiment, 1925

At the right time and in the right place, soldiering can be a satisfying profession. It was just that for the 15th United States Infantry, stationed in Tientsin, China from 1912 to 1938. Here, "soldiering was interesting and pleasant and not drudgery, even prideful."[1] The regiment's officers were picked and the enlisted men were regulars with long service.

The period depicted marks the halfway point of the Fifteenth's tour in China.[2] Officers and men alike were fashion plates: the sergeant's winter olive drab uniform was tailored in Hong Kong; the buttons were of English manufacture and his spiral puttees were purchased from the British canteen. All metal emblems and insignia are polished, even the dragon and scroll of the "Can Do," the regiment's distinctive insignia, which is larger than contemporary models.[3]

The summer field uniform worn by the captain is the standard infantry dress for the period. His tie is tucked between the second and third buttons. The buckle of his Sam Browne belt has rounded corners. On garrison duty, officers and first sergeants carried swords. The infantry wore neatly blocked Stetson campaign hats, untilted.

Although the olive drab shirt of the private was untailored, his breeches were meticulously pegged. He wore no organizational shoulder patch. His tin hat was buffed, shellacked, and stencilled with the "Can Do" insignia. The metal of bayonets was polished to a near-blinding sheen. Each soldier was issued two stocks for his Springfield: one had the standard issue finish and was used for training and qualification firing. The second was for ceremonial use only and was kept in deluxe condition by being kept wrapped in linseed oil-soaked rags.

The corporal holds the Chickamauga Guidon that was awarded annually to the best company in the regiment and carried in addition to the company guidon for one year. Its red and gold colors are associated with Imperial China, and an acorn represented the Civil War badge of the XIV Corps. Like the company parade guidons, it was made of heavy silk. The guidon pike heads had extra long shanks.

On the rifle ranges enlisted men could wear ". . . soft laundered blue or brown denims, mix them or match them as you pleased. You could wear a campaign hat, fatigue hat, a garrison cap or no head covering at all."[4] During the winter, permanent parties stationed at Chingwangtao were issued fur caps, sheepskin coats, and felt overshoes.[5]

Captain William B. Tuttle's mounted patrol, consisting of ex-cavalrymen in the service company, wore boots, spurs, and campaign hats with the straps under the chin instead of at the back of the head. They rode shaggy Manchurian ponies. Lieutenant Colonel George C. Marshall, founder of the patrol in 1925, called them, "a sporty-looking cavalry troop."[6]

As long as a 15th Infantryman was dressed in his olive drab shirt, spiral puttees, and campaign hat, no one would or could mistake him for an officer. But once he put on his dress tunic with its gold buttons, his well-pressed slacks, his white shirt and black tie, his patent-leather-billed Pershing cap, it took a nice eye to discern that he was still a private.

Trousers, leather garrison belts, and swagger sticks were part of the off-duty uniform the year round. The overcoat was cut in the British Guards pattern. In the summer, tailored "golden Hong Kong khaki, buttons shining, leather gleaming," were worn.[7] Occasionally, a tailored golden khaki shirt substituted for the tunic and white shirt. Only American ribbons were worn; all others were forbidden. It would not do to have a sergeant sporting the Iron Cross, as some could have. Unique to the Tientsin garrison was the "Chung" patch awarded for proficiency in Mandarin Chinese. The patch was sewn on the left sleeve.

Frederic E. Ray, Jr.
John R. Elting
Edward S. Jones

[1]Elbridge Colby Colonel U.S.A. (Ret.), *Military Affairs*, vol. XXV no 4., 213, 214. General Matthew B. Ridgway, U.S.A. (Ret.), letter to author dated 23 June 1959. When Captain Ridgway joined there were NCOs who had come out with the regiment in 1912.
[2]Mr. Charles G. Finney, Private, 1927-1929, very kindly furnished seven photographs of Company E.
[3]Summarizing the shield: blue and white infantry colors with four red acorns (Shiloh, Murfreesborough, Chattanooga, and Atlanta). The XIV Corps acorn badge origin is in Daniel Butterfield's Memoir. "The Rock of Chickamauga" is self evident. The dragon refers to Imperial China. "Can Do" is 19th century pidgin English.
[4]Forrest G. Pogue, *George C. Marshall, Education of a General, 1880-1939*, New York, 1963, 240.
[5]Finney, 173.
[6]Pogue, 235.
[7]*Ibid.*, 87.

Sergeant, Winter Parade Uniform

The "Chickamauga Guidon"

Private, Summer Field Dress

Captain, Summer Field Dress

15th U.S. INFANTRY REGIMENT
(The Forgotten Fifteenth)
American Barracks, Tientsin, China, circa 1925

16th U.S. Infantry Regiment, 1930

The 16th Infantry is probably the most decorated unit of any size in the entire U.S. Army. It has won twenty-eight Distinguished Unit Citations (one by the regiment and twenty-seven by its various companies), two Meritorious Unit Citations, four French Croix de Guerre, two Belgian citations and the Belgian fourragère. It is one of seven outfits in the army which can wear the fourragère of the French *Medaille Militaire.* It has been repeatedly commended for its intrepidity in such widely separated actions as Gettysburg and Tunisia, Luzon and the Meuse-Argonne, and Kasserine Pass and the Beaches of Normandy.[1]

Much of its renown is due to long assignment to the celebrated 1st Division, which it joined in June 1917. But another source of fame is its tour of garrison duty between the world wars in New York City. There it marched in most of the big city's parades and took part in welcoming many of its visiting dignitaries.

In the plate we see the Sixteenth as it appeared on the streets of New York on Army Day, 1930. For such occasions it developed its own form of parade order, stretching the uncompromising olive drab and khaki clothing to the maximum.

The private wears the regulation olive drab serge with matching coat and breeches, tightly rolled puttees with white bindings, dark brown shoes with white laces, russet leather belt, and accoutrements. His first sergeant has the same and has reverted to the nonregulation practice of wearing a sword, perhaps only for this parade. Apparently the sword he carried was a cavalry officer's saber of the model of 1872. All men wear the fourragère of the French Croix de Guerre.

The field officer wears a darker coat with cream colored Bedford cord or elastique breeches and dark cordovan boots. Shirts were white and ties black in those days; the notch lapel collar had been introduced only four years before, in 1926.

It was the regimental band that received the greatest number of additions. White cross belts, caps, and leggings, plus brass fittings, added a lively note; all were, of course, strictly nonregulation. The white bearskin hat on the drum major was the crowning touch but, alas, it seems only to have been worn for a few years. Perhaps its owner didn't get enough practice in keeping it on his head.

John Severin
Frederick P. Todd

---

[1]This was the total of awards as of 1958.

Officer, Drum Major, Bandsman, Private and First Sergeant in special parade uniforms

16th U.S. Infantry Regiment, 1930

American Expeditionary Force, Siberia, 1918-1920

America's second expedition to Russia began on 2 August 1918, when General William S. Graves was ordered to assemble a force to be sent to Siberia.[1] On 3 August 1918 Colonel Henry D. Styer, commander of the Philippine Department, was cabled to send, on the first available transport for foreign service, the 27th and 31st U.S. Infantry Regiments, Field Hospital No. 4, Ambulance Company No. 4, and Company D of the 53rd Telegraph Battalion equipped for "winter service."[2] The 27th and 31st Regiments were to be recruited to wartime strength and additional support units were also assigned to the force.[3]

On 1 September 1918, General Graves and his staff arrived in Vladivostok.[4] American forces were not officially withdrawn until January 1920, with the last elements departing from Vladivostok harbor on 1 April.[5]

The first troops to arrive in Siberia were posted to Sviyagino in their "tropical garb" of model 1910 cotton uniform, felt campaign hat, cloth leggings, and russet leather shoes.[6] Many of these uniforms, which were custom made in the Philippines, were distinguished by white bone buttons on the trousers' calves, fly, and waist. The padded cloth leggings were cross-stitched for the sake of durability and distinctiveness.[7] The second figure from the left illustrates this uniform.

The third figure shows the standard wool uniform subsequently issued to all members of the expedition, including regulation "roughout" hobnail shoes, wool wrap leggings, and Model 1907 winter caps.[8]

Due to the haste of the expedition's departure for Siberia, obsolete model 1876 buffalo overcoats and model 1879/1902 muskrat caps and mittens were sent out.[9] The right-hand figure is equipped with specimens of cap, mittens, and officer's boots of 1st Lt. Norman C. Streit, M.G. Company, 31st Infantry, in the collection of Company Member Hayes Otoupalik, which served as models.

The Quartermaster Corps produced special uniform items for this expedition. Since there was insufficient time for the manufacture of additional buffalo overcoats, suitable substitutes were used. "The division sent a man to the north woods country of Minnesota and Wisconsin . . . There he bought sheep-lined coats with [olive drab cotton] moleskin or duck shells."[10] The left-hand figure illustrates such a coat, based upon a specimen in the Otoupalik collection, made by the Monarch Manufacturing Company of Milwaukee on 26 August 1918; it bears a Quartermaster's inspection tag to that effect. The muskrat cap is of the revised 1918 pattern and has longer ear flaps and an affixed visor, and it is based on a cap in the collection of Company Member Christopher C. Bruner.

The fur-covered mittens were attached to the wearer by a neck cord to prevent them from being lost when action necessitated their removal. The rubber and felt shoes, with horseshoe buckles, are the 1907 pattern adopted for Arctic wear.[11]

The shoulder sleeve insignia shown are both drawn from surviving patches and represent the two styles worn. Research with veterans indicates that the S/AEF patch was used by those troops posted to the interior, while the standing bear design was worn by units based in the Vladivostok area and by some "individuals" who returned from inland posts. Although variations still exist from uniform to uniform, our plate attempts to show the four modes of dress commonly worn by members of the American Expeditionary Force to Siberia.

We wish to thank Company Members Christopher C. Bruner, B. William Henry, and Paul J. Schulz for their aid on this plate. A special thanks is also extended to the following Siberian veterans: Thomas A. Shotwell, Alphia W. Goreham, Elmer B. Moe, Elmer E. Kobold, Malcolm Currie and Mrs. Norman G. Streit and Mrs. Eline Lamson.

Ralph Heinz
Hayes Otoupalik
Orton Begner

[1]Plate #444, MC&H, Fall 1976; General William S. Graves, America's Siberian Adventure, 1931, 3.
[2]Edith Faulstich, The Siberian Sojourn, 1970, 126.
[3]Colonel William S. Strobridge, Golden Gate to Golden Horn, 31. These additional units consisted of Infantry Replacement Battalion (Companies A and B); Evacuation Hospital No. 17; Medical Supply Depot No. 7; members of the Army Nurse Corps, Dental Corps and Veterinary Corps; 146 Ordnance Depot; Service Park Unit No. 333, Motor Transport Corps; Supply and Labor Companies, QMC; Bakery Company No. 391, QMC; and War Prison Guard Detachment.
[4]Robert Maddox, "Doughboys in Siberia," American History Illustrated, August, 1977, 12-14.
[5]Ibid., 17-21.
[6]Faulstich, op. cit., 56. The companies posted to Sviyagino were F and G, 27th US Infantry.
[7]The uniform of Alphia Goreham, Company D, 31st US Infantry in the collection of Hayes Otoupalik.
[8]Ibid., Hayes Otoupalik Collection.
[9]Benedict Crowell, America's Munitions 1917-1918, Washington, 1919, 461-463; Gordon Chappel, Museum Monograph No. 5, Arizona Historical Society, 1972, 29-32; letter from Colonel William McCaskey Chapman, USA, retired, dated 11 Feb 1977, in the files of Hayes Otoupalik; Edgar Howell, United States Army Headgear 1855-1902, 76-79; photographs of Thomas Shotwell, Ambulance Company No. 4 and an overcoat marked HQ Company, 31st US Infantry in the Hayes Otoupalik Collection.
[10]Crowell, op. cit., 461-463.
[11]Secretary of War, The Uniforms of the Army of the United States, 1 Oct 1908, Arctic Overshoes, Par. 103, General Orders 167, W.D., 1907, plate 139.

American Expeditionary Force, Siberia, 1918-1920

501st U.S. Parachute Battalion, 1941

In May 1940, the German blitzkrieg swept over Belgium and Holland, and Hitler's airborne troops seized defensive strongpoints to secure the headlong advance of the ground elements. This turn of events spurred the U.S. War Department to action in an area where it had been complacently vague. On 25 June 1940 the formation of the Parachute Test Platoon was directed, with personnel to be drawn from the 29th Infantry Regiment at Fort Benning.[1]

While the Air Corps assembled a few aircraft, technicians, and parachutes at Fort Benning's Lawson Field, the required forty-eight men were selected from 200 applicants.[2] The Test Platoon gained momentum rapidly, perfecting jumping techniques and developing a training routine by mimicking German methods. Adaptations were made by trial and error with American equipment. Encouraging progress and growing anticipation of American involvement in the European war prompted the activation of the 501st Parachute Battalion in October 1940.

The fledgling airborne arm showed an early interest in its uniforms, due to the personal pride of the parachutists in their calling as well as to consideration of the practicalities of what the uniforms had to withstand. The plate shows the working dress of the Battalion as it appeared during most of 1941. Three figures wear the experimental olive "balloon cloth" jump coveralls. This garment boasted a profusion of pockets for grenades, pistol magazines, and other equipment and was made of a shiny sateen. Field tests proved it to be impractical and it was replaced by a two-piece combination which was later adopted as standard.[3] The first sergeant, private, and jumpmaster also wear an early form of the Corcoran jump boot especially developed for parachutists. The standard service shoe was its basis, with features of the cavalry boot intermixed. Sponge rubber insoles seemed a clever way to absorb landing shock, and thick rubber soles and heels were used for better traction on aircraft surfaces. The strapped ankle reinforcements proved a nuisance around parachute impedimenta and were abandoned in favor of tighter lacing and added stitching.[4]

Parachute packs were tan or olive drab with white harness and static lines and galvanized fittings. The Riddle crash helmet was usually painted russet or olive drab with a black stripe. The specimen illustrated has a white pad at the nape and a cream-colored horsehide bib attached to the brown leather chin strap. The flap was worn to fend off pine trees encountered in Benning's drop zones and guard against riser burn.[5] The emplaning private wears an aviator's tan cloth toque with yellow-orange goggle loops. The warrant officer has a cap and shirt of dark olive-brown and pink-beige trousers and necktie. His brown leather flight jacket is embellished with the red and white arrowhead emblem of Wright Field.

The staff sergeant wears pale grey-green herringbone twill mechanic's coveralls with white name tape. He has sewn olive drab on blue-black chevrons over a previous expedient painted in ink. His overseas cap is tan, piped in infantry blue. His ankles are braced with lace-on anklets as used before the advent of the full boot. He carries a revolver tucked into the thigh-side tool pocket and fastened with white tape.

The duties of the jumpmaster required that he poke his head out the exit door into the slipstream and check the winds and landing zone before allowing a drop. This necessitated issue of goggles, which served as the jumpmaster's badge of office.[6] The distinctive unit insigne has a silver escutcheon charged with a blue Ojibwa thunderbird trimmed in red. The motto "Geronimo" is inscribed on a blue scroll. The silver parachutist qualification badge is shown on a cloth background of scarlet, edged in infantry blue. This oval backing dates to the awarding of the wings in early 1941, when it was felt that what the jumpers' brevet lacked in size could be made up with a display of the organizational colors.[7] The cap disc was infantry blue with embroidered white parachute and rim.

This plate was prepared with the generous aid of Company Fellows Lieutenant General William P. Yarborough, who served as a company commander and test officer in the 501st Parachute Battalion, and Sidney C. Kerksis, one of the test platoon volunteers from the 29th Infantry. General Yarborough was responsible for the design of the two-piece World War II jump suit and insignia shown in the illustrations.

John C. Andrews

[1]Albert G. Alderton, A History of the Airborne, Amherst College thesis, Amherst, Mass., 1951, 107.

[2]John T. Ellis, Jr., The Airborne Command and Center, Army Ground Forces Historical Study 25, Washington, D.C., 1946, 3.

[3]Thomas M. Pitkin, Quartermaster Equipment for Special Forces, QMC Historical Study 5, Washington, D.C., 1944, 245-247.

[4]Ibid., 247-248.

[5]Correspondence with Lieutenant General William P. Yarborough.

[6]Interview with Sydney C. Kerksis.

[7]Correspondence with Lieutenant General William P. Yarborough.

Private   Warrant Officer

1st Sergeant   Staff Sergeant   Jumpmaster

501st U.S. Parachute Battalion, 1941

Alamo Scouts, U.S. Sixth Army, 1943-1945

As 1943 began to draw to a close and the Sixth Army prepared for the Admiralty Island Campaign, commanding General Walter Krueger conceived the idea of organizing and training a highly specialized group of soldiers to obtain much-needed intelligence of the Japanese forces and Allied objective areas. The concept was daring. A small group of men, all volunteers with special training, would land by night in enemy territory, reconnoiter for several days or weeks and bring out eyewitness information.

Orders were issued on 28 November 1943 establishing a scout training center at Kalo Kalo on Fergusson Island, a half-hour boat ride from Sixth Army Headquarters, for the purpose of qualifying individual officers and enlisted men for the "efficient performance of scouting and patrolling under all conditions of terrain, weather and vegetation found in the Southwest Pacific area; and to train teams capable of landing near and reconnoitering, areas of probable future operations."[1]

The course lasted a rigorous six weeks. During the first four weeks specific subjects, including cover and concealment, Judo, handling of rubber boats, scouting, patrolling, swimming, quick-fire marksmanship and night landings from PT boats were covered in detail. The last two weeks were devoted to practical exercises such as the landing of reconnaissance teams on hostile shores and the location and annihilation or capture of such teams. Throughout the course physical conditioning and utilization of local resources were stressed.

To the best of our knowledge, the first field operation that the Alamo Scouts took part in was a reconnaissance in force of Los Negros Island on 27-28 February 1944 prior to the landing of combat elements of the 1st Cavalry Division. Their pinpoint intelligence of Japanese strength and dispositions in this prelude to the Admiralty Campaign established the Scouts as a formidable force which would shadow the Japanese constantly through the remainder of Sixth Army operations in the war.

An action team usually consisted of one officer and six or seven enlisted men although for an operation in Dutch New Guinea, the team consisted of two officers, eleven enlisted men and three native guides.

The plate illustrates an officer, in the left background, and two enlisted men operating as a reconnaissance team. When on operation, all team members wore "herringbone twill utility fatigues,"[2] although the writers have seen a poorly reproduced photograph allegedly showing scouts in one-piece camouflage jungle suits which were briefly tested in the Southwest Pacific theatre before being reclassified as limited standard issue, as tests found them "too heavy, too hot and too uncomfortable."[3] No distinguishing badges of rank were worn.

The figure in the foreground wears the old style Army canvas leggings as they were originally issued to his parent organization. These, in all likelihood, have not been turned in for standard two-buckle boots inasmuch as they more effectively discouraged insect attacks than the lower-topped boot. He carries the M1 carbine with fifteen-round magazine and extra ammunition in pouches attached to the stock of the carbine. Additional ammunition would be carried in the M1923 cartridge belt. All Scouts carried the incendiary grenade AN-M14, and each of the three carries two suspended from standard issue web suspenders. These grenades had a two-second delay igniting fuse, a sheet metal body, and a filler of thermite. They were designed to start fires or melt metal. While not shown, Scouts also carried the fragmentation grenade MKII. The .45 ACP U.S. M1911A1 pistol was offered to all Scouts as an optional weapon and most did actually carry one. For this particular mission, the team leader himself did not carry a sidearm. Dog tags were covered with black tape to eliminate noise and reflection of sunlight off the bright metal. The twill utility cap was found to be satisfactory for defense against dense undergrowth and insects and was certainly more comfortable than the steel helmet when on long-range missions in a tropical climate.

The private first class in the right rear carries the model 1942 M1 Thompson submachine gun with 50-round drum magazine. Five additional box magazines, each containing fifteen rounds of .45 caliber ammunition, are shown in the cartridge pouch which existed in three, four, and five compartment styles. This was suspended from the M1936 pistol belt. Other equipment is standard issue web, including the canteen, and the private wears the well-known G.I. two-buckle boot.

The 1st lieutenant in the left background prefers the M1 Garand rifle, a first class semiautomatic 30-06 caliber rifle originally adopted by the Army in 1936.

Within nine months of their formation, various Alamo Scouts had earned a total of nineteen Silver Stars, eighteen Bronze Stars, and four Soldiers Medals without losing a single man.

Raymond S. Johnson
Alfred Hahn

[1]U.S. Army Field Forces, Observer Board Reports, Pacific Ocean Areas, Number B-3-24 (5 January-17 February, 1944).
[2]Personal correspondence with CSM (Ret.) Galen Kittleson, former Alamo Scout.
[3]Report of First Lieutenant Robert L. Woodbury, Quartermaster Observer in the Southwest Pacific Theatre — 1 February 1943 to 15 May 1943.

Officer

Private First Class

Private

Alamo Scouts, U.S. Sixth Army
1943-1945

Company Aid Men, European Theater of Operations, 1945

In April 1945, a chance meeting occurred between elements of the 45th (Thunderbird) Infantry Division and the 20th Armored Division near Munich, Germany. The former was a veteran outfit, while the latter was soon to see its first combat. This plate depicts that meeting and shows the evolution of uniforms and equipment of the company aid man.

The men wear no packs because the armored infantry stored theirs in their half-tracks and the 45th had requisitioned a German truck to carry their excess baggage. A company aid man carried two aid kits slung on suspenders from the shoulders. He did not carry weapons because of the Geneva Convention, and his helmet and armband were clearly marked with the Geneva Cross.[1] The usual practice was to paint red crosses in white circles on the front, rear, and sides of the helmets; and the aid kits were frequently marked with the same device. Two white armbands with the Geneva Cross were worn on the sleeves. This was designed to clearly identify the noncombatant medical corpsman and it was then assumed that he would be relatively immune from fire. His other equipment consisted of a gas mask (soon discarded), pack, pistol belt, canteen, and a personal first aid kit.

One of the first things that any new medic picked up as soon as they became available was a pair of infantryman's cartridge belt suspenders. It was thought that the medic would be perfectly happy with the pistol belt alone and would need no support for it, but the medics usually felt otherwise. A second item of equipment usually picked up was an extra canteen. The first item to disappear from his equipment was his personal first aid kit.

A new unit going into combat for the first time in this season of the year was equipped with the standard issue field jacket. While these were worn by most of the veterans, there were a few of the older, shorter style to be seen. The one item which every infantryman desired was the tanker's lined jacket with knit wrist and collar. Whenever possible, these were begged, borrowed, or otherwise requisitioned; by the end of the war, approximately one quarter of the men in I Company, 180th Infantry, had tanker's jackets.

The details of the men of the 45th Division were taken from the personal photographs and souvenirs of the author. Additional assistance, particularly on details of an armored division, was obtained from Company Fellow Colonel John R. Elting and Company Members Arthur P. Wade and Major Vorin E. Whan.

Eric I. Manders
George A. Snook

---

[1]The pistol held by the central figure (and, alas, also the wristwatch displayed by his comrade) may be classed as "souvenirs."

20th Armored Division
Shoulder Patch
Oklahoma National Guard

45th Infantry Division

Riflemen

Medic, 20th Armored Division

Medics, 45th Infantry Division

Company Aid Men, E.T.O., 1945

1st U.S. Armored Division, 1940-1942

In 1941, the 1st Armored Division was one year old. It had been created as part of the Armored Force, formed in July 1940 out of the emergency brought about by happenings in Europe. As represented in its tri-color insignia, it was composed of troops drawn from mechanized cavalry, artillery, and infantry regiments.[1]

This plate illustrates the basic uniforms and equipment worn at this time, including outmoded items, soon to be replaced. The infantryman on the extreme right wears the basic field service uniform: olive drab shirt and trousers; black tie, tucked between the first and second buttons; brown service shoes; and the M1938 canvas dismounted legging. The sergeant on the extreme left wears khaki summer service dress. In the Armored Force, however, the herringbone twill suit shown on the mechanic and the winter combat suit shown on the tanker, intended as special uniforms for their particular jobs, were also used as field uniforms.[2] In the thirties, mechanized units were authorized to wear the overseas cap for field service in place of the campaign hat worn by the rest of the Army.[3] This distinctive cap was high-crowned and worn on the left side of the head.[4] It was edged with braid in the branch color and bore a brass branch or "U.S." disc insignia on its left curtain. Troops still wore the "old style tin hat — the kind you couldn't wash in," but the following year, the M1 helmet and liner combination came out, and they received them before landing in North Africa.[5]

The officers' dress still reflected the "Old Army" although some officers had given up the breeches and boots for field wear. As in the plate, an olive drab or "green" blouse and "pink" breeches, boots, Sam Browne belt, and officer's saber comprised the normal dress uniform. Cavalry insignia and regimental insignia were still worn. On the left curtain of the overseas cap, officers wore a circular piece of fabric under their rank insignia, in the color of their arm of service. If there were two colors, the main one was worn on top of the secondary, with the first piece being smaller and leaving a narrow border of the secondary color around it. Generals wore black velvet circles.

The field equipment issued was either the M1910 haversack and pack carrier combination or the musette bag, known correctly as the M1936 canvas field bag. The infantryman wears the former in an arrangement known as the "haversack without rations."[6] This contained toilet articles and the meat can in its pouch on the flap. The tanker has the musette bag issued to officers and motorized enlisted men. This bag could be carried at the side by its shoulder strap or on the back when attached to a set of suspenders. The tanker, however, usually stowed his musette bag in the vehicle or attached it on the outside.

This being a period of rapid expansion and mass procurement of uniforms, there was great variation in the supposedly standardized shades of uniform clothing. Officers' blouses ranged from yellowish-drab to very dark green, "pinks" through the whole possible spectrum of grays. Nonregulation gray or forest green shirts, trousers, and caps appeared; the yellowish "chino" khaki became popular. Herringbone twill had many variations, especially after it had been washed several times. The winter combat suit often was the palest brown. Incidentally, it was not particularly warm; if you wore the cap's neckpiece tucked into your collar, as prescribed, it led cold rainwater down into the seat of your pants; also, the QM genius who designed the suit forgot that field soldiers occasionally needed to relieve themselves and would have preferred not to have to disrobe to do so.[7]

The 1st Armored Division, even though then only in existence one year, was by no means void of a heritage. Two of its units held unique distinctions in the Army. The 1st Armored Regiment (Light), formerly the 1st Cavalry Regiment, held sixty-one Battle Honors by 1941, more than any other regiment; and the 6th Infantry Regiment (Armored), formerly the 6th Infantry Regiment (Rifle), was the oldest regiment of continuous service.[8] The division went on to distinguish itself in North Africa and Italy and to become known as "Old Ironsides."

H. Charles McBarron, Jr.
Walter H. Bradford

[1]Historical and Pictorial Review, First Armored Regiment (L), First Armored Division of the United States Army, Fort Knox, Kentucky, 1941, 15.
[2]Thomas M. Pitkin, Q. M. C. Historical Studies No. 5, Quartermaster Equipment for Special Forces, 1944, 150-151.
[3]Thomas M. Pitkin and Erna Risch, Q. M. C. Historical Studies No. 16, Clothing the Soldier of World War II, 1946, 78.
[4]The Story of the First Armored Division (World War II unit publication), 6.
[5]Ibid.
[6]FM 21-15, Equipment, Clothing, and Tent Pitching, 1940.
[7]Comment from personal experience, Colonel John R. Elting. Note: The combat jacket shown here is the second model, authorized in March 1942. The original model had patch pockets.
[8]Historical and Pictorial Review, op. cit., 20.

Tanker, Winter Combat Uniform   Cavalry Lieutenant

Tanker, Summer Uniform   Mechanic, Herringbone Twill Fatigue Uniform   Infantryman, Field Uniform

1st U.S. Armored Division, Fort Knox, Kentucky, 1940-1942

Feigl Battery, 7th U.S. Field Artillery Regiment, 1925-1926

"Feigl Battery," one of the very few organizations in the Regular Army of that era to have a distinctive name, was so called in honor of Lieutenant Jefferson Feigl, the first American artillery officer to be killed in action in World War I, 21 March 1918. Its other designation was F Battery.

The mid 1920s were marked by a succession of minor changes in uniforms and accoutrements. In efforts to improve the somewhat drab aspects of the service uniform. The earliest of these were the introduction of the new garrison cap called the "Pershing style" and the changeover from bronze finish to brass for buttons and collar insignia. This was soon followed by improved tailoring of the service coat and breeches; by the winter of 1925-26 the roll collar was adopted for the entire U.S. Army.

The 7th Field Artillery was then serving at two of our northern posts; regimental headquarters and the 1st Battalion were garrisoned at Fort Ethan Allen, Vermont; the 2nd Battalion was garrisoned at Madison Barracks, New York. Several units had adopted branch color patches for collar and cap insignia, thus the 2nd Battalion of the Seventh had circular patches of scarlet felt under collar and cap insignia for all enlisted men, while officers wore similar patches only under the insignia for the garrison cap and underneath rank insignia on the left front of their winter fur caps. For officers, scarlet scarfs and linings for the overcoat and short coat were common to the 2nd Battalion but not to regimental headquarters and the 1st Battalion, which wore the familiar issue muskrat caps with vizor and ear flaps. Those worn by officers of the 2nd Battalion were of special pattern as shown in the plate, similar in basic design to the World War I overseas cap, and worn well down on the right eyebrow.

The bugler of the guard and the battery commander are shown wearing the standing collar blouse, the latter, as was frequently the custom, wearing a scarlet silk kerchief instead of a stock. The bugler's mounted leggings have been reworked by the battery saddler to add leather binding around the tops and to cut away the leather reinforcing of the inner legs just above the ankles. The fourragère for enlisted men was the issue worsted type, with a single knotted cord for the "spike" and a single braided loop worn under the arm. The leather belt and attachments were reserved for dress formations and the additional chin strap on the cap was a "Battery purchase" item. For "Post Calls" and dress formations the trumpet, key of "C-" with slide to "F," was used; for all mounted drill maneuvers, etc., the short artillery bugle, key of "Bb" was substituted.

The fourragères worn by officers were of silk with two additional loops of cord worn outside of the arm. There were many slight variations in the cut and hardware of the Sam Browne belts of that period. The predominant trend, as shown on the battery commander, was to eliminate the unessential. Thus the underside "D" rings for the British type sword sling and the suspension hook have been omitted and the sliding frog for the saber chain has been replaced by a single "D" ring sewn to the belt midway between the "D's" for the single shoulder strap. At this time the preference for sharply rectangular hardware was not yet prevalent. The battery commander carried his saber unslung, grasping it firmly by the grips with the guard forward, a custom peculiar to 2nd Battalion officers.

Buck strappings on officers' breeches were universal. Straight, short-shanked spurs and chains worn with gartered straight-leg dress boots predominated for all occasions except field duty.

For winter, steel stirrups were wrapped in sheep skin as a precaution against frostbitten feet. The same practical consideration dictated the use of single wrap-around leather spur straps rather than short straps and chains. The mounted officer's "three buckle" field boots were then just coming into high favor.

As far as is known, Feigl Battery was the only unit in our Army authorized the use of a steel lance as its guidon staff. During World War I the lance had been presented to the battery by a French dragoon as a token of his esteem and gratitude to the men who saved his life. His lance, embellished with the regimental coat of arms and a band bearing the battery designation, served for all occasions when the battery was in formation. Feigl Battery used its silk guidon for all battery formations other than actual service in the field.

The horses of the 2nd Battalion were matched for color as nearly as possible: Headquarters and Service batteries, predominantly chestnut; E Battery, all blacks; D Battery, all bays; Feigl Battery, predominantly bays with a few roans. During that period manes were roached short, tails were kept plucked at the base, and fetlocks were clipped clean. In addition to the "U.S." brand on the near shoulder, each horse had its serial number on the near side of the neck and its battery letter and number on the near fore hoof. As shown in the plate, the "winter clip" was in use.

The four guns (75 mm) were named Feigl, Flaherty, Fluff, and Fox.

The motto of the Regiment was taken from General Orders 201, AEF, 19 November 1918: "Never broken by hardship nor battle."

Harry C. Larter, Jr.

Bugler of the Guard   Lieutenant and Guidon, Winter Field   Battery Commander, Garrison Dress

Feigl Battery, 7th U.S. Field Artillery Regiment, 1925-1926

Lafayette Escadrille, French Aviation Service, 1916-1917

The Lafayette Escadrille was the 124th Scout Squadron (*Escadrille*) of the French Aviation Service during World War I. Its officers were French and its men American volunteers who, with two exceptions, were noncommissioned pilots.[1] Appropriately, the squadron took for its insignia the head of a war-whooping American Indian, which was painted on the fuselage of its Nieuport and Spad single-seater pursuit planes.

The Lafayette pilot had no distinguishing uniform or badge. He was merely another *poilu* who was qualified to fly an airplane. If some of the men made the most of this in their dress, it was because they were young, in a young service, and represented a young and·big country in a big war.

The figures in our picture reflect a norm arrived at by a study of photographs in conjunction with individual biographies which describe service affiliations prior to enlistment in the Flying Corps, and thus account for variations in uniform. For example, one Lafayette pilot favors the big beret of the *Chasseur Alpin,* to which one finds he was entitled by service in the American Volunteer Ambulance attached to the *Chasseurs.*

The first seven Lafayette pilots entered aviation via the 1914 red-trousered infantry of the French Foreign Legion. Neither picture nor text gives a positive proof that red trousers flew on American legs, but it certainly is probable that red trousers were worn. Our picture shows a French officer of the Lafayette Escadrille, wearing the red pants and dragoon tunic to which he was entitled, adapted for aviation and worn with the chic of a pre-war French career officer.

The regulation uniform for aviation is worn by the figure in the right foreground. He is correctly dressed, and he wears on his left breast the squadron insignia of "Spad 3": the silver stork with wings down-thrust. He is being given an enthusiastic welcome by "Whiskey" and "Soda," the lion cub mascots of the Lafayette Escadrille.

Although the dark blue-black of Aviation, borrowed from the Engineer Corps, was the correct dress, strictly speaking, horizon blue was the universal uniform color of the French army in World War I. The pilot standing behind the dragoon lieutenant wears this color. The sergeant in the left foreground wears the horizon blue tunic with collar and tie, in the fashion made popular by British officers. Many French soldiers, by preference, wore hunting stocks of horizon blue beneath either type of collar.

The usual headgear was the kepi (colored according to the branch of service) and the *bonnet de police.* The latter was always horizon blue. High laced boots were the ideal for the well-dressed pilot, though riding boots were also popular. For flying, however, spiral puttees, golf hose, or oxfords with slacks seem to have been adopted for comfort and warmth.

The two figures in the background wear flying kit. The furred overalls were usual, even in a war where the "Cavalry of the Clouds" was known to fly dawn patrols in gay pajamas. Be that as it may, the pilot or observer in an open-cockpit plane over northern France, even on *late* spring mornings, would consider himself lucky to have available a bearskin overcoat such as is worn by the other background figure.

The badge of the Flying Corps was the wing and star collar ornament. On the dark dress uniform, this was worn on an orange-colored patch, and on the front of the kepi, without the colored patch. The pilot's badge was worn on the right breast of all uniforms. A sergeant wore wings and propeller in red and white on his sleeve. Above the figures are drawn in detail the badge of a pilot and the Indian head of the Lafayette Escadrille, which also appears on the Spad in the background.

Medals, which were very numerous in the Lafayette, were worn either as ribbons or, in the French manner, as full decorations, even on working clothes. The figure standing with the dragoon wears, in addition, the fourragère of the Legion of Honor — a distinction given his squadron for multiple citations.

A careful appraisal of the uniform worn by the Lafayette pilots indicates the true character of that corps: a dash and élan which were reflected in his dress uniform, yet (especially in his "work clothes") a seriousness compatible with the job for which he had volunteered.

Frederick T. Chapman
Harrison K. Bird, Jr.

[1]This note is based upon James Norman Hall and Charles Bernard Nordhoff, eds., *The Lafayette Flying Corps,* Boston, 1920; and their *Falcons of France,* Boston, 1940. Also the paintings and etchings by Henry Farre contained in a catalog of his New York exhibition, 1918; material in the Musée de l'Armée, Paris; and the recollections of Company Member Colonel John H. Hunter, 2nd.

Sergeant Pilot

Lieutenant Pilot,
Dragoon Uniform

Sergeant Pilot
Forage Cap

Flying Clothes

Lieutenant, Aviation Service
Dress Uniform

Lafayette Escadrille, French Aviation Service, 1916-1917

96th U.S. Aero Squadron, 1917-1918

The 96th Aero Squadron was organized at Kelly Field, Texas in August 1917 and sailed for Europe in October. The squadron trained at the bombing training school near Lyon, France. Later, men and material moved to Amanty airdrome southwest of Toul in the Lorraine sector.

On 12 June 1918 the American Air Service made its first bombing attack. The target was the railroad yards at Dommary-Baroncourt. The mission was a great success in spite of German fighter opposition.

10 July was a catastrophe. The U.S. bombing effort ceased to exist when six Breguet bombers of the 96th landed in Germany by mistake. During the next three weeks the squadron was at an operational standstill. There was only one bomber available, which was used for practice bombing and flight training. In August, eleven new Breguet bombers arrived and the 96th resumed strikes against enemy targets.

The First Day Bombardment Group was formed in early September. It included the veteran 96th plus two brand new outfits, the 11th and 20th Aero Squadrons. The 166th Aero Squadron was added in October. The newer units operated De Havilland 4 all-purpose airplanes, while the 96th used French Breguet 14 B2 bombers, which were considered far better aircraft.

Brigadier General William Mitchell, Chief of the First Army Air Service, tried to maintain air superiority by making incessant assaults on the German rear areas. He refused to spread out the aero squadrons in a thin cover to corps and divisions. The concentrated attacks of U.S. bombers diverted large numbers of enemy fighters from the front line. In order to cut down losses, a large diamond formation was adopted. The 96th was supplemented by teams from the other two DH 4 outfits.

By late October the shortage of aircraft forced the group to return to smaller and more dangerous formations. Besides very aggressive enemy fighter planes, there was unusually accurate antiaircraft fire. In the last phase of the Argonne offensive the ground troops broke through the German lines, but weather grounded the bombers.

Thirty-nine bombers blasted the railroad center at Montmedy on 4 November. Seven enemy planes were shot down but two bombers were lost. The Breguets returned to Maulan completely riddled. The war was finally over for the battered 96th. It was unable to fly the last mission with the group.

Before 20 May 1918, the air component wore the Signal Corps insignia. After that date the Air Service became a separate branch. Officers wore a single-breasted high-collared brown wool coat with four patch pockets and dull bronze buttons. On each side of the collar there was a bronze "U.S." and a winged propeller insignia. A gold chevron on the lower left sleeve indicated six months spent overseas. Shoulder patches were sewn on after the Armistice.

Above the left breast pocket, pilots wore a pair of silver embroidered wings on a dark blue background. The initials "U.S." were in gold on a shield between the wings. This wing badge identified the individual wearer as a qualified military aviator.

Piping on the garrison or overseas cap was black and green, the branch colors for the fledgling Army Air Service after it left the Signal Corps. It was either a mixed cord or a narrow green strip below a narrow black strip. Officers wore their insignia of rank on the left front of the cap.

The Sam Browne belt and russet leather gloves were adopted from the British army. Wool breeches (khaki cotton for summer wear) were worn with laced boots or spiral wrapped puttees. For cold weather, officers wore short double-breasted coats or mackinaws with fur or dyed sheepskin collars.

Flyers wore a tannish brown coverall with black overshoes. Edges of the goggles were grey and the helmet was brown leather; gauntlets were black or brown leather.

Raymond S. Johnson

AAF - The Official Guide to the Army Air Forces, New York, N.Y.: Simon & Schuster, 1944.

J. Duncan Campbell, Aviation Badges and Insignia of the United States Army, 1913-1946, Harrisburg, Pennsylvania: The Triangle Press, 1977.

Alfred Goldberg, Ed., A History of the United States Air Force, Princeton, New Jersey: Van Nostrand, 1957.

James J. Hudson, Hostile Skies, Syracuse, New York: Syracuse University Press, 1968.

Thomas G. Miller, Jr., History of The First Day Bombardment Group, West Roxbury, Massachusetts: World War I Aero Publishers Inc.

Pilot (Officer)
Coverall Flight Suit

2d Lieutenant
Mackinaw

1st Lieutenant
Winter Service Dress

96th U.S. Aero Squadron, 1917-1918

278th U.S. Signal Pigeon Company, 1945

The subject of this plate is one of the lesser known World War II U.S. Army outfits. The Signal Corps pigeon companies were organized to supply an emergency means of communication on the various battlefronts. At their peak, the pigeoneers numbered slightly over 3,000 men with 54,000 homing pigeons. The soldiers shown here were attached to the XIII Corps of the Ninth Army. The company was first organized 15 February 1943 at the Army Air Base, Jacksonville, Florida, as the 1308th Signal Pigeon Company, Aviation. It was sent to Europe in August 1944, transferred to the ground forces, and redesignated the 278th Signal Pigeon Company. The company saw service in England, France, Belgium, the Netherlands, and Germany and was awarded battle stars for the Rhineland and Central Europe campaigns.[1]

Our plate covers a period of transition in uniforms. The soldier on the left is wearing the recently issued wool field tunic, or "Ike" jacket. Although intended as a field garment, the troops preferred to save it to use as a dress jacket while on leave.[2] The two-buckle field boots replaced the service shoe and lace leggings. The soldier with the buckled field boots is carrying the submachine gun (grease gun), caliber .45, M3, two of which were issued to each squad.

The technical corporal is shown releasing a pigeon from a captured German gas mask cannister held by the private first class. These containers were pressed into service as single-bird carriers for infantrymen going on combat patrol. The corporal is armed with the carbine, caliber .30, M1, issued three per squad. The remaining members of each squad carried the 1903 Springfield.

In the foreground may be seen the standard four-bird carriers. Plastic message capsules were stored in the top of each box.

The soldier on the right is wearing the knit sweater which was designed to be worn under the M1943 hiplength field jacket, and he is holding a 12-gauge Sportsman shotgun, which was issued to each squad in order to control hawks.

The lofts were made of plywood and could be easily dismantled. They were designed to fit into a jeep trailer, and could be moved as the battle lines fluctuated. The company was ordered deactivated, effective 1 November 1945, at Heidelberg, Germany.[3] Much of the material for the plate came from the writer's personal collection of photographs, taken during service with the 278th.

Eric I. Manders
Wayne A. Colwell
Bert Goodrich

[1] Wendel Mitchel Levi, *The Pigeon*, Sumter, S.C., 1957, 15-16.
[2] Erna Risch, *The Quartermaster Corps: Organization, Supply, and Services*, vol. 1, Washington, D.C., GPO, 1963, 94-95.
[3] Levi, *op. cit.*, 16.

Private   Corporal Sergeant   Shoulder Patch, Ninth Army

278th U.S. Signal Pigeon Company, 1945

Chicago Black Horse Troop, 1929-1940

Soon after assuming command of the 33rd Division, Illinois National Guard, in 1927, Major General Roy D. Keehn requested authority from the War Department to organize in Chicago an additional troop and a mounted band as part of the 106th Cavalry Regiment, Illinois National Guard. These units were to be specially uniformed, equipped, and mounted, to furnish a spectacular feature for Chicago civic functions.

General Charles P. Summerall, Chief of Staff, United States Army, secured War Department approval of the activation of these units, which were unofficially designated the Chicago Black Horse Troop and Mounted Band. The troop — officially Headquarters Troop, 106th Cavalry — received federal recognition on 27 April 1929; the band received recognition on 12 June 1929.

To fully equip a troop and band of this character, approximately 100 matched black horses were required. (The federal government could support a peacetime strength of only forty-two mounts.) The cost of the extra horses, additional care and facilities for them, and special uniforms and equipment was assured by a public-spirited group of citizens who, incorporating themselves as the nonprofit "Chicago Black Horse Troop Association," undertook the raising of $100,000.00 to cover the initial outlay, plus an additional $9,000.00 annually. During the depression, members of the troop and band turned over their drill pay to maintain their organization.

The Black Horse Troop and the Mounted Band played conspicuous parts in all Chicago ceremonials for some ten years. The troop was redesignated Troop E in 1935, and Troop A in 1940. In November 1940 it was inducted into federal service; in 1942, it was mechanized, serving in the southwest Pacific as the 33rd Cavalry Reconnaissance Troop. Inactivated at Camp Shanks, New York, in October 1945, the troop was reorganized and federally recognized as the 33rd Mechanized Cavalry Reconnaissance Troop (Black Horse Troop) in April 1947. A later reorganization transformed it into the 33rd Aviation Company, 33rd Infantry Division, as of 1 March 1959.

The distinctive uniform of the Black Horse Troop was the result of a series of compromises within a large committee appointed for the purpose. Company Fellow Hugh Charles McBarron, Jr., worked out several designs for the committee before it finally settled on the one shown here. Our plate is based on Mr. McBarron's original designs and photographs purchased from the Chicago Historical Society. The tall plume on the captain's shako seems to have been an addition to the original uniform design, according to which the officers' epaulettes were to be their sole distinction of rank. At any rate, it flaunts impressively in a 1932 photograph. Various differences also appear in the cut and decoration of the schabraque: the original design and a 1940 photograph of a painting (date unknown) show the style depicted here; a 1932 photograph shows a skimpier version, without the medallion in the lower rear corner. Likewise, white gauntlets, such as the captain wears here, appear occasionally.

In gathering information for this plate, the authors recognized a potential problem, which leads them to offer this warning. The Black Horse Troop dismounted for the last time only eighteen years before this plate was published, but it was far easier to secure the details of the average Napoleonic uniform than it was to locate those necessary for this plate. The Adjutant General's Office, Illinois National Guard, was very helpful, but had little information on uniforms. The Chicago Historical Society had little more. Information concerning the few nonregulation pre-World War II uniforms of the National Guard will have to be collected as soon and as carefully as possible.

Frederick T. Chapman
John R. Elting

Headquarters Troop, 106th Cavalry

Chicago Black Horse Troop, 1929-1940

102nd U.S. Cavalry Regiment, New Jersey National Guard, 1921-1922

This trooper, with his superb horseman's seat, well delineates the pride of all United States cavalrymen — whether Regulars, National Guardsmen, or Reservists — who once rode with that arm of the service. It also illustrates the late Company Fellow Harry C. Larter's mastery of drawing mounted men.

The 102nd Cavalry Regiment began in 1890 as the "Essex Troop of Light Cavalry." It was increased to a squadron in 1913. In 1919 it was reorganized as the 1st Squadron of Cavalry ("The Essex Troop"), New Jersey National Guard. Two years later (March 1921), this squadron was expanded into a full regiment, officially designated the 102nd Cavalry Regiment.

When World War I ended, the Army Quartermaster Corps had huge stocks of weapons, equipage, and uniforms available for issue to the National Guard. There was also a large reservoir of riding and draft animals for assignment to mounted units. The sergeant in our print wears a winter uniform of shirt, blouse, and breeches of olive drab wool.[1] His chevrons, not clearly visible, are olive drab stripes sewn onto a lighter colored background, worn on both sleeves. Blouses were form-fitting, single-breasted, with a standing collar that hooked together at neck, patch pockets placed two above and two below the waist, and two shoulder straps, all of which fastened with small bronze buttons. All metal buttons were embossed with the U.S. eagle. Bronze discs, one inch in diameter, were worn on the blouse collar; the disc on the right side was marked "U.S." in block letters, with smaller letters "N.G." superimposed. The opposite disc bore the cavalry's crossed sabers with unit identification. Breeches were pegged, laced below the knee for snug fit at the calf, and reinforced at thigh and seat.

For rainy weather, troopers were issued either a sage green, coated-fabric slicker, made with an inverted rear pleat to cover the saddle cantle when mounted, or a poncho of the same color. A campaign hat of olive drab felt, creased in a Montana peak, was held in place by a chin strap of brown leather and decorated with the yellow Cavalry hat cord. The laced canvas leggings were reinforced with brown leather; usually the troop saddlers re-tailored them for smart individual fit. Spurs were of nickel-plated steel, straight-shanked and without rowels.[2] Since only hobnailed field shoes were issued, all troopers bought brown-leather dress shoes. Many also purchased custom-made uniforms of better quality.

Summer uniforms were of washable cotton khaki. These, and the canvas portions of the leggings, were repeatedly laundered and scrubbed to obtain the much-desired faded look of those worn by Regular cavalrymen.

The russet leather horse equipment consisted of the M1904 McClellan saddle with hooded stirrups, a double-size olive drab wool saddle blanket, a pair of M1904 saddle bags, the M1909 halter with halter shank, and the M1909 bridle headstall with the M1904 bridoon (snaffle) and M1912 (curb) bits and reins. During 1920-1922, the regiment used only the snaffle, many officers believing that the average mount handled more easily without the curb. In 1921 the regiment adopted colorful chrome yellow brow bands and distinctive rosettes for their bridles. Horses were mostly browns or bays, between fifteen and sixteen hands, and averaging 1,100 pounds weight.

Weapons were the standard U.S. Springfield rifle, M1903, caliber .30; the M1911 Colt semiautomatic pistol, caliber .45; and the light, curved M1860 cavalry saber with blued steel scabbard. The latter was replaced in 1921 by the unpopular, straight-bladed M1913 Patton saber with an awkward checkered grip, heavy blued-steel guard, and scabbard of wood covered with khaki webbing.

Officers' blouses usually were of olive drab serge, and their breeches of light-colored Bedford cord, with buckskin reinforcing. Sam Browne belts and boots were brown or cordovan; hat cords were of mixed gold and black silk. Saddles were a matter of personal preference.

The 102nd was the first National Guard Cavalry regiment to complete its coat of arms. The yellow shield signifies a cavalry unit; the horse's head in blue was the crest of the Essex Troop; and the red fleurs-de-lis commemorate the Alsace and Argonne campaigns of World War I. The lion's head crest derives from both the Dutch and English arms of the original colony.

After years of efficient service as an armored cavalry regiment, the 102nd became the 102nd Armor, New Jersey Army National Guard, a "parent regiment" to several units of the 50th Armored Division, NJARNG.

Grateful acknowledgment is made to Company Members Lieutenant Colonel Walter J. Landry, Jr.; George A. Rummel, Jr.; and Bruce Halsted for their help.

James P. Simpson
John R. Elting

---

[1] The guidon usually was carried by one of the platoon sergeants or a corporal, usage varying with the unit. By 1920 it was a purely ceremonial item.

[2] Some of the earlier (M1911?) "swan-necked" or "goose-necked" spurs still may have been in use.

In Memoriam
HARRY C. LARTER JR.
1902·1960

102nd U.S. Cavalry Regiment
New Jersey National Guard, 1921-1922

369th U.S. Infantry Regiment, New York National Guard, 1918

During World War I, most black soldiers served in labor or service units, however, Harlem's own 369th Infantry was an outstanding combat unit. Originally it was planned that the regiment would serve as part of the all-colored 93rd Division, but the division was never organized. Instead the four black infantry regiments were brigaded into French divisions and did all their fighting under French command.

The 15th New York Infantry was authorized by the state in 1913, but it was not until 1916 that the unit began to be formed. The armory was a cigar store with a dance hall above it on Seventh Ave. and 131st Street, Harlem. Two hundred Negro residents in the city, who had previous military service, became the nucleus for the new regiment. Overcoming many obstacles, Colonel William Hayward, a former Nebraska National Guard officer, succeeded in obtaining rifles and uniforms. After the declaration of war 6 April 1917, the 15th New York was the first unit in the city to be recruited to war strength.

After federalization, the regiment trained at camp Whitman, Poughkeepsie, N.Y. This was followed by a tour of guard duty around New York City. Public works were protected against sabotage. The Machine Gun Company guarded interned Germans on Ellis Island.

After performing monotonous guard duty, the 15th New York was sent to South Carolina for training, but rather than risk racial incidents the unit returned north and was shipped overseas. It was the first black combat unit to reach France, arriving on 27 December 1917.

Already the regimental band was considered the best in the A.E.F. The band instructor was Lieutenant James R. Europe, who was really a line officer. Band leading was considered to be his relaxation. The tables of organization called for twenty-eight bandsmen. Actually there were forty-four. The band played for American troops on leave in Paris for Washington's Birthday. This was followed by a tour of France. Traveling 2000 miles, music was furnished in twenty-five cities. The band did much to publicize the arrival of American troops and lift sagging French morale.

During their first two months in France, the men worked as laborers. On 15 March 1918 the regiment was redesignated as the 369th U.S. Infantry and was sent to serve with the French. For a month, fifty French instructors taught the men the use of French weapons.[1]

The men were issued French helmets and brown leather belts and pouches, although they continued to wear their U.S. uniforms. The canteen (*bidon*) was covered by dark blue cloth. The French gas mask was in a dark metal container. They were armed with Mannlicher-Berthier model 1916 rifles.

On 8 April 1918 the 369th went into the trenches as part of the 16th French Division and served continuously until July 3rd. The regiment returned to combat in the second battle of the Marne. Later the 369th was reassigned to General Lebouc's 161st Division in order to participate in the Allied counterattack. On 19 August the regiment went off the line for rest and training of replacements.

On 25 September 1918 the Fourth French Army went on the offensive in conjunction with the American drive in the Meuse-Argonne. The 369th turned in a good account of itself in heavy fighting, sustaining severe losses. They captured the important village of Sechault. At one point the 369th advanced faster than French troops on their right and left flanks. There was danger of being cut off. By the time the regiment pulled back for reorganization, it had advanced fourteen kilometers through severe German resistance.

In mid-October the regiment was moved to a quiet sector in the Vosges Mountains. It was there on 11 November, the day of the Armistice. Six days later the 369th made its last advance and on 26 November it was the first Allied unit to reach the banks of the Rhine.

Although one Medal of Honor and many distinguished Service Crosses were awarded to members of the regiment, the most celebrated man in the 369th was Private Henry Johnson. In May 1918, Johnson and Private Needham Roberts fought off a twenty-four-man German patrol, though both were severely wounded. After they emptied their three-round clips, Roberts used his rifle as a club and Johnson battled with a bolo knife. Johnson was the first American to receive the Croix de Guerre.

Photographs show that the 369th carried the New York Regimental flag overseas. The French government awarded the regiment the Croix de Guerre with silver star for the taking of Sechault. It was pinned to the colors by General Lebouc at a ceremony in Germany on 13 December 1918.

Today the lineage and tradition is carried on by the 369th Transportation Battalion, 2366 Fifth Ave., New York City.

Raymond S. Johnson

[1]Painting of Corporal C. Thompson, West Point Museum.

Band Master

Colors, 15th N.Y.N.G.

Drum Major

Corporal

Officer

R.S. JOHNSON

369th U.S. Infantry Regiment (15th New York National Guard) 1918

U.S. Naval Railway Batteries, 1917-1918

The importance of long-range artillery became evident in World War I, when the Germans were bombarding vital facilities behind the Allied northern lines. Counterbombardment was ineffective, for Allied guns did not have the necessary range.

On 26 November 1917 the Navy Department approved the construction of five railway carriages to carry fourteen-inch, 50-calibre cannon with six locomotives and enough cars to support the staff and carry supplies. The cannon had been used to arm battleships and new battle cruisers. Contracts were awarded to the Baldwin Locomotive Works of Philadelphia for the gun carriages and locomotives. The support cars were to be built by the Standard Steel Car Company of Pencoyd, Pennsylvania.

Work moved along rapidly and the equipment, knocked down, was shipped to France beginning in July 1917. The first battery was assembled and left St. Nazaire on 21 August; the others were soon completed as well. There was no problem moving them over French railway lines, for the gauges were compatible. The guns did an excellent job against the Germans and destroyed German railway centers and ammunition stores.

The dress of the personnel of the naval Railway Batteries conformed basically with the Navy Uniform Regulations of 1913, revised 15 January 1918.[1] Section 65(b) stated that Naval officers and men serving with a Marine expeditionary force could wear the field uniforms of the Marine Corps, with bronzed Naval insignia. Although the batteries were not attached to a Marine landing force, Rear Admiral Charles P. Plunkett, head of the Naval Batteries, decided that the Marine gear would be better than that of the Army, which was prescribed for the American Expeditionary Force. Brigadier General William Chamberlaine, who was in command of the Army railway guns, considered that the naval guns were under his command and that the Army dress should be worn. Plunkett claimed his orders came from the Secretary of the Navy, and the uniform should be that prescribed by the Navy uniform regulations.

Admiral Plunkett is shown in the winter field uniform of the Marine Corps. On the standing collar appear the bronzed devices "USN" and the foul anchor of line officers. On his shoulders and overseas cap are the two silver stars of his rank. Around his cuffs are strips of black braid (worn by members of the General Staff; other officers wore brown braid).[2] The coat buttons were not bronzed, as required by the Navy uniform regulations. His leather boots had been bought in England, and were not the military issue.

The lieutenant is wearing the Marine Corps summer field uniform of olive drab. His leather puttees were used by many instead of the "wrap-around" leggings available from the Army. The collar insignia is, like Plunkett's, bronzed. The two bars of his rank are silver. His cap is the Navy type, with the cover of the Marine Corps.

The enlisted man in the center is wearing faded blue dungaree trousers and the field dress summer jumper for men of the Marine Corps. The dungarees were specified by the 1913 regulations, and they faded when washed. The leggings are those specified for men on duty in a landing force. The helmet was made available to all persons on duty in the field in Europe. While the enlisted men could wear the insignia of their ratings on their sleeves — in black instead of the regular red or white — alone with the white eagle and specialty marks, photographs do not show any men with sleeve marks.

The coveralls worn by the sailor, second from the left, were supplied by the Army; the Navy did not have any such work clothing. They were of olive drab cloth and, when washed, faded a bit. To cover his head he is wearing the dark blue knitted watch cap which is included in the 1913 regulations.

The enlisted man at the far left is wearing the Marine Corps enlisted man's shirt, and Navy dungaree trousers. His hat is the Marine Corps field hat, with no cords for enlisted men. His black boots are prescribed by the 1913 regulations.

The dress of the officers and men of the Railway Batteries was basically that of the Marine Corps, with working gear of the Navy.

The authors would like to thank Lieutenant Colonel H. C. Brown, USMC—OINC Marine Corps Museum Branch, Quantico, who gave data on uniforms and color samples for field dress, and Colonel Donald L. Dickson, USMC, Ret., who gave data and sketches of the uniforms of 1917-1918.

Ronald E. Spicer
James C. Tily

[1] *Uniform Regulations*, U.S. Navy, 1913 (rev 17 January 1918).
[2] Rear Admiral Garret L. Schuyler, USN, Ret. He served with the Naval Railway Batteries and gave the information on sleeve braid.

Petty Officers

Lieutenant,
Summer Field Dress

Rear Admiral,
Winter Field Dress

Naval Railway Batteries, 1917-1918

Lieutenant, U.S. Marine Corps, 1937

This sketch of a young 2nd lieutenant, rendered by the late Colonel John Magruder, illustrates in faithful detail a typical commissioned company-grade officer of the 1st Marine Brigade at Quantico, in summer field service uniform. Scores of photographs were reviewed to insure accuracy of detail, and the opinions and recollections of the writer were incorporated, inasmuch as he had served as an officer of Battery B, 10th Marines, at that place and time. The governing factors in the making of this sketch were *Uniform Regulations, U.S. Marine Corps, 1937,*[1] modified to an insignificant degree in accordance with then current Brigade uniform regulations and other local "ground rules" which permitted certain variations.

To insure uniformity in the color of its leather equipment, the Quartermaster, U.S. Marine Corps, contracted with a civilian firm for the manufacturing and bottling of a dark brown dye, officially termed *brown, USMC, 141 shade,* which was sold over the counters of Marine Corps Post Exchanges, to be applied by the individuals concerned. Unfortunately, the shade of *blanco* issued for web equipment and canvas field gear such as canteen covers, first aid kits, and automatic pistol clip pouches was not subject to the same degree of strict uniformity, with the result that it varied in color from true khaki to a straw hue (obtained by washing and sun bleaching) in some instances, and from a deep olive drab shade to a distinct grass green in others. The bleached effect being considered "regulation" at Quantico in the summer of 1937, this sketch shows it.

The summer service field uniform for commissioned officers consisted of (from top to bottom): the campaign field hat with flat, broad brim and Montana peak,[2] bearing the large (cap) size Marine Corps emblem in bronze, with a double hat cord (scarlet and gold) with acorns, secured by a leather hat strap (dark brown) worn around the rear of the head (not under the chin); the usual regulation issue khaki cotton shirt and field scarf,[3] with insignia of rank (small size) on both collar tabs; starched khaki cotton breeches for officers, secured below the knee by either small bone buttons or cotton laces and eyelets (at the discretion of the manufacturer), and with

provision for reinforcing material along the lower inseam. Footgear consisted of high-top leather laced shoes with either leather shell puttees (with clip and strap fastening gear) or laced puttees; field boots were optional.[4] Naturally, the footgear shade of dark brown corresponded with that of the holster for the Colt .45 Automatic, model 1911 and attached leather leg strap. The type and manner of wearing of the regulation web equipment (pistol belt with shoulder braces, crossed in the rear) are shown, with pistol ammunition clip pouch on the wearer's left, first aid pouch on his right. The canteen and cover usually were worn on the right hip, to the rear of the pistol holster, to partially offset the additional weight on the wearer's left side occasioned by the presence of map case, compass, binoculars, haversack, or officer's musette bag, not to mention a gas mask. The pistol lanyard, worn over the shoulder as depicted, was a required item of equipment whenever the pistol and holster were carried.

Perhaps the only distinguishing items which denote the individual as a member of an artillery battery, as distinct from a rifle company, are the wearing of the bronze-colored whistle and chain in the left-hand shirt pocket,[5] and the carrying of a leather or bamboo riding crop. All things considered, the field uniform was a sensible rig, and it was essentially that worn throughout the Haitian and Nicaraguan Campaigns of the 1920s and early 1930s.

Roger Willock

[1]*U.S. Marine Corps, Uniform Regulations, 1937,* U.S. Government Printing Office, Washington, D.C., 1937; also, Colonel Robert H. Rankin, USMC, *Uniforms of the Sea Services (A Pictorial History),* U.S. Naval Institute, Annapolis, Md., 1962.

[2]The average officer purchased his own Stetson, disdaining the issue model provided by the quartermaster. Brims were worn flat — ironed stiff, if necessary — and were kept perfectly blocked, especially the creases in the peak.

[3]"Field scarf" was Marine-ese for "necktie."

[4]In the field, laced boots were acceptable. Riding boots (without spurs) were permitted but not when on duty with troops. Riding boots with spurs could be worn only by mounted officers, i.e. field officers or others actually assigned to mounted units.

[5]The noise of the Holt tractors which towed the Pack Howitzers was so great that whistles were required to give even the simplest command.

J. MAGRUDER '62

Lieutenant, United States Marine Corps, 1937

American Field Service in Italy, 1943-1945

The American Field Service began its life as a volunteer ambulance corps in August 1914 as a step in the creation of a military hospital by Americans living in Paris. With the assistance of Mrs. William K. Vanderbilt and the Ford Motor Company, ten home-made vehicles were ready by early September.[1]

From this simple beginning the organization, soon designated the American Field Service, had grown into a volunteer force operating 1,220 donated ambulances and a considerable number of camions when it was taken over by the U.S. Army in late 1917.

The service maintained its identity between the two World Wars, holding reunions and conducting a program of American fellowships in French universities. Thus when the second war came it was prepared once again to offer its services as volunteers to France. Under the directorship of Mr. Stephen Galatti, and with the United States Ambassador to France, William C. Bullitt, as Honorary President, the AFS set about raising funds, establishing liaison with essential authorities, and finding volunteers.

The operations of the AFS in World War II were far more widely dispersed than before, as befitted the character of the war. After a brief and hectic experience in France during 1940, the ambulance companies found themselves scattered around the world in the Middle East, in Africa, in the Mediterranean Theater, in India-Burma, and finally back in France. In this plate we see the companies which, commencing in October 1943, served with the Allied armies in Italy.

The artist was privileged to serve as an AFS driver in Italy and Germany during 1944-1945. The men he found himself with were an extraordinary group. The majority were college graduates or the equivalent and well represented in the arts, letters, and the professions. Their average I.Q. must have been far above that of any outfit of comparable size in World War II. Some were well over draft age, a few under. Some couldn't possibly have passed an army physical examination. Some were conscientious objectors. But for a noncombat outfit, the AFS per capita record of casualties and decorations was unusually high.

The AFS in Italy consisted of two companies of four platoons each, with roughly 120 ambulances per company, plus necessary service lorries. Major maintenance was furnished by the Royal Army Service Corps. The companies were considered Eighth Army troops by the British; they were never permanently attached to a regiment, brigade, division, or corps but were assigned by AFS HQ at Army request as emergencies demanded.

I have illustrated three uniforms more or less characteristic of the Italian service. The central figure wears the standard British army battle dress with officer's cap which as warrant officers we were entitled to wear. His ribbon is that of the Africa Star, shown enlarged. It represents the North African campaign from El Alamein to Tunis. The yellow background is for the sands of the desert, the wide red band for the Army, the narrow dark blue one for the Navy, and the light blue for the R.A.F.

The figure on the left wears summer-weight shirt and shorts, with tan stockings and web gaiters. The old-style cap he wears was gradually replaced by the beret shown on the figure at right whose garb suggests the liberties taken in combining regular issue clothing with whatever took the fancy of the wearer. The gray shirt obtained through barter or as a gift from a generous Kiwi (whose distinctive garment it was) was made of New Zealand wool. The corduroys probably stem from Cairo and the tennis shoes from A.G. Spalding.

The mess tins (British "dixies") were very practical, and when held properly in one hand could hold your complete meal — spam or bully on one side; bread and jam, well-laced with hornets, on the other, leaving a free hand for the cup of strong tea.

The figure with the blankets wears a wool-lined leather jerkin, not very dressy but an excellent windbreaker.

The ambulance is a Dodge four-wheel drive with an extra low speed gear — a life saver in mud and chewed-up landscape.

The army flashes hardly need explanation except in the case of the U.S. Fifth Army with which AFS units served together with British troops as part of that army.

The flash of 21st Army Group is added because Montgomery, its commander, insisted that one of the AFS companies, which had served the Eighth Army in Africa and Italy, join him again for the last push into Germany.

Frederick T. Chapman

[1]All historical information has been taken from George Rock, *American Field Service, 1920-1955*, New York, 1956.

Cap Devise

Eighth Army

21st Army Gp
Germany

U.S. Fifth Army

French First
Army

561 Coy.

485 Coy

American Field Service in Italy, 1943-1945

Lake Superior Regiment (Motor), Canadian Army, 1945

The figures in this print of our fellow North Americans in World War II represent the use of various combinations of the uniform for quick identification of subunits during battle.

All are soldiers of A Company, Lake Superior Regiment (Motor), armed, equipped, and dressed for a daylight raid across the Maas River, The Netherlands, at 1230 hours, 17 January 1945. No. 1, No. 2, and No. 3 Platoons took part, each having a different role in the operation, each uniformed and armed distinctively for its role.[1]

No. 1 Platoon made the initial river crossing and seized and held a bridgehead on the snow-covered foreshore. The men wore snowsuits and were armed with Bren guns. The officer leading No. 1 Platoon (central figure) has let his white hood fall back, revealing the woolen scarf and toque. The caliber .38 Smith & Wesson revolver is the officer's personal weapon, which he has supplemented with pockets full of grenades and a #4 Mark 1 rifle. At this time the revolvers, either Smith & Wesson or Webley, were being called in and 9mm Canadian-manufactured Browning automatics issued.

The figure on the right, wearing battle dress and khaki beret, is a private of No. 2 Platoon, lightly dressed and lightly armed for the assault over the dike and the seizing of a firm base on the edge of the town of Hoenzedril, the objective of the raid. He is armed with a Bren gun, though half of this platoon carried rifle and bayonet. He also carries a small pack filled with fragmentation grenades.

The company commander, with his headquarters and signals and artillery communications, wore the dress of the No. 2 Platoon, from whose position the raid was to be directed.

No. 3 Platoon was given the job of getting into the town of Hoenzedril, seizing prisoners, and being as disagreeable as possible. For this role they were armed with P.I.A.T.s (Projector, Infantry, Anti-Tank), flamethrowers, phosphorus and fragmentation grenades, and — as personal weapons — Sten guns. The kneeling figure on the left is a P.I.A.T. man, as is the Cree Indian who is coming up with more bombs. They wear tin hats, netted; the nets are garnished with brown and green strips of camouflage cloth. They are also wearing felt-lined leather vests as protective armor against flying rubble, as well as for quick identification of this group.

All distinguishing marks of rank, regiment, and division were removed for this raid. The "Canada" patch, however, was never taken down. As this was a river crossing, everyone wore a deflated Mae West (not shown in the print) over their clothes but under their web equipment, and all carried a razor blade or an open, sharp clasp knife in an outside pocket for quick escape from weighty gear should a reconnaissance boat capsize or sink.

Battle-dress trousers were made with a special pocket on the right thigh for the first field dressing. These dressings generally were found to be too small to cover a wound. All ranks, therefore, were issued khaki-covered "shell dressings," approximately 7 x 3 x 2 inches, which were carried under the helmet net or tied under the left shoulder strap. Shortly before H-Hour there was a rum issue!

In this print, the regimental badge of the "L.S.R." is shown against the green background of the 4th Armoured Division patch. The "Lake Soups" were the Motor Battalion of the 4th Armoured Brigade, 4th Armoured Division.

Today the "L.S.R." has returned to its armory at Port Arthur, Ontario where, as the militia regiment of the lakehead area, it carries on the tradition and honors of the Algoma Rifles of the Riel Rebellion and the 52nd Battalion of World War I. The regiment, because of the recruiting value of the kilt, has become Scottish, and now is correctly designated "The Lake Superior Regiment (Scottish) (Motor)." As such, it wears a new badge and kilts of the Macgillivray tartan.

Frederick T. Chapman
Harrison K. Bird, Jr.

[1] The uniforms and equipment shown are taken from the author's personal knowledge and collection, checked against the holdings of the Imperial War Museum, London.

THE LAKE SUPERIOR REGT.

Dark Blue

CANADA

Khaki

Green

INTER PERICULA INTREPIDI

Lake Superior Regiment (Motor) Canadian Army, 1945

Imperial Japanese Forces, Aleutian Islands, 1942-1943

The forces of Imperial Japan occupied the Aleutian Islands of Attu and Kiska in June 1942 and thus established a tenuous foothold on America's northernmost territory. Troops from the 7th U.S. Infantry Division landed on Attu in May 1943 and destroyed the fanatically resisting Japanese garrison in a bitter battle that raged over the rugged terrain. United States and Canadian troops landed on Kiska on 15 August 1943, only to find that the entire Japanese garrison had been evacuated.

The accompanying plate depicts a visiting major general inspecting defenses on one of the islands. The superior private on the right is wearing the Japanese army uniform adopted in 1938. The turn-down collar is worn open in the summer or in the tropics. His olive drab wool single-breasted coat has five buttons and four flapped pockets, the two breast pockets having buttoned flaps. His wool trousers are styled like breeches and he wears the puttees that were usually worn by dismounted enlisted men. His field cap, worn under his helmet, is of wool with a chin strap and, on the front, the gold star of the Japanese army, which sometimes appears in the color of the headgear item on which it is worn. His steel helmet has long tapes which tie under the chin or at the back of the neck.

Over his right breast pocket he wears the zigzag chevron that was used to denote arm or service; different colors identified the various branches — red for infantry and tanks, yellow for artillery, sky blue for aviation troops, dark green for medical personnel. His two cartridge pouches are made of rubberized fabric, a third one with an oil can is in the rear. His gas mask is in a canvas carrier under his left arm; his rifle is the 6.5mm Arisaka, Model 38 (1905), a modified German Mauser easily identified by its unusually long length.

The Marine leading seaman on the left wears the same uniform as that used by the Army, except for the use of Navy insignia. Though the well-known *tabi* (split-toe sneakers) were issued in all climates, both he and the Army private wear high marching shoes of unfinished leather with either leather hobnailed or cleated rubber soles, for better protection against mud and cold. Strictly speaking, there was no Japanese Marine Corps, though a corps performing Marine duties did exist, but from an administrative viewpoint it remained regular Navy personnel. The gold anchor worn on caps or helmets was its primary identifying feature. Though naval insignia was prescribed, some units used Army rank insignia and sometimes even combined both — army insignia on the collar and naval insignia on the right sleeve. He is carrying the Model 99 (1939) 7.7mm light machine gun.

The uniforms of the three officers in the center are not government issues, but are privately furnished. For this reason, wide variance in color, quality, and cut existed among all Japanese officers' uniforms. The major on the left is wearing an olive drab wool uniform and fur-lined leggings, similar in style to that issued to enlisted men. His map case, binoculars, and pistol are carried at his sides; the straps across his chest indicate that his haversack, canteen, and gas mask are in the rear. The gilt on the metal star on his service cap has worn away, giving the appearance of a silver rather than a regulation gold star. Behind him is a captain, wearing a typical officer's overcoat, which is double-breasted with two rows of six buttons on each side, two flap side pockets, and a slot on the left side for a sword sling. Though not visible here, his cuffs have single bands of brown braid. The major general wears a service cape of greenish khaki. On his left hip is a leather map case; a rubberized fabric pistol holster is at right front. The decoration at his throat is the Order of the Golden Kite, granted in recognition of conspicuous service against a foreign foe. The officers all carry nonregulation swords, a practice sometimes followed by NCOs as well.

In combat areas great latitude existed in the use of both uniforms and insignia. Frequently pre-1938 uniforms were worn as fatigue and combat uniforms until they were worn out. Marks of rank or specialty were sometimes omitted altogether. Marine officers and men, regardless of regulations, wore pretty much what they pleased, especially ashore. The seaman in the left rear, who presumably ferried the general ashore, wears a dark blue uniform and white canvas leggings. His field cap is similar to that worn by Army personnel.[1]

Donald A. Burgess

[1] J.A.N. No. 1, *Uniforms and Insignia;* Joint Army and Navy Publication. See also Military Intelligence Service, Special Series No. 27, "*Soldier's Guide to the Japanese Army,*" November 1944.

Seaman

Leading Seaman (Marine)

Major

Captain

Major General

Superior Private

Imperial Japanese Forces, Aleutian Islands, 1942-1943

German Navy, U-Boat 537, Labrador, 1943

During the evening of 22 October 1943, a German IXC class U-boat, *U-537*, slipped into remote Martin Bay on the northern tip of Labrador and dropped anchor. Its visit, in the midst of World War II, was to establish an unmanned, automatic weather station. Data transmitted from this and similar stations in the Arctic would be of considerable value to the Kriegsmarine in planning U-boat operations. The station components were quickly landed, assembled, and tested. The crew embarked and *U-537* made for the relative safety of the open sea.[1] Some months after the successful Labrador mission, *U-537* was transferred to Far Eastern waters. While on patrol in the Java Sea area during the night of 9/10 November 1944, *U-537* was attacked and sunk by the American submarine USS *Flounder*, with all hands lost.

Our plate depicts several crew members as they set about assembling the station. *U-537*'s commanding officer, Käpitan-leutnant Peter Schrewe, is shown wearing an officer's double-breasted reefer jacket. The anchor-embossed buttons are gilt, as is the national emblem on his right chest and the two wide and one narrow bands of rank lace on the lower arms. The star indicates a line or sea officer. He wears gray-green denim working trousers and black leather jack boots. Traditionally U-boat commanders wore white tops to their visored caps. Befitting his rank grouping, a single line of yellow embroidery is seen on the edge of the visor. Above the chin strap is the gilt national emblem and black-white-red cockade.[2] Many U-boat crews designed and had manufactured semiofficial badges that were distinctive to their particular crew. *U-537*'s badge was a pair of crossed swords and an anchor, which can be seen pinned to the left side of the commander's hatband.

Though no insignia of rank is seen, the figure to Schrewe's left is identifiable as an officer because of the gilt braid edging on his wedge or side cap. The *U-537* badge and national eagle and rosette are also on his cap. Thigh-length, double-breasted leather coats were generally worn by nontechnical personnel.[3] Under this, he wears a sheepskin coat.[4]

The petty officer wears gray-green denim working fatigues, said to be patterned after British battledress, with plain buttons. Sewn above the right breast pocket is the national emblem in yellow cloth. The waistband can be tightened by means of a slide-type buckle. He is recognized as a petty officer by the yellow lace on his collar points, which sometimes were made from brass strips. Though not present on the jacket, rank badges could be worn on the shoulder straps.[5] Petty officer cap peaks were unadorned.

The center figure wears a sailor's tufted wool knit watch cap and the single-breasted, short leather coat and trousers worn by U-boatmen designated as technicians. In his right hand he carries a 9mm, MP40 submachine gun. The weather station cannister on which he rests his left hand is marked, in English, "Canadian Weather Service."[6] This, and the leaving behind of a few buttons, empty cigarette packs, and American matchbooks was intended to give the impression, in the unlikely event of the station being discovered, that it was a U.S. or Canadian establishment.[7]

The *U-537*'s largest armament was a 10.5cm gun mounted just forward of the conning tower. When the voyage began, the boat also possessed a pair of single-barrel 2cm antiaircraft guns just behind the tower, plus a four-barrel 2cm antiaircraft gun on the lower platform, known as the *wintergarten*. The latter was torn from its mountings by a storm and lost overboard while the U-boat was enroute to Labrador.[8]

We wish to thank Werner Bendler of Bremerhaven, West Germany and Franz Selinger of Ulm, West Germany for their kind assistance on this plate. Mr. Bendler served on the *U-537* prior to its transfer to the Far East and Mr. Selinger is an authority on Germany's wartime Arctic weather stations.[9]

Eric I. Manders
Wayne A. Colwell
George A. Snook

[1]*Canadian Geographic*, Ottawa, CI, No. 6, 42-47; *Marine Engineering Digest*, Ottawa, I, No. 2, 29-30.
[2]Among the general works consulted on German Navy uniforms were: Andrew Mollo, *Naval, Marine and Air Force Uniforms of World War II*, Poole, England, 1975; Andrew Mollo, *The Armed Forces of World War II*, New York, 1981; Editors: We, *German Military Uniforms and Insignia 1933-1945*, Old Greenwich, CT, 1967.
[3]J. P. Mallmann Showell, *U-Boats Under the Swastika*, New York, 1973, 131.
[4]Photograph, F. Selinger collection.
[5]U-boat "battledress" jacket on exhibit Canadian War Museum.
[6]Photograph, F. Selinger collection.
[7]Unpublished W. Bendler report, Bibliothek fur Zeitgeschichte, 10 Sept. 1981.
[8]Bendler report, *op. cit.*
[9]Mr. Selinger's archival sleuthing resulted in the rediscovery of the Labrador station. In July 1981, many of the rusting components were brought out of Martin Bay by a Canadian Coast Guard helicopter and ship. The parts are presently stored in the Canadian War Museum, Ottawa.

Officer   Petty Officer   Seamen   Captain

German Navy, U-Boat 537, Labrador, 1943

THE MODERN WARS, FROM 1946-

Korea

Lebanon

The Berlin Blockade

The Cuban Missile Crisis

Dominican Republic

Vietnam

Grenada

3rd U.S. Infantry Regiment (The Old Guard), 1966

The 3rd Infantry, the oldest regular infantry unit in the United States Army, serves as the Army's security and ceremonial unit for Washington, D.C. This plate depicts its ceremonial uniform, worn for such duties as personal escort to the President of the United States, guard of honor for the reception of high-level foreign dignitaries, wreath-laying ceremonies at the Tomb of the Unknown Soldier, or formal military funerals.

In the central foreground is the 3rd Infantry's commanding officer, Colonel Joseph B. Conmy, Jr., who held that assignment during the period, 1964-1967. Colonel Conmy wears the standard infantry officer's dress blue uniform. Around his left shoulder is the 3rd Infantry's distinctive insignia, the "Buff Strap." This is a strap of black leather, one-half inch wide, through which is woven a one-fourth-inch-wide strip of buff leather. Other regimental distinctions are the gold belt and the gold braiding on the top of the cap as can be seen at the lower right of the drawing. The front of the cap is at the top of the plate.

The master sergeant on the colonel's right and the private to his left rear wear the same basic ceremonial blue dress uniform worn by the United States Army Band. The dark blue coat and sky blue trousers have the same cut as the officer's and are decorated on the cuff and along the trousers' side seam with two bands of one-fourth-inch golden yellow braid. The cap is dark blue, trimmed with the same braid. The top of the cap is braided like the officer's. The chin strap, chevrons, and shoulder knots also are golden yellow. Belts are sky blue with golden trim, keepers, and buckles. Both enlisted men wear the buff strap and infantry blue shoulder cord; both are armed with the M14 rifle. (Effective in 1967, all 3rd Infantry noncommissioned officers in the grade of platoon sergeant and above now carry the noncommissioned officers' sword, model 1840, on ceremonial occasions.) The silver badge on the private's breast pocket marks him as a member of the select detail of sentinels which maintains the eternal vigil at the Tomb of the Unknown Soldier.

In the left background are two members of the 3rd Infantry's famous Fife and Drum Corps. Members of the corps wear white wigs, instead of powdering their hair as would have been done on ceremonial occasions in the late 18th century. (One anachronism mars the corps' appearance: an individual who had sufficient authority and a greater devotion to noise than to historical accuracy insisted on the inclusion in the corps of a section "armed" with bugles.)

The drum carries the 3rd Infantry's arms:

> . . . within a bordure of the United States, a hill vert crowned with battlements gules on a field argent. on a chief azure three crosses patee of the field. Encircling the escutcheon an infantry officer's full dress belt (para 2, Special Regulation 42, 1917) with plate in chief proper inscribed with the motto "Noli Me Tangere" in base, and in Chief "3d Infantry, 1784" all sable. The escutcheon and belt to be displayed in front of an old pattern bayonet and drum major's baton from the Mexican War, crossed in saltire proper.
>
> Crest on a wreath argent and azure an infantry officer's cocked hat with white plume proper.[1]

The charge symbolizes the 3rd Infantry's service at Cerro Gordo, Churubusco, and Chapultepec during the Mexican War. The crosses recall its Civil War service with the 2nd Division, V Corps, the badge of which was a white maltese cross. It should be noted that the 3rd Infantry is the only regiment in the Army which is permitted to use the shield of the United States as part of its coat of arms. The crest of these arms in brass (see upper left-hand corner of this plate) is worn as regimental insignia on the shoulder straps of service uniforms.

In the center and right background is the color party, likewise dressed in a facsimile of the regiment's 1784 uniforms. The coats are blue with red facings. Waistcoats and gaiter-trousers are white. A red canteen is carried on the left hip.

The colors shown here are, from left, the national colors, the U.S. Army flag, and the regimental colors. The second of these, with its mass of streamers, is a major load to carry even on a still day.

The 3rd Infantry has another unique distinction, its caisson section, the Army's last mounted unit. This unit, with its twenty-eight carefully trained horses, is a vital part of state and full-honors funerals, and it occasionally appears mounted during regimental reviews.

H. Charles McBarron, Jr.
John R. Elting

[1]AG Letter 424.5, Coat of Arms, 10 January 1921.

Fife and Drum Corps

Sergeant

Colonel

Color Team

Private

**3rd U.S. Infantry Regiment (The Old Guard)
Ceremonial Dress, 1966**

18th U.S. Infantry, Regiment Colors and Drums, 1949-1953

The 18th Infantry, the "Vanguards," was one of the regiments formed at the outbreak of the Civil War. It fought through most of the Western operations and was at Chickamauga, Chattanooga, and Atlanta. It carries battle honors for four Indian campaigns. It served at Manila in 1898 and thereafter on other islands of the Philippines. But probably the greatest single event in the life of the Regiment was when, on 8 June 1917, it was assigned to the 1st Expeditionary Division, that remarkable outfit which later came to be called the 1st Infantry Division. Since 1917 the story of the 18th Infantry has been, to a considerable extent, the story of the "Big Red One."[1]

The Eighteenth is one of the most decorated units of any size in our entire army. It has been awarded six Distinguished Unit Citations (our top unit award), one to the regiment, three to its organic battalions, and two to individual companies. Four times has the French government pinned the Croix de Guerre on its colors, twice in each of the two World Wars. This has given its men the right to wear a fourragère in the colors of the French *Medaille Militaire,* a distinction which only six other United States units enjoy. It boasts two Belgian citations and on its colors hangs a Belgian fourragère. Its battle honors, from 1862 to date, total thirty, and in its ranks have served nine winners of the Medal of Honor. Quite a record for an outfit just over a century old.

When World War II ended, the 18th Infantry looked back on a remarkable three years of scrapping and the knowledge that in doing all this it had lost 1,498 men killed and 5,490 wounded.

After 1945 the Regiment served in Germany. There, as early as 1946, it was given the job of furnishing honor guards for the European Theater Headquarters at Frankfurt, and it is to this side of its life (rather than its side devoted to training and maneuvers) that the present plate is dedicated.

The drum and bugle corps shown here is a ceremonial unit not found in the Tables of Organization, but authorized in this and other regiments. Its members wear the regulation olive drab service uniform but with special white waist belts, gloves, scarfs, fourragères (on the right shoulder), and boot laces. Their chromium-plated steel helmets have the divisional patch on the front and the regimental device on each side. On their left arm, above the Red One patch, is a special arc flash in infantry blue bearing the white letters "18th/Drum-Bugle Corps/Inf."

Both the honor guard and the color party wore at times a quite similar parade uniform, the belts being web pistol belts stripped and whitened. Their arc tabs carried the words "18th/Honor Guard/Inf."

In the drum and bugle corps there were one bass, two tenor, and four side (snare) drums; from four to eight buglers; a cymbal; and a drum major. In the plate are shown a tenor, a bass, and a side drum, in that order. The Puerto Rican tenor drummer, a corporal, is the commander, as his green shoulder strap loops indicate. The drums were rope-rigged but still retained four metal strainers to keep them true. On their barrels were painted the regimental insignia and battle honors. The bugle tabards also had the distinctive regimental device.

The entire regiment, on parade, wears the divisional insignia on the front and the regimental insignia on each side of their helmets, the yellow and green fourragère of the *Medaille Militaire,* regimental insignia on the shoulder straps and divisional insignia on the left shoulder sleeves, and the prescribed brass insignia on the lapels.

Milton Caniff
Harry C. Larter, Jr.

[1]*Army Lineage Book, II, Infantry,* 115-17. We are indebted to Hqtrs., 18th Infantry, for supplying a complete file of photographic material and for verification of details.

Colors and Drums

18th U.S. Infantry Regiment, 1949-1953

351st U.S. Infantry Regiment, 1951

Following the end of World War II, western Europe saw itself threatened by communism on numerous fronts. Taking advantage of the weakened state of Italy, Yugoslavian forces moved to control the port city of Trieste at the head of the Adriatic Sea. In 1947, the Council of Foreign Ministers (created at Potsdam), established the Free Territory of Trieste, which would be under United Nations administration. The city and a small strip of land would be garrisoned by a small American and British force which would try to keep Yugoslav troops at bay until some other arrangement could be worked out.

In 1951 American forces defending the Free Territory consisted of the 351st Infantry Regiment, a small quartermaster unit, and an occasional Navy destroyer or cruiser which was to provide offshore fire support. The 351st had become "soft" from occupation duty, and were dubbed "chromium plated soldiers" by certain observers. It was at this point that the late Colonel Paul W. Caraway became commanding officer. Caraway immediately began a program to strengthen the unit and make it a combat-ready force. Battalions were rotated in and out of Austria for training, and within a short time the Regiment had achieved an excellent reputation. The 351st could also be counted on for quick deployment to any point of the Free Territory menaced by Yugoslav troops. Rocket launcher training was especially emphasized to meet possible thrusts of Tito's armor. Caraway's men were indeed, "showing the flag, and keeping the peace."[1]

The winter uniform was general issue, with mountain bags used in place of blankets. Helmet liners were marked in front with insignia of rank, while steel shells were marked on the rear with stripes to indicate combat leaders. The 1st Battalion had the company letter or battalion number stenciled on the right side in luminous paint for night identification. Soldiers are wearing neckties since this plate shows them leaving for Germany to take part in combined field exercises. This was to meet off-duty European Command regulations, since the collar was normally left open and unbuttoned while in the field. The uniform consisted of heavy twill field trousers, and field jackets worn with woolen underwear and shirts. Men often wore double-soled wool socks and sometimes a woolen sweater under the field jacket. Parkas and overcoats were not worn during field operations by the 351st. White stripes on the helmets of the sergeant and corporal indicate NCO combat leaders. The men are armed with the M1 Garand, Browning Automatic Rifle, and the M1 Garand with grenade launcher.

American forces were withdrawn from the Free Territory shortly after Colonel Caraway's tour of regimental command ended. In 1954 the city reverted to Italy, and Yugoslavia received the disputed area to the south. The 351st remains an active part of the Army Reserves today, and has battalion headquarters in Milwaukee, and Fond du Lac, Wisconsin.

Artist unknown[2]
Dale E. Biever

[1]Phone conversation with Lieutenant General Paul W. Caraway, U.S.A., Ret., 22 Dec 1980. General Caraway was a Fellow of the Company.
[2]Phone conversation with Lieutenant General Caraway, 22 Dec 1980. While commanding the 351st, General Caraway had the men photographed wearing a variety of uniforms. The drawings were made by an ex-Fascist who had formerly designed wine bottle labels. He had been relegated to menial work in the city when Caraway asked him to do the art work from the photos.

116

351st U.S. Infantry Regiment (Winter Field Uniform), 1951

1st U.S. Cavalry Division (Airmobile), 1966-1967

The 1st Cavalry Division (Airmobile) is basically an infantry division without heavy equipment, with the addition of the 11th Aviation Group. The combat maneuver battalions are conventional infantry units with cavalry designations for historical reasons. The 11th Aviation Group, comparable to a regiment in size, consists of the 227th, 228th, and 229th Aviation Battalions, the 11th General Support Company, and Headquarters and Headquarters Company, 11th Aviation Group. The three aviation battalions give the division its special "airmobile" capability.

A major component of the 11th Aviation Group's Headquarters Company is the division's pathfinder section. This unit conducts three types of operations. When required, members can parachute into an objective zone to mark the landing area and guide aircraft in. A second mission is to control all air traffic into and out of forward area landing zones, supplying such pertinent information as wind data, traffic patterns, and artillery fire data. A third mission is to accompany infantry companies in the field and control the arrival and departure of support helicopters.

Three examples of commonly improvised equipment can be seen in the drawing. The pathfinder is carrying ammunition in a cloth bag originally used to hold a claymore antipersonnel mine; this bag can hold a dozen eighteen-round magazines. Less obvious is his substitution of a general purpose carrying strap for a rifle sling. Both the pilot and the pathfinder carry survival knives.

All of the men shown are wearing special uniforms commonly called jungle fatigues. This uniform was cooler and dried faster than standard fatigues and had extra carrying pockets, placed to be accessible when wearing a pack and load-bearing equipment. Individuals could wear the sleeves rolled above the elbow or completely down. After extended field wear, these uniforms became dirty and torn and were usually replaced with new, unmarked fatigues. As a result, enlisted infantrymen often wore no insignia or drew insignia directly on the uniform with a ballpoint or marking pen, as the company commander has here added his rank on his helmet cover.

The basic infantry weapon in Vietnam was the M16 rifle, the weapon carried by the pathfinder. Some combat leaders, like this company commander, carried the experimental CAR-15, an M16 with a shortened barrel and a collapsible stock. Privately owned pistols were popular with many officers, especially those not in the infantry. The pilot wears his own pistol with a locally made holster and belt. The machine gunner carries an M60 machine gun and all members of the squad carry extra machine gun ammunition in addition to that for their individual weapons.

Officers and troops in Vietnam produced a variety of improvised insignia in addition to standard items. Subdued insignia, with the central design in black on an olive drab background, were used throughout the 1st Cavalry and were usually of the same general size and shape as standard insignia, but they varied considerably in quality as they were usually hand-made locally. All three individuals in the foreground of the picture wear the subdued 1st Cavalry patch on their left sleeve. The pathfinder wears the combat infantryman's badge above his left pocket and immediately below it are US Airborne wings. The pathfinder badge is worn on his left pocket. Vietnamese Airborne wings, awarded for at least one jump with Vietnamese troops, are worn above his right pocket. On his right sleeve the pathfinder wears an 82nd Airborne Division patch, showing he served with that unit during the Dominican Republic service. Both of the captains wear rank and branch insignia on right and left collars, respectively. The pilot wears an aviator's badge above his left pocket and, on that pocket, the distinguishing patch for the 229th Aviation Battalion.

Three examples of unique identification are also evident. The black baseball cap worn by the pathfinder has gained the unit the designation "black hats," and the black neck scarves with white winged skull and legend "Death from Above" were used by members of the 1st Battalion, 8th Cavalry, during this period. Another identifying symbol in the picture is the blue circle on the door of the helicopter, indicating that this ship belongs to Company C, 229th Aviation Battalion.

Peter F. Copeland
William K. Emerson

IN MEMORIAM
LTC VORIN E. WHAN
KIA VIETNAM, 1968

Pathfinder, Corporal   *Company Commander*   *Helicopter Pilot*

1st U.S. Cavalry Division (Airmobile), 1966-1967

1st Battalion, 77th U.S. Armor Regiment, 1969-1970

The 1st Battalion, 77th Armor, was assigned to the 1st Brigade, 5th Infantry Division (Mechanized), which arrived on the eastern coast of the Republic of Vietnam in the summer of 1968. Stationed in the northern I Corps area, the battalion participated in operations on the DMZ (Demilitarized Zone) in such places as Wunder Beach, "Rocket Ridge," and Khe Sanh. With a lineage from Company A, 753rd Tank Battalion (Medium) of World War II and Company A, 77th Heavy Tank Battalion of the Korean War, the unit was authorized to carry on its colors three streamers and a fourragère of the French Croix de Guerre for campaigns in Italy, and two streamers of the Presidential Unit Citation, Republic of Korea. Reflecting this heritage, the distinctive unit insigne consisted of a blue shield mounting a silver tiger sejant (sitting), with claws and tongue of red, supporting a silver battle-ax trimmed in red; a silver scroll below the shield heralded the motto *Insiste Firmiter*.

The figures in the plate represent typical field troops of a tank unit in Vietnam. Their dress is marked by an emphasis on comfort and utility and an antipathy to the spit and polish of "wire hangers" (nonfield troops). As in conflicts of the past, there was a definite contrast between what was prescribed by regulation and what was actually worn.

The platoon leader on the right wears the prescribed uniform of shade 107 olive green, rip-stop poplin jungle fatigues — many times in the field his appearance would have differed little from his enlisted men. Conferring with a tank commander, he holds his map enclosed in a plastic case, and, in his right hand, a CVC (combat vehicle crewman) helmet.

His fatigue jacket carries a name tape and "U.S. Army," embroidered in black and sewn horizontally above the breast pockets.[1] Also in black are a 1st lieutenant's bar on the right collar and the Armor branch insignia on the left. The blue-and-white distinctive unit insignia on the left pocket was a nonregulation cloth item made by the Vietnamese and commonly worn by the entire battalion. The 5th Infantry Division (Mechanized) insignia — the "red diamond" on the left shoulder — is significant in that it was not "subdued"; combat insignia were normally black, brown, and olive green. In the left breast pocket, attached by a cord in the prescribed manner, is the brigade S.O.I. (Standing Operating Instructions), a book of signal call signs, frequencies, and codes. In the opposite pocket, in a protected location, hangs his wrist watch. The jungle boots, laced to prevent constricting the ankles, carry an identification tag.

Uniforms of enlisted men in the field resembled closely that of the platoon leader, except for a conspicuous lack of regulation insignia. When these items were worn, they usually took the form of black metal grade devices pinned to the collar, or even the older black sleeve chevrons.

The tank commander wears an olive green jungle hat decorated with embroidery. The ever present towel about the neck protects from the burning sun and mops up perspiration. His unbloused fatigue trousers have been tapered by Vietnamese tailors. The boots have zippers, another Vietnamese item, for ease in donning, especially in emergencies, but they quickly wore out in the mud of the monsoon. On the tank commander's right wrist is a metal Montagnard bracelet that symbolized friendship with these mountain people. The other jewelry items, peace symbol medallions, love beads, and the like, were the nemesis of troop commanders, but still commonly seen since they reflected the subculture of the young troops.

The tank driver, inspecting the track, wears a similar uniform. Contrary to policy, he rolls his trousers instead of blousing them. His jungle hat, stitched around the edge of the brim and crown for shaping, has its string hanging in the back. The bracelet on the left wrist is a "power band" of braided boot lace, signifying a common spirit among black troops.

The individual weapon of a tank crew was the M1911-A1, caliber .45 pistol, issued with a black leather shoulder holster. Carried in the turret were two M3 or M3A1, caliber .45 submachine guns, assigned to the driver and loader, respectively. The main weapon was the M48A3, tank, combat, full tracked. Its armament included a 90mm main gun; the M73, 7.62mm machine gun, mounted coaxially with the main gun; and the caliber .50 M2, heavy barrel, turret type machine gun, removed from its cupola and mounted on top. The tanks of each company carried a variety of markings, numbers, and slogans. The vehicle in the plate is recognizable as belonging to Company B, which marked its tanks with "Armor" yellow numbers enclosed in a circle, the inscription "Steel Tigers" in white on the gun tube, and three bands of "Armor" yellow encircling the bore evacuator. Increased to four in 1970, these bands signified major engagements in the DMZ.[2]

Walter H. Bradford

---

[1] USARV later changed position to parallel with the pockets, but only new men were required to conform.
[2] Author served as a platoon leader in Company B, 1969-1970.

1st Battalion, 77th U.S. Armor Regiment, 1969-1970

U.S. Special Forces, 1963

Early in 1952, the Army Chief of Staff authorized 2,500 personnel spaces for the establishment of Special Forces units, to give the Army a clearly defined capability in the field of guerrilla warfare. The first such unit, the 10th Special Forces Group, was organized at Fort Bragg, North Carolina, on 20 June 1952. Thirteen months later, it was alerted for movement to Germany.[1]

At Fort Bragg in 1954, a committee from the 77th Special Forces Group organized from personnel left behind by the Tenth, met to consider selecting an item of uniform to distinguish Special Forces men from other airborne troopers. With concurrence from men of the 10th Group in Germany, they chose a beret, believing that the American people identify such headgear with a high degree of military professionalism and an unconventional military mission. They chose forest green, the color popularly associated with Rogers' Rangers, dating from early in America's history of unconventional warfare. (Historically speaking, blue would have been a more appropriate color.)

Men of the 10th Group in Germany have worn the beret since that time; other units waited until late 1961 to wear it officially.

On 11 October 1961, President Kennedy made an inspection trip to Fort Bragg, having indicated previously that he desired the Special Forces contingent to wear green berets. The next day, he telegraphed the contingent commander, Brigadier General William P. Yarborough, that " . . . I am sure that the green beret will be a mark of distinction in the trying times ahead."[2] Two months later, the Department of the Army authorized wear of the beret with most uniforms by Special Forces men who qualify for that right. All Special Forces units — Regular, National Guard, and Reserve — are now part of the First Special Forces, which carries the traditions, lineage, and honors from the Ranger units of World War II and Korea, as well as those from the Canadian-American First Special Service Force of World War II.[3]

Shown in this plate are a Special Forces captain and two sergeants (on the right a master sergeant, E-8; in the center, a sergeant first class, E-7) wearing the green beret with the army green uniform. The flash of color on the beret indicates the Special Forces Group to which they are assigned. Thus, the officer and one sergeant wear the red flash of the 7th Special Forces Group;

the other sergeant has the teal blue flash, edged in white, of the 2nd (Reserve) Group.

Shown at the upper left of the plate on the beret flash of the 2nd (Reserve) Group is the distinctive black and silver crest of the First Special Forces.[4] Emblazoned on the scroll forming the outer part of the crest is the motto: "De oppresso liber," — "To free from oppression." Attached to the scroll are two crossed arrows symbolizing the Special Forces' unconventional warfare role. The fighting knife, issued to only the First Special Service Force during World War II, is the pattern for the knife which is attached over the crossed arrows. Enlisted men wear this crest centered on the beret flash; all Special Forces personnel wear it on both shoulder tabs of the army green uniform.

Over their left breast pockets, all three soldiers wear the silver wings of qualified parachutists, mounted on a background of teal blue and gold, the Special Forces' colors. (Teal blue was chosen because of the Special Forces' branch immaterial status.)

On their left sleeves, from top to bottom, the captain and master sergeant display Airborne tabs denoting completion of that specialized course of training and the Special Forces shoulder patch. The arrowhead shoulder patch, in Special Forces colors, bears vertically that First Special Service Force knife and horizontally three lightning flashes denoting air, sea, and land infiltration capability.[5]

In all other respects, the army green blouse, khaki shirt, and black necktie are standard issue. The army green trousers, bloused, are tucked into black parachute boots.

Frederick T. Chapman
Irwin C. Nye
Benis M. Frank
John R. Elting

---

[1]Colonel Aaron Bank, "Founder of Special Forces," provided this data in a letter he wrote from retirement in 1961.
[2]Copy of this telegram from The White House is on display in the Special Warfare Museum, Fort Bragg, North Carolina.
[3]Official statement of lineage and honors of First Special Forces, from Office of the Chief of Military History.
[4]Authorized by Heraldic Branch, Department of the Army. A crossed arrow collar insignia was worn by the Canadian-American First Special Service Force.
[5]As above, 1954.

AIRBORNE

Captain
7th Special Forces Group

Sergeant
7th Special Forces Group

Sergeant
2nd Special Forces Reserve Group

U.S. Special Forces, November 1963

U.S. Army Band (Pershing's Own), 1948-1958

The Army Band's original uniform, designed under General John J. Pershing's grim eye, was of a blue-gray shade which soon was termed "Pershing Gray," but which actually was the regulation "Cadet Gray" of the United States Military Academy cadet uniform. This uniform was first worn on 6 June 1924, the band having used issue olive drab uniforms for its first three years.

Even with white trousers and cap covers, the Pershing Grey uniform proved hot and uncomfortable in average Washington weather. Also, there was some difficulty in obtaining replacements for its special shades of cloth. By 1943 it passed from use, but was resurrected in 1948 for General Pershing's funeral.

A slate blue uniform of summer-weight wool was adopted in 1943 and was worn as a dress uniform during the Army Band's overseas service (1943-1945). This uniform lacked distinction, and its material also was an odd shade, difficult to procure and match. It therefore was discarded after the war.

The Army Band thereafter went from one improvisation to another. It was a time of low military appropriations, with not enough money for essential weapons, let alone band uniforms. In 1948 the band wore shade 33 olive drab "Ike jackets" and trousers, with one-eighth-inch yellow piping at the top and bottom of the cap band, along the sides of the shoulder straps, around all sleeve insignia, and down the trouser seams. The drum major had no special uniform. Officers (like the third figure from the left) had gold piping on their shoulder straps. This uniform was made up with both blouse and jacket and included a special olive drab overcoat. So dressed, the band was at least soldierly, if drab.

In the early 1950s, a stock of surplus Cavalry yellow material was discovered and converted into new uniforms which made the Army Band "a glory in the sunlight seen afar." The cap was blue with a yellow band and chinstrap; the coat was yellow with blue collar, shoulder knots, cuffs, and braid. The cuffs and collar were braided with yellow. Trousers were blue with a yellow stripe; buttons and insignia were yellow metal; waist belts were blue. The blue used in this uniform was the brilliant "cobalt" or "Chemical Corps" blue. The drum major shown here is in semifull dress. On parade he wore a black fur busby with a gold tassel and two loops of yellow cord on its front and a red plume on its right side.[1] In addition, he had blue cross belts with a brass plate at their intersection on his chest — a singularly graceless contraption. White gloves (adopted about 1948, when the band began appearing in ceremonies with the 3rd Infantry Regiment) were worn with this uniform, much to the musicians' discomfort. The bandmaster had a double braided blue cord draped across his chest from shoulder to shoulder. The drums had a natural wood finish and red hoops and were decorated with the national coat of arms.

At about the same time the band adopted a summer uniform of Palm Beach-type cloth. Originally, it was identical with the yellow uniform, except that white cloth was used in place of the yellow. Later, its blouse was modified to give it an open collar with lapels, to be worn with white shirt and black tie.

Unfortunately, both new uniforms soon suffered strange and unpleasant afflictions. The overage yellow cloth turned various nonregulation shades and began falling apart. When the white summer uniform was dry-cleaned, the blue dye ran, and the blue-and-white material shrank in disproportionate degrees. Both, therefore, were discarded and replaced by the official dress blue uniform designed for enlisted wear throughout the Army (see the second figure from left). The band had worn this on occasions since 1949, but it was distinctive only because very few enlisted men had purchased it. The cap and coat were dark blue; the trousers were light blue; the cap band, braid, aiguillette, and trouser stripe were yellow. Officers wore the same uniform, "differenced" with a double loop of gold cord across the chest—and red flaps on their breast pockets! In turn, this uniform was replaced by the special blue uniform developed about 1957 for division-level and higher headquarters band and honor guards. (Not shown.) Since a total of some forty units wore it, it was hardly distinctive.

H. Charles McBarron, Jr.
John R. Elting

---

[1] This "plume" was of stuffed red cloth–not feathers.

Drum Major, 1953

Bandsman, c.1958
(Blue Ceremonial Uniform)

Officer, 1948
(Special OD Uniform)

Bandsman, 1953
(Summer Uniform)

U.S. Army Band (Pershing's Own), 1948-1958

U.S. Army Band (Pershing's Own), 1970

On its own initiative, during 1965-1968 the Army Band developed a new uniform, beginning with that of its drum major. This uniform was researched at the Army Institute of Heraldry and the Army Uniforms Division of Natick Laboratories. General Harold K. Johnson, Army Chief of Staff, ordered the somwhat fussy original shoulder cords simplified to the type shown and directed that all band personnel wear miniature medals instead of regular-sized ones.

The new uniform has returned to the military collar—which, besides being smarter looking, eliminates the cost of issuing and maintaining over one thousand white shirts. As shown here, the drum major and the bandsman from the Herald Trumpets section wear the winter uniform. The coat is standard dark Army blue, shade 150; the trousers the lighter shade 151. The coat has no exterior pockets; the braid on its shoulder straps, front, bottom, and lower sleeves is gold; buttons and insignia are yellow metal; shoulder cords are gold braid. There is a single three-fourth-inch stripe of gold braid on the outside seam of the trousers. The specially styled chevrons are gold braid on dark blue for winter, on white for summer. The collar ornaments (see inset at top of plate) are a new, distinctive design, being the crest from the band's coat of arms. When the band is in its "duty" (green) uniform, these are worn on the shoulder straps.

The drum major's H.M. Guards officers' model bearskin is black with a gold-chain-covered chin strap. On its left side is a white-over-red plume. A black hackle is worn during state funerals. His baldric is scarlet, edged with gold and decorated with miniature silver drumsticks and the band's coat of arms and the "Rhineland" battle honor in gold. The baton is gilt silver; gauntlets are white.

The summer uniform consists of a white coat and shade 151 trousers in lightweight material. A lightweight shade 150 coat may be worn if considered more suitable for the occasion. The white coat has dark blue cuffs and collar patches.

All band personnel, except the drum major, wear a scarlet cap braided with gold. This color was selected as representative of the red coats frequently worn by musicians up to the time of the Civil War. The cap ornament is a yellow-metal miniature of the Band's coat of arms, identical in design with that on the drum major's baldric.

Officers and warrant officers assigned to the Band wear the same uniform as the enlisted men, except for their appropriate cap ornaments, more elaborate sleeve braiding and shoulder cords, and shoulder boards with their insignia of rank. The shoulder boards are those of the Adjutant General's Corps—dark blue, piped with red.

The Army Band's new tabard — a "squared" version of the shield of its coat of arms — is shown in the left background. Within its dark blue border there are eight alternate white and red bars, signifying an octave in music. These are surmounted by a gold-hilted silver sword and a gold-decorated silver mace. The small escutcheon at the top, yellow with a wavy black bar, is a memorial of the Rhineland campaign. The deep fringe is gold. The band's drums carry its coat of arms in place of the national insignia.

Research for these plates began in 1966 with the devoted and intelligent help of the then Associate Bandmaster Lieutenant Colonel Gilbert H. Mitchell, Jr. The project proved far more complicated than any of us expected. Assisted by retired Sergeant Major Charles Kline, the last original member of the Band, Lieutenant Colonel Mitchell quizzed retired bandsmen, hunted down old uniforms, and shook out forgotten files for photographs. Every new discovery involved a half-dozen additional questions. A useful result of our mutual labors has been the Army Band's historical program, begun by Lieutenant Colonel Mitchell before his retirement.

H. Charles McBarron, Jr.
John R. Elting

Drum Major

Herald
Trumpet

Officer
(Summer Uniform)

Bandsman
(Summer Uniform)

U.S. Army Band (Pershing's Own), 1970

U.S. Marine Corps Detachment, Washington, D.C., 1955

This plate illustrates men of the U.S. Marine Barracks, 8th & I Streets, S.E., Washington, D.C.[1] With the exception of the guidon bearer, all are members of the Drum & Bugle Corps.

First authorized in 1934 at the direction of Major General J. H. Russell, Jr., USMC, Sixteenth Commandant, in 1955 there were thirty drum and bugle units spread throughout the regular Marine Corps, ranging from the original unit stationed at Washington to those at Atsugi, Japan and Port Lyautey, French Morocco.

All field musicians are products of regular boot training and then go on to Field Music School, but as the qualification badges shown in the plate indicate, they remain first and foremost Marines and secondarily musicians.

While the normal T/O strength for these corps was twenty-five musicians plus one drum major, the Washington unit had an authorized strength of thirty members but actually carried forty-three. This overage permitted a band of approximately thirty men at any one time, since the excess personnel generally were absorbed by rifle range details, watch lists, and those on leave or sick status.

The T/O allowance for a twenty-five-man drum and bugle unit was as follows:

4 snare drums	3 baritone bugles
2 scotch drums	8 soprano bugles
2 tenor drums	2 bass bugles
2 cymbals	2 French bugles

The guidon bearer is shown wearing the blue undress "A" uniform; the drummer (carrying a tenor drum) wears blue undress "C"; the drum major wears blue dress "B"; and the bugler wears blue dress "C".[2]

It will be noted that the plate is dated precisely "1955." The drum and bugle unit at Washington was constantly undergoing some alteration in equipment or uniform subject to the fancy of barracks COs or commandants. Since this unit is primarily ornamental in nature, that is to be expected.

General L. C. Shepherd, Jr., USMC, Commandant from 1951 through 1955, took especial interest in the 8th & I Barracks Detachment, and under his personal supervision many modifications were made in the interest of both appearance and comfort. The drum major, for instance, experienced considerable difficulty and discomfort with his original baldric. Between 1951 and 1955 several baldrics of varying design were tried, crossing both the left and the right shoulder. Finally adopted was a white leather one on which are mounted three rhodium-plated ornaments. White leather gauntlets were decreed for the drummers as well as the drum major, while buglers and the cymbal player continued to wear white cotton gloves. General Shepherd also prescribed black cap visors and shoes (instead of dark cordovan as is specified in uniform regulations) and directed that all personnel of the 8th & I Barracks have double-soled shoes with metal heel plates.

Once General R. McC. Pate, USMC, assumed the office of commandant on 1 January 1956, a number of changes were made in the Corps: all leather was changed back to regulation cordovan; single-sole shoes without heel plates have been reinstituted; the tassels on the ends of the musicians' breast cords have been replaced with metal tips similar to those worn on the fourragère.

Such is the problem that faces the historian in regard to this unit; in fact, each time this artist visited the barracks to check details, he encountered some new change. As a result, the year 1955 was chosen as representative and details are in accordance with practices in effect at the close of that year.

John H. Magruder, III

---

[1] It is necessary to differentiate between the Marine Barracks at 8th and I Sts. and the Marine Barracks at the Naval Gun Factory, both in Washington and located less than one half mile from each other.
[2] In designating uniforms, all dress uniforms involve the wearing of medals while undress call for ribbons. With "blues" the designation "A" specifies dark blue cap cover and sky blue trousers; "B" stipulates white cap cover and sky blue trousers; "C" uniforms include white cap cover and white trousers.

Guidon Bearer   Drummer   Drum Major   Bugler

U.S. Marine Corps (Barracks Detachment, 8th and I Streets, Washington, D.C.), 1955

U.S. Air Force Pipe Band, 1965-1966

The United States Air Force Pipe Band was undoubtedly the most colorful special musical unit in our armed forces. The Pipe Band was officially organized in 1960 as a unit of The United States Air Force Band. Previously, the Air Force Band's field music had included a number of pipers, whose effectiveness led to this recognition of the Pipe Band as a separate unit. Pipers were recruited throughout the United States, and only highly qualified men were accepted for membership. Drummers for this unit originally were drawn from The Air Force Band's Drum and Bugle Corps, but received special training in the difficult, intricate, and fast style necessary to play with the pipes.

This unit did not represent a new trend in American military music, but rather a revival of something older in American tradition than the United States itself. The pipes came to America with the first Scots settlers. They spurred the avenging rush of Oglethorpe's Highlanders at the Bloody Marsh in 1742, and led the Highland regiments through the French and Indian War and Pontiac's Rebellion. There were pipers with the militia of the western Virginia counties in Lord Dunmore's War of 1775, and a piper played defiance that last evening from the Alamo's battered walls. The 79th Regiment, New York State Militia, marched behind its pipe band into the Civil War.

The USAF Pipe Band was authorized Highland dress by special order of General Curtis LeMay. The original uniforms were made in Scotland and were delivered to the band in June 1960, while it was on tour of Great Britain. The tartan chosen was the "Mitchell" tartan, in honor of General "Billy" Mitchell, the original great champion of an independent Air Force. It was formed of blue and green squares with narrow stripes of red, white, and black. The kilts were pleated up to the vertical white stripes which are most predominant at the back of the kilt. During 1965 the original kilts and plaids were replaced with the same tartan in a heavier wool which has somewhat different color shades. Both varieties are illustrated (within the capabilities of our colorists) in our plate.

The Highland doublet was dark blue, laced in traditional fashion with white. All leather was black, and all metal white or silver. Hose was of the Mitchell tartan with scarlet garter ribbons. White spats were worn except with the evening dress uniform. For evening dress, the bandsmen replaced the doublet and plaid with a black evening mess jacket, black cummerbund, white shirt, and black bow tie; the military horsehair sporran was replaced by a sealskin evening sporran.

Bonnets were the newer Glengarry type, very dark blue with red "toorie" and black ribbons. The drum major had a feather bonnet with four tails and a white feather plume on the left side. He wore the traditional skean dhu in his right hose. The drum major's staff (or "mace"), topped by the figure of a crowned lion, was of unknown origin. It was obtained in Europe by the unit's original drum major, and is of black-finished Malacca wood with silver top and chain. The bass drummer's leopard skin had a broad red edging. The sporran was white, with two black tails. The original plain clasp (worn by the drum major on this plate) was later replaced by a somewhat more ornate model.

The cap emblem was the same insignia which is shown enlarged on the bass drum: the traditional US Air Force Band emblem of a lyre backed by a pair of wings, which in turn were superimposed on a propeller. On Pipe Band ceremonial appearances it anchored a black ribbon cockade and black cock's feather.

In the late spring of 1966 the pipe bag covers were changed from the wool Mitchell tartan to velveteen Saint Patrick's (royal) blue with gold fringe at the stocks and back edge. The pipes' cording was in tartan colors.

The Pipe Band's skill and striking appearance made it a favorite throughout the United States and overseas. Its somewhat sudden disbandment in June 1970 has subsequently been hotly argued.

The unit history and uniform descriptions in this text were furnished by Major A. D. Gabriel, Commanding Officer of the United States Air Force Band, and Company Member Technical Sergeant James J. Neary, Drum Major and Non-Commissioned-Officer-in-Charge of the Pipe Band.

Ronald E. Spicer
John R. Elting

Bass Drummer
(Full Dress & Old Tartan)

Piper
(Full Dress & New Tartan)

Piper
(Evening Dress & New Tartan)

Drum Major
(Full Dress & Old Tartan)

U.S. Air Force Pipe Band, 1965-1966

Aggressor, the U.S. Army's Maneuver Enemy, 1960

The U.S. Army organized its maneuver enemy, Aggressor, in 1946. This force, built around a small cadre, evolved into a full-fledged "enemy" with its own uniforms, tactical doctrine, order of battle, and a language, Esperanto. The Army defined Aggressor as " . . . a training aid consisting of an imaginary enemy nation with a history, government, armed forces, and an undefined homeland." [1]

The basic Aggressor uniform was a government-issue combat uniform that was dyed jungle green. The Agressor helmet, with a ridge running from front to rear over the crest of the helmet, was probably the most distinctive item of equipment. With some exceptions, this helmet was worn by all Aggressor troops. Occasionally an officer wore the service cap. As with many foreign armies, certain units wore caps that set them apart. All fusilier units (fusilier being the designation of elite troops) wore red garrison caps. Personnel of airborne units were also permitted to wear the red cap. Troops assigned to tank and reconnaissance units wore black garrison caps; however, the men of fusilier tank and reconnaissance units wore the red cap. The fusilier cap, because it symbolized high unit esprit de corps, was frequently worn in place of the helmet.

Shoulder straps were in three colors: red, worn by fusilier officers only; white, worn by marshals and general officers only; green, worn by all other officers and by all other ranks. The Aggressor soldier could be readily identified by his collar tabs and sleeve patches. Colored cloth tabs were worn on the collar to designate branch; black Arabic numerals indicated the numerical designation of regimental-size units and below. The branch colors were Mechanized Rifle, including mountain and ski units, red; Airborne, blue; Tank and Reconnaissance, yellow; Artillery, including missile units, white; Engineer, green; Signal, tan; Chemical, purple; Other Services, orange. Divisions were identified by a rectangular colored cloth patch on the upper right sleeve with black Arabic numerals to indicate the number of the division. Higher echelons, such as corps and army, followed the same scheme used for divisional units.

Aggressor officer rank insignia was worn on both the shoulder straps and on the cap. Officers of company grade were identified by gold bars, field grade by gold leaves, and general officers by a combination of gold leaves and crossed cannon. Enlisted grades were designated by a combination of chevrons and pips worn on the sleeve of each arm. A sergeant major wore a gold leaf in lieu of pips. The chevrons were worn point down with the point four inches from the lower extremity of the shirt cuff. Some units adopted berets, stripes on trousers, sateen shoulder straps, and collar tabs to show their unit pride.

The emblem of the Circle Trigon Party, a white circle with a green equilateral triangle superimposed, was used as a "national" insignia, at times on the uniform, and was also used to mark vehicles and other equipment.

The men depicted in the plate represent units listed in the established Aggressor order of battle, reportedly active in Aggressor's California lodgement area. The private represents the 4th Fusilier Mechanized Rifle Regiment, 19th Fusilier Mechanized Rifle Division. The staff sergeant represents the 119th Mechanized Rifle Regiment, 60th Mechanized Rifle Division, and his map bears the proper Aggressor symbols. The senior sergeant, whose rank insignia is covered by his partially rolled up sleeves, is wearing the markings of the 104th Medium Tank Regiment, 2nd Tank Division. The major, identified by his single gold leaf, is on the staff of the 172nd Mechanized Rifle Regiment, 18th Mechanized Rifle Division. [2]

Aggressor is still active, but has been "reconfigured" to duplicate Russian organization, weapons, equipment, uniforms, and tactics.

Donald A. Burgess
Albert W. Haarmann

[1] AR 350-177, paragraph 2.
[2] The plate and text are based upon the following Department of the Army publications: AR 350-177, 11 October 1960; FM 30-101, 27 April 1961; FM 30-103, 16 September 1960; plus material and photographs provided by the U.S. Army Aggressor Center, Fort Riley, Kansas.

Private   Staff Sergeant   Senior Sergeant   Major

Aggressor, The U.S. Army's Maneuver Enemy, 1960

Canada: Royal 22e Régiment, 1965-1966

On 7 November 1914, the 22nd (French-Canadian) Battalion was organized for service with the C.E.F.[1] As part of the 5th Infantry Brigade, 2nd Canadian Division, it fought in most of the more important engagements of World War I, two of its members winning the Victoria Cross. The battalion was disbanded on 20 May 1919.

Because of the distinguished service and outstanding record of the 22nd (French-Canadian) Battalion, the Canadian government authorized the organization of a regiment, entirely French-Canadian, to carry on the traditions of this battalion. General Order No. 30, dated 1 April 1920, designated this unit as the 22nd Regiment and made it a part of the permanent active militia. Redesignated Royal 22nd Regiment on 1 June 1921, it was renamed Royal 22e Régiment on 15 June 1928. As such, it fought in Sicily, Italy, Northwest Europe, and Korea as well as carrying out various U.N. peacekeeping duties. To the public it is affectionately known as the "Van Doos."

On 8 November 1927, King George V authorized an affiliation with the Royal Welch Fusiliers. Shortly thereafter, a full dress uniform similar to that of the Fusiliers was adopted. On 1 July 1928, the regiment paraded for the first time in this uniform, which has changed little in the intervening years and is shown on the field officer, drum major, and goat keeper, in this plate. Other ranks' uniforms are like that worn by the goat keeper, but without the shoulder wings, with gloves in lieu of gauntlets, and with chrome bayonet and scabbard, worn at the left hip; they carry the FN 7.62mm rifle with white slings and sight cover. The cuff, which is obscured in the plate, is blue, pointed, and edged with white lace with a trefoil knot at the top. The band's uniform is like that of the goat keeper, with the addition of a white shoulder belt and music pouch worn over the left shoulder, and white gloves. Band NCOs wear gold lace on the shoulder wings and the base drummer wears the traditional leopard skin. The drum major's baldric was taken into use in 1959, along with two color belts of the same pattern. The scrolls carry the battle honors from World War I through Korea, written in French, in keeping with the regiment's heritage. Officers and warrant officers class I wear the uniform as shown on the field officer, except that the warrant officers wear an epaulette like those of other ranks. Adjutants and field officers, only, wear spurs. Senior noncommissioned officers and warrant officers class II wear a red sash over the left shoulder. Badges of rank, other than officers', are of gold lace or embroidery worn on the right sleeve only. The white leather belting was replaced with plastic for reasons of economy.

The blue uniform pictured here forms the basis for three orders of dress worn by officers of the regiment. It consists of a forage cap; jacket, of patrol pattern; trousers or overalls; white gloves; and Wellington boots. The breast pockets, unlike those of other regiments, have no center pleat. The peak of the forage cap carries a one-inch band of gold braid, following the curve of the peak, for field officers.

The summer equivalent of the previously described uniform is shown on the right-hand figure of this plate.

The mess dress consists of the forage cap, jacket, waistcoat, overalls, Wellington boots and white gloves. The jacket is of Canadian army universal pattern. The corps and regimental distinctions are in the badges and the color of the waistcoat. For field officers, the shoulder straps, and front and bottom edges of the jacket are edged with gold Russian braid; a double line of this same braid runs down the front of the waistcoat, and a single line along the bottom edges. Rank insignia are embroidered in silver on the shoulder straps and miniature medals are worn. In summer, the waistcoat is replaced by a plain white shirt, with a cummerbund, the same color as the waistcoat.

The crest of the regiment, shown in the inset, is worn on practically all types of headdress, including the bearskin, as well as on buttons, waist plate, and music pouch. The collar badge consists of a silver fleur-de-lis above a triple scroll inscribed "Regiment Canadien-Francais," all in silver, or white metal for other ranks. Other ranks' shoulder badge, of brass, is shown in the lower left; the officers' badge, of silver, is shown in the lower right of the inset. Warrant officers class I wear the officers' pattern shoulder badge, but in brass.

Like their comrades of the Royal Welch Fusiliers, the R22R have a goat mascot. He came to the regiment from the Royal Goat Herd at Windsor Castle. For parades, his horns are gilded and his hooves are blackened. Between his horns rests a silver plaque, surmounted by the regimental badge, on which is inscribed the details of his presentation. On certain special occasions, he will wear a coat of royal blue, embroidered with the badge of the regiment, silver fleur-de-lis in the corners, the whole coat decorated with gold lace.

In the background is the original Vimy Cross, erected in honor of the dead of the 2nd Canadian Division and its 13th Brigade. It is the custom within the regiment to salute the cross when passing.

Donna Neary
Ernest J. Owen

[1]Unless otherwise indicated, the information contained in this article was supplied by La Régie, Royal 22e Régiment.

Officer
Order of Dress, 2B

Officer
Mess Dress
Order of Dress, 3A

Field Officer
Full Dress

Officer
Order of Dress, 2C

Major
Dress

Goat Keeper
Full Dress

Regimental Crest and Shoulder Badges

NEARY

Canada: Royal 22e Régiment, 1965-1966

Index

Helmets
  French, 96
  steel, 70, 78, 82, 98, 104, 114, 116
  sun (cork/pith), 20, 26, 30, 32, 42, 66
  U.S. Prussian-type, vii, 4, 10, 14, 16, 18, 34, 38
Horses, 2, 4, 16, 84, 92, 94, 112
Hoseney, Don, 8
Hutchins, James S., 2

I

Illinois Troop Units
  Chicago Black Horse Troop, 92
  106th Cavalry Regiment, 92
Indian Scouts (See "Scouts, U.S.")
Indian Wars, v, vii, viii, 2, 4, 6, 8, 28, 114
Infantry, vii, 10, 12, 14, 18, 30, 46, 48, 50, 74, 78, 80, 82
  Canadian, 22, 104, 134
  Japanese, 106
  Mexican, 62, 64
  Spanish, 60
  U.S. 3d Regiment, 112
  U.S. 15th Regiment, 26, 28, 70
  U.S. 16th Regiment, 72
  U.S. 18th Regiment, 114
  U.S. 351st Regiment, 116
  U.S. 369th Regiment, 96
  U.S. Porto Rico Provisional Regiment, 30
Italy, 102

J

Japanese Troop Units, 106
Johnson, General Harold K., 126
Johnson, Raymond S., viii, 58, 78, 90, 96
Jones, Edward S., 26, 28, 70
Jones, James T., viii, 36

K

Kennedy, President John F., 122
Knives, 8, 32, 118, 122
Korea, v, 134
Krueger, General Walter, 78

L

Labrador, 108
Lafayette Escadrille, 86
Larter, Harry C., viii, 4, 14, 84, 94, 114

Leggings (See "Puttees")
Lewis, Edwin S., 6

M

McAfee, Michael J., v, ix
McBarron, H. Charles, viii, 12, 14, 16, 38, 54, 56, 82, 92, 112, 124, 126
McKeever accoutrements, 4, 10
McMaster, Fitzhugh, 36
Machete, 60
Machine gun, 26, 64
  Bren, 104
  M2 (Cal..50), 120
  M16, 118
  M73, 120
  Model 99 (Japanese), 106
Magruder, John H., viii, 6, 100, 130
Manders, Eric I., viii, 18, 80, 90
Maples, Philip G., 10
Marrion, Robert J., viii, 22
Marshall, Lt. Col. George C., 70
Mascots, 14, 86, 134
Massachusetts Troop Units
  6th Infantry Regiment, 46
  Naval Militia, 58
Medaille Militaire, 72, 114
Merritt, General Wesley, 50
Mexican Border Campaign, 16, 52
Mexican War, 112
Mexico, v, 62, 64
Mitchell, Lt. Col. Gilbert H., 126
Mules, 6, 36
Mulligan, Robert E., 12
Musket, smoothbore, 40

N

National Guard
  Connecticut, 10
  Illinois, 92
  Massachusetts, 46
  New Jersey, 94
  New York, 12, 14, 48, 96
  Ohio, 16
  Pennsylvania, 18, 50, 52
Naval Militia, 58
Neary, Donna, viii, 134
Neary, Sergeant James J., 130
Necktie, viii, 70, 72, 82, 100, 116
New Jersey Troop Units
  102d Cavalry Regiment
New York Troop Units
  7th Infantry Regiment, 48
  10th Infantry Regiment, 12
  69th Infantry Regiment, 96
  369th Infantry Regiment, 96
  Naval Militia, 58

New Zealand, 102
Nicaraguan Campaign, 100
North African Campaign, 102
Northwest Rebellion, 22
Nye, Irwin C., 122

O

Ohio Troop Units
  First City Troop, Cleveland, 16
"Old Guard," the, 112
Otoupalik, Hayes, 74
Owen, Ernest J., 134

P

Packer, civilian, 36
Panama Canal Zone Police, 44
Pathfinders, 118
Pennsylvania Troop Units
  1st Infantry Regiment, 18
  10th Infantry Regiment, 50
  2d Troop, Philadelphia City Cavalry, 52
"Pershing" cap, 84
Philippine Constabulary, 40, 42
Philippine Insurrection, v, 28, 50, 114
  P. I. A. T., 104
Pistol, automatic
  Browning, 104
  Colt, 54, 78, 94, 100, 120
Plunkett, Admiral Charles P., 98
Porto Rico Provisional Infantry Regiment, 30
Powers, Kenneth H., 14
Puerto Rico, vii, 30, 46
Puttees
  canvas, 44, 64, 74, 78, 84
  leather, 42, 44, 48, 64, 100
  spiral (wrap), vii, 40, 42, 48, 70, 72

Q

Quartermaster Department/Corps, vii, 36, 42

R

Ray, Frederic E., 70
Red River Expedition, 20
Remington, Frederick, viii, 32
Revolutionary War, 50, 52
Revolvers, 32, 36, 46, 76
  Colt, 4, 40, 44
  Lefaucheux, 60
  Smith and Wesson, 4, 104
  Webley, 104